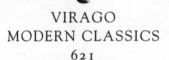

VIRAGO
MODERN CLASSICS
621

Mary Renault

Mary Renault (1905–1983) was best known for her historical novels set in Ancient Greece with their vivid fictional portrayals of Theseus, Socrates, Plato and Alexander the Great.

Born in London in 1905 and educated at the University of Oxford, she trained as a nurse at Oxford's Radcliffe Infirmary where she met her lifelong partner, fellow nurse Julie Mullard. Her first novel, *Purposes of Love*, was published in 1939. In 1948, after her novel *Return to Night* won an MGM prize worth £150,000, she and Mullard emigrated to South Africa.

It was in South Africa that Renault was able to write forthrightly about homosexual relationships for the first time – in her last contemporary novel, *The Charioteer*, published in 1953, and then in her first historical novel, *The Last of the Wine* (1956), the story of two young Athenians who study under Socrates and fight against Sparta. Bo̶ṷṵthese books had male protagonists, as did all her later wo̶ȿenhone. no̶ṣ. end h̶᷉———–᷂᷉ ᷉hemes. Her sympathetic treatme   in Renault a wide gay ·

By Mary Renault

KIND ARE
HER ANSWERS

Mary Renault

Introduced by Sarah Dunant

virago

VIRAGO

This edition published by Virago Press in 2014
First published in Great Britain by Longmans, Green and Co. Ltd in 1940

Copyright © Mary Renault 1940

Introduction copyright © Sarah Dunant 2014

The moral right of the author has been asserted.

A CIP catalogue record for this book
is available from the British Library.

ISBN 978-1-84408-954-3

Typeset in Goudy by M Rules
Printed and bound in Great Britain by
Clays Ltd, St Ives plc

Papers used by Virago are from well-managed forests
and other responsible sources.

MIX
Paper from
responsible sources
FSC® C104740

Virago Press

Little,
100 Vi
Lo

An Had
ww

ww

INTRODUCTION

At a white-tiled table a young girl was sitting, sucking a bulls-eye and sewing a shroud ... She was nineteen, pretty, undersized and Welsh; hideously dressed in striped cotton, a square-bibbed apron that reached her high collar, black shoes and stockings and a stiff white cap

... the child who presently would wear the shroud was lying with a pinched, waxy face, breathing jerkily through a half-open mouth. An apparatus of glass and rubber tubing was running salt and water into her veins to eke out the exhausted blood. It was all that could now be done ... The little nurse stitched doggedly away ... She had made plenty of shrouds; the first few had made her feel creepy, but they were just like the rest of the mending and darning now.

Mary Renault was in her early thirties when her first novel, *Purposes of Love*, was published. That quiet but dramatic opening was also a mischievous one. Neither the young nurse nor the child would make it past page two. Instead, the story is thrown down a staircase, along with a heap of soiled laundry, into the

v

hands of Vivian, a trainee nurse, whose experience of both hospital life and an intense relationship with Mic, an assistant pathologist, makes up the core of the book. So far, so hospital romance conventional. But it isn't long before a fellow female nurse seduces Vivian and we discover that Mic has had an affair with her brother. By anyone's lights, such a book, coming out in 1939, marked the arrival of a bold new voice.

For those who, like me, grew up gorging themselves on Mary Renault's historical stories of ancient Greece, it may come as a surprise that for the first twenty years of her career she wrote only contemporary novels. For others more attuned to the homosexual subculture that the Greek novels explored, or having read *The Charioteer*, published in the 1950s, it will be less of a revelation to learn that even as a fledgling popular novelist she was interested in issues of sexuality and sexual orientation, writing with a directness that made some people, including an early reviewer of *Purposes of Love*, wonder if the author's name might be a mask for a man.

In fact, Mary Renault *was* a pseudonym, but not one designed to protect her gender. She was born Eileen Mary Challans, the first daughter of a middle-class doctor, in 1905 in London's East End. Her early memories show an intelligent, strong-willed child with an independent streak, no doubt exacerbated by her ringside seat on an unhappy marriage. 'I can never remember a time ... when they seemed to me to even like each other,' she wrote later in life to a friend. Though her fiction often takes the knife to frustrated, resentful mothers – both classical and contemporary – she could also be understanding. In her third novel, *The Friendly Young Ladies* (the euphemistic title refers to two women in a sexual relationship), she dramatises elements of her own childhood, but not without sympathy for the wife who, though she is intrusive and manipulative, is also clearly unloved.

Mary's escape from her parents came through education: at the insistence of her university-educated godmother, Aunt Bertha, she was sent to boarding school in Bristol and then went on to St Hugh's College, Oxford, subsidised by her aunt, as her parents considered the expense wasted on a daughter. An early love for history and literature would colour her whole life, allowing her later to meet the challenge of immersion in Greek history. She became involved in theatre, another passion that was to persist, but in other ways Oxford University in the 1920s was a conservative establishment, especially for the few women who went there, and there was no hint from her friendships with both men and women of the more radical way her life was to develop.

Her first attempt at serious writing came in 1928, when, during her last term at Oxford, she began work on a novel set in medieval England. J. R. R. Tolkien was perhaps an influence, as Mary had attended his lectures and clearly admired him. She was later to destroy the manuscript, dismissing the story as 'knights bashing about in some never-never land', but she was still working on it at twenty-eight when, looking for a way to support herself independently from her parents, she started to train as a nurse at the Radcliffe Infirmary.

It was to be another defining experience. Nursing was extremely hard work, but it offered the burgeoning writer a richness of experience that would have been well nigh impossible for a woman of her class elsewhere at that time. While others were marrying and starting families, she was deep in the business of life and death, meeting people from all backgrounds. It also gave her first-hand knowledge of the human body, in both its wonder and its fragility. All her fiction would drink deeply from these experiences. When she turns her hand to Greek myth and history she will confidently inhabit their overwhelming masculinity, celebrating athletic, erotic male beauty side by side with the heroism and agonies of battles and death. Meanwhile, the dramas of medicine and illness would permeate all her early novels.

Purposes of Love, not surprisingly, draws heavily on the training she has just come through; even the novel's title is taken from the prayer that the nurses recited every morning. Peopled by a beautifully observed cast of minor characters ('Sister Verdun was a little fretted woman with an anxious bun, entering with a sense of grievance into middle age'), it plunges the reader into the gruelling physicality of hospital life, contrasting the drama of sickness and injury with relentless rules and routine. Near the end of the book we sit with a nurse in night vigil over the mangled body of a dying, but conscious, young man. The scene is rich with the authenticity of detail, but it is clever as well as upsetting, since we know the man much better than the nurse does, which makes her mix of professional care and natural compassion even more affecting. The novel was an impressive debut, and became a bestseller, attracting fine reviews both sides of the Atlantic.

Kind are Her Answers was published the following year. Mary was under considerable pressure to write it quickly, as both publishers, especially Morrow in America, wanted it delivered before the outbreak of hostilities. In the end, it came out the week of the evacuation of Dunkirk, in 1940, which meant that it was largely critically ignored. Perhaps for Renault's long-term reputation that was no bad thing, as *Kind are Her Answers* is a much more conventional love story. It has its moments, though. Kit Anderson is a doctor locked in an unhappy marriage, who meets the woman with whom he will have an affair on a night visit to her seriously ill aunt. For a modern audience, the sexual passion is the most convincing part of the story. Their hungry young bodies make a painful contrast with the old woman's ageing, fading one and the adrenaline of risk and proximity of death adds to their abandon; during his unofficial night visits they must keep their voices down when they make love in case they are heard.

Return to Night (1947), which won Mary the MGM prize, a whopping £150,000, is a doctor–patient romance, though it cunningly inverts the stereotype by putting a woman, Hilary, in the white coat. The book opens with a riding accident and the time-bomb of internal bleeding inside the brain, which Hilary must diagnose in order to save a handsome young man's life. Renault had done a stint working on head injuries and the drama of the diagnosis and the tussle of wills between the complacent matron and the woman doctor is expertly played out.

In her fifth novel *North Face* (1949) nursing becomes character rather than plot. Inside a love story between two guests in a Yorkshire boarding house after the war, Renault uses two women in their thirties as a kind of spatting Greek chorus, ruminating on the morality (or not) of the affair. Already very much professional spinsters, one is a desiccated prissy academic, while the other is a blowzy, more down-to-earth professional nurse. Though the satire is at the expense of them both (at times they are more entertaining than the rather laboured love story), the nurse at least feels in touch with life. If Mary Renault had ever considered academia, this is surely her verdict on the choice she made.

But nursing did more than fire her fiction. It also changed her life. It was while training at the Radcliffe, living inside a set of rules to rival the most oppressive girls' boarding school, that Mary met twenty-two-year-old Julie Mullard. The coming together of their fictional equivalents after an evening tea party in one of the nurses' rooms is one of many perfectly realised scenes in *Purposes of Love*. Mary Renault and Julie Mullard were to be a couple until Mary's death. In England they mostly lived apart, often working in different hospitals, snatching precious weeks in holiday cottages or visiting each other under the radar of the rules. Then, in 1948, helped by the money Mary had won for *Return to Night*, they moved to South Africa.

Despite the fact that they would live openly and happily together for the next thirty-five years, neither would refer to herself as lesbian, nor talk publicly about their relationship (though elements of it are there to be read in Mary's fiction: the character of Vivian is clearly a mix of both of them, even down to the dramatisation of the short affair that Julie had with a hospital surgeon soon after they met). Some of their reticence can be explained by Renault's own personality: private and contained, with success she became more so. Some of it was no doubt a throwback to the difficult moral climate in which they began their relationship; the only contemporary public example of lesbian culture had been Radclyffe Hall's provocative *Well of Loneliness* and both of them found it 'self-pitying'. But it was more nuanced than that.

In 1982, a year before her death, Renault was the subject of a BBC film directed by the late writer and poet, David Sweetman, who later went on to write a biography of her. I was a good friend of David's at the time and, like many gay men I knew, he was eloquent about the place Renault's novels had played in his life. When he asked her about the sexuality in her work, she had this to say: 'I think a lot of people are intermediately sexed. It's like something shading from white to black with a lot of grey in the middle.'

The words describe perfectly much of the shifting sexual territory Renault fictionalised in her first five novels. For the sharp-eyed, *The Friendly Young Ladies*, published in 1944, is a portrait of a sexual relationship between Leo(nora), writer of cowboy novels – Mary herself loved cowboy fiction – and Helen, a lovely and talented nurse who has the odd dalliance with men. We meet them first through the eyes of Leo's young sister, who runs away from home to stay with them. Suffused with Mills & Boon sensibility, she sees only what she wants to see; Leo's tomboy manner and clothes, the shared bedroom and the domestic familiarity are all taken at platonic face value. A young doctor, full of his own psychological insights, is equally blinkered, trying his hand with both women (and being turned down more because of his personality than his gender). It makes for playful story-telling as it divides not only Renault's characters, but presumably also her readership. In the end, this cosy set-up is broken apart by the rugged American writer Joe, who has a night of passion with Leo that results in what feels like a conventional but unconvincing happy ending.

Interestingly, in 1982, when, on the recommendation of Angela Carter, Virago reissued the novel, Mary herself wanted to alter the ending. In a letter to the publisher, written barely a year before her death, she said: 'You will see I have marked a cut of several pages near the end, and will I am sure agree that this was a thoroughly mushy conclusion ... far better leave Leo's choice in the air with the presumption that she stays with Helen. The ending I gave it looks now like a bow to convention, which it wasn't, but it was certainly an error of judgement.' A compromise was reached, and instead of changing the text she wrote a new afterword, which is reproduced again now.

The same criticism of an imposed happy ending might also be levelled against *Return to Night*, where the heroine doctor falls in love with Julian, the young male patient she saves. Breathtakingly beautiful, emotionally quixotic and under the thumb of a domineering mother, Julian yearns to be an actor and a halo of sexual ambivalence hovers over him throughout the novel. Hilary meanwhile, eleven years older, in a man's job with what could be a man's name, finds herself cast as half lover, half mother. As they head towards the happily-ever-after of marriage you can't help thinking that they would both benefit from more wriggle-room to experiment.

Mary Renault was eventually to find that wider sexual and imaginative freedom in her Greek novels, but not before one last, extraordinary, contemporary book. Freed from the grey British skies of post-war austerity and culture, in 1951 she wrote *The Charioteer*, an explicit portrait of homosexuality during the war.

Its rich backdrop is drawn from her experience nursing soldiers in a hospital partly staffed by conscientious objectors, and it tells the story of Laurie, an intelligent, introspective young man, who comes to understand his sexuality through a platonic but profound encounter with Ralph, an older prefect at his public school. Injured at Dunkirk, he goes on day release from hospital and is introduced into a homosexual subculture, in which Ralph, now a naval officer, is a player. The hot-house atmosphere of this hidden society is brilliantly, though not always flatteringly, observed (Renault had had experience of such a world in her early years in South Africa).

Laurie's continued self-analysis and his struggle as to how to live as a gay man, dramatised as a choice between his love for Ralph, who he learns had saved him at Dunkirk, and the growing connection with a young conscientious objector working at the hospital and yet to realise his own homosexuality, make up the rest of the book.

Reading *The Charioteer* now is to be blown away by its intensity and bravery. In 1953, when it came out in Britain, it was a cultural thunderbolt (in America it took another six years to find a publisher); reviews were overwhelmingly positive and Mary received scores of letters from appreciative readers. By then, though, she had moved on and was submerged in two years of research for her next book, which was to be something altogether different.

From the opening sentence of *The Last of the Wine* (1956), ancient Greece and the male voices through which she enters it burn off the page with an immediacy and power that will characterise all her historical fiction. Homosexual love, sacrifice, companionship and heroism abound in a culture which accepts, encourages and celebrates sexual diversity. At nearly fifty, Mary Renault had at last found her world.

Sarah Dunant, 2014

I

Kit Anderson crossed the landing from his wife's room to his own, and, too much occupied with his thoughts to switch on the light, walked through the dark with the accuracy of habit to his bed. He untied the knot of his dressing-gown, stood still for a moment, knotted it again, and put on the bedside lamp to look for a cigarette. Smoking last thing at night was not a habit of his – it was one of the small things about which he was rather fussily hygienic – but tonight more important habits had been broken. It would take him more than the length of a cigarette to sort and reassemble himself. He had not fallen seriously out of love since he was twenty, not a good age for analyzing the experience. This time he found it as complex, as interesting, and (to his momentarily shocked surprise) as satisfactory as falling in.

At this point it occurred to him that with the light behind him, and the street in front, his meditations were probably public. After two years of general practice, he was still not quite acclimatized to the mild spotlight trained upon doctors in small towns. In his own mind he always, unless he reminded himself, slipped back into the strenuous anonymity of his London hospital, a way of life which he secretly preferred.

He put the light out and settled himself again, invisible now except for the point of his cigarette, to the private disappointment of a passing housemaid returning from the cinema, who had thought the circle of light round his fair head not wholly an anticlimax. Kit for his part was not much attached to his personal appearance, which was a professional liability. He was nearly 30, but the stranger's casual estimate was likelier to be 24. His hair was the chief trouble, being of the raw-silk color and texture that hardly ever outlasts childhood. His eyes were the most obviously adult part of his face; they had a definite air of being willing to continue an acquaintance with reality. But, unaware of this, he was fond of concealing them behind superfluous horn glasses in the consulting-room to make himself look older. Soon it would make little difference, for his mouth was on the way to looking the same age; its pleasant line had become somewhat voluntary and determined.

Kit was well aware of what his looks cost him in annual income and it led him to eke out the horn glasses with a professional primness which people who knew his work thought amusing, as well as unnecessary. Such patients as he got, he kept, and often a friend or two of theirs as well; but most clung to his senior partner, Fraser, who had a head like an advertisement for tonic wine, and addressed them as We.

There had been a time when Kit had ceased to be annoyed with his physical envelope. While he and Janet were first in love he had felt much more kindly toward it, because the fact that she seemed to like the look of it had made it, indirectly, a part of her too. But that was gone, almost forgotten, though it was of Janet he was thinking as he leaned out among the slight breezes and hidden sounds of the chilly moonless night. With a confused sense of loss, of release and self-reproach, he was trying to accustom himself to the discovery that she no longer had the power to hurt him.

Nothing had happened. It was because it had all been so simple, so lacking in situation or crisis, that he knew it must be true. The day had been like other days: evening surgery, bridge with the Frasers – a crushing weekly rite from which he had hoped as usual for an emergency call to deliver him. As usual, no call had come; they saved themselves for his evenings with McKinnon, which he enjoyed. Afterward, for an hour or so, he and Janet had talked desultorily about the impersonal thing which had become their safety valve, and had gone up to bed. It was while he was brushing his teeth that he suddenly remembered the name of a book which during the conversation had eluded him. Janet had heard something about it and wanted to read it, and by morning he might have forgotten, so, noticing on his way from the bathroom that the light still showed under her door, he had knocked. She said 'Come in' with the moment's hesitation which had become so habitual that now he scarcely noticed it.

'Oh, Janet – can I come in a minute? – I've just remembered the name of that book. I knew it was some sort of tongue-twister. I'll write it down on your pad, shall I?'

Janet was sitting up in bed and filing her nails. Her straight heavy dark hair was brushed smoothly into the plaits which, by day, she wore coiled together at the nape of her neck. Now they hung over her shoulders, giving her a schoolgirl air. Her white crepe-de-Chine nightgown and bed-jacket were dainty and immaculate. He noted vaguely their quality and good taste, and thought, without emphasis or realizing that it was for the first time, how impalpably delight had evaporated from her, like the scent from a flower.

She looked up. 'What – oh, do you mean that education thing? I couldn't think what you were talking about—'

'Yes, the F. M. Alexander one you wanted. May I?' He sat down on the end of the bed with the memorandum pad on his knee.

3

Her voice had been subtly defensive; he knew she had been trying to cover the uneasiness she had felt at his appearance. She did not look at him as he wrote, but picked up a nail-buffer and began to polish her nails and curve them against the light. Kit wrote down the title, carefully rounding out his cramped medical scribble to make it legible. He ought to have remembered how careful she was not to meet him when she was in her night things. No doubt she was right. Then a slow surprise took hold of him, because he *had* forgotten tonight. He had walked in casually, with an untroubled mind and half his thoughts elsewhere, thinking only of the book she had seemed anxious to read.

'Thank you, Kit.' She took the pad and studied it, with a kind of blank concentration which betrayed that she had only wanted another excuse to look away from him. 'You shouldn't have bothered at this time of night.'

'I was afraid I might forget,' he said. 'The Times Book Club will get it for you without any trouble.' It was too steep for her, he was thinking. She would stick at the first chapter.

He got up. Suddenly – no doubt the word 'education' had been working in his mind – he thought how maladroit it was to have brought to her notice a book so much concerned with young children. Hesitating a moment, he said, 'You may find it rather solid going. It's very technical. Bore you, perhaps.'

She looked up with the bitter-sweet smile which had, at last, become involuntary. 'Never mind, Christopher dear. If I find it beyond me, you shall explain it all in words of one syllable.'

'I didn't mean it like that,' he said. But at that moment, like a breath of cool wind in a stifling room, the knowledge broke in on him that he no longer cared what she believed him to mean. It was all external to him. He only wanted to make her mind at ease, as he would have wanted to relieve a patient of pain or restlessness, and to get back to bed and to sleep. He felt this with a strange mingling of liberation and lostness; it was like

4

finding oneself outside the gates of a prison after serving a long term. 'Well,' he said, 'I'll be going. Are you sleeping better, by the way?'

'Yes, a good deal, thank you. I very rarely hear midnight strike now.' She put her manicure things away; he recognized one of her gestures of dismissal.

'Better keep up the tonic for a while. Just let me know when you want some more. Good night.'

'Good night ... The bottle's still half full; it will last some time yet.' He was moving away, when she put out a sudden hand and caught at his sleeve. 'Kiss me good night, Kit. I'm sorry. I don't mean to be unkind.'

'Of course, I know.' He bent and kissed her cheek; then, because she looked reproachful, her mouth. She took hold of the lapel of his dressing-gown, and he knew by this sign that she was about to make one of those gestures to which from time to time she seemed impelled. These were the moments to which, for a year now, he had been learning to brace himself; sometimes aware hours ahead of their approach, sometimes taken off his guard, so that his mind had, by now, pitched itself to a constant, almost unconscious watchfulness. But tonight there did not stir in him the swift, secret signal for defense, the fear of self-betrayal, the set expectation of pain. He simply wanted to keep her from hurting herself if possible, and for his part, to get to sleep.

He put his arm round her shoulders. 'Why don't you settle down straight away? You know, women keep too many of these fiddling odd jobs to do last thing at night: nails, and so on. It leaves your mind restive and then you stay awake.'

Leaning her cheek against him she said, with a deliberate little sigh, 'I try to keep myself looking nice for you, Kit—'

Oh, God, he thought, *not now*, and the old habit of sudden control made a stiffening in his throat. But next moment his

5

caution relaxed; there was no danger any more. 'You always look nice, to me,' he said, and patted her shoulder.

Ignoring it, she put her arms round her knees, and twisted her fingers together. 'You must often think hardly of me, I know, though you pretend not to. You think I don't realize – or that I don't care.'

He stood beside her, lightly caressing her shoulder, remembering times like this in the past, amazed that it should be recollection now and no longer reality: the almost unbearable strain, the bewilderment that she should be willing consciously – for he was sure that she was aware of it – to inflict this hurt, the half-understanding of an emotional need which drove her, tangling unendurably the pain of compassion with his own pain. But now only compassion moved in him.

'I think you should sleep, my dear,' he said, 'and not imagine what isn't there.'

She looked quickly at him, and then away; and he knew, with an almost impersonal shock of discovery, that his calm had disconcerted her, that the evidence of his suffering had been – unknown to her perhaps, perhaps only unacknowledged – a necessary satisfaction and release. In the past he had half suspected this, but, because the thought was impossibly hurtful, had thrust it aside from his mind. She sat twisting her fingers, restless lest he should leave her, thinking of something more to say; and it was then – watching the light strike sideways on the smooth ivory plane of her cheekbone that had once in itself been able to take his breath away – that he knew he was free of love, and had been free, perhaps, without his knowledge, for a long time.

'I've failed you,' she said, 'I know. I expect you always think of me like that. But I do try to make up for it, Kit, every way I can. You know that. Don't you?'

'Please,' he said. How distant it all seemed: her voice, her

6

shoulder under his hand, like a memory, cut off from the present by a wall of glass. 'I never think that. How could I?' He took away the book she had been reading, and, withdrawing his arm, settled her into the pillows. 'Go to sleep, Janie my dear. I'll give you something to take if you'd like it. Shall I?'

She did not answer for a moment, then, turning her head to look at him, said, 'You've stopped loving me.'

Even this had happened before; so that when he said, 'Don't, Janie, you know I love you,' he did not think till later about its not being true. He was more occupied with its strangeness; it was like looking at a healed scar on one's body, and recollecting that this had once been the seat of intolerable pain.

'Kit,' she murmured, 'if you like—'

He moved away, discovering in some hitherto unguessed corner of himself the capacity for despising her. 'I wonder what you take me for. I could be a lot more use to you if you'd trust me now and then.'

'I'm sorry.' She gave her little sigh again. 'I know I've treated you badly. But you have to make allowances, Kit.'

The earnestness of her voice – as if she were revealing to him some new possibility that could never have occurred to him – made him want suddenly to laugh. But instead he kissed her forehead, said, 'I love you a lot, Janie,' and went away.

Now, against the blankness of the sky at the open window, this terminal moment took its place against the pattern of the past. Their marriage, which ended in his heart tonight, had ended physically a year ago, when Janet had borne their first and last child, dead, and had nearly died along with it. From the very beginning, something had warned him that she ought not to attempt motherhood. It was pure instinct, a flair his calling had developed in him, for there were no obvious contradictions. But he had been sure, and, because he loved her desperately, had used every persuasion against it, until one day a chance phrase or look had brought him the sudden certainty that it was what, from the first, marriage had meant to her; that he himself was secondary. He scarcely realized the force of the blow this dealt at him, because he accepted it. He knew little of women, beyond a few tentative adventures in his student years, to which something had kept him from committing himself. To Janet he had committed everything, receiving her values with so complete a faith that he supposed them common to all women as good as she. That she should want a child more than she wanted him seemed to him neither strange nor a matter for reproach, and he protested no further.

When the disaster happened, he cast aside, casually almost and unnoticed, his few half-conscious reservations of himself. The utmost he could offer, he felt, was a small consolation and her due. He was a single-minded person, young for his years and, within the limits imposed by five years in hospital, an idealist.

Because he went on allowing for her convalescence long after it had passed, it only filtered in on him gradually that his acceptance of the blame was taken for granted by her. The discovery was a catastrophic shock to him. His feeling had been sincere, but he had assumed, without thinking about it, an equal sincerity in her, a readiness to confront her own consequences which was the natural complement, in his mind, of his desire to confront them for her. When he found that she met necessity as a stream does rocks, by a progress of avoidances, he taught himself, as with an unwisely loved child, to deflect from her those realities of which she was afraid. She forgave him, very sweetly, for spoiling her life. He remained hopelessly in love with her, to the point, sometimes, of taking himself at her valuation.

Since then, Janet had been 'delicate.' She was delicate still. It was now, almost certainly, too late for her to be anything else. She had let the time slip by within which, if at all, they could safely take up married life again. That was a period about which Kit preferred not to think too much. In retrospect even, her gently deprecated martyrdom, the implications about himself which she had not needed to underline, still had the power to make him feel rather cold. Yet he had continued to love her, mostly in a finely drawn silence, for another year.

She had never retracted her unspoken accusations, only added to them as the time passed. He had accepted them silently, because their injustice was irrelevant to the hurt they inflicted – that she should be willing to inflict it was the final thing. Tonight, thinking it over, he knew they were only part of her defense against reality, and was glad not to have torn it from her. She was insufficient to life without it.

He had perceived, too, the secret fear she had not admitted to herself, that she should go too far and lose him. He felt it in the little crises and stresses, leading nowhere out of nothing, with which she tested him. She had become an artist in evolving and justifying them, seeming to find in them both reassurance and a drug-like stimulation. On Kit the effects, and the effort of concealing them, had often been devastating. He had always been unable to tell her that it was only at such times, in the emotional turmoil they produced, that he sometimes wanted other women. He had done nothing about it, even when they had rather evidently wanted him.

But now, as he leaned in the window, he did not consciously recapitulate these things. They were no more than the background of a mood, and it was the mood which engaged his mind because the rest was weary with custom while this was new. He thought with relief that his real life would never be conditioned by someone else again. It was no way to live; one should rest on one's own center.

He must be careful with Janet, he thought. She must never know these discoveries he had made about himself and her. He could be better to her now that he was free of her. He felt possessed suddenly by a great kindness for her.

He discovered that after all he was ready for sleep, and threw his cigarette-end out into the dark.

Janet turned out the rod of light inset at the head of her bed, lay still for a few minutes, and turned it on again. As a rule, it was soothing to look at her green and silver room; she had pretty, elegant taste, and was quick to recognize and imitate originality. But tonight there was little to choose; the darkness seemed printed with the past, the light with the present. At the side of her *eau de Nil* taffeta eiderdown was a squashed depression where Kit had been sitting; she twitched at it with little sharp jerks till it fluffed out again.

The truth, she thought – and the truth should be faced however unwillingly – was that Kit was growing hard. She had felt this several times lately, though never so strongly as tonight. Tonight for the first time he had been cold to her. It was the only word. She had met him, as she always tried to, with sympathy and understanding; one must make allowances for men; and he had been utterly unresponsive, snubbing her with cold kindness. She asked so little, she thought: only some affection and warmth, and to know that he minded about her. He had always showed that he minded; till tonight.

For Kit to grow hard seemed so *wrong*. It didn't suit him. He was egotistic, of course, as all men were; it was something to do with sex that made them so, and women, being more perceptive, learned to make sacrifices quietly and to expect no thanks. But he had never been hard. That was what she had liked about him when they first met, a freshness, something romantic and unspoiled. He had had such beautiful thoughts about her. She had been careful of his illusions, taking pains always to be gracious in his presence, avoiding anything undisciplined or crude. But it had gone for nothing. Well, men were more physical; one learned not to expect too much.

She put out the light again, but began to be sure now that she would not sleep. She wondered whether to go across to his room and ask him to give her something from the dispensary after all. Perhaps he would guess then that he had upset her, without being told. He would be in bed, she supposed, by now. She had a sudden vivid picture of him, switching on the light half in his sleep as he did when a night call came, and sitting up with his fair hair silkily tangled and his pajamas falling off – he was not an obviously restless sleeper, but always contrived partly to detach himself from his clothes. She remembered how his gray eyes darkened with sleep; his brows and lashes were a kind of tarnished-gilt color, almost brown, and did not disappear against his skin like those of most fair men. She had noticed them again tonight, while he was writing out the name of the book. Reaching again for the light switch, she picked up the pad and looked at it: large round letters, not like his, as if he had been writing for a child. But she had always complained about his writing; illegibility, she maintained, was a form of bad manners.

It would be tragic, she thought, for Kit to become coarsened and spoiled, as, if she lost her influence on him, he might. This was the first time she had thought explicitly that she might not hold him; he had always been so unalienably there. But tonight there had been a moment as he stood over her – tall, flexible like a boy with the kind of grace that is just over the border from awkwardness, smelling familiarly of Pears soap and toothpaste – when she had newly, piercingly imagined life without the certainty of him; the cold, dull reflection of herself that everything would give back without the interposition of his love; the dreadful narrowing of herself if he ceased to be an extension of her. She had wanted, for a moment, at any cost to keep him there, to find out what he was thinking about that made him so unlike himself, so sufficient and self-contained. But he had not understood, and that of course was best. Men ceased to respect you if you abandoned your reserve. She had always been careful about that.

She sat up and turned her pillow, which felt hot and tumbled, and put out the light again. But she still found herself remembering his hair, soft and shining under her fingers, against her shoulder, and his sleepy weight for which, when she woke him, he would apologize. Perhaps last year, if she had pretended a little – but when she knew it could not give her a child she had hated it all. And he had said it should make no difference to his loving her. He had promised.

What could have changed him? A suspicion began to grow on her that this deterioration was due to the influence of someone else. She had never cared much for his friend McKinnon. He was always bringing over bleak, frightening books, which she hated, for Kit to read. He looked at her too in a way which made her feel sure he was cynical about women, no doubt because he knew the wrong ones. Did he ever introduce them to Kit? Kit was so simple about women, so naïvely generous in his judgments. He didn't see through people.

The hall clock struck twelve. She had been lying awake for more than half an hour. She wished she had not told Kit that she was sleeping better. Kit was forgetting, among McKinnon and his friends, how sensitive she was, how acutely she felt small coldnesses and failures in response that most women would never even notice. He had been so sympathetic when she was ill, sitting on the edge of the bed when she couldn't sleep and talking and holding her hand. Perhaps if she were to be ill again – as she easily might be, with the cold weather ahead and all this worry – he might realize. She noticed, now, that her head was aching. She felt cold, too. She must not let herself be ill again, for Kit's sake. She would ask him for the tablet after all. He would hardly be asleep yet. Or, if he were, he was so used to being called up that he would soon drop off again; how lucky men were to have no nerves!

She put on the light, and bent for her green satin slippers.

2

On Thursday mornings, as near twelve o'clock as possible – for she liked regularity – Kit used to visit Miss Heath. He noted the day with a certain pleasure; calling on Miss Heath was rather like re-entering one's childhood as a grown-up visitor. Miss Heath, her maid Pedlow, and her cook, lived in 6 of the 26 rooms of Laurel Dene. It was a smallish Victorian-Gothic castle, walled away at the end of a cul-de-sac in what had been, 60 years before, the best part of the town. Now the Keble-ish houses on each side of the road had all been turned into offices or maisonettes; but behind the wrought-iron gates and spiked brick wall of Laurel Dene nothing had altered much, except that little Amy Heath had grown into Miss Heath, a very deaf old lady with chronic heart trouble.

Kit, as he turned into the mossy drive, thought how implac-ably hideous the grounds must have been in their youth, when the gravel and geraniums and lobelia were paint-fresh. Now the flower beds held only lush, tangled perennials, the month-high lawns were powdered with daisies, and the white paint was flak-ing from the conservatory and the garden seats. Noticing the poplar leaves plastered moistly to the bonnet of his car, Kit had the year's first feeling of autumn, and said to himself, *Of course, she'll never go through the winter.*

He tugged at the brass bell-pull, whose pattern had been smoothed by palms and fingers to a soft ripple like ebb-tide sands, and thought about conversation, which was important. Ten years ago Kit's predecessor had explained to Pedlow that Miss Heath was not to be worried, and Pedlow had taken it to heart and remembered it every morning when she read aloud from the *Times.*

Pedlow opened the door. She was a subterraneous-looking creature with a cachectic skin, and moved with faint crepitations which Kit could never certainly assign to her black alpaca dress, her corsets, or her bones. She still wore the little round cap, like a frilled doily, of two generations back, and two lumps of hair in front and one behind to support it.

Because Miss Heath so often misheard his questions, or rambled on about something else instead of answering them, Kit had reduced them to a formality and always collected his real report from Pedlow in the hall. He could tell at once, from the way she fiddled with the bib of her apron, that things were not going so well. Miss Heath, it seemed, had been taken quite bad during the night.

'Well, I wish you'd sent for me,' Kit said. 'Don't hesitate if it happens again. Miss Heath's in a condition when it's impossible to be too careful. What exactly happened?'

A blush, brownish and dim like sawdust, crept into Pedlow's sallow cheeks. 'That's what I can't forgive myself, doctor; I never knew anything about it till morning. Miss Heath rang the handbell by her bed for me, but I sleep so sound. I have from a child and I can't break myself. And Miss Heath doesn't like the idea of anyone sleeping in the room with her. I've kept thinking all morning how I might have come in and found her passed away. And so good she was about it. When I didn't come, she said to

15

herself – so she told me – no doubt it was the will of God.' A rim of moisture formed round her pale eyes.

'Well,' said Kit hastily, 'I don't think there's any need to assume that. The solution seems to be that Miss Heath should consider getting a nurse this winter. It's been in my mind for some time, and this morning I'll suggest it to her.'

Pedlow's face underwent a curious setting and buttoning process, and the points seemed to lock with an almost audible click all over her body. She explained that Miss Heath didn't like the idea of a nurse. She had had one some years ago, and the arrangement hadn't answered, it hadn't answered at all.

Kit sighed inwardly. He might, of course, have known. Pedlow was just of the class and period to whom trained nurses were an upstart kind of domestic servant, giving themselves airs above their station, and demeaning to wait upon. If he imported one there were obviously going to be ructions.

'Sooner than have Miss Heath upset like she was that time,' Pedlow said, 'I'd sit up with her myself and just take a little nap in the day. That's what I'd been meaning to do.'

'I hardly think that's an ideal arrangement. We shall be having you ill too. Perhaps Miss Heath has some relative who could come for a time. Well, I'll see what she thinks about it.'

He crossed the hall to what had been the morning room, but was now Miss Heath's bedroom because of the stairs, trying as usual not to feel like a small boy in the presence of the towering wrought-brass bed, with its crochet counterpane representing as many years' work as an altarcloth; the rusty silhouettes of Miss Heath's parents at its head; the thunderous steel engraving of Moses on Sinai; and Miss Heath herself, throned in her great plush armchair in the bay window, her dropsical legs tucked away under a red and green wool rug, the thin silver hair parted and combed back from her pale moon-face, which was like the face of an old Buddha who had outlived his wisdom with undisturbed calm. Beneath her stuff dress were visible the superimposed ridges of many woollen garments, conjectural in function and in form.

He talked to her about a companion, but she did not seem much impressed, and he refrained from bullying her in the matter, having perceived, as soon as he saw her, how little difference it could really make.

Janet had read F. M. Alexander and ten or twelve other books in the last fortnight. She had taken to reading voraciously, indiscriminately, and, apparently, without any unifying personal taste or even much enjoyment. She read what was being talked about, good or bad, light or heavy, but nothing she read seemed to undergo a digestive process. Yet she did not read apathetically; the most diverse things could leave her in a state of defensive indignation. Kit, who had been accustomed to take refuge in this kind of discussion when things were difficult, now found it as full of pitfalls as any other. It was as if the walls of her ego were closing in on her; she seemed incapable of disengaging any idea from its personal attachments. She had a naturally quick intelligence, and could wrest even from moderately difficult works just enough of their purport to find some application to herself or him. She never began by stating this directly, but would open some seemingly abstract discussion with a strung-up insistence that gave her away at once. Under such conditions conversation ceased to exist, and became, as far as Kit was concerned, simply a series of exercises in passive defense. He often made efforts to conquer his caution or ignore it, but it was no use. He could feel behind all she said the tension of something waiting to pounce, and it was impossible to relax while one watched to see where the spring was coming from.

There was very little room in their home for getting away from one another. They had chosen it without reference to this need, as people in love will, unless one at least of them has pronounced habits of solitude already. In any case, they had little choice. They shared with the Frasers a solid, two-story Georgian house, taking the upper floor and the front garden. The rooms were well proportioned and lit with fine square windows, but there were very few of them. Kit slept in the room which had been meant for the nursery, a fact which Janet, he knew, always silently remembered; she seldom entered it. They had only one guest room, a living-room, and a small dining-room not adapted for anything else. There remained his consulting-room downstairs; it was cramped and rather bleak, containing chiefly a roll-top desk, examination couch, and steel filing-cabinets, but it was useful as a last resource. Unluckily, Janet knew, by now, the times when he really needed to be there. Even when it had evidently averted a break of control on one side or the other, his disappearance really hurt her. Kit knew that this at least was genuine, because she often tried to hide it; and it left him at a loss.

He hated to hurt her, partly because he disliked hurting anything – a fact which sometimes made his work more wearing than it need have been. Besides, he always had more knowledge of her moods than she of his, being less concerned to fit them to a pre-conception, and the mere fact of minding about them died hard.

That evening an extra-heavy surgery, which he spun out as far as possible, gave him a decent excuse for working late. At dinner she was subdued, and Kit, who felt tired, was glad to be quiet. Over the coffee she said, 'Whatever were you doing to that poor little boy who was screaming downstairs?'

'Just feeling her tummy over. It was a girl.'

'She must have been in terrible pain. What was the matter?'

'Half a pound of licorice candy.'

'I think children should only be taken to women doctors.'

'Very likely.'

'She sounded absolutely terrified.'

'She was. Her mother had been telling her for years that if she wasn't good the doctor would come and take her away in a black bag.'

Janet stirred her coffee in silence. Her head bent lower, and presently he saw that she was struggling with tears. For a moment he felt simply an exhausted refusal to cope with it; then he came over and sat on the arm of her chair.

'I'm sorry, Janie. Honestly I am.'

She took out her handkerchief and said, half under her breath, 'You find me easy to score off now, don't you, Kit?'

'Why do you let yourself be?'

'I don't know. It's so – unfair. Men have everything.'

'Have they?' said Kit. In their courting days he had found her generalizations about 'men' and 'women' faintly exciting, because of their purely personal implications; besides, he had been a few years younger and more prone to make them himself. Now his mind had ceased to move, except clinically, in these channels, and his response consisted mainly of patience. But her grief troubled a loyalty in him which had little to do with the obligations of marriage. He had never examined its sources, or reflected that it came from a kind of personal coherence woven into his self-respect. He had loved her, and, in fact, bet his life on being right about them both. If he had not foreseen her response to this or that it was as much his responsibility as anyone's. 'How do you mean?' he asked.

'Well, you've got your work; it never stands still; always something new being discovered. You never have to think that everything will be the same for you in ten years, except that you'll be older.'

'But, my dear—' As if she had been struggling in the sea and had stretched out a hand to him, Kit's apartness, his resolute toleration, melted. He bent toward her, with a sudden sharp pang of returning tenderness.

She looked quickly up at him, and took his arm tightly

between her hands. 'Don't get tired of bothering with me, Kit. I know I say things sometimes, but—' She turned away and finished, half to herself, 'One has to have somebody.'

Kit took her on his knee and stroked her hair, taking care, because he had been well trained, not to disarrange it.

'You don't have to worry about that,' he said.

She rested in his arms for a few moments, unrelaxed, her eyes closed; then said quickly, 'Why do you let me be so childish? And I've so much to do this evening.' She slipped away from him, and, going over to her neat pretty little desk with its painted pen tray and colored sealing waxes, started to make out her library list.

When the telephone rang very early that morning, it roused Kit from a sleep so deep that he did not remember, in the first moment of waking, where he was; he imagined himself in his little room at the top of the hospital, called by the casualty-bell; and beneath his sleepiness and irritation had a feeling of well-being and of reluctance to become conscious, as one has at the end of a pleasant dream. Perhaps because of this, instead of putting on the light with the notebook and pencil beside it, he rolled over and reached for the instrument in the dark. 'Hullo,' he said sleepily.

'Is that Dr Anderson?' The voice had a low pitch, not exploding in the ear like most women's voices on the telephone. He disliked being wakened by a metallic squawk. Feeling pleasantly drowsy again, he got back under the clothes, propping the instrument on the pillow.

'Speaking,' he said, with a half-hearted effort to sound alert.

'I'm so sorry to wake you up.'

'It's all right,' said Kit, jolted a little; the voice had neither the panic of the distraught relative nor the crisp impersonality of the nurse. 'Who is it?'

'It's about Miss Heath. Pedlow says you asked to be called if she seemed worse. I think she must be – she's so out of breath, and her lips are blue.'

Kit heaved his legs over the edge of the bed, and, telephone in hand, felt for his slippers. 'Right, I'll come straight over. Will you give her a dose of the special mixture at once, please?'

'The dark brown one? I've given her that. It seemed to do her good.'

'Splendid. Don't worry. I'll be there in ten minutes.'

A quick dresser, he was there in seven. It had rained, and would rain again. A wet, furred moon filled in the spaces between the poplars with its thin wash of light. Leaves were still falling, and the trees showed now in patches the stripped outline of branch and twig against the sky. The lamp in the porch had been switched on; its yellow spread fuzzily, like a blot, in the mists of the night.

As he stepped out of the car the front door was opened by a girl in a Chinese-blue dressing-gown of quilted silk. She looked smaller than she was in the high hall, with its stag heads ten feet up and still far from the ceiling, the towering carved coat-stand, the assegais, and the palms; small but concentrated, the silk of her gown and dark red sheen of her hair focusing the light like spar in a cave. For a moment her unexpectedness linked itself in Kit's mind with the colors of the night, and the place looked different, as if he were seeing it for the first time.

'How quick you've been.' She spoke with ordinary, pleasant courtesy, but her voice was hushed because of the stillness of the house, and the slight words took from this a reasonless significance.

'Has there been any change since you rang me?' he asked.

'Yes. She looks so much better that I'm ashamed to have got you out of bed.'

'Oh, that's all right.' He scarcely knew that he had smiled as he spoke, so that her answering smile seemed sudden and surprising.

Her face in repose was compact and grave, square-boned, but clear in outline, with eyes widely spaced, the brows slanting up a little. He had thought it unrevealing, but her smile was as open as a small boy's, a personal enjoyment rather than a social gesture. Her eyelids looked drowsy, and her skin, unpowdered, had a childish bloom of sleep. She had on a white silk nightgown which showed a little at the hem of her wrap but was too low to show at the neck.

Kit said, 'Well, I'd better take a look at her anyway,' in his hospital voice. As she led the way to the door he felt he had been loitering a long time, though Pedlow would have delayed him minutes longer.

Miss Heath was awake. Propped in her high pillows – she had difficulty with her breathing if she lay flat – she had reached for the heavy Bible with its brass clasps and embossed black boards, which lived at night on the table beside her bed. She was still panting with the effort of lifting it onto her knees. When Kit came in she marked the place carefully with her finger before she looked up.

'Why, is this Dr Anderson? Christie, my dear, you don't mean to tell me you've been sending for poor Dr Anderson at this time of night? Why, it must be after twelve o'clock.' She moved about in the bed, trying to peer at the alabaster and gilt clock on the mantelshelf, which said fifteen minutes to four. The Bible slid sideways out of her lap, and Kit and the girl moved forward at the same moment to catch it. They got it between them just as it reached the edge of the bed; the girl's fingers became caught for a moment between Kit's hand and the book. He had forgotten about her when he entered the sickroom, and found himself caught back into a confusion of impressions, sharp, but too rapid for definition: a light warm scent of bath powder just too complex to be the scent of a flower; a smooth wrist, the bones scarcely traceable; the texture of the blue satin slipping against his sleeve.

He relieved her of the book with the slight brusqueness he would have used to a probationer who had done something clumsy. Miss Heath had clutched feebly at the thing as it fell; her breathing made a little fluttering sound in her throat.

'This is really too heavy for you, you know,' Kit said; and, over his shoulder to the girl, 'Surely there must be a lighter one somewhere in the house?'

'You mustn't take that away from me,' said Miss Heath. 'That was my mother's Bible.' For the first time Kit saw in her wide placid face a contraction of fear. 'All her marks are in it, and all mine since I was confirmed. Yes, my dear mother gave me this Bible for my confirmation. I could never get used to another one. It wouldn't *read* the same, though perhaps it's wrong of me to say that.' Her lips were bluish gray and shrunken, crossed by fine deep furrows; her voice had the shake of very old age. Kit reassured her, and took his stethoscope out.

The girl had walked away to the other end of the room, where she was almost drowned in the shadows. There was a faint clicking as she put something away, the medicine and glass perhaps, in a cupboard. Kit fumbled perfunctorily with the ribbon of Miss Heath's bed-jacket and said, 'Now we'll just have this back,' in the manner accepted for recalling a nurse to the sense of her duties. The girl came back unhurriedly and bent over the bed. The stooping loosened the edges of her gown a little. He widened the gap in Miss Heath's pale-blue crochet with a half-jerk of impatience, and laid the rim of the stethoscope against the loose limp old body underneath.

What he heard was very much what he had expected. The acute phase of the attack was over; the murmur of the regurgitating valves was a little, but not very much, more audible than before. Kit was interested in hearts, and even played sometimes with a secret ambition to specialize. He moved the stethoscope about, happy in a single-minded concentration.

'Now the back, please,' he said crisply. The girl took the weight of Miss Heath's body, raising it forward from the pillows against her shoulder. She was close to Kit as he leaned forward to listen. The light warm scent of the powder reached him again; her hair too had a delicate aura, of itself or of some wash that she used, different but having somehow the same personality.

Miss Heath began to say something. Her shaking voice boomed and rumbled at him through the tube. 'Do you know, Dr Anderson—' Kit was filled with a violent, unreasonable irritation. 'Just a moment, *please*,' he said sharply.

Miss Heath's voice trailed away; magnified in his ears, Kit could hear the startled acceleration of the laboring heart. He felt, without seeing, the quick movement of the girl's head as she turned to look at him. He took the instrument away and pulled down the garments he had displaced.

'I'm so sorry, I was rather—' he began, just as Miss Heath said, 'I beg your pardon, doctor.' When he smiled, Miss Heath forgave him, although she had been shocked at his speaking to her in that tone. He was always so courteous, so unlike the young people of today.

'Now there's no occasion to worry,' he told her as he always told her at these things. 'Everything's settling down very nicely. Just try to get off to sleep, and send for me at once whenever you need me. But mind, no lifting heavy books about by yourself, or anything of that kind. Will you?'

Her old lama's smile spread smoothly over Miss Heath's gray face. 'I'm well cared for, doctor. I'm waited on far too much. I've my little Christie to look after me.' She laid a hand, with the skin like fine yellow crepe, over the hand of the girl resting on the eiderdown beside her.

The door opened behind Kit, a smooth sound, for the old lock was the work of a leisured craftsman, beautifully made.

'I beg your pardon, madam. I thought I heard—'

It was Pedlow, though it took Kit a second or two to recognize her. Her tight, rigid uniform had been so much a part of her that her emergence from it was slightly shocking, as if she had shed part of her skin. She had, in fact, in her haste left her teeth behind, and lisped a little. She was wearing a white calico nightgown, with a buttoned frill in front and a little round collar, and was holding bunched round her a dressing-gown of dark crimson wool. Her faded hair, dragged into two thin plaits, showed the pink scalp between its strands. Kit had not noticed before that the puffs which supported her cap were false. He saw her for the first time as a woman, and felt a faint shock of repulsion; it was as if something that had lived for years underground had been disturbed into daylight.

The girl looked up at her, and smiled. 'It's all right, Pedlow. Don't worry. Dr Anderson says Miss Heath will be all right now. You go back to bed again. There isn't anything more to do.'

Pedlow stood still for a moment. Her lips, drawn back a little from her shrunken gums, showed a tiny black hole in the middle. Her eyes were like narrow black spaces too, as they shifted, traveling past Kit, to the girl. They passed over her face and body and the triangle of white skin where the lapels of her gown crossed.

Kit had, for a moment, a creepy feeling. His life had freed him almost entirely from squeamishness of the simple kind, but the very naturalness of this made him more sensitive to certain kinds of undertone. They showed up against the well-disinfected surfaces of his mind, like a thumb-mark on clean enamel. Looking away, he occupied himself with coiling his stethoscope and returning it to his pocket. When he straightened himself, Pedlow had gone.

'Poor Pedlow,' said Miss Heath. 'She's always so distressed if she thinks I've been unwell. But she sleeps so soundly. She was always a poor riser as a young girl. I remember it well, and the trouble it gave my dear mother. Fancy her waking tonight. Now, Dr Anderson, you'll take something, won't you, before you go? A glass of sherry? Christie, my dear—'

Kit thanked her, and declined. He was feeling tired, vaguely disturbed and irritable, and looked forward to making up the rest of his night's sleep. The girl saw him out. They crossed the antlered cavern of the hall in silence.

Under the clearer light of the porch her hair looked crisp and shining with life. It grew strongly back from her brows, falling in deep waves behind the temples and covering her neck. She had brushed it back without fastening of any kind, and a strand of it was beginning to stray down over her forehead. He wondered how she wore it during the day.

At the inner door of the porch they both paused, in the kind of silence when people seek not for something to say but for some excuse to separate without saying anything. At last the girl said, 'I hope this wasn't too unnecessary.'

'Certainly not.' He spoke with a needless emphasis, as if she had said something highly controversial. 'If she has similar symptoms again, please send for me immediately.' There was another pause. Kit said, 'Well—,' made a movement to the door and stopped again. 'Are you a relative of Miss Heath's?' he asked.

'I'm her great-niece.' She showed no disposition to elaborate this.

Kit, with his hand on the door, said, 'I'm afraid this is rather anxious work for you. You realize, of course—'

'Of course,' she said. 'That's why I had to come.' She spoke impersonally, as if her choice had not been exercised.

'I hope you get proper rest,' said Kit a little abruptly. 'Where do you – how do you manage about waking up?'

'I sleep in the old drawing-room, on the other side of the hall.' She added, like an afterthought, 'There's a bell fixed up from her room to mine. The end's fixed to her bed.'

'Well, that sounds effective . . . Don't you find it rather eerie? It's a very large room.' Once or twice, on early visits, he had been put to wait there.

'No. I like it.' Her face lightened with one of its sudden simplicities of enjoyment. 'I can have the big doors open straight onto the garden.'

Kit had been brought up by a careful mother and wife. He started to say *But someone might get in*, and stopped in the middle. He began to talk quickly and clearly, addressing himself chiefly to the stag's head on the wall behind her left shoulder. 'It's a responsibility that should really be taken by a trained nurse. You mustn't think I don't fully appreciate that. But there were objections, as you know, and it was difficult to insist. One has to avoid any possibility of shock, or of inducing symptoms. You see, the heart is to a great extent under nervous control, and if the patient is led to anticipate—'

'Yes,' she said. 'I see.'

Kit's eyes returned to hers, which were smiling. He had not known till then that he was blushing, transparently, as fair people do, to the roots of his hair. It had been a trouble to him at school, but it was ten years since he had grown out of it. Her small, unconscious smile, revealing it to him, made him feel suddenly and blazingly angry, with his own sensations, the night, the house, with Miss Heath, with her.

'I'll look in sometime tomorrow,' he said, 'if I can manage it. I shall be busy. Send for me if you think it necessary. Good night.' He heard her answer and thank him as he swung through the outer door to his car.

The drive, planned for the sweep of broughams and victorias, embraced three sides of the house with its curve. As he rounded the apex of the bend Kit turned his head; a glimmering space of lawn, pale with dew and the long straight strands of low-lying mist, ended in the deep windows of the drawing-room and the blank gap of its open doors. In a top-floor room a thin wedge of light divided the edges of the curtains. Pedlow, he supposed, performing whatever her preparations for bed might be. *Poor old Pedlow*, he thought; *she'd have a fit if she knew those doors were left open all night.* There was a jar as one of his front wheels mounted the turf beside the drive. Kit swore, and returned his eye to the road.

He put the car away and crossed the garden to the house. It still wanted an hour to daybreak, but the darkness had the unreal, transitory feel of morning.

He crossed the landing quietly, but just as he reached his room he heard the click of a switch and saw the line of light show sharply under Janet's door. He stood still for a moment with his hand on the knob of his own. As he passed on he reflected suddenly that only a few months, perhaps weeks, ago, if this had happened, he would have stood irresolute on the landing, wondering if he might knock at her door, whether she would be pleased to see him or would make him feel that his coming had been an intrusion. He knew how glad he was that it had all ended. Never again, he thought; for anyone.

It surprised him to find his bed scarcely cold; he seemed separated from the moment of waking by many hours. He thrust his head down into the pillow to shut out the noise of the wind; it was rising and beginning to whine among the chimney stacks. *She won't be able to keep those great doors open*, he thought, *on a night like this.* For a moment before he slept he saw her throwing back the bed covers and moving like a swimmer through the stream of the wind, her hair lifted, gasping and laughing at the sweep of it past her sides.

3

A few mornings later Janet looked up from a letter at breakfast. 'What conference is being held here next week?'

'None that I know of. Nothing medical, anyway.'

'Peggy Leach says she's coming over for it, and wants to know if we can put her up.'

'I expect it's an educational thing. They use the old Manor for them sometimes. I don't know her, do I? Does she teach?'

'I haven't met her lately. We were at school together. She was senior to me, very popular and good at games. Fancy her remembering me.'

Kit laughed. 'Did you have a crush on her?'

'How unkind you are, Kit.' She put the letter down. 'Everyone's sentimental at school. It isn't anything to sneer at.'

'I didn't mean to. We're all products of the system.'

'There again. All your criticism is so *destructive* nowadays, Kit. I do so wish you hadn't changed like this. That's how Dr McKinnon always talks.'

Kit got up. 'I've a heavy round this morning,' he said. 'Don't wait lunch for me if I'm late.'

'I shall see you get a proper meal, dear, whatever time you come in.'

She picked up her next letter and slit the envelope with neat-fingered precision. Kit went down to his consulting-room.

In the course of his morning round he visited Laurel Dene and was received, as he had been each time since the night call, by Pedlow. Evidently in the mornings the girl, Christie, went out. Kit was glad to have avoided her. His brief disturbance had settled, and everything had shrunk to the reasonable proportions of morning. He had analyzed and dismissed the incident, feeling detached and clinical. He felt safe from entanglements; he looked forward to an uncomplicated future, devoted chiefly to work and ideas. He had had enough of personal relationships to last him the rest of his life, and had never taken easily to the kind of episode in which no personal relationship was involved.

He was pleased with his work that morning. X-ray confirmed a diagnosis which had been a long shot; a new vaccine treatment was getting results; his worst diabetic was sugar-free for the third day. Miss Heath had looked better too, and he had walked out of the house unconcerned with anything else. He was whistling under his breath as he drove through the principal shopping street of the town. There was a Belisha crossing in the middle of it, and he slowed down for a group of pedestrians. The last one to cross was the girl from Laurel Dene. She was wearing a neat olive-green suit with a hat and shoes the color of gingerbread. Kit thought how average she looked, groomed into the uniform of the season; the angle of the hat, the face tints, the clothes striking the moment's balance between waist, shoulders, and hips; even the kind of walk that the clothes required. At this moment she saw him; they exchanged smiles. Kit drove on, unmoved as he would have been by the model in a gown-shop window, and experiencing a curious feeling of flatness. Dispassionately he noted that her ankles, which had been out of sight last time, were good, and returned to the consideration of his last case.

He went to bed tired with a good day's work, and dreamed disturbingly, as, when he was most pleased with the settled pattern of his life, he sometimes did.

A couple of afternoons later he met Janet carrying a bowl of bronze chrysanthemums into the guest room. She was humming to herself, and looked more animated than she had been for weeks.

'Those are nice.' He stopped for a moment to breathe their sharp frosty smell. 'You're good with flowers, Janie. Who've we got coming?'

Janet's song stopped. 'Oh, Kit! What *is* the use of telling you anything?'

'Did you? I'm sorry. Never mind, tell me again.'

'You *know* we discussed the *whole* thing at breakfast only the day before yesterday.'

Carefully tracking the conversation backward, Kit remembered. 'Oh, yes. Someone for an education conference.'

'Peggy Leach. And she never said it was education; that's what you said. You never pay much attention to the things that interest me, do you?'

Above the spread of the metallic flowers her pale face, sullen in its smooth frame of dark hair, had a strange perverse beauty. It found some flaw in Kit's practiced defenses. His mouth hardened.

'In the course of this morning,' he said, 'I've seen two people who are going to die, three who depend more or less on me to prevent them from dying, and one who'd be better dead. I'm sorry if I seem vague about the small talk at breakfast last Thursday week.'

Janet drew in a little quick breath. He tried before she should speak to gather himself together, but she remained silent, while something sharp and unknown flickered into her eyes. It was

31

beyond anger; it seemed to him for a moment to be fear. He saw that her lips were pressed so tightly together that the blood had gone out of them.

'That was a bit needless,' he said. 'I'm sorry – forget it.'

'Forget it?' She spoke as if she had only just found speech possible. 'You've never in your life spoken—' She stopped with a little sound of bewildered anger; she had tilted the shallow bowl toward her, and a stream of water was darkening on her dress.

'Here,' said Kit, 'let me take it.' He lifted the bowl out of her hands, found a place for it on a side table, and began to mop with his handkerchief at the wet stain. The dress, like all her things, was beautifully cut and modeled; he found himself thinking what a perfectly proportioned body she had, with a kind of objective surprise as if it had never had personal significance for him. He felt a sudden sense of relief and freedom, and his anger went, leaving a confused pity for which he dared not seek expression. He occupied himself with the handkerchief and the dress.

'It doesn't look as if it would stain,' he said. 'You'd better change it though, or you might get a cold.'

'Yes,' she said expressionlessly. He bent to give the place a final rub. She snatched the handkerchief out of his hand and stood still, pulling it through her fingers.

'My dear, is it worth it? I've said I'm sorry.'

She looked at him for a moment in silence, then said half under her breath, 'You humor me now. Like a bad-tempered child.' Before he could answer she had gone. His handkerchief lay at his feet on the floor.

He picked it up, damp and tinged very faintly with the correct and delicate perfume that she used. With the potency that scents have to involve all the other senses in memory, it brought back to him the first days of their honeymoon: the sound of deep broken water under the rocks of the Channel Isles, sun and blue air filling the curved spaces of the bays; Janet with her fragile, beautifully tinted hands full of tiny shells that seemed like miniatures of them. He remembered walking with her in the tree-roofed inland rides, where the sunlight dripped through like honey into round pools among the ferns. The churches had been lined with memorial stones to seamen drowned about the coasts; death had seemed to hang near like the other edge of a shining and sword-like life. Her rare concessions had been like the rewards of enchantment; he had not asked, had scarcely known that he desired, generosity of her or that she should attempt to adapt her way of living to his; not questioning what she offered, since she seemed to have given everything in choosing him to receive it. It had been a life lifted out of life. He saw it now, remote and complete as if it had been expressed in art by a stranger, detached from its consequences with the finality of death, and suddenly he felt the waste in himself of the power of wonder and delight. He remembered that he was young, and had been planning for himself the achievements of middle age.

The handkerchief was still in his hand. He put it in his pocket and, picking up the flower bowl, carried it into the guest room and put it down on the table where, he saw, she had already arranged a mat to keep it from marking the polish.

He had visits to pay in the afternoon; so it was a little after teatime when he got home. Janet's visitor had arrived, and they had started tea. Miss Leach greeted him warmly. She was a tall young woman with a pink outdoor skin, teeth that showed when she talked, and bright blue eyes shining with a penetrating kind of cheerfulness. She had on expensive tweeds spoiled by a bead necklet and a fancy wool jumper that just missed the color-tone. Kit felt a little enveloped by her friendliness.

After tea they talked round the fire. It was a cold day; Kit's round had been rather drafty and comfortless, and he would have liked to relax with a book; but Janet was looking warmed and expanded and, for her sake, he made himself as pleasant as he could. He excused himself when it was time for his evening surgery. Miss Leach dismissed him with a benevolent smile, as if he had asked whether he might now play with his trains.

The evening surgery was used chiefly by panel patients who came in on their way from work. He had grown to look forward to this part of the day. He found their directness restful; the hedgings and modesties of the private patients were too much an extension of his life at home. Among the servant girls and errand boys and the old workmen with dirty, knowledgeable hands, he could recapture for a little while the satisfaction of hospital life, where now he was only a semi-outsider giving anesthetics or taking an occasional clinic during someone's holidays. Sometimes, after a too-guarded day, the mere use by a navvy of some coarse physical term had a kind of nourishment in it.

There were fewer patients than usual tonight, but after they had gone he spent the best part of an hour in the consulting-room, filling in record cards, smoking and reading. His chair was hard, and the place radiator-warmed and a little cheerless; but he scarcely noticed it now.

When he went upstairs again, Janet and Peggy were sitting side by side on the sofa, talking in undertones. As he came in he saw Peggy reach over and give her hand a confidential little pat. At dinner she told, in a tactfully jocular way, anecdotes to show how sensitive Janet had been at school.

Kit was expecting a confinement call, and would not have been sorry if his patient had chosen tonight for the event, but the telephone was obstinately silent. About nine o'clock he tried recourse to the gramophone. After the first concerto Miss Leach said, with bright wistfulness, how much she admired people who *understood* good music. Some day she hoped she would have time to learn a little about it, but there always seemed so much— The effect was to make Kit feel faintly selfish and ostentatious, as if he had boasted of proficiency at some snobbish and exclusive game.

At ten, however, it fortunately turned out that Miss Leach had had a long journey, and would like to get early to bed. Janet took her to her room, and, when she did not return, Kit thought he might decently escape to his own. When he crossed the passage ready for bed, he still heard their voices murmuring through the guest-room door.

He did not settle quickly; he felt restless, unhappy, and disillusioned, and unable to escape it by turning the thing into a hackneyed situation and a music-hall joke. Long after the finish of their married life he had hoped for her friendship, and had a genuine respect for her taste. He was ashamed of the extent to which his feelings had been hurt, unsure of all his judgments, and lonelier than he had ever been in his life. He tried to read, but gave it up and, shutting off thought with dogged obstinacy, at last got off to sleep.

He seemed scarcely to have closed his eyes when the telephone rang. He thought with resignation that this was typical timing for a confinement, and, as he sat up in bed, collected his ideas about it and checked over in his mind the contents of his midwifery bag.

'Is that Dr Anderson?'

'Speaking.' His recognition of the voice had been so immediate that he seemed to have awaited it. He answered, feeling two distinct existences, one which listened attentively to a case-history and made appropriate deductions, another which followed its own reasoning, made its own decisions, and, thrust impatiently aside by the first, still moved in the darkness outside the circle of the lamp, tinging the color of the night.

'The symptoms have only just come on. Yes. Yes. And you've given her the digitalis mixture. Good. All right; don't worry. I'll be right along.'

When he was dressing he found himself looking out a clean collar – a thing he had never done on an urgent call in his life – and shut the drawer again with a slam.

The house was quiet and unlighted. He went softly downstairs and out to the car. He was in the garage before he noticed that it was his midwifery bag he had brought out. He ran back for the other, swearing at himself.

It was still raining. The light over the porch at Laurel Dene was reflected in a deep puddle in one of the sunken places of the drive. Christie opened the door as he drove up; she had on the Chinese-blue dressing-gown she had worn before.

For a moment neither of them spoke; then Kit said, 'Good evening,' and she answered and stood aside from the open door. Kit put down his bag and began to get out of his driving-coat, wet already in the distance between the car and the porch. She helped him to pull it off, then said, 'I don't think she's so bad this time as last. Perhaps I ought not to have sent for you.' Again it was as if her voice had broken a pause.

'Not at all,' Kit said. 'One can't afford to take chances with a condition of this kind. You were perfectly right to call me up.' He crossed the hall to Miss Heath's room, hearing, distinct in the silence, the movement of her silk gown behind him.

He opened the door quietly, and then paused on the threshold, instinctively barring the girl's passage with his hand on the jamb; for in the first moment he thought that Miss Heath was dead. Her round yellow face lay motionless in its mound of pillows, with closed eyes; her mouth, faintly blue, was a little open. He bent nearer. A faint, rhythmic sound disturbed the quiet. It was a gentle snore.

Kit tiptoed gently to the bed. It was true that her color was far from good. She might, he thought, have had an attack of some kind a little while before. Perhaps he was mistaken; she might be unconscious. Leaning close, he listened to her breathing. No, she was asleep.

He looked round. The girl had not come into the room, but was standing where he had left her in the doorway. Her face was set with what seemed a sudden fear. He came back to her and they went together into the hall.

'No,' he said. 'It's all right. She's fallen asleep.'

He saw her hands, which she had clenched tightly together, relax. She nodded her head. 'It was only just – when you went over quickly like that. I thought something might have happened when I was out of the room.'

'That did cross my mind for a moment. But there shouldn't be any further trouble tonight. If she can sleep— How long has she been sleeping, by the way?'

She looked up quickly. 'It can't have been for more than a very few minutes. Just since I went out.' She was twisting a little pearl ring on her finger. Women slept in their pearls, he remembered, to keep them warm. He tried to think of something professional and intelligent to say, but could only try to remember the color of her eyes, which were hidden, and see that her lashes were tinged with the dark red of her hair and that her lids were transparent and faintly veined with blue.

'Well,' he said at last, 'you needn't worry now.'

'No.' She played with the knot in the silk cord of her gown. They had stopped in the hall, halfway to the door; he could not remember how long they had been standing there.

He forced himself to go on talking. 'Do you get many of these disturbed nights? You ought to make them up in the morning.'

'Oh, I'm all right. I can sleep on if I want to. But you can't, can you? I'm sorry. You look tired.'

She looked up at him, meeting his eyes before he was ready. He would have to get away, to say something, he thought; but he did neither. It was she who, without seeming to have moved, was suddenly close to him. She looked up into his face with a cloudy smile.

It did not seem to him that anything new had happened when he took her in his arms. He had known how her eyelids would feel, cool and fragile, and the soft brush of her lashes against his lips.

This is insanity, he thought, half-awaking, and gripped her with all his strength because in a moment she would try to go away. But her firm silky shape only molded itself more closely to his hold, and one of her arms slipped round his neck. Her mouth was still smiling, distant and dreamlike, as he closed it with his own.

In the years of his marriage, and even before, he had forgotten what it was to be made welcome without reserve. A light cracked behind his eyes. He did not know that he had lifted her almost off her feet. She clung about his neck, her head falling back a little; he kissed her throat and the hollow of her shoulder.

They stopped at last for breath and she rested, unmoving, in the support of his arms; her lashes lifted a little and her eyes, deep and shining, seemed to include and pass beyond him. The blood began to flow back, clear and bright, into her lips which his kiss had whitened.

'Send me away,' he whispered. 'Do you hear? For God's sake send me away.'

'Not yet.' She slid her hand upward along his arm, and brushed her fingertips lightly over his hair.

He held her harder. 'Send me away. I've no right to be here.'

'I know.' She drew his face down again to hers. 'I know all that. Not yet.'

He could feel the stretch of her muscles, firm and flexible, as she reached upward in his tightened arms. He kissed her and felt her fingers move in a vague caress about his head. Her gown, loosened sideways, showed two ribbons of pale satin knotted at the shoulder. She shut her eyes and rubbed her face sideways, as a cat does, against his cheek. 'I shouldn't have called you,' she murmured under her breath.

The yellow glare of the light, high up in its cut-glass shade, dazzled in his eyes. 'Where can we go?'

Am I saying this? asked a distant and bewildered voice within him, intruding from the day. He let it fall silent. She turned softly in his arms and said, 'I'll—'

They both stiffened, fixed in an embrace which they no longer felt. There had been a sound – a step, or some other movement – on the floor above.

'Quick!' She slipped from his arms, folding her gown round her, and snatched his coat from the stand by the door. 'Quick, put this on; say something ordinary.'

'I—' His voice trailed off. He could think of absolutely nothing to say; he was dazed as if he had been wakened from deep sleep by an explosion. She shook the coat out and held it up to him, crooked, with the sleeves out of reach. Recovering himself, he took it away from her and threw it over his arm. The house was perfectly silent. 'It wasn't anything,' he said. 'A board creaking somewhere, I expect.'

She clutched him by the sleeve and pulled him toward the door. 'No. It was Pedlow. I could tell it was.'

He detached her clenched fingers and held them. They felt cold. 'You're not frightened of Pedlow, are you?'

'No. Not really. Of course not.' She smiled, looking past him at the stairs.

He warmed her hands in his. 'You mustn't be frightened. All these old retainers get a bit queer. I've seen a lot. She's only on your nerves because you're continually cooped up with her, and overtired. I'll make you up a tonic; you ought to be taking one.'

She laughed under her breath. 'How delicious you are. Will you really mix me a tonic?'

'No,' said Kit as a thought occurred to him. 'Better not. I'll find you a good proprietary one.'

'No? Why not?'

'Because,' he said slowly, 'it would make you technically a patient of mine.'

'Don't you want me to be?'

He dropped his coat on the floor, and pulled her to him by the shoulders. 'No. I don't.'

After a little while she pushed him away. 'I'm sure she heard you. You must go.'

'Yes. How shall I see you again?'

'Don't be a fool,' she said softly. 'You know when we wake in the morning we shan't be able to forget this fast enough.'

'That's impossible.' But he knew, as he spoke, that it was true. He looked down at her hair tangled behind her ears; her face was turned away. 'Life's hopeless, isn't it?' he said.

She nodded, and moved to free herself; but at the last moment he caught her back again. She struggled with unexpected strength. 'No. You don't . . . Go now. Please.'

Her arms slipped suddenly round him. He felt her hair against his throat and heard his own heart like some external noise.

'What is it, then?' She tilted her face upward against his shoulder. 'Don't you want it to be tomorrow morning?'

'My God.' He kissed her angrily; she put her hand over his mouth.

'It is tomorrow, you know, already. It must be after one.'

Impatiently, without thinking, he said, 'Oh, this doesn't count.'

'I know. The small hours never seem part of any day, do they? A sort of No Man's Land.'

'Yes, that's what I always—' He stopped, because the conversation between their eyes had taken a different turn, and the rest of the sentence had left his mind. They were silent; her hand, with which she had been idly caressing his shoulder, rested there motionless.

At last she said slowly, 'I'm so afraid Pedlow may have heard the car.'

He steadied his voice. 'She sleeps like a log. If she'd heard it she'd have been down by now.'

'Yes . . . I don't know.' She strained away, listening and staring into the darkness; then suddenly turned back and clung to him. Joining her hands behind his head she pulled his face down to hers. 'Listen. Drive your car away. Leave it somewhere else. Walk round the lawn, by the side of the shrubbery, where it's dark. I'll leave the glass doors open.'

Staring at her closed eyes, he whispered, 'We must be out of our minds.'

'Yes. We are, of course. You mustn't make any noise.'

'No. Don't worry. I'll take care of all that.'

'Well, go then. Go now. What are you waiting for?' She twisted out of his hands. 'Here, you've left your coat again. No, put it on. Don't you see it's pouring with rain? Do you want to get pneumonia? Don't leave the car too near the house. How long will you be?'

'I don't know. Six or eight minutes, I should think.'

'All that time? We shall both have long enough to change our minds.'

'No.'

'If you do you're to stay away. Mind that. I shall know if you have. I shan't want you.'

'Be quiet.' He bent to her, but she pushed him away. 'And if *you* change your mind?' he asked. 'What then?'

She looked up at him, thoughtfully and without protest. 'If I do I'll put the light out and close the doors.'

'All right,' said Kit. He turned toward the porch, then came back and caught her by the arm.

'What is it?' she asked. 'Oh, do go.'

'I will. But I had to – I wasn't sure. You do know, don't you, that I'm—'

'Oh, yes, yes, of course I do. Don't fuss, dear.' Then, seeing that

he still hesitated, 'Surely you're not going to begin telling me—'
She smiled. 'No, you never would.'

'Would what?'

'Oh, nothing. I meant – that tale about her being your wife only in name. But you wouldn't.'

Kit let go of her arm. After a little pause he said, 'I don't think, really, it makes any essential difference.'

She was staring at his face. 'My dear, have I— I didn't— Don't pay attention to what I say. I don't pay half enough myself.'

'It's all right. It doesn't matter. In any case, probably the less we relate this to real life the better.'

She was silent for a moment. 'You're refreshingly honest.'

'I don't know – I—'

'Are you going to stand here talking till it's light, or we've both got bored?'

She opened the door, letting in a swirl of rain. The wind lifted back her hair, as he had once seen it lifted in fancy.

'Did you have a hat? Or gloves? For God's sake don't leave anything about.'

'I didn't bring any.' He smiled at her. 'If you remember, I came in a hurry.'

'Did you?' she murmured vaguely. 'Oh – yes, you did.' She colored faintly. 'I'd forgotten you *could* hurry, we seem to have been at this door all night.' She gave him a little push toward it, then checked him by the coat lapels. 'You're sweet.' She kissed him without passion, tenderly and gently, and shut the door behind him. He went out into the rain.

4

'Hark to the rain,' she said. The wind had shifted, and was tossing handfuls of drops against the tall glass panes of the doors. Their voices rose a little under its noise, sinking to whispers in the silence between. 'Are you cold, my darling? Your shoulders feel cold.'

'Cold?' said Kit drowsily. 'Don't be silly.'

She fished up the eiderdown from the floor beside her and tucked it round him, murmuring, with childish tenderness, 'You mustn't ever be cold.'

'I never will be again.'

'You're going to sleep.' She drew her fingertips in the darkness exploringly over his closed eyes.

'Not really.'

'You mustn't go to sleep. I should have to wake you and I couldn't bear it. What a shame. Let's put the light on again.'

She leaned across him and switched it on; it stood on a low table beside the bed, a little gimcrack battery affair like a ship's lantern. He turned to look at her as she slid down beside him again; she lay with casual grace and well-being, as if she were resting after a swim.

'You're good,' he said, and saw her smile. But he had used the word as one might use it of bread. In the language which was, so far, the only one in which they had exchanged confidences, she had spoken with a perfect honesty and completeness. Seeing his eyes on her she stretched again, contentedly, as people stretch in the sun.

'I'm glad you like me.'

Exactly, he thought, as if she were a little girl who had given somebody a birthday present. She had a curious fortuitous innocence which had never left her, even in the moments which had most belied it.

He folded her into the eiderdown, and she curled herself into his arms. Over her head he could see the room, which had only been a vague, confused background before. The far end of it was almost invisible in shadow. He could just make out a great marble fireplace carved in high Gothic relief, and filled with brass, an arched mirror over it, reflecting innumerable silver oddments on the mantelpiece. Above their heads, like an inverted fountain of muddy water, hung the dusty crystals of an Empire chandelier, returning the small glow of the lamp. The carpet was pink, with a lattice of darker pink flowers; it seemed to stretch away like a sea; a gilded chair, a mahogany occasional table piled with knick-knacks and photographs, islanding its distances here and there. The bed, a stiff guest-room affair with high wrought-brass head and foot, looked accidental and lonely, like a raft.

'What a cavern to sleep in,' he said. 'Doesn't it give you the creeps?'

'Sometimes it's fun. I act costume plays when I go to bed. I remember, though, it did frighten me once when I woke in the dark and couldn't remember where I was. I wish you'd been there.'

'Mightn't that have been a bit upsetting too?'

'Not for a minute.' She tucked her head under his chin.

A yard or so from the bed was a gilt, spindle-legged sofa,

covered with faded rose brocade. Her blue gown was lying in a heap over one end of it, and it must have been the place where she kept her clothes at night, for, overflowing from behind one of the cushions, there emerged the top of a silk stocking and a pink satin suspender. A mahogany chest of drawers was the only other bedroom furniture besides the bed. Her brushes and cream jars were strewn at random over the top; one of the drawers had jammed because it was too full to shut, and from a corner protruded a bunch of crepe de Chine. On the tall footpiece of the bed the second stocking of the pair hung by itself, looking appealing, as if it were waiting for Christmas. She must be shockingly untidy, he thought, if this represented her party manners for a visitor; and pierced by a sudden irrational tenderness, he gathered her in and began to kiss her again.

'What is it?' she asked him.

He did not know, so answered, since it was true, 'I shall have to go in a minute.'

'Ah, no.' She wrapped herself round him, making herself soft and cherishing. 'I can't send you out into the rain.'

'Don't,' he said involuntarily, and pressed her face into his shoulder to silence her.

'Don't what? What's the matter?'

'Nothing.' He pushed the hair back from her ear. 'I really will have to go; I've a midder case that might come off.'

'But you can't go now. What is it? I make you unhappy?'

'Oh, God, no. I can't explain.'

'Why – what do I do?'

He shook his head. She raised herself on her arm and bent over him, leaning her cheek on his so that her hair fell darkly across his face. He whispered unevenly, 'It's nothing . . . It's only – you're very kind.'

'What? Oh, my sweet.' She lifted herself to look at him, and caught his face between her hands. Soothingly, as if she were

45

consoling a baby, she murmured over him, 'I'll always be kind to you, my precious, always. I promise I will. You're such a darling and I love you so much.'

'No,' said Kit quickly. He moved a little away from her. 'Don't spoil it. It's good enough as it is.'

'But I only said I loved you. Don't you want me to love you? Darling?'

'I don't want you to say you do as if you were offering me a lollipop.'

She looked round at him quickly. 'But I—' She slid away from him, and lay with her chin cupped in her hands. 'You frighten me,' she said slowly. 'People generally—' Her head jerked a little, as if she were flicking something away. 'Are you always as devastatingly sincere as this?'

'I didn't mean to be brutal. But from you it's too— Oh, well, anyway, don't do it.'

'You don't want to love anyone, do you?'

He was silent, startled that she should have perceived this. For a moment he cast about for some evasion, but in the end said simply, 'No. I don't.'

He was unhappy at the thought of hurting her, but she only leaned over and stroked his face. 'It doesn't matter, pet,' she said fondly. 'You don't have to. Don't get all worked up.'

'I wish I could tell you,' he said slowly, 'how you—'

'S-sh. I promise I won't love you if you don't like it. Cross my heart I won't. I only said it to be nice to you. Dear – what do they call you? What's your name?'

Kit looked into her earnest face, and was suddenly overtaken by laughter. He choked it down, till he found that she was laughing too. They clung to one another, shaking, till he forgot not to make a noise, and she stuffed a handful of eiderdown into his mouth. During this moment it occurred to him that he had never laughed in bed before.

'Well?' She ungagged him. 'What *is* your name?'

'I adore you. It's Christopher.'

'*Is* it? But mine's Christina. Our names are nearly the same.' She looked at him wide-eyed. 'That must *mean* something.'

'So it seems.' He kissed her, still laughing a little. 'People call me Kit as a rule.'

'Kit. That's nice. I like that. Do you know mine?'

'The important part. Christie what – or ought I to know?'

'Christie Heath, of course. My grandfather was Aunt Amy's brother.'

'Christie Heath.' He repeated it because the sound of it pleased him, and affectionately, without thinking much about it, stroked his hand over her side. He felt her flinch a little, and stopped.

'It's all right. It's only a bruise. You're stronger than you think you are, you know.'

Kit had heard something of this kind before, and his response was instinctive. With the prompt obedience of habit he moved himself out of the way and said, 'I'm awfully sorry.'

She was quite still for a moment; then with a little murmuring sound reached up and flung her arms round him with a violence that nearly throttled him. Her face was pressed tightly to his, and he could feel her lashes grow warm and wet.

'I didn't mean it; I was making it up. You didn't hurt me, dear, you didn't. You've been unhappy and I didn't know.'

'Hush,' whispered Kit, stroking her hair. 'Don't – please; I—' His throat hurt him and he could not say any more.

One of her tears ran, thinly salt, over his mouth. 'Dear, dear Kit. Everything's going to be all right. I'm going to look after you; you're never going to be unhappy any more.'

He wanted to laugh at her absurdity, but the tightness in his throat prevented him. Her warmth hung, heavy and softly clinging, about his neck; he shut his eyes, and bent to her lifted mouth.

Slowly and momentously, seeming to clear its throat beforehand, the grandfather clock in the hall struck the half-hour. The little battery in the bedside lamp was fading; the bulb had grown dim and yellow, and its faint circle of light hardly reached beyond the bed. Kit stretched himself, and gave a sigh into which a yawn intruded.

'Oh, darling, and you've got to work all tomorrow. Go to sleep for a little while. I'll wake you up; I promise I will.'

'No.' He shook himself awake. 'I must leave at once. I'm expecting a case.'

'What sort of case?'

'A woman having a baby.'

'Oh.' She let go of him. 'I wish you'd told me.'

'It's all right,' he said, made ashamed by her concern. 'It may not be for days, and there's a good nurse in the house.'

'I shouldn't have kept you.'

'Don't worry. If it were really urgent, my – someone would have rung for me here. I always scribble down the address before I start on a night call.' He had been meditating on this for the last few minutes, but Christie seemed consoled.

'Come here, darling, and I'll see to your tie.'

'Thanks; but I expect, really, I can do it better myself.' He pulled at it awkwardly; the necessity for having kept on most of his clothes made him feel a little self-conscious and boorish.

'Sweet, that's worse than ever. Let me a minute. Don't look so nervous; I'm very good at ties.'

She was. Kit got up and put on his coat, surprised to discover how angry it made him. 'Can I borrow your brush?'

'Of course. You can't see over there; give it to me.'

It was backed with painted wood, pale green with a pattern of tiny flowers, a cheap, pretty thing. She brushed his hair back, stroked it down with her hands, and kissed him. The brush she dropped, with a matter-of-fact air of dismissal, on the floor. Kit picked it up and put it back in its place.

'Don't get up,' he said. 'I can let myself out.'

He sat on the edge of the bed, looking down at her. He had not known, till the moment came, how hard it would be to leave her. She took his hand in both hers, and held it against her cheek. 'You'll feel all different in the morning. Next time we meet we'll pretend it never happened.'

'Next time we meet,' he said, 'we shall probably have to. But I'm glad it did happen and I always shall be.'

'You must go.' She moved her cheekbone softly in the hollow of his hand.

He made a movement to rise, then slipped to his knees and put his face beside hers on the pillow. 'I shall miss you,' he said, afraid at the sudden knowledge of it.

'I'll think about you,' she said in her warm comforting voice. 'I promise I'll be thinking of you and loving you, darling. Always I will.'

The wind rattled the rain-beaten casement impatiently behind him. He pressed his face into the spread of her hair, and did not contradict her.

5

'I can't tell you how relieved I was,' said the nurse, 'when I heard your car stop. Fancy your noticing the light and remembering which house it was. Those few minutes just made all the difference. I hardly dared leave her, even to phone. And having your bag with you and everything.'

'I happened to be passing this way,' said Kit, scrubbing his nails, 'from another case. The bag was luck, really. Brought it out by mistake and couldn't be bothered to take it in again.'

The maternity nurse handed him a clean towel, her plain face warm with appreciation and the solid friendship of those who have shared a skilled and strenuous job. The first crying of an infant sounded, thin, indignant, and lonely, from across the landing.

'You can't have been in bed at all tonight,' said the nurse with sympathy. She had only had an hour herself.

'Not to sleep.' Still enclosed in the concentration of the last few hours, he meant simply that he had been awake when the first call came.

Above the noise of water gurgling out of the bathroom basin came the sudden drumming of rain. Kit was still for a moment, with the towel held to the wrist he had been drying, then looked away quickly from the nurse's pleased, tired eyes.

'Yes,' he said slowly after a moment, 'it was lucky I came along when I did.'

It was nearly six when he got in. He woke in sunlight, to find himself being shaken by the shoulder. He blinked, dazed and scarcely knowing where he was. He had thrown himself on the bed meaning only to rest, but had fallen into a sleep so deep that waking left him dazed, like coming round from an anesthetic or a blow. The curtains had just been opened, and a patch of sun fell on his face. It hurt his eyes, and he threw his arm across them, longing for sleep again. Then, under it, he saw Janet standing there, dressed for the morning.

He moved his arm, narrowing his eyes in the light. She did not speak for a moment; she had taken her hand away quickly when he woke, but was still standing beside him. To his indistinct vision there seemed a kind of softness and shadow in her face, and a little droop at the corners of her mouth that he had not seen lately. He rubbed his eyes, gathering his mind together, dimly remembering that something had happened, that it was somehow wrong she should be there, that it made him unhappy to see her.

'I've brought you some breakfast,' she said. 'You won't get anything to eat before surgery begins unless you have it now.'

He realized that there was a smell of coffee in the room. 'What?' he murmured, his voice furred with sleep. 'What time is it?'

'Half-past eight. I left you as long as I could.'

Struggling with a weariness that seemed ten times what it had been when he fell asleep, Kit began to come to himself. He felt stiff and cramped, and remembered that halfway through undressing it had not seemed worth while, and he had lain down as he was in his trousers and loosened shirt. Janet pulled up the bedside table with the tray on it.

'I told Elsie to bring you up some fresh shaving-water. The first jug will be cold by now.'

'Thank you.' Kit sat up. Her voice had a gentleness that moved and confusedly hurt him. 'You shouldn't have bothered,' he said. 'I could have come down.'

'You looked absolutely dead. You never sleep on like that. What happened? What time did you come in?'

'I don't remember, about six I think. I had two night calls straight on, a heart case first and then a midder.'

'You mean you'd been out ever since that first bell went before twelve? No wonder you're tired.'

'It's all right. I'll wake up if I have a cold bath.'

'Have this first while it's hot.' She poured out a cup of coffee, moved to go, and sat down instead on the foot of the bed, a thing she had not done for more than a year.

She said, looking out of the window at the sun glittering on wet roofs and trees, 'It must have been a terrible night to be out in. I lay awake for hours listening to the rain.'

'I wasn't out in it very much. I'm sorry it kept you awake.'

'Look! The ends of your trousers are soaking wet even now. You'll make yourself ill, sleeping in damp clothes. Kit, what a stupid thing to do. Whatever made you?'

'I didn't notice them. It won't hurt me for once.'

'You *will* change them?'

'My dear, of course I shall – the crease is out for one thing. Don't you worry about me.'

'Oh, I don't do that. I know you're independent.' She smiled, a tight little smile more like her ordinary one. 'But you looked so— Well, I mustn't sit here making you talk, or you won't get anything to eat.' She got up, smoothed the pleats of her neat skirt, and walked away. At the door she turned for a moment, seeming about to say something, but changed her mind. Kit finished his coffee, disarranged the bacon and eggs as plausibly as he could, and hurried to make himself presentable.

He was not a success with himself that morning. His mind moved laboriously and in circles, decisions came stickily, and he found it easier to worry over his bad cases than to think constructively about them. He had a headache which, after he had been driving for a short time, extended itself to his eyes. Nothing untoward happened, because he pushed himself at the details of his routine with irritable obstinacy; but he had a precise technical standard, and did not tolerate muddled method any the better because it got approximate results. During the unhappiness and discomfort of all this, his recollections of the previous night became exceedingly objective.

At the time, the purely professional aspect of what he had done had seemed distant, fantastic, even, to the point of humor. Now, hideously lucid and concrete, it began to emerge. He could see it set out, in neat clear sentences of neat small type, in the lower half of a right-hand column in the *British Medical Journal*:

While visiting the house of a patient in a professional—

Toward the end of his round he checked over his notebook, ticking off the visits he had already made. He found with relief that there were only two left, but flicked over the leaf perfunctorily to make sure. At the top of the last page was, *Thurs. Miss H. Laurel D.? renew prescription.*

It was, he realized, the first Thursday morning for months that he had not turned in at the gates as mechanically as he dressed or shaved, never varying the time by more than 10 or 15 minutes. He looked at his watch; it was a quarter to one. He sat in the car, with the notebook propped against the wheel, staring at the almost illegible scribble. After a moment he took his pencil and, scoring out the words with long heavy strokes, wrote underneath, *Visit last night.*

That's that, he thought. It amounted to nothing in particular, since he would have to call within the next few days in any case, but it satisfied, momentarily, his impulse of recoil.

At lunch he found Peggy Leach's place empty. She was lunching with some of the people from the conference. He expected to feel relieved, but did not; he had, in fact, unconsciously counted on her as a buffer between Janet and himself.

It was the first time he had deliberately concealed from her anything more concrete than his own unhappiness. He had found deceit difficult once; even the needs of his own self-respect had got him no further than reticence. But, later, the demands of her weakness had coaxed his integrity from him step by step. He had made himself more and more an accessory to her flights from truth, till at last he lied to her instinctively, kindly, without mental apology, as naturally as he handed her checks for the housekeeping. So, now, he felt strained rather than ashamed when she began to ask him about his night calls, whether one of them had been to the old lady with the weak heart, and whether she had been very ill. It was a ritual of hers, once in every day or two, to take an interest in his work. She never remembered what he told her, so he was used to suppressing anything complex or personally absorbing. He gave her a lucid, inaccurate account of the night's work, shifting the times, almost automatically, to sound plausible. She listened with a bright, kindly little smile, sitting straight and graciously in her chair. She was as beautiful, still, as she had ever been. Now that it was all over, he remembered the happiness she had given him rather than the pain, and the thought that he had broken his promises to her distressed him. That he was deceiving her, it did not occur to him to think. It was a condition of his life; he took it for granted.

No (he explained), Miss Heath wouldn't have a trained nurse. She had a sort of companion who looked after her if she was taken ill in the night.

'Poor woman,' said Janet sincerely. 'It must be terrible to grow

54

old in other people's houses, picking up the fag ends of other people's lives. I think I'd rather be almost anything than a companion.'

'Yes,' he said absently. The visit as it had really been had passed before his mind, and with it, suddenly, a picture of Miss Heath's placid sleeping face. It occurred to him for the first time that Christie might not have told her he had called at all. He had not thought, in the night, of making any arrangement about it. In that case Miss Heath – and Pedlow – would have been expecting him this morning. He always called on a Thursday. It meant that he would have to go this afternoon. 'This one isn't so very old,' he said.

'That must make it almost worse.'

'I suppose so.' He ate something which he did not taste and found difficult to swallow. He knew, now, that he had wanted all the time to go more than he had wanted to stay away. But he was too much at war with himself to feel pleasure at the thought of it. He resented the rather painful disturbance of his nerves, and told himself that she would probably be out, or in some other part of the house or the grounds; in any case, he was almost certain not to see her alone. He began planning conversational openings for Miss Heath or Pedlow which would be safely ambiguous. He would have to be careful, if he did not see Christie first. But in his heart he was sure that he would see her. She would manage it somehow. Against his will he thought of her comfort and her promises. While he was at work he had wanted to be free of her, but here at home, where every familiar thing had its own association of disappointment and loneliness, he knew why she had been necessary to him, and that she would be again.

'—after all,' Janet was saying, 'in practice it seems to work out, doesn't it? They all seem such happy, contented people. Look at Peggy, for instance.'

'Yes, don't they?' murmured Kit, wondering to what, and how

long ago, she had changed the conversation. 'It's a question of what suits one, I suppose.' He was thinking that he would ring up, after lunch, to say he was sorry he had not had time to get over in the morning, and would be along shortly. Whoever answered, Christie would probably get to know. After all, he reasoned with himself, she had been extraordinarily good to him. When he broke the thing off it would have to be very gently indeed. He was bound to see her today. Put like this, it all looked simple and straight-forward, but longing and resistance continued their conflict, unreconciled, within him.

The meal got to an end without Janet having noticed anything unusual. He had trained his face and his voice, by now, to look after the amenities when he himself was elsewhere.

He put the call through from his own room, because there was just a chance that Christie might answer. While he listened to the bell ringing in the empty hall his hands felt cold, and there was a constriction in his chest. He was angry with himself for not being able to take it humorously. But when the receiver clicked he started as if he had been shot. It was Pedlow, after all. He tried his most ingenious gambits on her, but she was completely – almost carefully – noncommittal. Miss Heath seemed a little better, she thought. She said nothing about last night's visit, and nothing to convince him that she did not know of it. He told her he would be there between half-past two and three.

That would give Christie time, he thought, to wind up any-thing she might be doing and get out to meet him in the drive. As the time drew near, and he got out to the car, his mind felt smoothed-out and secure again. He thought that she would be pleased to see him – the first conviction of the kind he had known for years – and felt warmed, uplifted, and protective. Again he decided that he must put an end to it. This time he was thinking not of himself, but of her.

He saw her when he was halfway up the drive. She was standing just as he had imagined her, in a gap of the laurels on the other side of the lawn, wearing a light soft dress, the color of meal, and a little yellow jacket. She was too far off for her face to be clear, but he knew at once that she had seen him. He slowed down – he had not come in sight of the house – and lifted his hand to wave to her. At the same instant she turned and disappeared into the trees.

At first he did not take it in. He thought she was coming to meet him by some hidden path, to avoid being seen. He stopped the car, and waited. Presently he caught a distant glimpse of her through the trees. Her back was turned; she was walking in the opposite direction.

There was a moment in which he appeared to himself to be accepting this quite naturally and calmly. Yes, of course, she was walking away. He had known this was quite likely to happen all the time. He started the car, contemplating the event reasonably, while the surrounding scene underwent a curious contraction, deadening the chill. His dread of self-betrayal, his painfully vulnerable pride, had been waiting for something of this kind all along.

He found he had reached the porch, stopped, and, catching a glimpse of himself in the driving-mirror, waited a moment to settle down.

Pedlow opened the door. She seemed more drawn-in and buttoned-up than ever. Even her stays did not squeak.

'How's Miss Heath?' he asked. 'Any change since I last called?'

'None, sir, as far as I am aware.' It was not like Pedlow to be so noncommittal. She was a woman of definite ideas. Probably, he thought, she was put out by having the girl in the house. Now he would have to glean his information from Miss Heath, a much more complicated matter. His resentment grew.

Worse was to follow, for Miss Heath turned out to be having

one of her vague days. Her faculties fluctuated a good deal, as old people's will. When he congratulated her on looking better than she had last time, she told him how thankful she was to Providence for not letting her suffer as her dear mother had done, and went on from there to a hunting accident her father had had when she was six years old.

'How did you sleep last night?' he asked her at last.

'Oh, I can't complain of my sleep, doctor. But I have disturbing dreams sometimes, very disturbing dreams. I dream sometimes that I've been thrown into the sea and that I'm just about to drown. And then one night this week I dreamed I heard you and Christie talking in the hall. Just the voices. It seemed quite real at the time; so foolish.'

'So long as you don't actually stay awake,' said Kit evenly, 'I don't think we need worry about that. You must let me know, though, if you have any more restless nights.'

'It's really of no consequence, doctor; I can always make it up in the day.' Her round face smiled at him, deprecating and kindly. He realized that he had become, in the last year, exceedingly fond of her. He hated lying to her as he had not hated lying to Janet, quite apart from the professional side of it, which had left him no peace all day.

'Now, I wonder where my little Christie is. Naughty girl, she must have forgotten the time. I particularly told her you were coming; I know you like to have someone to help with the lifting. But I'll ring for Pedlow.'

'No, please don't bother. I think the chest will be enough for today.' He listened, made out a fresh prescription, and left quickly.

Driving rapidly down the drive, he rounded a blind bend and saw Christie, walking well in the middle and quite oblivious of him, a few yards ahead. He just managed to avoid running her down by jamming on the brakes.

She was dressed for the street, wearing a long loose coat that swung pleasantly as she turned to smile at him. Her escape seemed not to have impressed her much. On Kit the effect of seeing her was like that of a violent blow in the diaphragm, uncomplicated by pleasure of any kind. 'Good afternoon,' he said. Aiming at pointed formality, he ejected it like an insult.

Her smile disappeared. It was the only alteration in her face that anger allowed him to notice. 'Good afternoon. Forgive me for delaying you.' She prepared to walk on.

Kit made a half-gesture toward his hat, but it never arrived, nor did the frigidly polite formula on his tongue take shape. He found them inadequate. What he wanted was a scene. He discovered in some astonishment that he had no intention of leaving without one. *I can't behave like this*, he told himself, and was pleased, in a hot and painful way, by the certainty that he would. 'It really isn't a very good idea,' he said, 'to go to sleep in the middle of the road.'

In the first moment of meeting, Christie had gone rather white. Now the color returned, with interest, to her face; she thrust her hands into the pockets of her loose coat, and planted her feet apart. 'This is a private drive. If you hadn't been tearing along, you'd have had room to pull up.'

'I did pull up, or you wouldn't be here. But it helps if the pedestrian makes *some* contribution.'

'Yes, I expect so. Don't let me keep you; I know you never have any time to waste.'

Kit had reached a stage when even this was not sufficient to dislodge him. 'If you'd ever seen a really bad road smash,' he said obstinately, 'you'd be more careful.'

'I have. My father and mother were both killed in one.'

'Oh. I'm sorry,' said Kit inaccurately. He was, in point of fact, furious with her for taking such a low advantage. As there seemed nothing to add to this, he said at last, 'Well, I'll say good-by.'

'That made you look rather an ass, didn't it?' she remarked as he was moving to go. 'I thought it would. That's why I made it up.'

Kit stopped in his tracks and, when he could speak, said, 'Well, my God.'

'You looked so silly and smug, I had to get some sort of a rise out of you. Now do go home.'

Kit drew in a sharp breath through his nose. He wanted, quite simply, to get his hands on her and beat her. Being normally even-tempered, he was somewhat shattered by the experience. He stared at her, his face setting.

The girl took a backward step which brought her up against the laurels at the side of the drive. 'I'm not frightened.'

Slowly Kit's years of cultivated restraint reasserted themselves. He said at last, with deadly calm, 'Possibly you might like to let me know, before you go, what you propose to tell your aunt about last night. She appears not to know that I called. It might be an advantage if we stuck to the same lie.'

She looked up quickly. 'But she was asleep.'

'But you happened not to mention whether you'd told her I was coming.'

'Oh.'

'And, incidentally' – Kit's voice shook a little – he was out of breath – 'old people, and people with weak hearts, sleep very lightly.' He paused, and added with a rush, 'You'd better remember that – another time.'

'What do you mean, *I'd* better remember it?'

'What do you suppose?'

She stared up at him; he saw her hand clenched round the gloves she was carrying. But they were both still, and during this pause the distorting lens of anger was removed for a moment from Kit's eyes. He saw that she was shaking, and that her face had the hopeless naughtiness of a child who dare not stop and let the accumulated reaction burst. It was a mood he was able to interpret, since it was his own.

He found that he was slightly sick; his head felt light, and he had the sensation, generally, of having been at the scene of some explosion whose wreckage he had not had time to view. 'I'm sorry,' he said.

'So I should hope,' said Christie unfairly. But her voice sounded miserable, and without conviction.

'I didn't mean what I said then.'

'I know, but you shouldn't have said it.'

'Come here a minute.'

'No. I won't; let me go. How *can* you be so absolutely beastly and then think you can just kiss me as if nothing had happened?'

'Keep still. Who said I was going to kiss you as if nothing had happened?'

In a little while there was a necessary pause, during which Christie said, 'But what was the *matter* with you?' and Kit said, 'What made you *do* it? That's what I can't make out.'

'Do what, walk in the road?'

'Are you crazy? Walk away without speaking to me when I came.'

'Was *that* what you were annoyed about?'

'You're incredible. You thought I'd like it?'

'I suppose I can't have thought'

'Well, then, why?'

'Oh, it was silly. It doesn't matter now ... I never thought of you minding like this. It was only – you'd been rather sweet before, and I was afraid you'd be different in the morning.'

In her embarrassment she was twisting a handful of his hair, which she happened to be holding, tighter and tighter; but Kit did not notice it. After a while she looked up at him, and let the piece of hair go. 'What is it, sweet?'

'Nothing,' said Kit abruptly, and kissed her to hide his face.

'But, my precious, you *are* funny. Didn't you think it would probably be something like that?'

'No. I—'

'Well, what *did* you think?'

With overdone casualness, Kit remarked, 'It was all a storm in a teacup. You get touchy when you've given yourself away.'

She moved her face back from his. 'But don't be silly, you're a man.'

'What has that got to do with it?'

'You don't have to feel that sort of thing. That's what I'm supposed to feel.'

Kit, who was feeling foolish, merely kissed her.

'I've been a cow,' she said suddenly, with a crack in her voice. 'You always make me feel a cow. I can't get used to you being so much nicer than anyone else.'

'Oh, for the Lord's sake—'

'I've been beastly to you. I've made you unhappy. I wish I were dead.'

Her voice shook with a passionate sincerity. Moved but bewildered, Kit embraced her. To be in her emotional neighborhood gave him the sensation of wandering among a medley of shining objects in a thick fog. It excited more than it exasperated him. She clung to him, murmuring remorse and love.

'How are we going to meet again?' he said.

They began discussing plans. He would come to her room through the garden on his way back from his next night call, or she was to dial for him on the telephone in the hall after the house was asleep. There would be no need to say anything, he explained; she could tap on the mouthpiece and he would know who it was.

'Yes. We'll do that. That will be lovely.' Her voice was absent.

'What's the matter?'

'Nothing. We'll fix it like that.'

'Don't worry. I'll see everything's all right.'

'Of course, I know. I was only thinking – I'd like to meet you in the day somewhere, and – and talk to you.'

'What about?'

'Just talk to you.'

He stroked her hair, not answering because he was both touched and taken by surprise. She went on: 'I could be out for about an hour.'

The concreteness of this brought him down to the ground. It was impossible; the town was a small one, and he and his car were known everywhere.

'You don't want to,' she said.

'You know I do. But in a job like mine everyone knows me by sight. You'd be surprised how many people will know you too by now. People in a place like this have nothing to do but talk. I doubt if we could get far enough away in the time we'd have. I could hardly drive you out from here.'

'No. Of course. It was a mad idea anyway. Don't bother about it.'

'We'll have to leave that part for a bit, I think. Which night will you ring for me?'

'I'll think about it.'

'It'll be better if we fix it up now.'

'I'd rather wait a bit.'

'Why?'

'Oh, because— Darling, don't be angry with me, or anything, will you?'

'Of course I won't.'

'I'm not going to see you again.'

'Don't be silly,' he said affectionately, and rumpled her hair. She remained oddly unresponsive. Suddenly it was borne in upon him that she meant what she said.

'But why?' he asked. 'What have I done?'

'I'll have to leave this week. I must get back to my job.'

'How can you? What about your aunt? She'll be terribly upset.'

Amid his confusion, this really meant something to him.

'She'll have a nurse. Pedlow won't mind, now, if it means getting rid of me.'

'You don't ask if I mind.'

'You'll be all right if I go now. Just kiss me.'

He kissed her, and she yielded with her usual completeness, as innocent of wantonness as she was of reserve. It gave to all her responses a kind of inevitability. With her, he seemed to take in some long-needed element, as simple as water or oxygen, and the weariness of years relaxed in him.

'Why do you want to leave me?' he said. A thought went through him like a bitter taste. 'Have you got someone else?'

'Oh, don't be such an *ass*.' She drew in her breath with a little hiss of exasperation. Her hands pushed at him, jerkily, as if she were trying to push in her words. 'Can't you *see*? I won't have you creeping about and lying. You're different; do you think I don't take anything in? It would make me sick to see you. And I might put up with that if I didn't know it would make you sick too. You'd hate me for it. You *have* hated me for it, already. Haven't you?'

Kit lacked practice in the routine evasions. He said, 'Only when you weren't there.'

'That's what's important.'

He was made ashamed by the truth of this, and sought escape from it in rebellion. His mind went back over the last years, and the effort with which he had carried himself through them seemed barren and sterile. He thought of a procession of future years like the last, in which he would grow old, set, and censorious.

'Oh, God,' he said aloud. 'What does it matter?'

She stepped back. 'Yes. I thought sooner or later it would come down to that.'

'Christie, I didn't—'

'Oh, yes, you did. You couldn't not be honest if you tried. It would be hell for you. Always having to pretend it was good and beautiful and we could really be something to each other, and making excuses and sneaking about in the dark. The first time just happened, that was fun, but to live like that— You'd be a lot better off with some woman where you could put the money on the mantelpiece and go bawdy and forget it. Why don't you? You'd be happier that way.'

He stood looking at her, astonished, hurt, and slightly shocked. He could only say at last, conventionally, 'You wouldn't talk like that if you knew anything about it.'

As if he had not spoken, she said, 'Well, good-by.'

'Christie – please.' He made an uncertain movement to take her back into his arms. She struck his hand away; he saw, now, that there were tears in her eyes. 'Let me alone. I tell you, I don't want you, I don't want to see you any more. Go back to your— Oh, go to hell.'

Her place was empty. A branch of laurel swung back behind her, stinging his face. He caught and broke it, and pushing through after her, found himself alone in the hollow underbrush, dried twigs and weeds under his feet, and the skeleton insides of the bushes arching over his head. Everything was very still. The sun splintered through leaves into his eyes. He became aware of Christie's receding feet passing from the grass to the gravel of a path, and of his own breathing, which in the silence sounded discordant and noisy.

His car was waiting, looking patient and unexpected, like a friend one has forgotten one promised to meet. He got in, and by a reflex born of long habit, flicked open the notebook in which he noted his work. It turned back at Miss Heath's name and the entry, *Visit last night*. He stared at it a moment, then added, in the appropriate space, *Visit, Thursday, 2:30 p.m.*

6

Janet sat on the edge of her wooden chair, looking round the hall. Beside her Peggy Leach's place was empty; she had gone over to talk to some people a couple of rows in front. Janet could see the group of them all standing up, two young men in plus-fours and a plump girl with a high color and a yellow jersey. They were telling Peggy some desperately exciting news; Peggy was congratulating them, jubilant, looking quickly from one to the other. Her gloves were on the empty chair at Janet's side. Everyone was circulating, greeting people, comparing notes, waving across distant stretches of the hall.

On each side of Janet were women, deep in conversations of their own. Those on the left were hatless, and gave the impression of encouraging each other brightly, like people not quite at ease. The three on the right were older, the committee type. They carried papers and periodicals, and were having a long, earnest consultation. Looking round her, Janet seemed to herself the only solitary person there. It made her feel conspicuous and uncomfortable. Occasionally someone would glance her way, as they searched the hall for somebody else. When this happened she looked away quickly, or pretended to be getting something out of her bag. She had never moved among large gatherings of people; the surge and impact of so many personalities made her feel exposed and on edge. She thought of the silk housecoat she was making, and wished herself at home, doing something planned and predictable, sheltered by the frame she had built for herself, a defense she had gradually grown to take for granted as a snail might the pink smooth lining of its shell.

Peggy was coming toward her, down the central gangway. Janet felt relieved; to have someone to talk to would make her feel less different from the rest. Then she saw that the healthy girl and the young men in plus-fours were coming too. As she watched, Peggy was pointing her out to them. They looked enormously self-assured, friendly, and expectant.

Quickly and almost unconsciously, as one tightens one's coat against a draft, Janet assembled a social smile, a gracious manner, and prepared a pleasant, noncommittal remark about the number of people who were there. She felt suddenly vulnerable, as if a trusted mackintosh had begun to let in the rain. Confusedly she sensed that a structure of conventions and taboos whose safety she had scarcely thought about, like the lock on her front door, had somehow become uncertain. She did not examine the feeling; consciously she registered the fact that the girl's hair was untidy, and her voice a little loud.

The introductions were over before Janet had had time to recover from their impact; she only took in the fact that the stockier of the young men was married to the girl, and that Peggy had introduced everyone by Christian names.

They asked Janet if it was the first Group meeting she had been to. She said it was, and produced the social remark she had had in mind about the fullness of the hall. She felt pressingly anxious to establish herself as a visitor, an onlooker, someone who has come to approve in a friendly but detached way. With her smile, her manner, her way of sitting and glancing about, she drew round herself a delicate little fence, composed of the small symbols which the people to whom she was used – Kit, for instance – might be expected not to ignore.

The married ones were called Bill and Shirley, the lanky boy Timmie; their surnames never emerged. Bill and Shirley said they *must* talk to her properly, and displacing Peggy, surrounded her, one on each side. They devoted themselves to encouraging her. She was probably feeling pretty queer, they said, a bit of a fish out of water. They had themselves the first time. They knew now that it was part of the resistance they had been putting up. They expected she must be putting up a bit herself. Peggy had explained to them that she was a reserved sort of person; that always made it more difficult. But didn't she think, really, that reserve was a form of Selfishness? (Selfishness was one of a set of words to which they gave clearly defined capital letters.) When you had learned to Share, you realized you couldn't keep yourself to yourself. In a way it was stealing, keeping what didn't really belong to you.

'I don't think so,' said Janet. 'Not necessarily.' She had not thought about it at all; the words were a defensive gesture, like the closing of one's eyes against a dust storm. It was all quite impossible; it was like sitting down to play bridge, and finding out after the game had started that it was strip-poker and everyone supposed you had known.

'It's just amazing,' said Shirley (or it might have been Bill; it was always quite difficult to remember, when answering, which of them had spoken), 'how many people are guided to come in just at some big moment, when they have to face up to things or smash. Bill and I were, weren't we, Bill?'

'Sure thing,' Bill agreed with his sociable grin. 'Our marriage was just about on the rocks.'

Janet looked vaguely pleasant. As if one of them had had an

accident with a set of false teeth, she tried to pretend that nothing out of the ordinary was taking place.

'Shirley was the first to get Changed.' Bill looked at her proudly; Shirley reproduced the look with the fidelity of a mirror. 'Then she got right down to changing me. I can tell you, I put up a fight.'

'I'll say you did,' cried Shirley, with hearty fondness.

'But when we really got down to Absolute Honesty, we found—' Cheerfully, Bill explained what he and Shirley had found. He had lowered his voice slightly, but not enough to make any impression on Janet, who felt each word reverberating through the hall. If they had fallen dead on either side of her, her first sensations would have been of grateful relief. When Bill stopped, she gathered her whole store of outrage into an icy 'How interesting!' She had used it, exactly like this, on the first and last occasion when Kit had tried to tell her an improper joke. Its effect had lasted the rest of the day. Fortified by the recollection, she looked at Bill, waiting for him to crumble. He turned to Shirley; their eyes met in a comradely, understanding glance, the look of kindly people making allowances.

Shirley put a plump, pink hand on Janet's arm.

'I expect it seems pretty funny to you, talking it all out like this. But that's only because you've got all tied up in yourself. All those knots will come out when you've Shared a bit. You see, Peggy's told us all about the tough time you've been having, and we just want you to know we understand and we're right in it all with you.'

Janet looked from one to the other. Her stomach felt inverted. Her bag was lying open on her lap, the contents sliding out. She did not know when she had unsnapped the catch. She collected the things, put them back, and looked about; at first, vaguely, for escape, then for Peggy to tell her she was going. But Peggy had, as it happened, crossed the hall immediately after the introductions; Shirley was occupying her seat.

Janet said, 'I think, really, I—' and felt for her gloves. Only one of them was there; the other must be somewhere on the floor. She reached after it, swimmingly. The lanky young man, Timmie, dived for it too, bumped against her, apologized, and pulled it out from under Bill's feet. He handed it over, and she noticed him for the first time. There had not been a chair for him, so he had been sitting perched on the back of the empty seat in front. She saw that he was much younger than the others, probably not more than nineteen.

'I say,' he said suddenly in a gruff boy's voice, 'you don't look awfully well. I was just thinking myself it was pretty hot in here. Wouldn't you like to go out for a minute and get a bit of air?'

He looked down at her, slithering awkwardly on the chairback. He had ginger hair, a wide, serious, uncertain mouth, and a light band of freckles over the bridge of his nose. His limbs looked clumsy and not very well fitting, as if the bones had not finished knitting up. He looked very pink, perhaps from stooping. Up till now he had said nothing at all.

'Yes,' said Janet. 'Thank you, I think I should.'

She got up. Bill and Shirley bounded to their feet around her. What rotten luck, they cried; why hadn't she said so? They had got all warmed up, yarning away, and hadn't noticed. They would all take her out, get her a glass of water, or a drink of something. They closed her in, boiling with helpfulness.

'No, please. I shall be quite all right in a moment. Please don't move.' She shrank back a little against Timmie, who was being squeezed on one side. He slipped between, put a self-conscious, heavy hand under her elbow, and bundled her away in front of him. Indistinct with shyness, he muttered, 'Better not all of us. Crowd isn't a good thing, makes you feel worse sometimes.' Janet said, 'Yes, I shall be all right, thank you,' and groped her way past the committee ladies, who clutched the papers on their knees in irritation. She looked round; incredibly, Bill and Shirley were no longer there.

Outside the hall was a little open space, with thin grass and a forlorn iron seat. Timmie led her over to it, gripping her elbow with tense nervousness which put her teeth on edge. She was glad when he let go of her to extricate a crumpled handkerchief from his pocket and dust the seat. She sat down, and he stood over her anxiously.

'Thank you so much,' she said, 'but I feel much better now. Don't let me keep you from the meeting. I shall just rest here for a minute, and then go home.'

'That's all right. They don't get going all at once. I think I'd better stay for a bit; that is, if you don't mind.' He leaned a big raw hand on the back of the seat, which creaked under its uncertain pressure. Janet looked at the grubby privet hedge, longing to be alone and to reassemble herself. She had a vague expectation of finding her hat out of place and her clothes crumpled, as if she had been rescued from a street accident. In evident terror of a gap in the conversation, he went on jerkily, 'As a matter of fact, I've got a sister who quite often passes out in hot theaters and places like that. She always says she feels better if she puts her head between her knees. I don't know if you've ever tried doing that.' He stopped, obviously fearing that he had suggested something undignified, which might offend her.

'Really,' she said, 'I feel perfectly well now. It's so nice of you to have looked after me.' She meant this for a dismissal; but he looked encouraged and sat down beside her, with his long legs straggling out in a semi-detached way in front. Dissatisfied, it seemed, with the look of them, he drew them in quickly and tucked them under the seat.

'I know what it's like, passing out, because I did once, when I got a kick on the head playing left wing. I'd been tackled, you see, and a chap behind was coming on rather fast and couldn't stop. The coming round's the worst part, really. But I expect this sort feels different.' Janet cast about in her mind for something efficacious that would stop just short of the obvious; her gratitude had not quite evaporated. He screwed himself round toward her. 'I've only known Bill and Shirley about three days. I expect, seeing us all roll up together like that, you thought we were all great friends.'

'Aren't you?'

'Well – of course in the way everyone is in the Group; it's pretty good that way. At least it's pretty good for me, because usually I'm rather on my own. I'm cramming for Oxford, you know, at home. This is my second shot; as a matter of fact, it's the Latin principally. Well, talking about Bill and Shirley, I don't mean that I don't think a lot of them. They've got a terrific way of tackling things that's all right for them because they're pretty tough. I mean, obviously there have to be tough people in the world to do the tough jobs. The only thing is about being tough like that, they don't always quite cotton onto it that everyone else isn't.'

The seat creaked as he shifted himself round to a more acutely uncomfortable angle. Janet looked at him, and suddenly her nervous irritability faded. He was watching the effect of his words with strained anxiety; he had the look of one who has had committed to him, as an awful privilege, the care of some delicate and priceless apparatus which is ordinarily entrusted only to technicians of the highest skill. To Janet it was like food to the starving. Kit had looked like that, only a little less nakedly, in the first weeks they had known one another. She had never allowed herself to become aware that it was for this she had married him; that she had wanted and expected it to be the note of their relationship; that the first demands of his passion had been a hideous disappointment for which she had never forgiven him, and, in the end, probably never would. Less than ever did she admit it to

72

herself now. What she believed herself to be thinking was that here was a charming, idealistic boy whom it would be cruel, after all, to snub, who needed someone to bring him out and preserve his illusions.

'Have you belonged to the Group long?' she asked.

'No. I only got Changed' – he shot out the word after a hard swallow – 'quite a few weeks ago. You know, I do absolutely understand you not being so keen about it at first, because of course you don't *need* something like that in the way I did. They'll try awfully hard to get you in, though, because of course you'd be such a help in it.' He removed his eyes from her face, locked his hands in a complicated way under one knee and over the other, and swallowed again. 'I was at a school in Canada, the last few years, because my people had to be there.' (This explained a few incongruous intonations of voice which had been puzzling her.) 'I don't know what the others were like, but at the one I was at, it was the done thing to be pretty hard-boiled. When I say hard-boiled, I mean the real thing, you know.'

She gave an understanding nod. Encouraged, but going pink at the ears, he went on, 'By that I mean that a lot of the seniors, anyway, had done pretty well everything.'

She nodded again.

'If you hadn't, you talked as if you had, and told stories and all that.'

She smiled at him; in his face she saw a reflection of herself inclining very slightly from a very high altar. 'I can't imagine you,' she said, 'telling any story that you couldn't repeat, for instance, to me.'

'Well, as a matter of fact, I know about a dozen that I'd rather die than let you hear, and some songs too.' Both of them were happily unaware of a substratum of modest pride beneath this claim. 'Sometimes' – he colored more deeply than before – 'I used to keep thinking about those things when I didn't want to. Of course we all thought religion was siss – pretty soft.'

'What made you change your mind?'

'Well, I met a rather marvelous chap who quite obviously wasn't soft. He's an International, as a matter of fact. So I thought if it was good enough for him, why shouldn't it be for me? He's speaking this afternoon. It's too bad you're not well. I think you'd have felt different about it all if you could have heard him.'

'But I'm keeping you from hearing him. Do please go in; it would be such a shame for you to miss it.'

She waited for his answer. The delicious sense of power, that essential vitamin whose deficiency she had, lately, begun so terrifyingly to feel, once again lit and warmed her.

'Oh, that's all right, he's sure to be speaking again at another meeting. You know, really, I do think somebody ought to see you home. It would be pretty grim if you suddenly felt wonky in the street somewhere. I'd love to, if I might.'

'That's very unselfish of you.' She smiled, gracious and indulgent, while he protested incoherently. 'Really, you know, it isn't necessary.'

They rose. Without exactly planning it, she got to her feet a little hesitantly, with the least suggestion of difficulty and limpness. He leaned over her, his freckled face quite drawn with solicitude. A noise of hear-hearing drifted out from the hall. Janet heard it in a sudden access of kindly toleration.

When she got home she brushed out her hair and combed it down a little lower and smoother over her cheeks. It made her look frailer, and accented her pallor a little. She turned away from the glass, satisfied, and convinced that the alteration had been an accident.

The silver was not looking quite as it should. The maid used too much plate-polish, and Janet was sure she did not wash the polishing cloth regularly. She gave her a little talk about it, pleasantly aware of her own patience set in relief by Elsie's stupidity. While she was in the kitchen the front door closed; it was Kit coming in. She ordered some fresh tea for him – he was late again – and went to her room. She intended to be lying down when Peggy came in; genuinely, she had a slight headache. But after she had rested a little while with eau de cologne she felt restless, and went into the sitting-room.

Kit had finished his tea, and was reading a new book he had bought about diseases of the heart. He looked up as she came in, smiled, said abstractedly, "Lo, Janie, meeting go off well?" and went on reading.

On the table was the novel he had changed for her at the library. She picked it up and sat down with it, then looked at him again. With an uncomfortable jar she perceived that he was quite oblivious of her. She had grown used to his pretending not to pay much attention when she came into a room, but it had never deceived her. She had always felt the shift of his concentration from what he had been doing, his expectation silently surrounding her. It had given a sense of importance and drama to all her small movements, to the first trivial remark she made. Often she had thought how irritating it was to be focused on like this, but the absence of it was quite surprisingly disagreeable. She opened her book, read the title page without taking it in, and looked at him again.

Suddenly she saw him as one sees people after an absence: imperceptible day-to-day changes accumulated themselves in a single impression. She remembered how Timmie's face had made her think of his. Everything of which it had reminded her was gone. How long had it been happening? He was not an anxious boy, but a man whose curiously fair hair only emphasized by contrast the decision of his face. There had been, in repose, a loose gawkiness about his wrists and ankles that disappeared when he moved. Now she wondered what had made her imagine it. He was chewing on

75

the stem of an empty pipe, absorbed in a page of diagrams. Presently he got out a pencil and made a note, or some small addition, to one of them. He might as well have been alone in the room.

She turned to the middle of the novel, tasting it here and there. It was a pretty, sentimental tale, pleasant enough but, she knew, a thing he would never dream of reading himself. She had often reproved him for bringing her back books which had excited him but which she thought heavy. Yet to realize that he must have chosen this one without interest, as the kind of thing she would like, made her feel neglected.

Turning back to the first chapter, she tried to read. It was, in fact, a book she might very well have chosen in default of something better for herself; but, perhaps for this very reason, it irritated her. There was a tickle in her throat, and she coughed, rather more loudly than its relief demanded. He did not notice. She coughed again, several times.

He looked up, half his mind transparently still in the book. 'Not caught a cold, have you?' he asked.

'Not a really bad one.' She took out the cologne handkerchief unobtrusively and patted her nose. 'I think it was when I got wet yesterday. It's only on my chest a little.'

'If it's on your chest you must look after it.' He put his book aside, fishing an envelope out of his pocket to mark the place. (Once, she thought, he would not have waited to do that.) In a detached businesslike way he got out a thermometer, uncased it, shook it down, and slipped it into her mouth. 'No, under your tongue.' His hand closed firmly and easily on her wrist. She remembered from earlier times the careful tension of his touch. 'Cheer up. You're not going to be ill.' He held her wrist tightly, waiting for her pulse to settle.

Her temperature was normal. She had been certain that at least it would be 99. 'But of course I'm all right,' she said pluckily. 'I told you it was really nothing.'

'I'll just go over your chest to make sure.' He ran down to the consulting-room, came back with a stethoscope, and held the metal end carefully to warm at the fire.

Her dress was a dark ninon that fastened to the throat with a little row of silver buttons. Slowly and thoughtfully she fingered the top one, and began to undo it.

Kit straightened, testing the end of the stethoscope against his palm. 'Oh, don't bother with that,' he said cheerfully. Evidently he had noticed what she was wearing for the first time. 'I can listen through that all right It's only thin.'

Janet fastened the silver button again and took her hand away from it as quickly as if it had burned her.

She stood up while he moved the instrument here and there, with silent precision, over the stuff, his face intent, his mind, she saw, a mile away from her, concentrated in his ears. She might, she thought with bewildered resentment, have been a patient. He moved round to her back, out of sight.

'Just cough once or twice, will you?' She coughed, a thin and, it seemed to her, pathetic little sound. He took the stethoscope away.

'That's all right. Nothing there. You've a spot of tracheal irritation, I expect. Wait a minute, I had a sample of lozenges today. You can try them out for me, will you? The formula looks all right.' He got them out of a coat pocket, opened and sniffed them, said, 'Not more than one an hour, I should say; they're strongish,' handed them over, and settled himself back again with his book.

Janet took a lozenge. It was bright pink, contained formalin, and had a sweetish-sharp flavor. She had expected something more medicine-like, menthol or eucalyptus. She was being kept quiet with a sweet, she thought, like a fractious child. The lozenge stung her throat a little. She was certain now that it really was sore, and remembered her headache, which she had allowed temporarily to lapse. It occurred to her that she had meant to be lying down when Peggy (who was taking tea at Shirley's) got back. It was nearly six; she might arrive at any moment. Janet thought, with inward shrinking, of her own confidences of a night or two ago. They had seemed possible then. She had got a little generous glow out of making excuses for Kit, explaining that, in spite of his insensitiveness and egotism, he loved her, she was sure, as deeply as he was capable of loving anyone; that she always tried, for that reason, to spare his feelings by hiding her own. Now, as she remembered it and watched him – so contained in himself, so suddenly an unknown quantity – she had a sickening sensation of the words appearing in his presence, twisting themselves, looking quite different from the convincing and touching picture they had made at the time. Presently Peggy would be coming in, fresh from talking to Shirley about it.

In her heart she knew that she never wanted to see Peggy again. She wanted to spend the evening, as she had spent so many evenings such a little while ago, sitting composedly, conscious of poise, of delicate grace and aloofness, aware of a secret audience, knowing that Kit was watching her under his lashes when he thought she was looking the other way.

She remembered how she had found him on the morning he had overslept. He had looked so vulnerable and so young, lying there tousled and half-clothed in a dead sleep of weariness. She had felt powerful and compassionate. His absorption maddened her. She got to her feet, moved only by the impulse to throw something at it.

'I think I shall go to bed,' she said. 'I've a headache.'

He looked round. 'Have you? Too bad. Yes, go to bed and sleep it off. Meeting tired you, I expect.'

'Perhaps it was that.'

'Peggy'll be all right I suppose? I'm seeing McKinnon this evening.'

How could he, she thought, how *could* he stroll calmly out of the house after she had explained to him that she was ill? It had never happened. He had loved to be depended on, to be allowed to gain a little importance with her. She pressed the handkerchief to her forehead. 'Yes, Kit dear, do go out and amuse yourself. I know I'm not very entertaining company for you when I feel like this. I'm sure Peggy will understand.'

He said nothing. She collected a few small things about the room, waiting. Surely he would apologize, or at least protest. As she got to the door she looked over her shoulder. He was glancing at the clock, regretfully putting his book away because it was time for the evening surgery. He looked neither angry nor hurt, simply a little tired. She went out.

In her own room she drew the green satin curtains, undressed, and lay down. The ordered prettiness of the place wrapped itself comfortingly around her. How generous, after all, the things she had said to Peggy had really been. It was for his sake, she reflected, more than for her own that she minded. Poor boy; in his self-centered way he loved her so much. Her mind drifted on to a little scene in which her cold got worse. She had pneumonia, double pneumonia; she was dying, and Kit leaned over her bed, asking for forgiveness, frantic at the thought of losing her. 'Don't have any regrets,' she was saying to him, very gently, in her dying voice. 'Some day you'll – understand.'

Her real illness – the blanketing weakness, the fading of thought and desire, the squalor and pain – she had long ago pushed into the basement of her mind. It had emerged slightly altered, tidied-up and refined, the dramatic values underlined and inartistic passages soft-focused.

How concerned the boy at the meeting had been about her! She smiled maternally at the thought of it. It had, she remembered, seemed to mean so much to him that she should come with him to the next meeting, and hear the International he admired. They could sit at the back, he had said, so that if she felt faint they could come out at once. If she did not come it might spoil the freshness of his enthusiasm. That would be such a pity. Really, she must try to be well enough to go.

7

It was next evening, while the International was dealing faithfully with the sins of his former state, that Kit's surgery was interrupted by an urgent call from Laurel Dene.

He found Miss Heath semi-collapsed, shrunken and blue in her high chair of pillows, clinging to Christie's hand. She scarcely noticed Kit when he came in. As he slipped the needle, with the almost painless speed of practice, under the withered skin of her forearm, Christie was saying in her warm comforting voice, 'I didn't mean it about going away. Of course I'll stay with you. I promise I will. Always. See, you're going to be all right now.' A faint gleam of relief mingled with the fear in the moist, shallow eyes.

When the worst of the attack was over, Pedlow came to sit with her mistress. As she went over to the bed to take up her charge, her body looked softer, less angular – mysteriously, almost comfortable. 'Well, there, now, Miss Amy,' she said.

Kit and the girl went out together into the gray twilight garden with its sweet evening smell of dusty leaves and dew.

'What now?' he said.

It was a last checking point for decision. They searched one another's faces in the shadow, both knowing it.

Kit found that he could think no further than the whiteness of Christie's face, and the little blue streaks under her eyes. She had been tired, and then badly frightened. The deadness of the half-light took the last trace of color from everything but her hair; she looked like a restless ghost. When he took her hands she blinked, swallowed, and began to cry.

The moment of choice passed. He comforted and held her. She was not to worry about anything tonight, he said. He would take care of it all. He would look after her. He wouldn't bother her; everything should be as she wanted.

She nodded, tightening her arms round his neck. It was no good talking about anything now, she said as she dried her eyes; they would feel different in the morning. She would be sensible then; she would do anything he said.

Everything, they promised one another, would be all right.

Three nights later, on his way back from a midnight call, Kit went through the garden at Laurel Dene, round the edge of the lawn, to the drawing-room windows. There was no need, he found, to tap on the pane; they were wide open.

'Darling. I've had an idea.'

'M-m?' murmured Kit, inclining half an ear. Christie always had ideas when he was feeling sleepy, but her voice was so pleasant that it didn't matter.

'I've got it under the pillow. Just let me put the eiderdown over your head, then I can put the torch on.'

Kit turned over, resignedly, while Christie arranged the eiderdown in a tent over their heads, and lit the flashlamp.

'I like your hair,' he said, 'with the light through it.'

Ignoring this side issue, Christie dived under the pillow and produced a crumpled piece of paper, on which were diagrams rather like the framework of noughts and crosses, complicated with arrangements of dots. 'Do you know what this is?'

Kit, who was still blinking in the light, recognized it after a moment as the commonest cipher generally used in preparatory schools. At the bottom was a simple sentence.

'It's a code,' Christie explained superfluously. 'Now we can write each other proper letters.'

'What, in that?'

'Yes, then it won't matter if anyone finds them.'

'Oh, good God,' breathed Kit. 'Give it to me.'

'Don't you think it would work?'

'Darling, if you have any more ideas like that, don't do anything about them before you ask me, will you?'

'Not if you don't like. But it *would* have been fun. How soon the air gets breathed up under an eiderdown, doesn't it?'

Kit had been astonished, at first, to find how quickly Christie had lost any kind of tragic feeling about their necessary deceit. Once she began, she had taken to stratagems as small boys take to playing Red Indians. There was something in it, he guessed, of escape from the crueler realities of the situation, but most of it was nature. Her favorite plots were concerned with the exchange of notes; he had assured her that there would be no harm in her occasionally using the post, but she preferred to conceal them in his gloves when he left them in the hall, to throw them, wrapped round stones, into his car as he came up the drive, or to put them in his bag, where they were liable to fall out embarrassingly at the next case he visited.

They agreed at last on a posting-box, a hollow tree in the drive. It was unsafe, but not more so than most of Christie's more ingenious ideas. He could not bear to hurt her feelings by asking her to write less often; besides, he enjoyed her letters, which had a wild originality of thought and spelling.

Since Miss Heath's last attack, he called there twice a week. Her hold on life was more tenuous than ever, but she was radiantly happy. 'I feel so much *younger*, doctor,' she confided to him.

'Perhaps it comes of being more in touch with the world. Christie's so good about reading me the papers. Poor Pedlow's intentions of course were *most* kind, but it seems she had been keeping the most *essential* facts from me for years, from some idea that I should worry. Yes, I'm thinking of buying a wireless set shortly; so nice for concerts, and the news.'

He managed to visit Christie about one night in seven. Their system, which they had evolved between them in one of Christie's more realistic moments, worked quite well. It was necessary that, if he went out in the night, he should have received a telephone call, since even the soft-toned bell he had in his room could be heard, if anyone happened to be awake, in other parts of the house. So in the small hours Christie used to dial his number on the telephone in the hall, tap on the mouthpiece when he answered, and slip back to her room; a quick and almost soundless procedure. A safer plan, when it was available, was for Kit to go round at the tail-end of a legitimate night call. If this turned out to be a scare needing little attention, he could risk the extra time.

At Christie's end of the business there was always the fear of the servants hearing something, though their rooms faced a different way. The house was full of the noises of old houses, sounds of mice, and cautious sounds of wood creaking as it contracted in the cool of the night. They never had, either of them, a moment's security or of what by common standards could be called rest. Kit wondered, sometimes, when he was alone, why he found it worth while. He never wondered whether he did.

The truth was that she was the first person in years who had given him any use for being young. Fraser, Janet, and the patients, if they had nothing else in common, seemed all alike in demanding from him the virtues of middle age.

One night, when they had not met for over a week, Christie rang him up at one in the morning. He had left a note asking her to do it, and had been lying awake for it, but the sound of the bell seemed an explosion in the silence and made him feel like a burglar who has trodden on the burglar alarm. The house was still quiet. He picked up the receiver, listening for the tap, but a sibilant whisper came through instead.

'Is that you, beautiful? Don't be long.'

'For the Lord's sake!' Kit, though not given to nervous outbursts, had felt the hair rise on his neck. 'Wait till I say something. If I'd been called out, Fraser would have got that.'

'Oh, darling, I *am* sorry. I didn't think, because you told me to ring. You're not angry?'

'No, dear, of course not. Look out at your end.'

'It's all right. Pedlow snores. Isn't it a good thing? What I wanted to say is, I've got a new scheme.'

'Well, don't – hullo, are you there? Hold it till I come, won't you?'

'It's practically finished.'

'Oh, God, I'll be right along ... Yes, darling, of course I do.' A board creaked somewhere in the house; raising his voice a little, he added, 'Just keep her warm and give her sips of water till I come. Good-by.'

When he tapped at the glass door, Christie met him with a dark coat thrown like a cloak over her nightdress. She took him by the wrist and led him outside again, finger on lip. Something had happened, he thought. Not daring to ask, he followed her toward a dark hump of shadow which he recognized as the summerhouse on the lawn. 'What's the matter?' he whispered at last, his heart pounding on his ribs.

'Nothing, love. Don't sound so worried. It's just my idea. Come in.'

The summerhouse was muffled in thick Virginia creeper, which rounded the angles of the roof and walls, and hung in a deep fringe over the doorway. He could just see it, in the faint glimmer of a half moon masked with clouds.

Fantastic as the notion was, it had its points. The place faced away from the house, and was in earshot of Miss Heath's bell. His chief feeling about it was an irrational satisfaction in not being actually under his patient's roof. It was absurd that this should seem any better, but somehow it did.

Christie lifted the curtain of leaves aside, pulled him in and kissed him. 'I haven't quite finished doing it yet,' she explained presently. 'I thought perhaps it might be noticed if I did it all too suddenly. But it seemed a shame not to be making the most of it before the nights get too cold.'

Kit got out the fountain-pen torch he used for examining throats, and flicked it here and there. Making startling and surrealist designs in the small beam, gaunt shapes detached themselves, trailing vast shadows, from the darkness. He picked out among them an old basket garden lounge – dangerously rickety and buttressed with a Tate sugar box at one end – covered with a fur carriage rug; a circular iron table with fancy legs; a croquet set with most of the paint cracked off and the balls split; a rotted tennis net rolled on a post, with cobwebs filling in the meshes; a racket of 1890 design, with five strings; and cushions in varying stages of decay.

'I shall cover the cushions,' whispered Christie, 'gradually. I've done two already.'

Kit moved the torch back and saw that two of the amorphous lumps had been freshly dog-stitched with what looked like the material of an old summer frock. On the top of the iron table the last of the Michaelmas daisies were arranged, with trails of creeper, in a jam jar.

'Lovely,' he said, and sat down on the basket lounge; it bent under him with a groan.

'It's all right really,' Christie assured him, 'now I've fixed it. I jumped on it this morning with both feet, as hard as I could, and it hardly gave at all. Do you like it in here?'

'Awfully,' said Kit.

'I'm so glad. I'll have it even nicer next time you come. It was such fun getting it ready. Come here and let me kiss you.' She sat down beside him on the basket lounge, which collapsed immediately. Fortunately dust, cobweb, and stray creeper muffled the sound.

'Are you hurt, darling?' asked Christie, embracing him tenderly. She had landed somehow across his knees.

The crash had shaken down a shower of dust and bits, stirring up a sharp, earthy, potting-house smell. Somewhere against the opposite wall the scurry of a startled mouse sounded. The cushions had their own smell of sun-baked plantings and old conservatories. A little wind swayed the creeper to and fro across the glimmering gap of the door, and a sweet, cold, dewy air blew in with it. On his knees, oddly emphasized by it all, was Christie, warm and sweetly scented and smooth in her satin nightgown. She clasped her arms round him and laughed softly down his neck.

'We'll have to mend it,' she said.

Kit pulled her down into the loose, musty cushions. 'That's a rotten idea. Let's have it where it can't fall any farther.'

He felt Christie's cheek fold into a smile.

After this they generally used the summerhouse on nights that were dry and warm. Christie became passionately attached to it, and lavished on it all the proprietary care that is expended in earlier youth on private tents, holes in bushes, and roosts in trees. She covered the cushions one by one with bits of frocks and petticoats, or remnants joined together, and decorated the jam jar with gold paint in a fancy design. The lawn-mower and tennis set she draped over with a colored dust sheet, and she kept a sort of treasure chest under the basket lounge. But her chief delight was entertaining Kit to a meal. For his better peace of mind he never inquired when, or how, she raided the larder to provide the thick tongue sandwiches, bits of cake, and chocolate biscuits which she arranged in tasteful patterns on two odd plates and a couple of saucers. Once she brought out cups as well.

'I'm going to do you really well tonight, sweetness. I've got some wine.'

'How marvelous. But I say, had you better? Wine's the sort of thing people really do miss, you know.'

'Oh, I wouldn't do that. That would be almost stealing. No, I got you this specially, myself. The man at the store said it was all right. It's Burgundy. Hold your cup, and I'll pour you some out. No, sweet, you have the one with the handle. Honestly, I like using this.'

'Is it nice?' asked Christie, watching him anxiously.

'A treat. But, darling, it's a shame for you to have to get it. I'll bring along a drink myself, next time. We've always got stuff in the house.'

'But, precious, I *love* giving you things. Have one of these biscuits. They've got coffee cream sort of stuff in the middle.'

Kit finished his cupful, and allowed himself to be pressed to a second. He ate two coffee cream biscuits, and a pink coconut one. The red potion, mixed with the scent of night and dry wood and leaves and Christie, took on a Swiss-Family-Robinson kind of charm. It was certainly warming. They were both laughing at nothing very much when Kit threw the carriage rug over them, and blew into the broken flower pot that shielded the candle.

'It's such a shame,' murmured Christie later on, 'that you can't sleep here.'

'I know,' said Kit. The cushions were as lumpy as field grass, but he meant it. He had recovered, lately, a gift for sleeping anyhow and anywhere, which had helped him through long stretches of heavy work in his hospital days. In the last two years he had found it forsaking him; it seemed, somehow, obvious and natural that now it should come back.

'Do you get bored,' she asked, 'playing house in here?'

Till she spoke, he had almost forgotten about the picnic. She had had one of her bewildering transitions to experience; when they were making love she seemed neither childlike nor sophisticated, but an ageless and necessary counterpart of himself. He stroked her hair drowsily and said, 'No, I like it. It's rather a rest.'

'Is it?' She pulled his hair – a sign of embarrassment – and said quickly, 'You get so sick of sharing a room, or using rooms that aren't yours. When I was a kid my room was really the spare room, and I had to keep it looking all polite. And at the Abbey, where I work, you're liable to sleep pretty well anywhere, especially when the Summer School's on. Once I slept on the stage. That was rather a lark.'

Kit suddenly found the evening's entertainment no longer amusing. He hugged her roughly and said, 'I wish I could—'

'Could what?'

'I don't know. Look after you, give you somewhere to be.'

'Would you like me to be more mistresslike, darling? Would I fascinate you more if I wore teagowns and black lace vests? And diamond garters?'

'You disgusting little horror. Would you like to?'

'Well, I'd look very nice in them. In fact, I never know why I don't do well as a kept woman. I always do something terribly bad form, laugh at the wrong moment or something. Oh, darling, I do love having someone of my own age.'

Such information as this remark contained Kit had guessed long before, and he did not want, particularly, to know anything further. 'Just how old are you?' he asked.

'Practically twenty-two. Are you laughing? Your face feels funny.'

She dug her fingers into his hair and rubbed it, with catlike pleasure, against her cheek. 'You always smell so nice. What's the stuff you scrub your hands with?'

'Dettol, I expect.'

'If I smelled that anywhere I should think of you.'

For Kit, the sweetish clean smell meant childbirth, infectious fevers, suppuration, death, and certain emergencies desperate enough to have survived the ruck of others in his mind. 'Would you?' he said. 'How funny.'

There was a little pause. Kit pulled his arm from under Christie to look at the luminous dial of his watch.

'You haven't been here very long,' Christie said.

In point of fact, he had sometimes stayed longer, but he felt, for no reason, suddenly keyed up and anxious; he could not settle down again, and left a few minutes later. On the way back he was annoyed with himself. Nerves were the last thing he could afford to cultivate. Next time it happened, he said to himself, he would take no notice.

But ten minutes after he was back in his room, the telephone rang, announcing an acute appendix. The call had been switched through from Fraser's flat; Fraser, he learned next morning, had been called out half an hour before.

It was one of several things which he had always known might happen, a long shot, but almost bound to come off once in a month or two. The nearness of it made all the other dangerous possibilities seem nearer. He hurried out, thinking about them, and found the patient on the verge of a perforation. That night he got very little sleep. He had put into his work, in the last two years, more of himself than he fully realized, including some of the emotions for which Janet had appeared to have no use. It did not occur to him as strange that he should lie awake in the creeping early light thinking not of Janet, but of the little shop assistant whose life he had saved by about three-quarters of an hour.

Before he got up he had decided to write and tell Christie he could not come again. He began a letter, and destroyed it. It would be too cruel, he thought, not to see her again first. For a week, and most of the next week, he made only his routine visits to Laurel Dene. At last he had a chance to go in the night again, and went, knowing that when Christie reproached him with his absence the thing would come to a head. He waited for it, having ready what he would say. But she never reproached him. She was merely happy, as if he were her reason for existing. Compassion turned his resolve aside, and desire melted it.

He compromised by shortening his brief visits, and hanging his watch on a nail in the wall where it could not be ignored. She complained of nothing, and seemed concerned only lest she should be unable to give him, in twenty minutes, the tenderness of half an hour. He found that seeing her less only resulted in thinking of her continually. In a meek woman her devotion would have been intolerable; in Christie, it gave him the sense of more than credible felicity, like an opium dream. If she had claimed power over him he would have been roused into resisting her, but she thought no more of claiming power than a child thinks with its mother.

Miss Heath had bought her wireless set. It sat on the table beside the large black Bible, looking rather lost and self-conscious. Miss Heath loved it, especially the plays. The mildest of these seemed able to give her an adventurous glow; her dear mother, she said, had disapproved of the theater.

'But, after all, things are so different now. So many nice people – I'm sure you'd never guess, for instance, that my little Christie had acted on the stage?'

'Really?' said Kit, thankful that astonishment, which he could not have concealed in any case, was the correct response. 'No, I don't think I should.' He could not help looking round at Christie, who was in the room at the time. She laughed a little.

'Well, I've acted on *a* stage. About the size of a tablecloth. The Abbey's only one of these People's Theater places.'

'Well, of course, dear,' said Miss Heath with fond reproof, 'Dr Anderson would hardly be likely to imagine that you were an *actress*. But she's played several important parts – haven't you, dear? – even Juliet. I still have the newspaper cutting that your poor father sent me.'

In Miss Heath's vocabulary *poor* meant *deceased*. This was another thing he had not known, though he found he had somehow taken it for granted.

'Why didn't you tell me you acted?' he asked in the hall.

'I didn't think of it. Besides, the Abbey's one of those indescribable places you need to see for yourself.' She gave one of her urchin grins. 'Why, does it give me more glamour?'

Kit had no chance to tell her, because just then Pedlow crossed the hall, and Christie shut into herself, as she always did when this happened. His own nerves were not so steady.

A night or two later, when he had meant to go to her, he had a call which he hoped might give him the chance. But it turned out to be a maternity case, a difficult obstructed labor, followed by hemorrhage, which kept him from just after midnight till nearly five in the morning. When he did get in he was (unusual for him) too tired to sleep soundly, and woke with a jerk half an hour earlier than usual. He was on edge all the morning; the new patients seemed incredibly stupid in giving their case histories, the old ones incredibly garrulous. At the end of his round he met Fraser in the drive, and had to listen to yet another summary of the political situation – the fifth that morning – lasting quite five minutes.

'—What can one hope,' concluded Fraser, 'from such an administration in a real emergency? Emergency, that reminds me; that call of yours last night detained you a long time. You got very little sleep, I'm afraid.'

'Oh, I got three hours.' Kit's throat felt hoarse and dry, and he swallowed. Fraser's room faced away from the garage and the road. He had not thought it possible for his comings and goings to be heard there. 'It was a midder,' he said, 'down in the council houses. Placenta previa. I had rather a job with her. The district nurse ought to have got me sooner.'

'Ah, yes, yes, I can well imagine it. A very self-opinionated woman. Both out of danger now?'

'Should be. I hope I didn't wake you coming in.'

'My dear boy, certainly not; I should say you make the minimum of noise. I remarked on it to my wife only this morning. I remember some years back I had an assistant – really, I might as well have taken all the calls myself, as I finally told him. But I don't sleep as soundly as I did – nothing in that; at my age one doesn't require it – and it occupies my mind to speculate on what I hear going on around me. I don't settle quickly, nowadays, after I've been called up. Yes, yes, of course, that was what I had been meaning to tell you. I took a call of yours while you were out. A chronic heart. Stout old lady with a red-haired daughter, lives in that big house at the end of Victoria Avenue. Mrs – Mrs – Oh, well, I've got it written down.'

'Miss Heath?' Kit's voice cracked a little on the aspirate.

'That's the name; I had it on the tip of my tongue. Mrs Heath.'

'Miss. The girl's her niece.'

'Niece? Mm – mh, yes, yes. I gave her a sedative. Highly nervous temperament. From her agitation on the telephone, I expected to find the patient *in articulo mortis*. Most unsuitable type of nurse for a heart case. You must find her trying.'

'Yes,' said Kit. His mind moved fast and confidently; he had noticed the same thing in patients suffering from the first stages of shock. 'Yes, she's had me up on one or two false alarms. As a matter of fact, I did make tentative moves in the direction of a trained nurse. But there isn't a hope; the old

93

lady's devoted to her. Started to throw an attack at the first suggestion.'

'Ah, well. The human element. At any rate, the patient has great faith in *you*. Looked quite blank when she saw me appear. But I succeeded, hm, in establishing confidence. By the way, I shall be attending an Insurance Committee meeting on— My dear boy, I shouldn't keep you standing here. That maternity case has used you up. You look positively green. Go in and take a rest, and I'll work in one or two of your visits this afternoon. No, no, not at all, nobody needs more than six hours' sleep after fifty-five.'

Kit thanked him confusedly and said he couldn't think of it; he would be all right when he had had a meal and a drink. He went on into the house, feeling, in point of fact, almost too sick to eat at all. It was no new idea to him that, if he and Christie were caught together at Laurel Dene, nothing could possibly prevent him from being struck off the register. Partly his phenomenal luck in getting away with it so far, partly Christie's gift for making the thing look like an excursion into a private island, had kept the idea at a comfortable distance most of the time. It had not occurred to him before that a public scandal would nearly kill Fraser. He had brought his standards of propriety intact from the 1880s. Moreover, he liked Kit and trusted him.

Kit took his coat off in the hall, and went to hang it up. It was a compact, artistic little hall, with a curtained alcove for the coat stand which Janet had copied from an illustration in *Woman and Home*. Kit replaced the curtain carefully after him; he had been in trouble about it so many times that he often caught himself looking over his shoulder to see if Janet were watching him. It reminded him, now, that it was Janet rather than Fraser about whom he ought to be worrying. He tried to imagine how she would feel, and thought instead that she had three or four hundred a year of her own to which, if the worst happened, he could add a little, and himself, if he went about it carefully, get a job as

94

a hospital porter or train as a male nurse. He could not think about her, he found, as he had thought about Fraser; it was an effort, indeed, ever to think about her longer than a day's contact demanded. He supposed that this was the measure of what he felt for Christie, not knowing that it was the measure of what he had felt for Janet herself. He had not experienced before the deep, the secretly satisfying, indifference that follows an exhausted love. He had, in the end, slipped into this last phase as naturally and as unconsciously as the tired body slips into sleep.

His mind eluded her again, and went back to Christie. Now, if ever, he thought, was the time to stay away. Danger, however casual, had a way of being cumulative. Besides, Fraser was still on his mind. But he could not leave her without a message about the night call; she must have had the fright of her life. He scribbled something reassuring to leave for her in the tree hole when he saw Miss Heath in the afternoon.

Lunch was an uneventful, and thus a restful, meal. The days were gone when he watched Janet's face as men watch the skies on which the harvest depends. He did not even notice that her preoccupation almost matched his own.

Laurel Dene was his last visit. The hollow tree was just in reach of his arm from inside the car. But the note was not posted; as he drew up, Christie slipped out of the shrubbery. She had been so still that he knew she must have been waiting there a long time.

'Is it all right?' she whispered.

'Yes.' He got out of the car and kissed her. 'Don't worry; nothing happened.'

'Really nothing? Didn't he say anything to you about me? Didn't he think I sounded funny on the phone? I was just going to say something to you, and then I remembered you'd told me not to, and didn't. And then he answered. All the time we were talking I kept thinking, supposing I'd said what I'd meant to say, and I felt so sick I hardly knew what I was talking about. Didn't he really notice? He must have; he gave me some aspirin, or something, when he went.'

'He noticed you were in a state, but he thought it was panic about your aunt. Cheer up, it might have been a lot worse. By the way, how ill was she? I must see her, of course.'

'Yes, of course. Don't go in for a minute ... Kit, I'm so miserable. She wasn't ill at all. I couldn't think of anything quick enough, except to tell him to come. I thought if he found her asleep we wouldn't disturb her, and I'd say she was better, like I did—' She stopped quickly. Kit pretended not to notice. 'I thought it would be all right. But he makes more noise than you do, and she woke up. She didn't recognize him at first – I suppose he hasn't been for ages – and it must have upset her heart, because he listened to it and didn't say I got him for nothing, or anything. And she's worried today because she thinks she's been ill. I thought I could always work it so that it shouldn't make any difference to her. I feel such a dirty crook. I don't know what to do.'

'It isn't anything to do with you. I'm running this show. I ought never to have let you send for me like that. I knew this might happen and you couldn't know.'

'I did know. I just hoped it wouldn't.'

A heavy bird, perhaps an owl, rustled in a tree. Kit looked quickly over his shoulder at the noise. When he turned back to her again she flung her arms round his neck and covered his face with kisses, childishly quick and clumsy. 'You're good for me,' she whispered. 'You're good for me.'

'Yes,' remarked Kit in some bitterness, 'it looks like it.'

Seeming not to have heard him, she said, 'I'm nicer when I'm with you than I am with anyone else. There suddenly seems more of me than I thought there was. I feel I could stop messing about and really be something. You make me feel good, and yet I can't be near you for five minutes without doing something wrong. How do things get mixed up like that? It seems so damned unfair. It must be my fault really, of course. If I were a real person I'd be able to tell.'

Her trouble, added to his own, had for Kit the force of a full stop. Everything seemed to have run to a standstill. He had been up most of the night, and his mind felt flat and gray. He said, colorlessly, 'You mean it's making you more unhappy than happy. I thought it would. Why don't you chuck it all? You will in the end, if that's what it does to you, whether you like it or not; and God knows I'd be the last person on earth to blame you. Let's say good-by.'

Her face, always so full of movement, was for an unnatural moment perfectly still. It was as if he had asked her whether she were ready to die. She turned her head quickly away.

Kit's heart seemed to stop. For him, what he saw was beyond joy or fulfilment; it went too deep to be felt except as a painful, almost physical, shock. Presently he would assimilate it, but its impact hurt him like sudden light. For years he had carried the shame of unreturned love about with him like remorse for an undiscovered crime. Most potent when he thought about it least, it had seeped even into his successes and tinged them with failure. He had written it off, like a bad debt. It had become part of his imagination of himself.

The look, quickly hidden, on Christie's face discharged this bankruptcy. There had been something absolute in it, drowning the physical, without calculation or reserve. He did not think about it; it went too deep into things painfully buried, shook him too radically, for him to know what it meant.

Looking past his shoulder she said, with bright, artificial politeness, 'You think we'd better not see each other any more?' She moved a little away from him, as if she hoped to slip out of his arms without attracting attention.

'I love you,' said Kit suddenly and loudly. He caught her back

97

to him so abruptly that she was taken off her balance and for a moment resisted him. He could hear the breath driven out of her in a gasp that ended in a little grunting sound. He kissed her face and hair furiously.

'What is it?' she asked breathlessly. 'What's the matter?'

'I love you,' he said. 'I love you.'

'Darling, what is it?'

'I don't know. I love you.'

'Hush, my sweet, I'm here. I won't ever go away.'

She stroked his cheek. He pulled her arm down and held it against her side.

'Dear, you're all tired out; go home and get some sleep.'

'No, I'm all right. I'll have to get on, I've got a lot to do.' He stood still, holding her arms above the elbow.

'What is it, darling? Tell me. You're upset about something.'

'No. I'm just going. I was going to say, do you—'

'Yes? Do I what?'

'It doesn't matter. Do you think you're being missed in the house?'

'No, I always go out about now. You look so worried. You're tired.'

Kit looked over the top of her head and said, with hard unnatural casualness, 'Do you love me?'

She looked up at him. '*Love* you? Don't be ridiculous, precious, I worship the ground you tread on. I never stop telling you.'

'Yes. But do you?'

'Darling, could you not hold my arm quite so tight? You're hurting it.'

'Sorry. I wasn't noticing.'

'Aren't you funny today? Haven't I been nice to you, or what? What made you ask me a silly thing like that?'

'I can't imagine. I don't think it's a thing I've ever asked anyone before.'

She laughed, and patted his face. 'Why should you, bless you? Who could help it, anyway? *Now* what's the matter?'

'Nothing. You haven't answered yet.'

'Dear, I keep saying, I'm crazy about you. Kit – don't. Come here; kiss me or something. Don't just stand looking at me like that; you frighten me.'

'I'm sorry, I – I'll have to go; we must have been here some time.'

'Hi, just a minute. Not with your hair like that, angelface. And there's a smear of dirt right across your chin; goodness knows where you got *that* from. Here, lick your hanky and I'll clean it off. What you need is someone to look after you.'

8

Just over a week later, walking home after the third Group meeting they had attended together, Janet told Timmie that she had been Changed. A receptive learner, she had acquired by now the full vocabulary as well as a good range of idiom, and could use both without self-consciousness, or with an embarrassment just slight enough to be subtly pleasant.

'I had a quiet time this morning,' she said, 'and it suddenly came to me, Timmie, that the guidance you had about me the other day was right.' She paused, to study unobtrusively the effect of her words. It was much as she had expected, but rather better. He had not got to the point, yet, of trying to say anything, so she went on: 'You remember what you said about my having done everything one person alone could?'

'Yes,' said Timmie. He swallowed. 'You mustn't think— I shouldn't dream— I mean, I don't really know anything about— Only, of course, it was obvious that if *you* didn't get on with somebody, it must be—' He stalled, blushed to the ears, and looked away.

'Never mind about that, Timmie. There are certain things it wouldn't be right for me to share with you. You're such a young, spontaneous, happy person, I want you always to keep that.' Her smile of secret courage turned like a knife in Timmie's heart. 'All I wanted to tell you is that I realize, now, the resistance I was putting up was just spiritual pride. I was selfish. It mattered too much to me that I should stand on my own feet, and fight my own battles without any help from anyone. I expect that seems foolish to you. It's just that I've always been – rather a lonely creature.'

'I don't see how you could ever be lonely,' said Timmie gruffly. 'I don't see how you could walk into a room without everyone in it wanting to know you. I did.'

'Perhaps you're rather a special sort of person, Timmie.'

Timmie looked like a dog, who is very seldom fed at meals, when a piece of meat comes over the edge of the table. He was beautifully predictable. She went on: 'And perhaps that isn't exactly what I meant. You can know a host of people, and still be lonely in yourself. You wouldn't understand that, Timmie. I wouldn't want you to.'

She had a moment's clear little glimpse of herself, as she spoke, dressed very simply in soft gray – or perhaps misty blue, or mauve – sitting enthroned and solitary in a noisy admiring crowd. Before Timmie it opened out whole planes of tragic mystery; he attempted no reply at all.

'But one shouldn't let courage become one's idol. One mustn't let it shut one off in oneself, and make one proud. One must put what one has into the common stock. There are a great many things I can learn from *you*, Timmie, for instance. That's why I've decided to join the Group.'

Timmie looked down at his right shoe and said, 'You know, I think this is about the best thing that's happened to me ever.'

'Oh, no, Timmie dear. As you go on, you'll have a message for much more worthwhile people than I am. I feel that about you, very definitely.'

'Not likely. And anyway, I didn't do anything. You were bound to, sooner or later, being so – the sort of person you are.' He walked for fifty yards or so in silence, then jerked out, very fast, 'I expect, now, you'll be able to change your husband, and then everything will be all right.'

'Change my husband?' Janet stared, startled, for the moment, half out of her wits. She saw Timmie's eyes fixed on her, anxious and innocent, and her phrase book came back to her. 'Oh – *Change* him. Ye-es, Timmie, perhaps some day.' She looked away, meditatively, trying to recover her poise. This new self of hers had made so lovely a pattern against the background of Timmie, it had not occurred to her, yet, to try the effect against the background of Kit. There was a pause, while she attempted to rearrange the design.

'It seems a bit hard,' Timmie was remarking with labored detachment, 'that right at the beginning you should have to lead off with a tough job like that. I mean, of course I don't know, but I should think it would be, fairly.'

'I don't think that's how I shall have to look at it, do you?' There was a shade of gentle reproach in her voice, which made Timmie crumple and go pink, and Janet herself feel somehow reinforced. 'Don't you think the only way is to forget about one's own selfish sensitiveness and reserve, and try to get guidance just for – for the other person?' This phrasing allowed her to preserve a half-illusion that she was speaking in general terms. It was, somehow, impossible to use anything even as definite as a personal pronoun.

'Yes, of course, I see you would think of it like that.' Timmie kicked a stray cigarette package across the pavement, and sank into another silence, from which he emerged to jerk out, 'What I was thinking was, how would it be if I had a shot instead. I mean, suppose he wasn't decent to you. I should feel it was in a way my fault, having more or less put you on to it. So I thought, if I sort of chipped in first and broke the ice— Not that I'd be any good compared with you, in the way of thinking things out and putting them, but sometimes if two men get together over a thing, they – Don't you think it would be pretty sound?'

There was a pause, filled for Timmie with high anticipations, and for Janet with a kind of turning over of the stomach. Her powers of thought were, for a moment, practically suspended, leaving in possession merely the instinct to remove the responsibility for what she felt to someone else. She drew herself together. 'No,' she said distantly. 'I think it would be useless, unwise, and most unsuitable. Really, Timmie my dear, you must wait till you're a little older before you assume responsibilities of that kind. Don't you think so?'

Timmie gave her one lost look, and accepted the divine chastisement. 'Sorry,' he said indistinctly. He looked on the ground for something to kick, but even this the well-kept pavement denied him. Janet glanced sideways at him, stiff at the joints with constraint and shame, walking a little lopsidedly because his eyes were fixed on his left shoe, his blush deepening till it clashed painfully with his hair. Her resentment left her. She had never achieved, completely, a victory like this before. With Kit there had always been a last shred of doubt. He had an incalculable pride which had made him elusive at moments of final humiliation. In Timmie, as in the sacrifice of some symbolic victim, she completed a dozen achievements that had lacked, at the time, their perfect crown. With no part of this process did her conscious mind have any traffic at all. She merely felt warm to Timmie again, wise and forgiving.

'But you mustn't be sorry,' she said. 'You meant it so kindly. I shouldn't have been cross with you. It's only that – one's unhappiness is so private. You wouldn't understand.'

'I'm going to learn to understand,' said Timmie, speaking with truer guidance than he knew.

9

A thunderstorm was creeping up, pushing its close air before it. The leaves in the garden dropped still, and the smell from every patch of rotten leaves hung motionless over its source, as if enclosed in glass.

Christie tossed in the close heat, throwing off the rug, and Kit's arm, from over her. She reached for his hand again, apologetically, and caressed it. 'It's so hot.'

'It will be better when the storm breaks,' said Kit.

'When it does I shall have to go in. It might wake her.'

'Oh, yes, of course.'

He had forgotten because for once he himself was feeling secure. It was his free evening. He and Fraser, when they relieved each other, had an arrangement which included the night calls as well. He told Janet he was going to see McKinnon, which, up till just after midnight, had been true. In this relief from guilt and tension, he had overreacted into a blissful sense of immunity. Christie saw his face change.

'Darling, what a shame,' she said. 'On your night off. Don't worry, it will be all right. The storm isn't coming any nearer.' Her voice, maternal and reassuring, suggested that she would attend to it herself.

The thunder sounded again, like huge casks being trundled round a cellar a long way off. A sheet of lightning threw into theatrical relief a low ceiling of cloud. For an instant as brief as the snap of a camera, the lovers saw one another, their eyes startled and darkly shining, surprised into strangeness as they were flung without warning from a world of touch into one of sight. When the flash had passed, they reached for one another like people reaching for safety.

She said under her breath, 'I used to be a bit frightened of thunderstorms.'

'Would you rather go in?'

'No. I don't mind things with you that I minded before.'

Tenderness and security warmed him. Looking up at the blackness of the invisible roof, he said softly, 'Tell me about that other chap. What was he like?'

She threw her arm over him. 'No. You don't want to know; you only think you do.'

'I don't mind tonight. Like you and the thunder. I want to know all about you.'

'You don't really.'

'Just as you like.'

She stroked his hair, then said, quickly and indulgently like a mother who has been asked for a bedtime story, 'All right. I'll tell you about Maurice if you want me to. But I don't think you'd get on with him.'

'Well,' said Kit tranquilly, 'I didn't ask with the idea of getting him to put me up for his club.'

She gave a soft little snort of laughter into his neck. 'He couldn't. He was a devout Communist.'

Kit grunted. 'What else was he?' Within him jealousy, like a stalking cat, waited quietly for something solid enough to put its claws in.

'He was about forty and dark and had a heavy sad sort of face. He did a rather exclusive sort of woodcuts; he had an exhibition of them once, called *Landscapes of the Mind*. Not many people came, and he was miserable. He had belonged to the Surrealists at one time, but they said he was irregular and had no place in the Movement. That was just after I met him. I couldn't bear him being so lonely. Besides, he said if I wouldn't have him he'd kill himself.'

Kit uttered a monosyllable under his breath.

'Don't be mean, darling, he quite easily might have. He'd tried once before, but he hadn't enough shillings for the gas and it ran out. He did a Landscape afterward, of what it felt like when he was almost dead. It was rather marvelous.'

'Oh. What was he like to live with?'

'Well, I didn't actually *live* with him, I only used to call in. I was working at the Abbey, and he shared a flat with a man who was on the *Statesman and Nation* or some paper like that. I just used to call in when this other man was away. He used to go away quite a bit, observing what people said to each other in trains and places, about whatever crisis was on.'

'How useful.'

'Yes, it was, except once when he forgot something and came back for it. Of course, Maurice did *ask* me to live with him – instead of this man, I mean, not as well – but I don't think really he could have afforded it, and though I was awfully fond of him, it was more restful, sort of, at the Abbey.'

'So I should imagine.'

'No, truly, he was terribly sweet sometimes. It was only that he had theories about me.'

'Did he tell you what they were?'

'Yes, all the time. That was it, really. You see, his most famous

Landscape – the one that made a lot of people say he was a genius – was called *Woman*. It was all in symbolism. And everything I did, nearly, he said was symbolical too. It was rather exciting, at first.'

'Must have been.'

'Look out, darling, that hurts.'

'Sorry. Go on.'

'You're not cross, precious, are you? I'm loving you like anything all the time, and you did ask me.'

'No, of course I'm not.'

'Well, about this symbolism; you could hardly blame him, seeing he was a sort of specialist, but he *was* inclined to overdo it a bit. For instance – there was a cobweb in one corner of his ceiling; it had been there for days and it was quite obviously getting larger and had more spiders in it, so naturally at last I got up on a chair to sweep it down. And he said that was tremendously symbolic, that I'd got up there to display my female form. I told him I hadn't known he was in the room, which was true – not that I'd have given it a thought. But he said that was symbolic too, my concealing my instincts. I suppose I shouldn't have argued, but it was just so *annoying*. I thought afterward I'd been rather unkind, because of course it was all part of his Communism, and if he didn't have set recipes for everything he couldn't make it work. So I made up, but we were never quite the same afterward.'

Below the horizon, the thunder made a sound like someone grumbling into a thick beard.

'I think it was good for me though, because since then I've never said men are like this or that, in case it was just as annoying for them. Though, as a matter of fact, most of them are. Except you, my darling. I do love you.'

Her cheek pressed against Kit's on the lumpy cushion, with its mingled smell of clean new cover and musty filling. He moved his head a little to one side, but not altogether away.

'Well?' he asked. 'What made you leave him in the end?'

She slipped her arm round his head to bring it nearer. 'Silly ass. *You* ought to know.'

'How do you mean?' said Kit, stiffening a little.

'Cuckoo. Of course, I met you. What's the matter?'

'Nothing,' he said presently. 'It's all right. I hadn't realized it was quite so—'

'Darling, I haven't seen him once since I came down here. What does it matter anyway, it's you I love. I wrote to him last week, saying it was all over. I haven't heard back from him yet, it's rather worrying.'

'Last *week*? But, good God, how many is it since—'

'Darling. I *know*. It does seem rather dreadful, but I couldn't bear to upset him. He does get so appallingly miserable; you never saw anything like it. I kept on starting letters to tell him, and then I'd tear them up and write an ordinary one instead. You know how it is.'

'You mean to say,' said Kit slowly, 'that all this time you've been writing—' He stopped, hearing his own voice saying, *Of course, Janie, you know I love you.* Aloud he finished, 'Well, you know best, I dare say.'

'Kit, darling, you're not upset with me?'

'No. No, of course not. I hope this chap doesn't put his head in the gas oven. He sounds a bit unbalanced, to me.'

'He hasn't got an actual oven, only quite a small ring. Besides, he's in the middle of a picture. I expect he'd want to finish it, and by that time he'd be feeling better. I wrote him a very *nice* letter, honestly I did. I wouldn't hurt his feelings for anything. I said I'd always love him too, in a way, but you were different from anyone else, and so you are, my sweet. Listen, didn't you think the thunder sounded nearer that time? . . . Kit? . . . Darling, for heaven's sake don't just lie there like an image looking at the ceiling. I suppose you think I don't know what you look like just because it's dark. I promise you, I can hardly remember what it felt like now. It's like something ten years ago. Oh, darling, what shall I do if I've made you miserable? Here, look, have some Turkish delight. It's rather special; I made it myself, as a matter of fact. Look out, it's rather sticky. You may have to sort of scoop it up with your fingers a bit.'

Kit took some, ate it, and, fishing out his handkerchief, began the still more difficult task of cleaning off the remains. In the course of these processes he found his emotions inclined to go off the boil. Just as he had finished, a flash of sheet lightning, more sustained than the others, revealed Christie to him. She was leaning over him, her face taken unguarded by the light, anxious and tender, pure devotion in her eyes. His thoughts of the darkness fled like ghosts at cockcrow, mocked by this candle flame of candid love. What he knew grew thin and inconsequent, what he guessed a dream. His too-sharp and dangerous happiness found relief in laughter. Christie caught him in her arms.

'Dear, dear Kit,' she murmured, 'if you knew how much I love you. Oh, I do. You're all that's real; I just imagined the rest, to pass the time while I was waiting for you.'

The air stirred, heavily, pushed from its sluggishness by the movement of colder air behind; the hidden birds shifted and scuttered in the leaves.

'You do still love me, don't you?' she whispered.

'Yes.'

'You didn't stop even for a moment?'

'No.'

'I should die if you did.'

The first heavy drops sounded on the roof above them, but neither of them heard till their first rustle and whisper had turned to a heavy sigh, and the sigh to great drumming gusts that made the empty spaces of the night solid with sound.

'It's raining,' said Christie lazily. 'Now there won't be a storm at all.'

'You'll be cold.' Kit reached for his overcoat and drew it over her; the air had freshened quickly.

'If I caught cold,' she remarked as she curled herself into it, 'you could come and look after me.'

'Even so, I'd rather you didn't.' He had wondered, sometimes, what her vague idea was of the professional risks he ran. Probably it amounted to some notion that gossip would be bad for his practice. He had never said much about it, thinking she had enough cause for anxiety at her own end.

'The General Medical Council,' he explained gently, 'is apt to take offense if one sleeps with one's patients.'

'Silly old codgers,' said Christie comfortably. 'Sour grapes, I suppose. All their own patients are royalty and cabinet ministers and bishops; and who'd sleep with them, anyway?'

'That's what I'm always telling them.' Kit grinned drowsily into the darkness; the strength of the rain, now that it had settled, had become rhythmic and hypnotic. He could stay, he thought, for another half hour. He drew a strand of Christie's hair through his fingers, and felt it curl round them of its own accord, like the caress of something alive.

It was pitch dark outside. The noise of the rain changed from a drumming to a wet hissing, as the surfaces it fell on grew saturated and overflowed. Through some crack in the roof above him a single drop fell on his face, startling because of its invisibility. It roused him a little; he shifted out of the way and shut his eyes again. But before he could settle, Christie twisted out of his arm and sat up.

'What is it?' he asked unencouragingly. They had fitted themselves into comfortable hollows between the lumps in the cushions, a process that took some time initially, and he did not want to move.

'Nothing; I was just thinking it must be time I went in.'

'What, now? It isn't very late.'

'I know. I think I'd better, though.'

'But you were just saying yourself— You're not annoyed about anything, are you?' This was instinctive, and slipped out before he thought.

'Precious, don't; you know you never annoyed me in your life. I adore everything you say and everything you do.' She rubbed her cheek against his hair. 'I must go in, though. I suddenly feel I'd better. I don't know why.'

'But do you realize there's a cloudburst, or something very like it, going on? You can't go in this. Apart from anything else, how are you going to explain a wringing-wet nightgown and pools of water all over the floor? Still less can you stroll in wearing my overcoat, willingly as I'd give it you.'

'Oh, I can hide the nightgown. Kit, darling, let me go. I want to. I feel frightened.'

'That's only the thunder. The rain will die down in a minute. If you go now you'll be mud up to the knees. You've only got satin shoes.'

'I'll carry them. I'll get rid of everything. I'm very careful.'

'Are you?' said Kit, his voice hardening. An imaginary portrait of Maurice, built up with vivid inaccuracy in the course of the evening, floated before his eyes.

'Oh, darling, no!' Christie cast herself on him, all solicitude. 'You can't go and be miserable now when you're going away from me. I couldn't bear it. I wouldn't sleep. I promise you faithfully I've never loved anyone a quarter as much as I've loved you. I never will, either. I'd rather die than make you unhappy, you know; you know I would.' She stroked him with little consoling gestures. 'Dear Kit. Say it's all right.'

'Of course it is. I didn't mean anything. I can't be quite rational about you, you mean too much.'

'That's nice.' She sighed contentedly, and curled up beside him again. 'I feel so safe with you.'

The rain still thudded over the garden, its even bass broken with the tinkle of odd splashes and drippings among the nearer trees. When another note threaded itself, clearly and insistently, into the noise, Kit heard it for a moment or two without attention. It was only after it had stopped that his mind snapped into recognition. Christie had let him go; now she gripped him again, not caressingly but in fear. They were both still, holding one another and listening to the silence, curiously defined among so many sounds, where this one sound had been.

Christie whispered, 'What shall we do?'

'Are you sure it was the bell?' He knew well enough, and was, indeed, hardly aware that he had spoken.

'Yes, yes, of course it was.' She pushed him away; he could hear her groping about the floor. 'Where are my slippers? I can't find them. Where did I put my slippers, Kit?' Her voice sounded as though her teeth were chattering.

Kit got out his torch, and picked them out in the beam. She slipped into them, blinking in the light and throwing up her arm to shield her eyes. Collecting himself, he said, 'Listen. You'll have to wear my coat. Take it and hide it and go in and see what she wants. I'll come over later on and collect it. You'll have time to change your shoes. Keep your hair dry; throw it over your head.'

'Yes,' she said mechanically. He threw the coat over her; she drew it dazedly about her.

'Hurry up,' he said. 'She'll ring again.'

'But how shall I send for you? How will you come?'

'I'll come when things have settled down.'

'But *now*. To see her. Don't you realize, she's ill?'

'How do you—' For a moment, accustomed to the many small needs for which nursing-home patients rang, he was simply impatient of the delay. The certainty in Christie's voice penetrated him slowly. He felt a constriction in his chest.

'Of course she's ill. She's never once rung in the night except for that.'

Kit got up and, with precise automatic movements, settled his clothes and his hair. Speaking not to Christie or altogether to himself, he said, 'It ought to be Fraser. Fraser's taking the calls.'

'It's you she—' Christie broke off. In the pause that followed, as if she had waited for it, the bell sounded again. She ran to him and whispered, 'No, of course. You mustn't let anyone find you here. You'll get into trouble. They can do something to you for it, can't they? Didn't you say they could? Go away. I'll get Dr Fraser. I know what to do till he comes. It will be all right.'

I haven't got anything with me, said a voice in Kit's head. He felt the pocket of his jacket, and encountered the tubular screw-case of his hypodermic. Beside it was a small, flat cardboard box. He remembered that, earlier in the day, he had called at the chemist's to replenish his supply of coramine.

Christie's hand was twisting a fold of his coat. He took her fingers in his and gently disengaged them. His mind felt curiously flat and commonplace; the ingrained habits of four or five years did not afford him even the luxury of an heroic choice. Much as if the casualty bell had sounded when he had just got to sleep, he said, 'Damn. All right, I'll come along.'

Christie was talking again. He did not listen much to what she was saying. The panic in her voice struck already, not on his emotions, but on the part of his mind accustomed to dealing with anxious relatives and people who lost their heads.

'Run along,' he said, 'there's a good girl. She ought to have someone with her. Just go in and reassure her, and then let me in at the front door. If it turns out not to be anything, wave through the glass and I'll go away. Don't worry, and hurry.'

Christie moved away. He could hear in the darkness the

small sound of the coat being drawn together around her. In the subdued voice of a schoolgirl who has been told to pull herself together, she said, 'Yes. I'll do that.' For a moment her shadow in the doorway made blacker a darkness which had seemed complete before; then he was standing, alone, listening to the rain, which seemed to approach intimately with a personality of its own, like someone who has been awaiting the chance of a private conversation. He turned up his collar, and went out, a stream from the roof drenching him before he was over the threshold.

Memory, and the heavy bulk of the house which he felt rather than saw against the blank sky, guided him till Christie had switched on the light in Miss Heath's room. Its beam leaped across the lawn, lighting up the outline of the porch. As he reached it, the light over the door dazzled into his eyes, and he heard the huge bolts rattle and scrape. The door swung back, and Christie stood in the archway, wearing the Chinese-blue dressing-gown, and separated from him by straight gleaming lines of rain. 'Quickly,' she said.

Kit went past her to the half-open inner door. The sound of the rain died as the thick door closed on it; and the thoughts that had accompanied Kit through the dark garden were cut off too like external things. Personality had nothing to do here; it was already leaving the face on the pillow, smoothed out by the uniformity of the act of death. He did not know Christie had come into the room behind him, till the pale straying eyes flickered for a moment of recognition. Without looking round he said, 'A glass of water, please,' and, breaking the paper seal of the box, got out an ampoule and a file.

As he bent over the bedside table, sawing at the fine glass by the light of the lamp, he heard a faint movement beside him. The old woman's struggle for her shallow breath had ceased for a moment; the fear in her eyes was superseded, as they turned toward him, by gratitude and surprise. With a fluttering gasp she whispered, 'Dr Anderson – how good – get here so quickly – such a trouble—'

Her yellow hand was picking and fidgeting at the sheet. He held it for a moment, slipping a finger up the wrist to feel the pulse. It was imperceptible; he had not expected anything else. He said, 'We'll have you feeling better in just a moment.' The graying face on the pillow gave back a remote reflection of his smile.

Christie had put down the glass of water beside the syringe. He rinsed it, and drew up the coramine. 'This isn't going to hurt you. Just the usual prick.'

He picked up a fold of skin and slipped the needle under it. Christie had gone round to the opposite side of the bed. He saw her hand close, warm and comforting, over the limp hand on the sheet. For a moment Miss Heath's eyes moved from one to the other; not very differently, seventy years before, little Amy Heath had looked from her dear Mamma to her dear Papa as, clutching their fingers, she walked toward the darkest, laurel-roofed bend of the drive. Then Kit drove the piston home. In the first instant after the needle was withdrawn that look of dream-shadowed, timid trust remained; in the next, a kind of lightning-flash of consciousness lit the flaccid face and the glazed eyes. They fixed themselves on Kit in a stare as of astonished realization; but what they saw he could not tell, for immediately there was a tremor of the limbs, and a jerking spasm of the breath which no other breath succeeded. Miss Heath's hand lay still, with a little fold of sheet under the fingers, and her mouth dropped open as it had been on the night when she had snored in her sleep. Her eyes, still fixed in their stare, became, with the strange definiteness of death, no longer eyes but simply part of the blank surface of a body. Kit bent and closed them.

He had known, as he gave the injection, that it was too late.

The syringe was in his hand. He glanced round the room, registering, almost unconsciously, the fact that there was nowhere to boil it.

'She's gone,' he said. He began to draw the pillow out from under the dead woman's head, not realizing that he had waited for a moment, instinctively, expecting Christie to support it as a nurse would have done.

Christie stood in the bay window, stroking the gray-green leaf of an ice plant between her fingers. She did not look up when Kit went over to her, and he did not look at her. He said the things that doctors say to devoted relatives after a death: that it had been inevitable for months, that she had been a comfort to her aunt, given her interests, prolonged her life. His voice had a practiced, professional kindness. Christie nodded, fingering the glaucous leaves. There was a tension between them, of fear for the moment when some personal inflection would first be used.

Kit said that he would call in the morning to make out a certificate and see if there was anything he could do. Christie said, 'Thank you. I should be glad if you would,' and looked at a small round rosette she had snapped away from the plant, as if she were surprised to see it in her hand. Turning it round she said, without any alteration of voice, 'She was frightened by herself. She rang twice. I came here so that she could have someone to come at once when she rang.'

Kit, looking past her at the blank dark of the window, said, 'If I hadn't been here, you'd have had to leave her to go to the phone.'

They both stopped, like people at the end of conversation.

Kit moved out past the lace curtain. The face on the bed seemed, to his questioning eyes, very remote from reproach or forgiveness. It was concerned only with itself, with being a thing in its final form, like print of which the manuscript has been destroyed. There could be no more emendations, no revision, no touching up. Kit went over and covered it with the sheet. Christie returned the bunch of leaves carefully to the flower pot, as if importance attached to the act.

'Shall you be all right,' he asked, 'here for the night?' This too was a formula; people were often afraid of being alone with a corpse; they got a relation or neighbor to come in.

'Yes, thank you.' They moved toward the door. 'You know, the servants are in the house.'

'Oh, yes,' said Kit. 'Of course.'

Christie opened the door. They both stopped, aware that something was different before they knew what it was. The hall was no longer dark, lit distantly, as it had been, by the light outside the porch. The big cut-glass lamp on the ceiling was burning, looking strident and unreal.

Just underneath it, in the middle of the red turkey carpet, stood Pedlow, fully dressed, her starched cap and clean apron standing out with wooden stiffness, her face as unmoving as the folds of her corseted black dress. She had something dark over her arm; Kit, in the first dulled moment, took it for a rug. He heard Christie, beside him, make a little sharp breath-sound. After a moment she said, in a little, high voice, 'Well – thank you, Dr Anderson. It was very good of you to get here so soon. I'm sure you did everything possible— Thank you. Good night.'

Pedlow moved forward, reaching the door, with her smooth well trained haste, a moment before him. She was handing him something, with such correctness that Kit had taken it from her before he awoke to what had happened. It was his overcoat, which he had lent to Christie. Christie's face would have told him, if he had not already guessed, where Pedlow had found it. 'Thank you,' he said. Neatly and silently, Pedlow lifted it for him to put on.

Without turning, he could feel Christie's eyes fixed on his face. He put on the coat slowly, delaying while he could the moment when he must turn and display his emptiness to her need. The time for playing house was over. He had no defense to make for her, no shelter to offer her even for this one night. 'Good night,' he said.

Christie straightened her shoulders, said 'Good night,' and tried to smile at him. As he went out he saw Pedlow stop for a moment to look at her, before she crossed to the closed door of the room they had left.

10

Once, in the morning hours, Kit knew that he had dozed for an odd half hour, because the sky in the window changed its color suddenly from black to gray, but his eyes felt wide open and fixed, as if he had been staring at something during the time. When it was just light he dropped into a heavy sleep, from which the maid's morning tap waked him with a protesting shock. At breakfast Janet looked at him thoughtfully, and asked if he had had a pleasant evening with Dr McKinnon. An inflection in her voice made it clear that she supposed him to have been drinking most of the night.

The post had presented him with a circular advertising a newish drug. He had been employing it in his practice for a year, but he read the explanatory matter from end to end, and, when he had finished it, the testimonials. Janet returned to her own correspondence. Her last letter was several pages long. When he happened, once, to glance at her, she shuffled the pages with self-conscious negligence, so that the blank sheet at the back was turned toward him.

He managed to eat a little. His body was too well organized to become, even now, a parasite on his nerves. It cleared his head enough to make him think a little of appearances; he tried to smooth the strain out of his face and attempt a kind of conversation. Because of the effort this involved, it did not occur to him at once that Janet's replies were almost as perfunctory as his own. It was not till the end of the meal, when she gathered up her letters and began to fidget aimlessly round the room, that he recognized the familiar symptoms.

She was about to make a gesture, something she had been saving for some time. Seeing it coming, his mind said, in simple protest, 'Not in the *morning*.' It was too much. It took him a moment or so to remember what else it might be. He took his pipe out of his pocket and began carefully to fill it.

Janet fingered the envelopes in her hands and said, 'Christopher, dear, couldn't we have a little talk? I think it would be good for both of us. We haven't got together over things lately, have we?'

She smiled at him. It was a smile which looked as if she had copied it from someone else; it had a kind of forced friendliness verging on the genial, which, chiefly because it was so unsuited to her, jarred sharply. In his surprise he actually forgot the fear it had relieved. She went on, still smiling: 'I know what you've been feeling these last few weeks.'

Kit thrust the tobacco down into the bowl in a solid block which, as he discovered later, prevented the pipe from drawing at all. Without noticing, he added another layer.

'You feel I've been neglecting you. But though it may have seemed like that, you've been a great deal in my mind.'

'Not at all,' said Kit. 'I mean, of course, I've thought nothing of the kind.' He glanced automatically at the clock, which made it just under a quarter of an hour to morning surgery. Keying himself up to routine had taken everything he had; there was simply nothing left for this. He felt incapable even of the effort necessary to stave it off, and stood helplessly with his pipe (which he never smoked at this hour of the day) cold in his hand.

'What I wanted to say,' Janet continued, 'is this.' She had lifted her chin and pitched her voice a little beyond him. It had a kind of rehearsed effect, as if she were addressing herself to several people rather than to him, which made him feel uncomfortable. 'I've realized that up till this last month I've never been absolutely honest with myself about the reasons for our marriage having drifted onto the rocks.'

What on earth has she been reading? thought Kit in dim astonishment. The magazine slang sat as startling on her as if she had walked into the room in trousers. The surgery jogged his mind; he glanced at the clock again.

'I haven't faced up to my own selfishness. I've clung to my reserve, and reserve *is* a form of selfishness, Kit. I haven't shared with you as I should have done.'

'Shared what?' asked Kit dazedly. His mind had little capacity, this morning, for curiosity or surprise.

'Oh, that's just a— Shared my thoughts with you, I mean. I shouldn't have kept my feelings secret from a mistaken pride in bearing things alone. After all, there's a very sacred sort of bond between us. It's a thing we ought to have got together over.' She seemed checked here, perhaps by Kit's face, perhaps by a momentary doubt of her phrasing, but went on, quickly: 'In fact, I've been selfish in many ways.'

'My dear,' said Kit, horror at last overcoming his inertia, 'you've done your duty to me fully, and if I've seemed not to appreciate it I'm sorry; I can only assure you I do. I'll talk over anything you like later on, but would you mind now? I've got one or two examinations to lay out for downstairs.'

'Kit, it's only ten to nine. You *must* face up to things now; we've both got into the habit of dodging realities. It won't take a minute to finish what I wanted to say to you. It was only to tell you how wrong I feel it was of me to have let the – the physical part of our marriage go, just because it didn't mean anything to *me*. I should simply have told you honestly that it didn't, and fulfilled my part of it for your sake. And that's what I've resolved to do, Kit. I'll see a specialist, or anything you think necessary. I've been unfair to you, and I shan't rest till I've got right with myself about it.'

Kit turned the pipe in his hand, rejecting, one after the other, the answers that occurred to him. The conception of himself as an altar-stone for his wife's votive offerings was not a new one, but it had not been presented to him before with just this cheerful bonhomie, or at just this crux of his affairs. His resentment and bitterness were almost swamped by his sheer embarrassment; the violence of the three left him with no very clear impression of what he did feel. He clung, however, to an idea that if he expressed it he would be sorry afterward, and, presently, the smoke within him dispersed. But he was no nearer knowing what to say. The situation, when he got outside it, was like things he saw in the course of his practice, and left him with the same feeling of futility and impotent pity.

'You don't think I'm sincere,' Janet was saying. 'You're afraid I shall regret it afterward, and perhaps resent things and reproach you. But I shan't, Kit. I've found a strength I never had before.'

I must say something, Kit told himself desperately. To state the bald truth, of which he had no doubt, that the thing was impossible by now in any case, would be simple but brutally inadequate. He believed she had meant it; if so, heaven knew with what effort she had prepared this sacrifice to her conception of herself. To miss the cue entirely would be too cruel. Any cliché would be better, even *My dear, I've learned to care for you in a different way*.

It stuck in his throat, however. In the old days his lies to her had been like his consulting-room lies, prescribed as he might have prescribed a sedative, untainted by interest of his own. He was not quite aware that he had come to treat her as a patient, and did not know, now, why he felt that his professional integrity was being damaged. But she was waiting.

'My dear,' he began as gently as he could, 'I've—'

There was a tap at the door. Janet looked irritably toward it. He could see her making up her mind not to say *Come in*. The thought of approaching rescue was too much for him.

'Come in,' he said.

The door opened, apologetically, to admit the elderly maid from the Frasers' flat. She scarcely ever came with messages; the men had a house telephone between their surgeries, and Fraser was overpunctilious about interference out of hours. Kit was delighted to see her, but wondered what she could want.

'Oh, Dr Anderson, sir, I'm so sorry to trouble you, but Mrs Fraser said would you be good enough to step down before surgery and see Dr Fraser? He isn't very well and she doesn't think he'll be able to see his patients today.'

'Of course,' said Kit. 'Tell Mrs Fraser I'll be down.'

He saw Janet looking at him as the door closed. Her face told him that she knew he would use this excuse to leave her without an answer, but after all she was relieved and determined not to admit it to herself. He went over and kissed her quickly on the forehead. Each, for different reasons, avoided the other's eyes.

'That settles it,' he said, 'I'm afraid. Surgery will start late as it is, if I have to look him over first. I hope there's nothing seriously wrong with the poor old boy.' Janet was reading the address on one of the envelopes in her hand. Looking past her, he said, 'Don't worry over things, my dear, you're everything to me that I need you to be.'

He had no time to think the conversation over, for at the foot of the stairs Mrs Fraser met him, with trouble sitting reluctantly on her broad healthy face. Fraser was in bed, looking pinched and yellow and, unusual for him, every year of his age. He said that he had a gastric chill; he had had a call in the early morning, and been caught in a sharp shower.

'Not one of my cases, I hope?' said Kit. His feeling of guilt was reasonless; he supposed it must be becoming a habit.

'No, no, one of my own.' Fraser, with his practice on his mind, was impatient of irrelevances. He had been working till the last minute on a sheaf of notes for Kit. Before going over them he apologized, with his careful and rather ponderous courtesy, for giving his partner the extra work. He would not, he assured Kit, be *hors de combat* long enough to make a locum necessary.

Kit, not liking a sunk look about his eyes, tentatively suggested examining him; but the old man waved him away. He had had similar chills before, a matter of 24 hours; a little bismuth and a fluid diet would settle it. His thermometer and watch stood on the bedside table, but, with an obstinacy Kit remembered from other occasions, he kept their findings to himself.

Kit, whose program had been fairly well filled already, went through to the small annex in which his consulting-room was built, and looked at Fraser's notes. He took out his own notebook, put it side by side with the notes, and tried to correlate them into some kind of plan. He stared at them, together and apart, and stared again; but each time the grip of his brain slipped like the grip of a hand with a cut tendon. He could only wonder how he was going to see Christie, and, when this brought him back to the notes on the desk, stare at them and think of Christie again, and of what had happened in the night. He had had 24 hours with negligible sleep, but was too tired even to sort its effect from the rest of his trouble. After five minutes of it he pushed the notes to one side and rang for the first patient to be shown in.

The surgery, even with summary treatment, finished an hour late. Fraser's patients, through contact or affinity, nearly all had a dash of Fraser about them. They were mostly middle-aged, liked to come to the point in their own time, and were full of leisured conversational gambits which had, in decency, to be followed up for a few minutes at least. The visits were the same, but more so. Additionally there was the case to which Fraser had been called up, a sub-acute abdominal on which Fraser wanted a second opinion.

The consultation, and subsequent arrangements with a nursing-home, dragged on till nearly the end of the afternoon, leaving two or three more visits that could not safely be postponed. He plodded round them, followed by the knowledge that Christie must have been expecting him since the middle of the morning. He could have called for a moment between these cases, but his fatigue had got to the meticulous stage when each detail has to be cleared up in its exact order, for lack of confidence in future effort. They carried him on through teatime; it was falling dark when he got to Laurel Dene at last. There was just light enough to show him the blank eyes of the windows with their drawn-down blinds.

He rang, feeling unequal to the effort, which had somehow to be made, of facing Pedlow out. As it happened, he had nerved himself for nothing. The cook let him in, looking self-conscious, short of breath, and resentful – of her imposed office, Kit thought, rather than of him. There was no reason, he supposed, why she should not have done it often before in the course of Pedlow's time off; but he had never known Pedlow to take any.

The cook asked him if he would kindly step into the drawing-room. Kit stared at her, and took an involuntary step down the hall. He supposed she meant the dining-room; he had waited there once or twice, since Christie came. 'This way, sir,' said the cook. She opened the right-hand door.

Kit walked in, and stood still for a moment in the doorway. The drawing-room had come back to itself. The bed had gone, the chest of drawers with its brushes and jars, the dressing-gown thrown over the sofa and the slippers underneath it. His memory moving back over a couple of months, he realized that every occasional table, every vase, every photograph frame and non-descript silver object of art, had been arranged in its former place with the exactness of sacred vessels on which a ritual depends. The doors into the garden were shut.

Kit walked up and down the long room, which the cook had left in its half-twilight. There was a deadness in his heart which was beyond anxiety or fear. He was gripped by the power that symbols of disaster have to be more frightful than disaster itself, because they leave the imagination free. He stared through the closed glass doors into the garden, and a procession of possibilities, each more horrible than the last, trampled his common sense underfoot. When the door opened at last, he seemed to swallow his heart while he waited for the news. But it was Christie, wearing a dark brown dress, her hair looking dark too in the shadows. She shut the door behind her and stood with her hand on it, as if she were afraid to leave it unguarded. Her face was pale and tightly stretched; she looked cold.

Shaken out of his own fears, Kit went over to her; but she was hard and unresponsive in his arms, looking not at him but over her shoulder at the door. He felt her hands resisting him as if they were doing it of themselves, and she would have restrained them if she could.

'It's all right, dear,' he said.

She whispered, 'Don't say anything now. Someone will hear. It doesn't take long to make out a certificate, does it? You'd better not stay longer than that.'

Kit tightened his hold. Her terror had jerked his reason into its needed reaction. 'Nonsense. No one can do anything to either of us.' He spoke with an assurance that almost convinced himself. 'Sit down here and talk to me.'

She pulled her hand out of his, and looked away.

'What is it?' he asked.

'Why did you leave me all day, Kit? It's been— Why didn't you come in the morning? I suppose you were busy, or something. But I just didn't think you *could*.'

He was dumb for a moment. She never reproached him, never asked for explanations. If he offered them, she always seemed to have accepted them beforehand. He felt, not so much a sense of injustice as a difficulty in finding his feet.

'Fraser's ill,' he said at last. 'I've had to see his patients as well as mine. You know I'd have come if it was humanly possible. I could hardly work for thinking of you, as it was.'

'You do look tired,' she said, and absently gave his arm a maternal pat. 'But, Kit, all day? Would all those people have actually died if you hadn't been there?'

'Well, no, of course not. But they were all people who had to be seen.'

She peered at him a little, as if she were trying to see him in a better light. Thoughtfully and without resentment, she said, 'You're different from me, aren't you? I mean, I see you were right, but if it had been me I couldn't have helped going to you.'

'I'm sorry.'

'No, it's all right. I didn't mean to be silly about it.' She looked up at him solemnly. 'I like you being better than me.'

'Don't be a baby,' he said; her candor touched him to the point of awkwardness. 'I've come to talk to you about Pedlow. Now listen. You're not to let her upset you. I'll deal with her. If she tries to start anything, come straight to me. What's she been saying to you?'

'Nothing.'

Kit nodded, his expectations confirmed.

'That's what's so horrible,' Christie said.

'What about this room, then?'

'She just did that. She moved my things to the spare room as soon as I was up. She didn't ask me, or anything. I've hardly seen her. She spent the rest of last night – in there – I think.'

'I see. What about having the light on?'

Christie went over to the switch. The dusty crystal chandelier leaped into life, its facets reflected in the silver on the mahogany tables. Kit narrowed his eyes against it; it accented a certain grimness in his face. He sat down beside Christie on the brocade settee. 'Have you got any money?' he asked.

'Yes, I've got about seventeen pounds, but most of it's in the post office. I could get some tomorrow if it wasn't more than three pounds. How much would you like?'

Kit's jaw relaxed a little in spite of himself. 'Little lunatic, I don't want any. I was only wondering whether she'd start by trying to blackmail you or me. Your being out of it simplifies things. If she tries it with me I shall go to the police. Anything's better; you agree to that?'

She stared. 'Blackmail you? *Pedlow?* You must be mad.'

'I don't think so. Doctors are favorite subjects, you know. I've been more or less prepared since last night. Don't worry; your name won't be dragged in.'

'But, Kit – you didn't think Pedlow was like *that?*' Her eyes were blank with bewilderment; she stammered as she sought for words. 'Why, Pedlow – Pedlow would die before she'd steal a safety pin off my dressing-table. How *could* you think – don't you see, that's why she frightens me.'

Kit looked at her, in compassion for her simplicity. 'I think you'll find—' he began.

'Oh, Kit, don't be *silly.* When you live with a person who hates you, you get to know them. Besides, Pedlow's got plenty of money. She won't know how to spend it, as it is. It isn't money she wants.'

'How do you know?'

'Aunt Amy's left her a lot of money. Most of what she's got, I think. She wanted to alter her will and leave some of it to me. It was terrible; she kept saying would I remind her to ring up her lawyer. I had an awful job, sometimes, to put her off. I— But to have had something of Pedlow's— It would have been like the gold they take from tombs, that kills you if you have it in the house. Thank God I managed not to let it happen.'

Kit patted her hand. He felt his whole body relaxing in relief. 'Why didn't you tell me that before?' he said.

'I didn't think it was important.'

'But it explains everything. Her dislike of you, and spying about. Naturally, she was afraid for her expectations. No doubt your aunt had told her about the will; she was open about things, and fond of her. Pedlow's idea in watching you was that if the lawyer actually called, she could produce something against you and get your aunt to alter it again. She was too discreet to act unnecessarily. Now she knows her money's safe she's got no reason to make trouble. Your natural honesty's saved the two of us. Queer that you didn't see it yourself.'

'It sounds simple, put that way. I don't know, though. I've thought, once or twice, that Pedlow *wanted* me to be after Aunt Amy's money. It would have given her a sort of advantage over me. Sometimes I think when she finds I wasn't, she'll hate me more than ever. I know it sounds silly when you're being so practical, but it seems to me there were only two things she cared about, Aunt Amy and being more righteous than anyone else. She got out all my boxes this morning, and dusted them.'

'Well, that was quite a natural thing to do.'

'I saw her face as she was doing it, before she saw me.'

'Darling, you've been through a lot; you're fancying things.'

'Yes, perhaps it will all look different in the morning. Only – well, this morning I wanted to go in to – to look at Aunt Amy. I thought I'd feel better in her room. I was happy with her, you know; I never had time to tell you much about that. Pedlow passed me in the hall, and just looked at me. It – it made me feel as if I were a murderer going to gloat over someone I'd killed. I haven't dared to go even near the door, since. I knew I'd find her waiting.'

'She's upset, that's all.'

'I suppose so. I wish I wasn't so frightened all the time.'

'It's the house – the blinds and everything.' He put his arm round her shoulders. Pedlow had grown dim in his mind, Christie near and warm. He could only remember that in a few days she would have gone away. The comfort he offered her covered a longing to demand it for himself. 'Get out of doors as much as you can. Look, that reminds me. I've brought you a bottle of pick-me-up, and a sedative for the night. Don't forget to take them. You'll feel better after a proper sleep.'

'Dear Kit.' She took the bottle and pillbox with an attempt at a smile. 'You always promised me a tonic, didn't you?' She looked up at him. The mist of fear cleared from her eyes; she caught him by the sleeve. 'I don't want you to go away. I want to stay with you. I'd sleep all right if you were here.'

Oh, God, said Kit under his breath, *I can't stand this*. He pulled her into his arms. The pillbox rolled away over the floor, making a little noise like a baby's rattle. She clung to him silently for a moment, then began to cry, blindly and inconsolably. He could feel a hot trickle of tears against his neck. 'Don't,' he said, and tried to say something more, but could not.

She rubbed her closed eyes on his shoulder, making a wet trail on the cloth of his coat. 'I can't bear to be alone again now you've been here.' She tried to whisper, but choked.

'S-sh. Careful.' He got out his handkerchief and dried her face; if she had cried with any sort of feminine art, with any reservations of prettiness or poise, he felt he could have borne it. He offered her what comfort he had, which was simple and physical; indeed, he could scarcely have spoken if he had had anything to say. But presently she stopped crying, absently, like a baby who has been given something sweet to keep it quiet. In a little while she was kissing him, her face still hot and sticky with tears, and, a few minutes later, was amusing herself by making a piece of his hair stand up on end.

'Isn't it too bad?' she murmured when she had arranged it to her liking. 'I can't put it back again. I haven't got a comb in here any more.' She never seemed, like other women, to carry the essentials of repair about with her. 'I'll just have to sort of smarm it with my hand. There, that hardly notices at all. You do look sweet. I feel so nice now you're here. It's a bad idea to cry; it makes a kind of bruise in your stomach.'

'I won't be gone long. We'll be able to meet somewhere, now you can leave the house. Look, I'll write you a letter tonight and you'll get it first thing in the morning.' He could not imagine when he was going to write it; straightening Fraser's records and his own would take him well on into the night. He had wanted to plan with her, discuss the future, and leave with something to look forward to beyond the blankness of the immediate present. He could not remember how far away the place was to which she was going back. He could not ask her now. Within the small circle of her art they were ageless equals; now, outside it, the eight years between them gaped like twenty. He felt only that he must tiptoe away without rousing her grief again, as if she had fallen asleep holding his hand.

Fortunately he had all the information he needed for the death certificate and had filled it in already. He put it into her hand with brief instructions which she acknowledged vaguely, smoothing down his hair again.

'Will you think about me tonight when you're in bed?'

'I always do that.'

'Do you, darling? What a shame. I'll be so nice to you next time.' She kissed him.

As they went into the hall, he heard the door opposite close softly. He knew that it was Pedlow, going into Miss Heath's room.

Once or twice, when he had been making love to Christie, he had paused at the thought of the old woman lying near them, and wondered a little that she could have forgotten. But when she took comfort, he had been too glad to think about it much. He drove out through the dark drive, remembering her hands about his head.

I I

It was five days before he met her again, and on the first of them
he had no time even to miss her. When he wrote to fix the time
and the place Fraser was still in bed, and he was doubtful even of
the bare half hour he hoped for. But on the third day Fraser got
up: he looked a little thinner and yellower, and moved with a
slight increase of his dignified stoop, but there was something
rocklike in the set of his back into his consulting-room chair
which discouraged comment or advice. *He'll kill himself one of
these days*, Kit thought as they were going through the work
together, and he reflected, not for the first time, how little Fraser's
most irritating mannerisms really mattered. He was solid, good-
wearing stuff all through, and, thinking about him, Kit felt his
loneliness and dread of coming loss suddenly lightened with a
flash of relief, because whatever trouble he ran himself into
henceforward, Fraser was out of it. The practice was no longer
involved. His illness, as it happened, had struck a lucky day for
Kit; Miss Heath's death slipped in with the general summary, and
there was no need to invent a reason for his having been there
on a night when he ought not to have been seeing patients at all.
Kit was not blind to the fact that his habitual honesty was an

unfailing passport for his lies, and it did nothing to increase his pleasure in telling them.

In the last two days the work slackened for no definite reason, as medical work will; so in the end it happened that they had a full two hours together.

They met in a lane they had agreed on, a little way out of the town. It was a fine day, flooded with the clear cool sunlight of autumn; already, at three o'clock, shadows were looking pointed and a solemn gold was flowing into the colors of things. Christie's face and hair were tinged with it too; her voice was a little muted, and for her she talked very little. It was enough for Kit that she melted, as if he had dreamed her, into the light and his own sense of shining tragedy. He drove out through quiet lanes where leaves swished and whispered. When he had seen her first, standing silent with the long light seeming to slant into her like light into a shell, he had made up his mind where he would take her.

It was a place of his own, an old camp hidden in a wood on a hill, which he had found for himself one day when he had felt particularly unhappy and had tried, as he did when he had time, to blow it off in the open air. The crown of the hill was covered in beeches, and between their trunks the old walls meandered, showing here and there the texture of archaic stonework dry-walled in diagonal courses. The place represented an island in his thoughts, and, not very consciously, he had liked to keep it so. Its remoteness and its quiet gave out something benign, which he would have liked to create in his own life. He had never met anyone else there, and never come there himself except alone, until today.

They left the car and walked up an old cart track toward it. Their conversation, when they talked at all, was chiefly made up of 'Do you remember?' By silent consent they avoided the future; it was a part of the struggle with circumstance, from which for the first time they felt a moment of freedom. The miracle was perishable, as they both understood.

They entered the camp through a gap in the wall, the ancient gate, perhaps, of the citadel. Within, the bowl-shaped circle of wood was filled to the brim with broken light. The sun on its downward course struck through open places between the half-stripped trees, and gave everything it touched a glow of metal without its hardness or its cold. The air was heavy with a good secrecy.

Kit stood and looked, thinking suddenly not of Christie but of the hours of solitude and peace he had experienced in this place alone, the few hours when his spirit had been free. He felt separated from them, and for a moment the happiness for which he had lived for days was tinged with a vague regret. He had a mind too simply practical for contemplation, but he had touched the fringes of it here, and felt now a sense of trespass which he did not define. He translated the feeling, dimly, into a fear lest Christie should say something to spoil it all. This struck him as over-emphasis, which he distrusted; he turned to look at Christie beside him.

She stood gazing across the hollow into the sun-entangled leaves, her lips parted in delight. Her body was at rest, but there was a lightness of joy in it which made her weight seem not quite planted on the ground. Her hair made a central point in which all the lights and colors around them met and were resolved. As the pupils of her eyes contracted to focus the horizon he could see the fine creases in the iris like pleats in brown-gold velvet. There was a faint gilded bloom on her cheek where it caught the light. Her hair, her eyes, the surface of her skin, seemed to be drinking light; he had a fancy that if he drew her into the shadow she would continue to glow. She turned and smiled at him in radiant, solemn thanks. Kit's cloudy doubts dissolved. He took her hand and led her down the slope of the hollow.

The slopes of moss round the tree roots were already dry, in this sheltered place, from the rain of a few days before. They sat down looking toward the west, in a place where the leaves filtered the sun a little from their eyes. Christie took his hands, and said under her breath, 'It's so lovely; even if I'd been alone I'd have felt you were here.'

He laid his head on her knees. All the mean expedients of their love seemed melted and washed away in a stream of blue and golden air, leaving only a clear sorrow that shone like a sword. He began to talk softly. He talked as he had dreamed sometimes of talking to Janet before he grew accustomed to the thought that when the moment came the words would fail. A river of thought – the secrets of a solitary boyhood – he had been the only child of parents already middle-aged when he was born – flowed out into the sun. The bitterness of the world that he had seen in his calling and endured in his life was lifted, and his thoughts were colored by a childlike rack of memory, distant and serene.

Christie listened. Her silence fell around Kit like a protecting cloak. When he ceased to speak she put her hands on either side of his forehead, and lifted his face to hers.

'I love you so much,' she said.

The words, which she had murmured over him a thousand times, seemed to answer everything and include it. He laid his cheek against hers; the sunlight dazzled through the mingled gold of the leaves and of her hair. He smoothed out one of her curls against the dark green moss at the roots of the tree. All the warmth left in the late sun seemed to have sunk into her; and in her arms, after he had closed his eyes, he could see against his eyelids the colors of the sunset and the leaves.

A cool blue shadow, spreading outward from the western rampart, widened from a crescent to a semilune. At last it touched them with its rim, and they saw that the gold on the tree trunks had deepened to copper, and every fallen leaf was throwing its shadow along the ground. Kit looked at his wrist watch. The invisible crystal that had enclosed them cracked. They kissed, stretched, laughed a little as they brushed leaves and fibers and beechnuts from each other's clothes, while past delight still hung, like a warm haze, between them and the chill of evening and of parting to come.

For the first time they began to plan their future meetings. They found they would be able to manage Sunday sometimes, and sometimes Kit would be able to get over on his free afternoon; this involved some complicated exchange and shifting round of Christie's free time, which she said was certain to be all right. One way and another, it did not average out at much more than once a fortnight. 'How shall we stand it?' they said, but they knew that they would have to move further away from the present before it would mean anything. 'It will be worth waiting longer for,' they said now; 'we shall be free at least, not listening all the time, and creeping about in the dark.' Their minds lulled by their warmed and comforted bodies, they almost believed that they were embarking on a new and fortunate stage of their lives. 'A fortnight soon comes round,' Kit said, 'and we shall have it to look forward to.'

'Of course we shall, and it will be all right for us because we shan't have to worry. We'll know neither of us can alter in between. It will make all the difference, being sure.'

'What right have I to be sure of you?' Kit pushed back the hair from her forehead. 'I can't give you anything; I can't look after you.' But it only seemed like an invented notion, and Christie laughed at it.

They stopped in the gap at the edge of the camp, looking back through the trees. Christie's eyes rested affectionately on the little hollow in the leaves where they had lain. A shadow of a branch fell across Kit's eyes; he slid for a moment into solitude. It came to him, passingly, that henceforward the place would be this to him, and no longer, except in memory, what it had been before; and it was as if a door had been closed on something that would continue without him. He searched the wood for its vanished imminence, scarcely understanding that in this moment his sorrow was for a present, rather than an approaching loss. Christie's fingers closed, gentle and warm, round his hand.

'Don't be unhappy, darling,' she whispered. 'I'm going to take such care of you. Everything will be all right. You'll never be allowed to be unhappy for a minute, even when I'm not there.'

He kissed her, turning from the trees toward the road.

I 2

The long low room was littered with dusty color like a fair. A scarlet military cloak covered one of its rush-seated chairs; over another a blue sari edged with silver, with a half-mended tear in it, hung in a classic curve. On a trestle table down the middle, dominating the boards with a swagger, stood a towering brass helmet with a horsehair plume. Gauntlets, greaves, mobcaps and cravats of dingy lace, a rapier, a pair of canary tights, a string hauberk, and a leopard skin, stravaged round it with a cowed look, like a crowd of supers. Sitting on one corner of the table, a dark wiry young man, wearing slacks and a grubby gray flannel shirt with the sleeves rolled up, was polishing a breastplate. The rag he was using was scarlet, and fringed with a remnant of gold lace.

The breastplate was decorated with a Gorgon mask in high relief. Among the coils of its entwined serpents the polish lodged in black oily pockets, eluding the pursuit of the rag. The young man swore irritably. Blue traces of makeup, lingering round his eyes, gave him a soulful, hungry look. He fished about on the chair seat which supported, besides his feet, two thumbed type-scripts and a swordbelt encrusted with glass jewels.

'Christie!' he shouted. 'Where's that damned brush?'

From the middle distance came the scrape of curtain rings and the sound of heavy fabrics disturbed. It brought with it stronger wafts of the room's characteristic smell, a rich compound of greasepaint, camphor, musty stuff, wood-rot and dust. The source of movement was hidden by a tall hanging-stand filled with clothes. Glimpses of velvet, fur, tinsel, and gauze, mellowed by a romantic grubbiness, burst out from inadequate dust sheets thrown over the top. The curtain rings rattled again.

'Chris-*tie!*'

'How the hell do I know? I haven't been in the room five minutes.' Christie's head was thrust out between an orange satin panier and a red velvet farthingale, catching the sun and making the colors of both look a little dejected. 'You're sitting on it, or something. What did you clean all that armor on the table with? And the helmet? Look under that.'

'Funny, aren't you?' snarled the young man, slewing round with a clank of metal. 'I haven't cleaned them yet.'

'What are you cleaning them *for*, anyway? There's nothing going out except *Quality Street* and the *Shrew*. If you'd tell me where the lute is, it would be some help.'

'Oh, my God!' One of the typescripts flew across the floor. 'Have I got to put on the whole of this emetic whimsy and paint the backcloth *and* turn up my guts acting in it, and send out the hampers as well? Ask Flossie where it is. She's probably gone off with it for the angels. Tell her she can't; she'll have to make one.'

Christie surged back through the clothes-stand and disappeared. There was a sound of creaking wicker, from which her voice emerged muffled with stooping. 'She won't do that. It wouldn't have a psychic emanation.'

The young man grinned. 'It's nice having you back,' he remarked. 'Don't take any notice of me; I'm not myself on a Thursday.'

'Poor sweet.' Christie came round the stand, with a pair of gold slippers hanging from one hand. 'Truly, Rollo, I haven't seen the brush.' She rummaged on a window sill. 'Here, have the spare clothes-brush, and I'll wash it sometime.'

Rollo took the offering, and turned it over. 'This *is* the brass-brush,' he observed without rancor.

'Oh, is it? Never mind, I've only used it for the quite dark things. One of these vile Bianca slippers has got a tear in it.' She got a needle and thread out of a tin box on the table, and swung herself onto the edge beside him, dangling her feet. 'Honestly, Rollo, what *do* you want the armor for?'

Rollo gouged savagely at a serpent's tail. 'To wear tomorrow,' he said bitterly, 'as Flossie's ruddy prince.'

'But, Rollo *dear*.' Christie tried to turn a giggle into a cough, jerked the needle in the wrong direction, and sucked her finger. 'But it's twice too big for you.'

'I know that too,' said Rollo. 'Thanks.'

'I thought it was supposed to be sort of medieval. The back-cloth is.'

'Only when I painted it I didn't know we were going to get a rush order for *Saint Joan*. You can't send that out without suits of plate for Joan and Dunois, anyhow. This is what's left.' He waved at the table.

'Why not a string hauberk? It only wants a lick of gold paint. I'll do it for you when I've finished the hampers.'

'Do you suppose I didn't think of that? But Flossie reminded me that I've got to take it off in the last act and dedicate it on the altar. Can you see me with my arms over my head, peeling? They can't expect a strip-tease on a silver collection. Blast them.'

'Couldn't you just dedicate your sword on the altar?'

'Tell that to Flossie. She says it's essential symbolism.'

There were footsteps in the passage. Christie took Bianca's slipper and dived with it behind the hanging-stand. Rollo made the noise associated with grooms.

A voice said, 'Oh, *there* you are, Mr Baines,' with silvery clear enunciation, ending with a short run up the scale. Florizelle Fuller never simply came into a room. She entered. The upward tilt of her chin, and gaze fixed on something a little above the eye-level of those present, suggested a pursuit of occult music. Florizelle was aware of this; an admirer had told her so during the period when Barrie was on the crest of the wave. She had swimming, deeply set brown eyes, spiritual concavities in her cheeks, and a vertical chest. Today she was wearing a smock of purple handwoven linen, held in at the waist with a belt of Hungarian peasant work. The neck was clasped with a large plaque of hammered pewter surrounding an art porcelain jewel. A thin tapering plait of hair was wound several times round her head. She was extremely proud of its length. Rollo's favorite story was to the effect that when applying for her passport she had filled in the space for Distinguishing Marks with *Hair Below Knees*, and that an official had returned the passport marked *Hairy Legs*.

'Don't let me disturb you two busy bees.' Her progress was arrested by a fallen typescript which had entangled itself in her sandaled feet. She retrieved it and patted it back into order with a reproachful tenderness, appropriate to an ill-used child. Her plays *were* her children, as she often said. This time she said it with her eyes. 'I just came to tell you, Mr Baines, about a little inspiration I've had for your entrance in the last act. Then I promise I'll leave you in peace.' She poised herself ethereally, as if for levitation. In the presence of urgent manual activity she always had an air of being about to dematerialize. Rollo, to whom these symptoms were familiar, blew on the breastplate.

'Don't you think it would be *rather* delightful if you made the entrance to the altar through the audience, with the Child-Angels round you?'

The packing noises behind the stand gave place to a crisp,

expectant silence. Entrance through the audience was fraught, at Brimpton Abbey, with a certain liveliness.

'Don't you think,' Rollo remarked to the Gorgon's head, 'the costumes need a bit of lighting?'

'The audience *like* it so much, don't they? It gives them the feeling of *participating*, you know. Then, you see, you could be led in with a chain of flowers. We have a chain of flowers, you remember, from *The Spirit of May*. And my idea was that you might have the smallest Child-Angel – little Gladys it would be – sitting on your shoulder.'

Rollo put down the breastplate and rose to his full height. He was five foot six, and sparely proportioned. A feverish sound of creaking wicker came from the corner. 'I don't *think* so. Not *with* the Greek armor. I shall look rather like a turtle in it, in any case. Even supposing I didn't fall over.'

Miss Fuller gave a fluting, reproachful laugh. 'You know, you really *are* very naughty. I *know* you and Miss Heath don't take my little playlets seriously, but I do think—'

'Oh, nothing of the kind, of course,' began Rollo rapidly. He looked over his shoulder, but this signal of distress was intercepted by the hanging-stand.

The delicate adjustment of influences at Brimpton Abbey lent itself to recurrent crises. A growth of the 1920s, it had burgeoned overnight in a soil richly fertilized with wishful ideals. Its mission had been the presentation of Art to the Folk, and in its heyday it had been a rallying ground for many eager and not untalented spirits; its foundress, the veteran Anna Sable, had still been vigorous, and the star performances had been attended by critics from the *Observer* and the *Sunday Times*. By unnoticeable degrees Anna Sable's arthritis had persuaded her from the stage to the drawing-room, where her genius was spent on persuading rich visitors that they had made contact with a center of creative art. Then came the slump, and for several months Brimpton Abbey had revolved, as far as it revolved at all, under the motive power of Anna Sable, a few voluntary enthusiasts, a procession of resident secretaries, and Florizelle Fuller.

At the nuptials of Anna Sable and the Abbey, Florizelle had been a sort of chief bridesmaid. She worked without salary, and was therefore, by now, cemented as firmly into the fabric as the supports of the stage.

Rollo was an accident. He had arrived as a local amateur, and had remained so, with the help of a powerful motorcycle, while he drifted in and out of a series of jobs, none of which turned out to be exactly adjusted to a vivid dramatic sense, an irreverent vein of humor, an almost total lack of business acumen, and a Heath-Robinson ingenuity for making do. During his periods of unemployment he had amused his leisure at the Abbey. Nobody noticed for some time, and Rollo himself last of all, that he had made himself indispensable. It was not until he arrived on his motorcycle one morning to say that he wouldn't be coming any more because his people were moving to Edinburgh next month that scales fell from the general eye. Rollo was taken onto a staff hitherto entirely vestal, and took up residence.

Christie was not an accident. She could type and do shorthand passably, but not well enough to command a better salary elsewhere; it was her first job, so that she was not in a position to make unkind comparison between the hours of work at the Abbey and those obtaining in non-resident posts; and, which was important, she looked and sounded pretty on the stage. Rollo and Christie could be cast for juvenile leads without initiating blood-feuds, and – except during the Summer and Easter Schools, the high peaks of the year – they invariably were. Florizelle clung to her specialty of black spirits and white, red spirits and gray; she also enacted noble mothers, goddesses, and queens. This time, however, Christie's absence during rehearsals had given her the chance to play the heroine, and it made her particularly sensitive, as Rollo was finding out.

He picked up the breastplate again and held it up, ostensibly to catch the light. It provided a sketchy screen from Florizelle's wounded eyes. Reflected in the side of it, he saw with relief Christie advancing to his support. They formed a useful mutual-assistance guild. Christie smoothed things over when Rollo's sense of the ridiculous ran away with him, which was once a week or so, and Rollo – who was permanently grateful to Christie for being an inch shorter than himself – was generally in time to save her from detection when she got something into an impossible muddle, which happened on an average every other day.

'Oh, Miss Fuller.' Christie smiled with Sunday-school sweetness through her hair, which, loosened by stooping over the hampers, was falling into her eyes. 'I was just coming along to ask you if you've seen the lute lately. I've only got the bashed-in one. I can't find the good one *any*where.'

Florizelle's eyes swam; her hands flew to her breast, as if protecting an invisible relic from violation. During the early *pourparlers* Rollo slipped away. He returned five minutes later to find Christie packing the lute. They exchanged acknowledgments which custom had reduced to a ritual.

13

Kit sounded his horn again. The petroleum van in front replied with a honk that seemed to come derisively from its belly, and continued to hug the crown of the road. Kit's own blast had been an expletive rather than a suggestion; the road surface was filmed with oily mud, on which it would have been madness to overtake if there had been room.

Kit looked, for the tenth time, at the clock on the dashboard. Half-past three. She would be out. She might not have got his letter. He had only posted it late last night. He had been determined to come, but had not dared to announce it. A dozen things might have stopped him; he had nearly had to see the Regional Medical Officer for Fraser; he had nearly been needed to give an anesthetic. He had been absent last week, and dared not make a routine of disappearing without explanation. The whole business of getting away had been something of a nightmare.

Two days after he had left Christie the week before, he had had a letter from her announcing that she had had an offer from a theatrical touring company. The manager had seen her at one of the Abbey's week-end performances, and had written next day. Kit, who was an informed though sporadic theater-goer and read the notices of plays he could not attend, had never heard of the company. The manager, however, seemed to have charmed Christie, whose account was full of a vague and airy optimism more alarming than misgivings. Amid much extraneous matter, some of the terms of the contract emerged. Kit, who knew nothing of theatrical methods but something of business, thought that spuriousness reeked from them. Christie added, in a postscript, that she had been thinking it over when he last came and had meant to tell him, but hadn't wanted to spoil the time. This took Kit longer to recover from than the proposition itself.

He sat down in his first free moment, and wrote her three pages of what seemed, at the time, closely reasoned argument. It happened, however, that he was called away before he could finish it, so that he had occasion some hours later to read it again. He stared at it for five minutes before he tore it in two and burned it. Had he really written these appeals, these confessions of dependence between every couple of lines? This was what he had promised himself should never happen to him again. This time it was all to be different.

Rapidly he convinced himself that he had not meant to write like this at all. It had been only concern for her that he had been trying to express. He wrote her another letter on these lines, reread it, was slightly sickened by it and tore it up in turn. Black curls of burned paper began to choke the fire.

In the end he wrote her a business letter. He dissected the contract dryly, and arranged the result with a few legal notes. He posted it with a feeling of relief. It was as if some impersonal agent had been pursuing him with a deed of great commitment, which he had managed to evade.

Christie's reply came promptly. The letters she wrote from the Abbey were mostly typed, but her typing was as characteristic as her written hand; certain letters were always banged down harder than the others, and she had a trick of absently allowing a long word to overflow the line, and carrying it on to the next from some extraordinary division in mid-syllable. This time haste and eagerness emphasized both habits. Whatever had made him write her such a queer letter? Was he upset with her about going away? But that was the whole idea; she was doing it really for him. When she had made a success in the provinces, she would get a part in the West End. Mr Cowen had assured her that this was practically a certainty. Then she would be quite free, and would have a marvelous flat of her own, where they would be able to meet. It would be so much nicer than being at the Abbey. (Here followed a page and a half about deficiencies in the Abbey wardrobe, and some trouble or other that Rollo was having with the scenery for the current play.) Mr Cowen had said that it didn't matter in the least her not having any training or experience apart from the Abbey. What audiences wanted was personality. And the company was *quite* sound financially; she herself was investing in it the hundred pounds she had had under her aunt's unaltered will. She was going to sign everything in two or three days, when Mr Cowen was taking her out to lunch. It was at this point that Kit had begun making arrangements to go next day.

Until quite recently, one of several obstacles to this would have been the necessity of excusing himself to Janet. His free afternoon had been earmarked, in the early days, for excursions to town or elsewhere, and long after she had started to make her own arrangements it would still have been unthinkable that he should not have kept the time until he had asked her if there was anything she would like to do. But in the last weeks she seemed to have found the Group activities so absorbing that she had to be reminded when Wednesday came round. She never questioned his movements and, if he made motions of interest in what she was doing herself, became vague and changed the subject. Still, he never approached the day without a certain anxiety. This

Tuesday he was relieved, when he got in from the afternoon round, to find that she had people to tea.

The guests were Peggy Leach, who was apparently staying in the neighborhood again, and a young married couple whose surname he discovered, with difficulty, to be Harrison; they were called Bill and Shirley by everyone else. When he came in they turned, simultaneously, and fixed him with identical gazes of bright, interested calculation, a little as if they were reckoning up the chances of selling him something, but not just yet. Kit, after polite exchanges, prepared hopefully to withdraw into the background of the conversation and his own thoughts; they had all seemed more than adequate to one another's entertainment when he came in. But this, it seemed, would not do at all. They centered on him, as if he were a new boy entering a study at school. With an engaging now-come-on-you-tell-me air, they flung him tidbits of information about themselves, and waited open-mouthed (like Mappin Terrace bears, he thought) for reciprocal buns. Kit, whose whole personality was feeling tender and sore, found himself quite unable to detach even superficial parts for inspection. His replies grew guarded to the verge of incivility. Presently he saw them – together, of course – exchange a covert glance with Janet, as who should say, *Ah, yes, we see.*

After this the assault stopped as suddenly as it had begun. Instead the two of them formed, with Peggy Leach, a compact little conversational team, and began to toss round stories about the Group, as if they were engaged in a kind of exhibition match. They described how a friend called Bridget had been guided to break off her engagement owing to the resistance her fiancé had put up (to the Group, Kit gathered, after a few ambiguous minutes) and become engaged to Bob, who had Changed her. Another friend, called Timmie, had been guided to give up the idea of trying for Oxford and to stay at home, working for the Group. At this Janet leaned forward a little, and a faint tinge of color appeared in her cheeks. Probably, thought Kit dimly, all this was rather much even for her. He floated a little way off into himself again. Shirley helped him to visualize Christie, being her exact converse in almost every physical trait.

At precisely a quarter to six, Bill and Shirley sprang to their feet with such dynamic decision that Peggy Leach was drawn up after them, like a lump of iron by a magnet. Probably they had been guided, Kit thought.

'Well,' said Bill, 'back to the daily round, the common task! We'll keep a lookout for you folks tomorrow. Five-thirty sharp. I fancy you'll find old Ted pretty fine value.'

'Both of you will,' said Shirley.

A pause, which no one filled, caused Kit to look up. Everyone was gazing at him expectantly. He perceived that it was himself, and not Peggy, whom the plural included.

'I'm so sorry,' he said. 'I didn't realize you meant me. I'm afraid I can't possibly manage tomorrow.' Three pairs of eyes regarded him with thoughtful interest; he could see them each framing the word 'resistance', in block capitals. Rather desperately he added, 'I should have been delighted, of course, but unfortunately I'm not free.'

Janet said, 'But it *is* Wednesday tomorrow, isn't it? I told Bill and Shirley we'd both come.'

Kit felt the pent-up suspense of the last days crackling dangerously within him. 'Well, I'm sorry,' he said, 'but if you'd asked me first I'd have told you. I shall be away the whole afternoon.'

'I see,' said Janet.

Silence fell. Kit sat staring in front of him. Accumulated emotions, and the effort of suppressing them, had made him go white. His reason for a moment in abeyance, he waited for Bill and Shirley to explain that they had known about everything for some time, and would be glad to share with him and Janet about it. They merely looked at him in a kind of regretful satisfaction.

Bill turned to Shirley. Both their faces lit up with a bracing smile.

'My dear chap, that's perfectly all right with us. Absolutely. As a matter of fact, Janet here pretty well explained to us that you'd feel this way about it. It takes time, of course. It did with me. I've been through it all, haven't I, Shirley?'

'Rather,' said Shirley. 'Worse, if anything.'

'Just think it over when you're alone. Turn up when you feel you want to. Don't bother to let us know. We'll all understand.'

Kit became aware that the thinness of a membrane divided him from some ineffaceable kind of scene. Murmuring something, he got up and left the room.

The consulting-room settled him in a matter of minutes. He found that the clock stood at five to six. Sounds of departure had just come from the hall. He went upstairs again, to apologize to Janet. It was not the best time to pursue a situation which might turn into anything, but he felt incapable of beginning two hours' work with the thing hanging over his head. He had never been publicly rude to her before in the whole course of their married life.

Janet had gone to her desk, and was preparing to write a letter.

'I'm sorry about this Wednesday business. I didn't really mean to be short about it. I was thinking of something else.'

Janet looked up. It was incredible, but evident, that for a moment she had forgotten what he was talking about. His feelings became deflated to mere embarrassment.

'It doesn't matter.' She tapped her mouth with a corner of note paper. 'Do you mean you'd like to come tomorrow after all?'

'No; I'm sorry. I couldn't have done that in any case.'

'Then there's no need to discuss it any more, is there?' She put the paper down on the table and picked up a pen. He realized that his anxiety had been wasted; she had been relieved by his refusal. It had discharged her of some self-imposed duty and now she wanted to put it behind her. He began to say something perfunctory, saw no point in it, and went downstairs again.

Without thinking about it much, he knew that a section of life was finished; their relationship, such as it was, had tapered away to its last thread, and today – probably for no stronger reason than it had to happen sometime – the thread had snapped. From now onward they would be associated acquaintances, knowing each other only in the past, as separate in the present as workers at neighboring desks in office or bank. He had seen it in other homes, but had not foreseen, in his own, a time when some kind of need would not be alive between them, at first his need of her, then hers of illusion. He had supplied it poorly, he supposed; it was better she should have turned to something that had, at the worst, potentials of truth. As far as he was concerned, it lifted somehow the guilt of his deceits; he felt in a confused way that they now became static and formal, like the lies of a servant answering a door. By the time surgery began he was thinking about Christie again. He had been thinking about her for most of the intervening time.

The petrol van swung ponderously round and vanished down a side-turning. Kit drew in a sharp breath of relief and put on such speed as the road surface allowed. The outskirts of Paxton came in sight; it was a largish town on whose farther edge Brimpton Abbey hung like an ornamental tassel, the center of an older village which ribbon development had turned into a well-to-do suburb. Already the glitter of tinsel in shop windows reminded him that Christmas was not many weeks ahead.

When he drove into Brimpton a few lights were anticipating the dusk. He looked up at the gable where Christie had showed him, the first time he came, the window of her room. Its darkness dejected him like an omen; unreasonably, since he knew she rarely had time to be there.

He rang, listening to the noises of the place, already familiar: feet and voices echoing on wooden stairs, a piano softly rendering the kind of accompaniment against which verse is spoken, the overtones of a declaiming voice, distance swallowing the rest. He wished it were possible to have some idea who was likely to answer the door; at the Abbey, this was the privilege of anyone who might happen to be passing the hall. The domestic staff was loosely defined in function, and subject to rapid change. Perhaps it would be Christie.

It was Rollo, in shirtsleeves, with a cigarette in the corner of his long mouth, and a heap of brocades over one arm.

'Oh, hullo,' he said. 'Are you looking for Christie?'

They surveyed one another with mutual lack of enthusiasm. On Rollo's side this was due to finding Kit, who was standing a step lower down, still on a level with himself. This was the third time they had run into each other in a month; he would be living at the Abbey at this rate. Now Christie would be fussing to get away before they had got the scene right. An idea broke in on Rollo's annoyance. Could the chap, since he seemed to haunt the place anyway, be induced to take St Michael in the prologue of the Christmas play? Coloring right; every bit of six foot, going on for seven in a helmet – what an eyeful to raise the curtain on! Kit stiffened under the sweeping and, to him, inscrutable stare with which Rollo – irritation melting in a proprietary glow – was dressing him and making him up.

'Is she busy?' he asked without warmth.

'Well, we're more or less rehearsing at the moment.' Perhaps not the helmet, after all; a metal sunburst behind the head, fixed with a circlet. Blue-green eyeshadow, a lot of it. Rollo removed the cigarette from his mouth and smiled, as he could when he gave his mind to it, with considerable charm. 'We'll only be about half an hour, though. Come along in and watch, won't you? We'd love someone to sit at the back and shout if we can't be heard.' Rollo's least whisper was audible in the last row of the sixpennies, but he contrived to charge the suggestion with diffident appeal.

Kit declined, with thanks. He did not want to sit and watch Christie being embraced and probably kissed by Rollo for half an hour. His reaction to Rollo was permanently colored by a knowledge that he and Christie had once played in *Romeo and Juliet* together. Besides, nearly a week of mounting anxiety made the thought of passivity suddenly intolerable. He said he had several things to see to in the town, and would be back.

'Well, come up and take a look at the theater. You needn't stay for the whole thing.'

'I saw it the first time I came, thanks.' He found he did not trust himself to greet Christie with Rollo, who looked offensively observant, doing the honors.

'Oh, Christie took you over. I expect she told you it's one of the three best private theaters in England. You want to see the cyclorama with the lighting, of course. But I forgot, you're coming to the Easter School, aren't you?'

'Yes,' said Kit, who, his attention wandering, had thought that *The Easter School* was the name of a play. 'I'll certainly run over for it if I can get away.'

'Good work,' said Rollo to his retreating back. 'I'll put you down.'

Kit got into the car again and drove about aimlessly. When he rang the Abbey bell again, praying that she might answer it herself this time, he got instead Florizelle Fuller. Here he made an almost embarrassing success. She wafted him into the drawing-room, sat him down under a shaded table-lamp, heaped copies of *Drama* before him, and had an earnest conversation with him about Mime, which she pronounced Meem. When she had gone he sat staring, for what seemed several hours, at a photograph of a setting for *Macbeth*, made of round and hexagonal broken columns with flights of steps running in and out of them.

The drawing-room door slammed.

'Oh, darling, isn't this *lovely*!' Christie ran the length of the room and flung herself into his arms with such force that she knocked him back into the chair from which he was still rising. Her hair tangled itself into his eyes, and the sleeve of her cotton smock, smelling of old greasepaint and none too clean, constricted his breathing. He assembled her into a manageable shape on his knee. All the anxieties, fears, and jealousies of separation concentrated themselves into the violence with which he kissed her. She clung to him with strong little hands, eager and warm. A telephone bell, distantly ringing, recalled them at last to external things.

'I *did* like that,' said Christie, loosening her arm.

As if they had been seeing each other for days, they began to talk. Kit remembered dimly that he had driven over in a different mood from this, but it seemed distant and artificial. He was back in the charmed circle again; nothing could go wrong, nothing outside was entirely real.

There were footsteps in the hall outside. Christie leaped from his knee and sat in a distant chair, affecting great social poise. A lock of hair trailed down into one eye. The footsteps passed.

'Oh, Kit, I do love you. I get so bored being with everyone else but you. Come on out of here. I want to devour you undisturbed. Come up to my room.'

'Of course I can't. They'd throw you out if they knew.'

'Who cares? I could get another job by crooking my finger.'

Kit realized that his victory was won without battle joined. It did not particularly surprise him. The circle was complete.

'I know what,' Christie said. 'I'll take you round the theater again. If we meet anyone I'll say you're thinking of coming to the Easter School. But they're all having tea.'

They went through mazelike passages, broken by purposeless stairs. The smell of greasepaint, old costumes, and dry rot seemed like part of the walls. Already it had taken on for Kit the magic of incantation. It would have made Christie present to him if he had smelled it at the Pole. Her dirty flowered smock, unbelted and short to the knee, with deep pockets bulging with string and safety pins and butt-ends of eye-pencil and carmine, had folded him in it along with her arms. He found it clinging to his coat when he got home.

The theater, really so small as to be almost miniature, seemed expanded by emptiness to the size and solemnity of a church. They tiptoed through it, talking in undertones, and climbed the steps into the wings. More steps led down to the junk rooms under the stage, where oddments of furniture and properties were stored. Christie guided him with the stealth of a smuggler, and switched on a yellow light, by which they picked their way. Fragments of scenery divided the space into secret alleys and caves. The heating pipes went through, wrapped in sacking, and the air was close and full of dry smells. The ceiling was just half an inch from the top of Kit's head.

'This way.' Christie navigated him round the corner of a small crenelated tower. Behind it the light was filtered to dimness. He could see on one side a terrace wall festooned with paper roses, on the other a throne draped with threadbare brocade. In the space between he saw, after he had nearly fallen over it, a canvas bank covered with remnants of fiber moss. An ass's head leered on the floor behind it. Some old cotton cushions and a striped rug, arranged against it, were hollowed from being lain on, like a hare's form. A packet of cigarettes, a thin book which looked like poetry, a pocket torch poked out from folds of the rug. Kit remembered the summerhouse at Laurel Dene.

Christie sat down on the bank, which made a sound of creaking shavings, and pulled at his hand. 'I come down here,' she confided, offering him a crinkled cigarette, 'when I get a bit sick of them all, to think about you.'

'Have you been lately?' A recollection of the last few days tinged Kit's voice a little.

'Oh, my pet, don't be cross with me.' She curled down beside him, arranging a dubious cushion under his head. 'Isn't it funny, now you're here I can't think how I could have been such an ass.'

'You know,' said Kit with the mildness of security, 'that contract was obviously phony.'

'Oh, I shouldn't think so. Mr Cowen was awfully sweet about it. I mean, how did I think I could go away from you for all that time? Why, I might not have seen you for months. Of course it was a chance and all that, but I must have been mad to think I could. As soon as I saw you in that chair looking so lovely under the lamp, I knew I wouldn't go. Oh, darling, I *am* so glad you came. Suppose you'd come after I'd signed up everything and it had been too late. I should have died. Honestly I should.'

Her eyes shone in the half-darkness. Kit pulled her into his arms. His sense of power frightened him with a feeling of having offended fate. He tried to placate the gods with a reasoned exposé of the contract and Mr Cowen. Christie absorbed it all. Presently she found the defeat of Mr Cowen's designs outrageously funny. She mimicked his mannerisms, and speculated vividly on his probable connection with dens of vice in the Argentine, and the methods by which his victims were transshipped. Kit found himself actually defending Mr Cowen, but she waved it away.

'I knew he was a crook as soon as I started talking to you. You show people up. Like a lodestone – isn't it a lodestone?'

'Touchstone, do you mean?'

'A touchstone, of course.' She pushed her head under his chin. 'Kit, darling, I've been so silly about people. I've been fooled lots of times. Stop me if I do it again. Don't send me letters like a *Times* leader; they frighten me. When I got it I nearly wrote off to that shiny little man straightaway, I was so upset.'

'I didn't want to influence you,' said Kit carefully, 'in the wrong way.'

'Is this the wrong way?'

'Probably.'

'Well, it's the way that works with me.' A clock struck the quarter. Christie smiled, and patted the two cushions together. 'They won't be out of tea for another half hour.'

14

It had occurred to Kit sometimes that his life was developing a rhythm which, if he had charted it, would have made a neat and regular graph, rather like the graph of a recurrent fever. He had amused himself one day by tracing it on his blotting pad. It would start with 98.4 on the second day or so after he had seen Christie; then there would be a sharp little rise, say to 99, on the morning when he expected a letter. If, as sometimes happened, the letter did not come, it might go up to 100 or so, or, on the other hand, drop to sub-normal. A letter – a satisfactory letter, that is – would keep the line horizontal until the two or three days before his next visit to the Abbey, during which it would climb steeply to 103 or 104, according to the difficulty and danger he encountered in getting away. But during the time he was with Christie, the graph ceased to operate. He lived on a different scale then, to a different time; when he was with her, he seemed to have been with her always. Even the moment of parting did not become real to him till she was gone; it took a dozen gradual steps back into separate life – the road, the garage, the stairs, his own room – knocking at him in succession, to return him to loneliness.

Since the business of Mr Cowen, however, the graph had

tended once or twice to lose shape. The hours he slept with Christie still had their charmed completeness, but the intervals between were subject to sudden disturbances set in motion by nothing in particular; a couple of days' delay in her letter made him absurdly anxious, and, when it came, he would torment himself over some doubtful phrase which had its origin in nothing graver than Christie's slapdash methods of composition. He took to worrying four days beforehand, instead of two, over the chances of getting away to see her. When he was with her, the memory of all this faded, so that he did not perceive the undercurrent of strain threading even through his happiness, and, when it broke the surface, could not imagine what had happened to him.

One day he was driving Christie out to tea in a small hotel they had found – a friendly place where, in the off season, they generally had the little tea lounge, and a log fire, all to themselves. It was on the other side of Paxton, so that they had to pass through the town. In the middle of a shopping street Christie gripped him by the elbow and said, 'Look. Look there.'

Kit corrected the swerve that had threatened, and heard an indignant sound of brakes from a car behind.

'For heaven's sake,' he said, 'don't ever grab anyone's arm when they're driving. I nearly ran over a woman then.'

'But didn't you see who it was? No, don't look now.'

Kit gave an irritated and perfunctory glance at the pavement. The middle-aged woman he had avoided had turned on the curb to look at the car. It was Pedlow, dressed in black from head to foot: flat black hat, black sealskin coat, black stockings, flat black shoes. Even so briefly, he had time to notice that she had contrived to merge into prosperity without making a single essential change in her appearance. Under the elderly, conservative lines of the fur coat her body still had the same look of being made of leather bands strapped tightly over an iron frame. He could almost believe, from where he was, that he heard her squeak. Her head was turned away, but something about its angle suggested that she had just looked at him, or was just about to look. Then the car moved past, and she was gone.

Christie was sitting pressed back in her seat; she looked quite white. 'What's Pedlow doing here?'

'Shopping,' said Kit shortly, 'by the look of it.'

'She's come here to watch us,' Christie said.

'Of course she hasn't. You can't even be certain she saw us. She's probably visiting an invalid sister. Pedlow would be sure to have an invalid sister or two.' Privately he thought she was as likely as not to be living in Paxton; there had been, somehow, a resident air about her. But he knew it would be tactless to suggest it.

'It was horrible seeing her like that. I don't like it.'

'Don't be a baby,' said Kit a little irritably, because he had not liked it himself. 'Pedlow's settled. We know what she wanted, and she's got it. She'll have just about as much interest in you now as people have in a rainstorm after it's blown over. Darling, we've only got a few hours. Don't let's waste them getting into a fuss over Pedlow.'

'I know. I'm sorry. It *was* a bit soft of me.'

They talked about other things, but a vague discomfort worked like yeast below the surfaces of both their minds. When they got to the hotel, their special table was taken by a couple of middle-aged American women; they raked the room, every minute or two, with eager birdlike glances, anxious that no oddment of Englishness should escape them. Kit and Christie talked in under-tones, freezing up altogether when the conversation at the other table stopped. Both of them wanted to go to some quiet place and make love, but the Abbey was particularly impossible because a party of visiting schoolgirls was being shown over it, and the country was sodden after a spell of rain. Both of them disliked the thought of what Christie always described as 'messing about in the car'; knew it would end with that; and felt a kind of self-distaste which infected their mood. Christie tried to entertain Kit by describing the progress of the current play; this she did quite amusingly, but with too much recourse to Rollo's bons mots at the expense of the cast. Kit received the first two with polite amusement, the third and fourth with strained toleration, and, at the fifth, said, 'Well, I wonder he's not on the London stage if he's so damned superior to everyone here.'

'Rollo? He isn't superior; he just enjoys the comic side. He'd go mad in a job like his if he didn't.'

Kit recalled, with annoyance, Rollo's cool and roving stare.

'He liked you, too,' Christie said. 'He wanted to get you in for the play. He was awfully disappointed when I said you wouldn't be able to. It was St Michael he wanted you for; you'd have looked perfect, he said.'

'Oh. Well, I'm sorry to have done him out of a laugh.'

The American ladies paid their bill and went, leaving behind them privacy and peace. But neither of the beneficiaries were made happy by it. Christie's soft sparkle had gone; her face had a compact look which made her seem suddenly older.

'Don't be silly,' she said. 'You can't just invent things about people you've hardly seen. Rollo isn't a bit like that; I've known him for years.'

'I'm sorry. I didn't realize you were so intimate that you couldn't discuss him.'

'Of course I could discuss him. *You* don't want to discuss him. You've got some fixed idea of your own and you don't want to listen to anything else. You're talking just like Maurice did.'

'Thanks,' said Kit, hurt as one can only be hurt by a blow on a surface already raw. 'It seems quite a pity you had all the trouble of changing over. However, there's always Rollo.'

'Oh, Kit, stop being so *maddening* or I'll throw a plate at you.'

162

They confronted one another, with set faces, across the table. Behind the hard surface of Kit's anger a tiny voice made itself heard, reminding him of the moment of release from Janet, the happy rediscovery of solitude. Sickened, even a little frightened, by the violence within him and its wasteful stupidity, for the first time he regretted the freedom which had slipped so imperceptibly away. Something of it must have showed in his face, for the surface flurry of Christie's temper dispersed in sudden fear. She leaned across the table and caught his hand. 'Darling, don't. I love you, you know I do.'

'I'm sorry.' The anxiety in her voice, the return of dependence, slid him back into security. They exchanged uncertain smiles, then laughed. Somewhere, distantly, the still small voice that had spoken to him out of the whirlwind still sounded; but he let it fade.

'Fancy being jealous of old Rollo,' Christie said.

'I'm jealous of anyone who sees you every day.'

'Honestly I believe you thought Rollo made love to me.'

'He's a bigger fool than he looks if he doesn't try.'

'Rollo—!' She laughed delightedly. 'My dear, if you tucked Rollo in bed with me and locked the door, he'd just go on till midnight telling me how he'd like to produce *Hamlet*, and fall asleep talking. Honestly. It always amazes me that he can do love scenes as well as he does on the stage; I've never seen him look at a woman off it. Fancy picking on old Rollo.' She stroked the back of his hand with the tips of her fingers. 'No, if I hadn't you, I expect I'd cast an eye at the man we've got now playing Satan. He's new this year. Rather lovely, black-and-white and haggard with a voice like a passing-bell. When he comes on and says, 'How art thou fallen from heaven, O Lucifer, son of the morning,' it's like water running down your spine. He's unhappy, I think.'

'Don't tease me. We've only got three more hours.'

'Oh, darling, I wasn't. I was only talking off the top; I can't help talking to you as if I were talking to myself. I've hardly spoken to him. Kit, darling, you weren't really unhappy about Rollo, were you? I can't bear to think of you being unhappy about me when you're alone. I want to make you only happy. Don't you see, that's what I'm *for*, for you?'

She took his hand in both hers; her face glowed as if a deep light shone behind it. There was a hard tightness round Kit's heart. 'If you—' he began.

The waiter came in and began to clear the things from the other table. They each pulled their hands back and sat with them fixed stiffly on their knees. Presently Kit beckoned him over and paid the bill.

'Where shall we go, darling?' asked Christie when he had gone.

'Anywhere by ourselves. In the car somewhere?'

'Yes,' said Christie. 'Please.'

Kit was happy for the next three or four days. It was an obstinate, enclosed kind of happiness, a little like the pleasure of hugging a fire in winter, when a disregarded voice tells one that a better kind of warmth is to be had by walking in the frost outside. But Kit hugged his fire. He wrote to Christie, and got back, two days later, a letter overflowing with expressions of love. There was hardly room in it for anything else, even for her usual report on the progress of the play. He read it over many times, and kept it to read again; but when he returned to it, it was always with a fear at the bottom of his heart of finding something different between the lines. He never did, and put it away comforted. But some undertone in it – not insincerity, but rather a kind of over-anxiety and solicitude – would send him back to it in the same disquiet.

By the next time he went over it was mid-December, the last chance he was likely to have until after Christmas. The day beforehand he walked about the lighted shop windows, looking for something to give to Christie. There were several things he fancied – a little moleskin jacket, a gold watch the size of a sixpenny bit – which somehow he was shy of. They had a kind of hackneyed suggestion, were in fact what Christie would call mistresslike. She was liable to sudden and illogical fits of embarrassment about such things. In the end he found, almost by accident, something exactly right: a box for theatrical make-up, large and flat and businesslike, enameled pale green and full of flaps and drawers and unfolding mirrors and trays, unspillable compartments for powder of every shade, round pots for grease, thin slots for eye-pencil and thick slots for greasepaint. He had them all filled with the appropriate things, and, in secret that night in his room, unwrapped it and opened up all its lids and hinges and flaps and drawers; picking up the bright clean sticks of greasepaint with their gilt labels and cellophane covers, peering in gingerly at the powders (he was astonished to find that one was green), and imagining Christie's face looking back at him from the mirror in the lid. The only unfilled part was a large compartment in the bottom, for trinkets and oddments. He grinned to himself as he imagined the kind of thing with which Christie would fill it.

He enjoyed himself so much with this toy that, by the time he started for the Abbey, all his vague uneasiness had blown away. It sat on the seat of the car beside him, and had already a companionable air, like something she had worn. He sang to himself along the empty stretches of the road.

Christie met him at the Abbey gate, dressed for the cold; she had on a bright green hood of soft leather lined with fleece, and gloves to match. Her hair, escaping round the hood, shone like a smoky sunset, and her cheeks were pink with the frost. She got into the car (Kit had hidden his parcel under the dashboard), and looked up to say, with a little sigh, 'Oh, Kit, how *nice* you always are to see again.'

She looked, to Kit, so lovely that he felt incapable of talking about it. 'Where would you like to go?' he asked. 'Shall we drive out somewhere?'

'Let's go on the hills. I've been quite *sore* with wanting to be out all day.'

They drove west, away from the town, between beeches whose fallen leaves made a red border to the road, and up beyond them to the bare hills.

Christie was very gay. She talked incessantly, telling Kit anecdotes about the Abbey – which seemed to grow a fresh crop, like exotic fungi, every week – and getting Kit to tell her stories in exchange. She had an inexhaustible memory for characters, and he brought her all the tales about odd contacts in his practice to which Janet had listened, in the days when he still tried to amuse her, with strained politeness. Even when the joke depended on a technical point, she was quick to take it up from his simplified explanation. She had a kind of unsophisticated shrewdness like that of an intelligent child who has been much with his elders; nothing he said to her fell with the dead drop which marks the gulf between personalities.

On a bare stretch of hill they got out and walked, enjoying the last of the sun which sparkled through the thin air like bubbles in wine. Just before it was time to turn back, they stood in a clump of firs and looked at the light slanting along the hills. Kit watched the skyline, content with the world; at rest in the present and without demands on the future. After a minute or two he turned to look at Christie, expecting to see his thoughts reflected in her face as, all afternoon, his other thoughts had been. She was looking not at the golden grass but at him; her face was strained with compassion and, it seemed, with fear. His exaltation left him, he became suddenly aware that the sun was setting coldly and that the blue of twilight was creeping up from the valleys.

'What's the matter?' he asked.

She squeezed his arm quickly. 'Nothing, darling. I'm getting hungry, aren't you? Let's go somewhere and have tea.'

There was a big farmhouse standing back, in a smooth garden, from the road; a famous place in summer, but hibernating sleepily now in the shelter of a ridge of pines.

'Let's go there,' Kit said. 'It looks peaceful.'

'It looks as if it was closed for the winter, to me.'

They were made welcome, however, with cordial surprise, put into a plushy parlor with a Georgian brass curb and a log fire, and served with toasted scones, bread-and-butter both currant and plain, two kinds of jam, and a towering homemade cake. They both ate a good deal, but Christie found time to chatter with even more animation than before. Kit said very little; he looked at Christie, drank tea from a thick white cup with a gold clover leaf in the bottom, and laughed when required. The farmer's wife, who had things to do in the back kitchen, left them to themselves.

At the end of the meal Kit said, 'Wait here for me. I've got something outside in the car.' He brought back the parcel with the make-up box, and put it on her knee.

'What's this?' she asked, fingering the string as if she were frightened of it. 'Is it for me?'

'You ought to have it at Christmas. But I shan't be here.'

'Kit, what have you been doing?' She pressed the other hand, unconsciously, against her heart.

'Open it,' said Kit happily. 'It won't bite you.'

'No, but, darling, I—' She turned and smiled at him quickly, cleared a space on the table, undid the string and paper, caught her breath, and opened the green enamel lid of the box. Kit, standing behind her, saw her face framed, just as he had imagined it, in the mirror inside the lid.

'Oh, *Kit*.' She opened the folding trays, lifted out the sticks of make-up and put them reverently back again, dipped her finger in the powder and made a little smooth dent. 'It's lovely – I—' Suddenly she turned from the treasures in front of her as if she had forgotten them, and looked up at his face. His hands were resting on the back of the chair; she pressed her cheek against his arm. 'Oh, God,' she said, 'why do you have to be so sweet?' Her voice broke on a quick violent sob; he could see its passage through her lifted throat. She flung herself forward, her elbows on the table, her head in her hands. Her hair fell down over the bright sticks of greasepaint and the green enamel edges of the box.

'What is it?' Kit smoothed the loose hair back against her cheeks, and tilted up her chin. 'Don't be silly,' he said softly.

'I'm not being silly.' She shook his hands off and turned away. 'You don't know what I'm like or you wouldn't be good to me like this.'

'Of course I know what you're like.'

She went on, her voice muffled and indistinct through her hands: 'I had a feeling you were going to do something like this. I kept thinking if it was something bitchy you'd bought me, jewelry or something, I wouldn't feel so awful. But it's even more like you than I was afraid it'd be. I wish I'd jumped into that quarry we passed just now.' Even in her grief, youth and vitality ran in her voice like water.

He knew she had never imagined death for herself in all her life, and smiled. 'What *is* all this?' He pulled gently at one of her ears, through her hair.

'You're so good. You're always the same. Don't you see, I'm not. I'm different whoever I'm with. And I don't want to be. I only want to be the sort of person I am with you. Oh, Kit, why do you have to be away from me?'

'God knows why. Something I did wrong in a former life, I dare say. I never am away from you, really.'

'But I've been away from you.'

'How do you mean?' said Kit. He drew away from the chair and stepped back, so that the brass fender almost tripped him. He

168

steadied himself with an arm on the edge of the mantelpiece. At the sound of his heel against the brass Christie started round in her chair, and looked at him with wet, frightened eyes.

'Kit, *don't*. I can't bear it.' She jumped up and caught his other arm between her hands. 'Nothing's happened really. It all seems so senseless now you're here.'

'What exactly has happened?' He felt the plush fringe of the mantelpiece give dangerously in his fingers, and loosened their grip.

'Nothing that you could call anything. It's only that this Lucifer man's been sort of hanging round me a bit. Lionel Fell his name is. He's all right, not bad. Really it was because I felt so sorry for him. You see, he's always wanted to go on the stage, and he's good too, but his people are dead and he's got a sister in a sanatorium with t.b. and has to work at insurance, or something, to pay for her. His father died of it and of course secretly he thinks he will too in the end, though he doesn't actually say so. He came an hour early for rehearsal one day through muddling the times, and told me all this while he was waiting about. I couldn't not be nice to him. I didn't mean him to take it seriously. And when I found he had, it seemed a bit brutal to choke him off all at once. But truly nothing's happened except we've gone for walks round the grounds after rehearsal and he's kissed me once or twice. Darling, say you don't mind.'

'Why should I mind?' asked Kit in a dead level voice. There was a little round ornament made of Goss china on the mantelpiece, just on a level with his hand. He picked it up and turned it over, looking at the red-and-yellow arms of some seaside place or other, stamped on the foolish fat curve of its belly. He did not look at Christie. He was contending with a part of his brain which wanted to make him say, *Good Lord did you fall for a tale like that?* If he said it he would say other things in support of it, and before long would believe them to be true. This mattered, somehow, even more than the distrust it would inevitably sow between Christie and himself. He did not reason it all out as consciously as this; it was simply that two images fought for possession of his inner eye, one hot and poisoned, the other clear.

He put the little china pot back on the mantelpiece, turning it round carefully so that the crest came outside.

'Poor chap,' he said. 'I should go gently with him if I were you. People with that tendency are usually emotional, you know.'

'Yes, he is.' She stared up at him, hanging on his arm. 'Kit, aren't you shocked with me? Playing around with other people when I love you all the time?'

'No,' he said. 'Not particularly.' He had been neither shocked nor surprised, not even surprised by his own lack of astonishment. He had felt, in an expected place, an expected pain. But this he did not admit to himself.

'I feel such a beast. I didn't think I could look at anyone else after knowing you. He was so unhappy, that's how it all started.'

'Well, of course,' said Kit lightly. He laughed, and removed a teardrop from her face with the tip of his finger. 'Damn it, you don't have to come to me in sackcloth and ashes every time you kiss someone good night. So long as I don't actually see it happening.' Imagination at once presented the picture to him; he laughed again, quickly. 'I thought, from the way you carried on, you were going to tell me you'd been to bed with him every night for a week.'

She pressed her cheek against his shoulder. 'Darling, I won't. Oh, I'm so glad you came today. I feel I know what I want and what I am, when you're here.' She felt his body harden under her arm. He said nothing. She went on, eagerly: 'Truly, Kit, I won't, no matter what he says.'

Kit was staring intently at a large engraving on the opposite wall, of Wellington and Blücher shaking hands. He could have drawn it afterward from memory, though he did not know he saw it at the time. He said, speaking to a bandaged soldier in the foreground of the picture, 'Had you made the appointment?'

'No, not really. Not in so many words. He isn't the sort of person who'd ask you like that. I only said I'd come to tea and look at his acting books and things. Probably nothing would have happened when it came to the point.'

'No,' said Kit gently, to the soldier, 'of course not.'

'No, I feel sure it wouldn't really. But all the same, I won't even go to tea now. Probably it would only unsettle him more. You'd like him, Kit, I feel sure, if you met him. I've made him sound a bit of a misery, but he never talks about it in the ordinary way. He'd do well on the stage if he had a chance; he moves beautifully.'

'Perhaps I'll see him act sometime.'

'Yes, if I can I'll—' She stopped and looked up at him. 'My precious, what is it? You look as if something were walking over your grave. You aren't upset with me after all?'

A straying part of Kit's subconscious was examining the rag with which the soldier's wound was bound, and substituting a surgical bandage of correct pattern. He said, 'You're not by way of falling in love with this man, are you?'

'In *love* with him? Darling, don't be fantastic; I've got you. Here, let's sit down.' She pushed him toward the big plush armchair by the fire, and climbed on the arm. 'It's all right; I'll jump off if I hear the woman coming. No, don't you see, it's like being in love in a play. He does it all rather well, you know – I don't mean he ever actually poses, he's quite a sincere sort of creature, but he has what you might call a sense of situation. And when he reaches a specially artistic moment, I think what my part ought to be as you might remember your part in a play, and before I've time to think, I've picked it up. I'm often like that.' She paused, looking reminiscently into the fire. 'But when I see you again, I suddenly realize, like after the curtain, I'm hot and tired and covered with make-up, and I want to get it all off and change because there's my own comfortable room waiting for me. I've never felt like that before.'

Kit pulled her down, silently, into his arms. She clung round his neck, murmuring that she loved him. He looked down at her hair, shutting himself into the warm shell of the instant's touch and sight, wondering how long he could make it last before something broke through it, and let the future move in on him again. It lasted for just three minutes, before the rheumatic tread of the farmer's wife sounded in the passage outside. Christie wriggled away from him, jumped back to the table, and began to shut up her box. He looked after her, longing to bring back the moment that was over. She winked at him, with affectionate vulgarity, over her shoulder.

For the rest of the day she lavished herself on him, perfectly; the hours became dreamlike, and passed with the smooth speed of a dream. Once she said, 'I want to be so good to you. I want to be nicer to you than anyone ever was to anyone. I want to be as nice to you as the houris are, who lie about in Paradise and do nothing but learn how to be nice.'

A frosty white moon shone in through the window of the car, silvering the highlights of her hair. Kit pulled the rug closer round her. 'The houris,' he remarked lazily, 'have to renew their virginity every time. So Mahomet said, I believe.'

'How jolly unfair. I'm glad I'm not a Mohammedan.'

'You couldn't have a soul if you were. Mohammedan women aren't allowed souls. That goes for houris as well.'

'Sometimes I miss my soul when you're not there.'

The moonlight seemed to pass through her face, lighting it palely from within. Belying her soft, heavy warmth in his arms, she looked like a creature of spirit thinly clothed with mist and light. He looked down at her, trying to print her face on his eyes, knowing that, as always before, it would be blurred by the very longing with which he tried to recall it.

'Kit, darling, I'll never go away from you any more. Until I see you again, I won't think for a single moment of anyone but you. I'll always be the person I am for you; it makes me so much happier than all the other people I've tried being. I promise I will. You do believe me?'

'Yes,' said Kit. He would have believed her if she had promised that the moon would come to her hand. Afterward when he was driving back through the dark alone, he still gathered belief round him, like a garment which the wind tugs at and pierces more and more with fingers of cold.

15

On the afternoon of Christmas Eve a caller was announced for Kit.

The work had fallen to its festival minimum of emergency cases. He had nearly finished his work in the morning, and had allowed himself an hour before winding up those that were left. Janet had gone out, to sing carols at Shirley's house; a couple of visitors were staying there for Christmas. Kit had an unconscious habit of expanding in her absence, like a large, well-trained dog who for once has got the hearth-rug to himself. He lit a pipe, pushed his chair round to the middle of the fire, pulled a table up to his elbow, and strewed papers and oddments round him on the floor. Having done this, he found the effect so pleasant that he did not read any of the things he had accumulated, but put his feet on the fender and sprawled with his eyes half-shut, looking at the flames.

There was a knock, and Elsie the maid came in, looking flustered – she had been caught in the middle of changing for the afternoon. She eyed the scene of comfort nervously, and said that there was a gentleman downstairs to see him.

Kit gathered himself partly together, grunted, and put his feet back on the fender again. 'Not a call, is it?' he said.

'No, sir, I think he just wanted to see you.'

'Well, find out if it's urgent, and if it isn't tell him I'm just going out and there's no surgery today.'

Elsie looked defensive. 'I did tell him that, sir, but he said he particularly wanted to speak to you personally and Friday wouldn't do.'

Kit swore silently and said aloud, 'Who is he?'

'A young gentleman, sir. A Mr Curtis.'

'All right. Show him into the consulting-room and tell him I'll be down.' He pulled resentfully for a minute or two at his pipe, which had been drawing well, propped it in the fireplace, stretched, and got up.

Timmie, balanced tensely on the outside inch of a chair, heard the brisk footsteps on the stairs and shot upright, licking his dry lips with the point of his tongue. His hands felt very cold, and he was individually conscious of the difficulty of disposing of each of them. He arranged them at his sides, clenched in positions of outward ease, and fixed his eyes on the door. When he had started from home he had felt slightly larger than life, and round ringing words had succeeded one another, with the fluency of a carillon, in his head. The consulting-room, carrying in its spare neatness the aura of an unknown personality, had been subtly undermining. The footsteps unsettled him still more; they ought to have been heavier and more aggressive. He suddenly wished he had not imagined it all quite so vividly; the impalpably different approach of reality made his splendid rehearsals fluffy in his mind. The footsteps were crossing the hall. Timmie set his jaw. Even if the chap did look different, it couldn't alter the fact of what he was. Timmie had that on authority which, as far as he was concerned, might as well have descended from heaven on tablets of stone. There was the guidance, too, under which he had come. He was trying desperately to recapture the certainty of this when the door opened.

Kit's professional curiosity had had just time to surmount his annoyance at being disturbed. He gazed with interest at a tense youth with light ginger hair, whose blue eyes were fixed on him in what looked like a mixture of desperation and blank surprise. Perhaps, he thought, it was Fraser the lad wanted after all. The pipe on the fender beckoned again, more hopefully. He smiled.

'It wasn't Dr Fraser you came to see, was it? I'm his partner. But if you're a patient of his, I think he's available.'

'Er – no, thanks.' Timmie swallowed with a muscular constriction so violent that it hurt Kit to look at it. 'You – you *are* Dr Anderson, aren't you?'

'Yes. Sit down, won't you?' Kit indicated the usual chair beside his desk, then noticed that the boy's face, where its color could be seen for freckles, looked chalky white, and added, 'Or why not lie down, there's a couch over here. Then you can tell me about it comfortably.'

A crimson blush flooded the caller's neck and face, ending with burning intensity at the ears. 'Oh, no. No, thanks very much. I haven't – I mean, I'm perfectly all right.' There was a pause, while his Adam's apple rose and fell like a piston.

Kit looked tactfully away, and pretended to be doing something with the note-pad on his desk. On his side, the interview was not proceeding abnormally. He had received several patients of the same age and sex, and with an equal degree of reluctance in coming to the point. They had a way of choosing him, rather than Fraser, for their deplorable confessions, because he was younger and, presumably, less likely to moralize. He prepared the helpful responses which generally succeeded in speeding matters up, recollected that he had poured away after morning surgery the bowl of antiseptic for his hands, and got up to mix some more.

'Actually,' said Timmie, getting it out with a hoarse crack, 'I haven't come to – to see you professionally. I came about a personal matter.'

Kit looked up sharply. Only one matter was personal to him at present. His visitor's nervousness, which could almost be heard to vibrate like a tuning fork, pointed his own absurdity. Probably the boy had got a girl into trouble, or she said he had. Poor little devil. He sat down at the desk again. 'Well, if there's anything I can – will you smoke, by the way?'

'Er – no. No, thanks. I've given it up.' Timmie worked his hand down over the side of his chair seat, and grasped it firmly. 'I came because I feel I ought to tell you – as a matter of honesty – that I've fallen in love with your wife.'

He awaited reply. Kit could have produced one more readily to a sandbag at the base of his skull. He sat in his revolving chair, dazedly watching the tweed jacket rise and fall, in jerks, over the boy's thin chest.

'I'm sorry to hear that,' he said at length.

Timmie blinked his sandy lashes, and licked his lips again. He looked like someone in an extremity of stage-fright who has been handed the wrong cue, and is racked for some means of linking to it his proper lines. A light of purpose suddenly transformed him. He said, loudly, 'Well, I'm not sorry. I may as well tell you at once that, though I've felt bound to come to you about it, I can't alter what I feel, and I don't want to. And nothing will make me.'

The first blankness of concussion left Kit's mind. He looked at the face in front of his, noting, with distant attention, the dry skin, the signs of sleeplessness round the eyes, and a fine tremor which nervous strain does not produce in a few hours only. He asked, 'Have you known my wife long?'

'Since the twelfth of September.'

'Yes; that's some time.'

'Probably you think I ought to have come clean about it before. I've been thinking about it for weeks, as a matter of fact, but she—' He stopped, staring at the carpet.

'Quite.'

Timmie looked up, and braced himself in a kind of relief. At last something was conforming to plan. If the man was angry he would presently say something in character, something typically insensitive and callous to which one would know the answer.

'You've told her about this, I expect?' said Kit gently.

'Mrs Anderson' – Timmie opened his shoulders – 'is absolutely innocent in every way.'

'Yes, naturally. That isn't what I wanted to know.'

'I haven't made any dishonorable suggestion to your wife, if that's what you mean.'

The corners of Kit's mouth moved faintly.

'No; I – er – gathered that from your coming to me.'

(*Cynical brute*, thought Timmie, *I expect he grins at her like that.*) 'If you mean does Mrs Anderson know I admire her and sympathize with her, yes, she does.' Kit nodded; Timmie experienced the uneasy resentment usually roused by the sight of someone else arriving at a private conclusion, and went on rapidly: 'And I don't suppose I'm the first person to feel that way.'

'No, I don't imagine so.'

Timmie shifted in his chair. He sensed, dimly, a kind of divergence from the blueprint drawn up by his guidance of the night before; but no readjusted guidance came to replace it. He stuck, doggedly, to the original. 'I think you ought to realize – in fact, that's partly why I came – that Mrs Anderson has – a very rare nature, and other people feel that, even if—'

'Even if I don't.'

'Yes,' said Timmie. The effort of not looking at the floor made a kind of creaking sensation at the back of his neck.

'What exactly did you come to see me about?'

'That,' said Timmie, 'really.'

'Yes, I see.'

Timmie blinked again, from the effort of trying to prevent himself. Once he began, it was hard to stop. He fiddled with his tie, and remembered a very good thing to say which he had thought of on the way. But when it had occurred to him, he had imagined himself being shouted at. It was not the kind of thing one said to a man who looked at you as if he were seeing something else. It was queer to think that he must be quite young, as young anyhow as Dagger, the International.

Kit roused himself. 'Well,' he said, 'I should think you could do with a drink, couldn't you, after that?'

Timmie's hand dropped from his tie. 'Oh, no. No, really, thanks.'

'I would. How about a brandy-and-soda?'

'No, honestly. I mean, it's a thing we rather cut out in the Group, you know.' He blushed; he had not meant to excuse himself.

'Yes, of course. I'm sorry. I ought to have remembered.'

Timmie got out a handkerchief, made a motion to blow his nose, stopped, twisted the handkerchief and stuffed it back into his pocket. Speaking rather fast and indistinctly, because this was extempore, he said, 'Look here, I'm afraid I haven't gone about this very well. I mean, one ought to see a thing from the other person's point of view, that's the whole idea, of course. I do realize, absolutely, you do important work and naturally things get by you that a person notices who has time to get away by himself and think things out. I've been able to sit and talk to J— Mrs Anderson for hours, when I expect you've had to go dashing off with people's lives depending on you.' He looked up anxiously.

Kit got out a cigarette, and lit it with concentration.

'Talking of time,' Timmie continued, 'some of us find it helps a lot to get up half an hour earlier in the morning and have a quiet time, getting things straight with ourselves. I don't know if you've tried that at all. Sometimes things come to you that you wouldn't think of, just racketing around. I think you might see things differently, about – about your wife, and all that . . . What I'm trying to say is, I don't want you to think I came here from selfish motives, to make a breach between you and Mrs Anderson, or anything of that sort. On the contrary.'

'No. I quite realize you came entirely on her account. I'm sure she appreciates it too. You told her you were coming, I dare say?'

Timmie stiffened in his chair.

'Good G— No, certainly not. Of course she hasn't the least idea of such a thing. Actually, I chose this afternoon because I happened to know she was going to be out. You mustn't on any account think— As a matter of fact, she definitely said I wasn't to. But afterward I had gui— I decided I ought.'

'Yes, of course, I see.' Kit came out of himself, and considered the straining face that watched his own. Angry compassion rose in him. 'Look here,' he said, 'can't you possibly get away for a bit?'

Timmie whitened. 'You mean you forbid me to see your wife again?'

Oh, God, said Kit under his breath. 'If I did,' he asked, 'would it be likely to stop you?'

Timmie said slowly, 'I'd give my word, if you gave yours to – to try and make her happier.'

Kit was drawing a lizard on his blotting pad. Without looking up he said, 'As bad as that, is it?'

'If I thought it would be any use to her I'd—' He stopped, shocked by his own voice, which might almost have been that of someone confiding in a friend. He longed suddenly to get away, to be seeing the thing in retrospect and getting it straight in his head.

Kit looked up from the lizard. 'What would you like me to promise?'

Timmie's heart seemed to catch in his ribs. 'Well, I – I couldn't bind you to anything in particular. I expect you know best what would—' He stammered into silence.

'You seem bent on making it easy for me,' said Kit. He added sets of claws to the lizard's feet, and abruptly pushed the blotter away. 'No. One's got no right to short-circuit other people. You can take it, I think.'

'How do you mean?' asked Timmie, swallowing.

There ought to be something, Kit was thinking, *that I can do for him; or what's been the use of it all? I can save his dignity; that's always something, I suppose.* His horn glasses, which he only used for consultations, were lying on the desk; he wished he had remembered to put them on.

'I appreciate your coming to me like this. It makes me feel I—' – he stabbed an eye into the lizard; it was worse than he had thought – 'I can leave your relationship with my wife to your sense of honor. I expect you and she do very valuable work together. As you say, I haven't the time to give to her interests that I ought to have.' He got up. ''Look here, I don't want to hurry you, but I've got to start out on some visits in a moment or two. Thank you for coming, I'll think over what you've said.'

Timmie collected himself, inch by inch, to his feet. He found that his knees were shaking a little. 'Thanks awfully,' he said. 'I – it's good of you not to mind my butting in.' The exit speech he had prepared on the way there suddenly returned to his mind; he blushed again.

Kit held out his hand. Timmie's pink turned slowly to crimson. He took it. 'I'll see you out,' Kit said. 'Oh, by the way, I think I should be inclined not to mention this to Janet when you see her.'

'But—'

'It's all right. I won't let on.'

Timmie's face went through a moment of curious plasticity. It was blank; then the eyes and mouth opened in incredulous relief; finally it returned a dazed version of Kit's smile.

'Well – I do think, probably, if you wouldn't mind—'

'Right, that's settled.' They went out. Kit paused with his hand on the front door. 'There's an old English proverb,' he said. '"That passed; so will this." It's perfectly true.'

'Not of some things.' Timmie lifted his chin. 'I *know* that.'

'I envy you. Good-by.'

Timmie swung out into the street, bumping into people on the pavement in his bemused meditation. Kit stood, for a moment or two, staring out of the window, then turned with a jerk to look at the clock. He got his bag out of the corner, checked its contents, and then, remembering the mess upstairs and the sequels of previous messes, went to tidy it up.

He spun out his short round, yielding to patients whom the season made talkative and who were anxious to extend his visit into a social call. The last one offered him tea, and he accepted. He wanted to let his feelings settle before he saw Janet again; he hoped to avoid, if he could, anything – and a look might do it, while he felt as he felt now – that might turn their guarded neutrality to an established bitterness. The boy's simplicity, his lack of resource, had released stored-up forces of reaction too dangerous to be liberated on his own account. He resented his own helplessness; he too, he supposed, by escaping out of her reach, had been accessory to this slaughter of the innocent. The thing would have to run its course now; arrested, the child would immortalize it, and some girl who loved him would find, years later, a ghostly Janet in her bed.

As he thought this, the image of Christie returned to warm him. Even the memory of her presence was like a glowing hearth beside which he relaxed in contentment and in toleration for the world. Even in her passion there was friendliness, even in her small patches of sophistication a zest of youth which put the cold and the dry humors out of countenance. His anger against Janet faded; he found himself remembering, in pity, how much of her must be the unalterable substance of her blood. Some man very likely existed who was her counterpart, some dreamer with a streak of masochism, whose love was seated chiefly in his brain. He had imagination enough to conceive such a man and the kind of happiness they might have had together. He had deluded both her and himself with a transient promise of it, so that now she would never find it; and he had found Christie. He was ashamed of his own condemnation. As he drove back through the winter darkness he thought of his next visit to the Abbey, made happy by it even from its distance as sailors by the expectation of harbor a week away. Perhaps there would be a letter waiting for him; she had not written to him for Christmas yet. As he turned the car in at the gates, he heard the choir from the Parish Church singing carols in the drive of the house next door.

The salver in the hall was piled with envelopes. Most of them were Christmas cards, but there was a soft fat one at the bottom, addressed in Christie's sprawling hand. He pushed the others back into a pile and took it, smiling to himself, into the consulting-room where he could be sure of peace.

Christie had sent him a tie. It was a good tie, and the coloring and design were charming. It had, indeed, everything in the world to recommend it, except the casual circumstance that it was the choice, not only of Christie, but of the Coldstream Guards. A regimental tie, he thought – stroking the silk because she would have stroked it – would probably have cost more than she could afford. He would get her to change it; she was quite without petty dignities, and, when he explained, would think it marvelously funny. Her letter was inside the tissue paper, folded round the tie.

He opened it out, spread it on the closed cover of his roll-top desk, smiling through the opening, through the first two sentences, through the first part of the third. His smile stopped. He turned the pages quickly to look at the end, turned back to the beginning, read it through fast, skipping the words that were hard to read, read it through, in a last hope, slowly again. He looked up from it and stared in front of him, trying to fight off the knowledge that stared from it like a color in which the pages had been dyed. There was no arguing with certainty. Its feverish promises, its compassionate and remorseful tenderness, the cracked and desperate ring of its assurances, shouted what they tried to conceal as plainly as if Christie had printed it out in words of one syllable. He even knew the name of the man.

Neatly and blindly, Kit folded the letter into four and put it in his pocket, wrapped the tie in its tissue paper again and shut it in the bottom drawer of the desk. Everything became, suddenly, quite silent, as if his ears had been plugged with wool. He did not know how long it was before he became aware again of external sound. Then, as abruptly as if he had waked from sleep or an anesthetic, he found that the carol singers had moved from the house next door, and were singing just under the window. A boy's voice, pure and sexless, floated out alone:

> Sire, the night is darker now,
> And the wind grows stronger;
> Fails my heart, I know not how—

There were footsteps on the stairs. Janet was coming down, to hear better, perhaps, or to give silver at the end. His body seemed to shrink back of itself, like an injured animal hiding.

'—no longer.' The last notes of the treble died away; the tenor leaped into its confident answer. Kit walked over to the switch and put out the light.

16

While it was still dark, the Christmas bells began to ring. Kit closed *The Thirty-Nine Steps*, which he had been reading since four, welcoming the sound, as he would have welcomed factory hooters or the screech of a tram. They were like small nail holes piercing the wall of his private darkness with evidence of an external world. A little later he heard Janet leaving the house on her way to church. He dressed himself, and walked through the streets in the gray creeping light, on pavements that rang like iron under the delusive down of a white frost. He felt bitterly cold, and no increase of pace would warm him. The faces of the people he met looked pinched and withered; everything that moved seemed to be moving with feverish noise and speed.

He got in just before Janet, kissed her at the breakfast table, and gave her his present, a dress clip which she had chosen when he had asked her what she would like. She gave him a pigskin wallet, stamped with his initials. He admired it and thanked her for it with so much animation and charm that she glowed almost into warmth; he observed, curiously, that one part of him felt an overkeyed pleasure in their friendliness, like the bonhomie one feels in the middle stages of drink, while another part of him was

thinking that he would never be able to look at the wallet without being reminded of wizened faces and freezing streets. They
each had letters from relatives, and read aloud to one another
items of family news.

Janet's mother was driving over to lunch. She and Janet got on
badly. She had belonged to a rackety set in earlier years, and
Janet's character had been partly formed on violent reaction from
her. Since then she had mellowed, but still thought Janet a prig.
This morning, for the first time, Janet admitted aloud that she
wished her mother had decided to spend Christmas elsewhere.
Kit was cheerfully sympathetic about it, and promised to get back
as early as possible from the hospital to break up the tête-à-tête.
They talked on, sitting at the table, for half an hour. Kit clung to
the conversation, as sick men will cling to a chance visitor whose
gossip distracts them from the fear of death. At the end of the half
hour, the talk fell flat all in a moment, like an effervescence ceas-
ing; they were left looking at each other awkwardly, and presently
Janet made an artificial excuse and went away. The fact that Kit
had eaten nothing at all had escaped her notice, because of their
chattering and the scattered letters and cards.

Kit was left alone in the dining-room. He got up and stared out
of the window, waiting for the telephone bell to ring. His mind
pushed at it, like the mind of someone in haste pushing at a slow
train. In a minute it would ring and he would answer it, and it
would be Christie to wish him a happy Christmas. He would ask
what she had meant by her letter and it would all turn out to be
a misunderstanding, or some mood that she had had and would
almost have forgotten. He could go on pretending this for some
time, he thought; and at once turned away from it revolted, as the
talk and laughter with Janet had revolted him to the end. But his
mind was still stretched for the telephone; he found he could not
relax it. He wished it would ring for some complicated emergency
which would not allow him for several hours to use his brain for

anything else. But he knew that if it did, he would come back to himself with the same disgust as before.

He understood that this would go on till he had done something with his solitude, cleaned it and made it endurable to live in. He tried, but the effort ached in him, like the effort to focus one's eyes on some fine object when vision is blurred with alcohol or drugs. For a moment he could see causes and effects, relate this thing to other things, shake off the terrible feeling of uniqueness, of the universe spinning like the spokes of a wheel round the axis of his pain. He would hold it off for a moment, look at it distantly. Then it would come back again.

The maid came in to clear the table; he took up his letters and cards and Janet's present and tidied them out of her way. Time moved in curious jerks; five minutes would seem like half an hour, then half an hour would be gone as if the hands of the clock had jumped it. Once he heard Janet's feet in the hall, and sat down, lest she should come in, with a magazine which was lying about open in his hand. Suddenly he remembered the District Hospital, and that he was overdue.

As soon as he got inside the doors, hilarity and welcome teemed round him, insistent and unremitting, like a swarm of flies. Christmas had got under way earlier here than anywhere else. It had started at one or two in the morning, when night nurses had whispered and giggled with housemen doing their final round, and furtive toasts had been drunk behind the ward-kitchen doors. The crescendo, at half-past eleven when Kit arrived, had got nearly to the top of its curve. The residents' common room sucked him in as noisily as a vacuum cleaner, providing drink and rude stories hot from the source. He thought, when he had finished his first whisky-and-soda, that it must have been given him nearly neat, and amid shouts of protest refused a second round. At last he escaped, leaving a limerick trailing off into distance behind him.

In the afternoon, Janet's mother thought him most amusing, and congratulated Janet on him in private when she was putting on her things.

The next day brought in the usual acute abdominal case and the usual case of cerebral hemorrhage, but there was still a great deal of it left.

After lunch, in duty spurred by desperation, Kit asked Janet whether she would like him to drive her up to town for a film or a show. She turned round from her thank-you letters and declined absently. It meant getting to bed so late; the drive back in the dark through crowded roads would be so long and cold; all the plays she particularly wanted to see were taken off for the holiday; she always preferred a matinée, in any case. She began to write again, but found that the question had broken her train of thought. It occurred to her that Kit had made quite an effort yesterday, had gone out of his way to be pleasant at breakfast, and (in the intervals of odd silences when he lost the thread of the conversation entirely) had been most helpful, even if in rather a silly way, with her mother in the afternoon. It would be wrong, she thought, to let this fall to the ground. Besides, if she did (though she put it somewhat less bluntly to herself) it would impair her sense of injury when she needed it next.

A forgotten idea revived in her mind. She looked up.

'I've just remembered, Kit, there is something on this evening that I really should like to see. And it would be a much shorter drive than going to town. The Brimpton Abbey Christmas Play. They were advertising it in Paxton when I was doing my Christmas shopping, and I made a note of the— What is the matter, Kit? That was the Frasers' telephone, not ours.'

'Nothing.' Kit stared at the book on his knee. 'I doubt if you'd care for it. It's a semi-amateur thing. I don't suppose it would be much good.'

'Oh, I think so. There was a whole column about it last year in the *Paxton Times*. I believe they put them on quite beautifully. You remember, I went with Mrs Cleaver to see their Summer School do *The Tempest* and told you how good it was. Such a dear little boy was Ariel. I'm sure I'd enjoy it.'

Kit continued to gaze at his book. A three-word phrase of print fixed itself across his eyes and repeated itself, like a cracked gramophone record, again and again.

After a pause Janet said, looking in front of her, 'Unless, of course, you prefer not to see a semi-religious play. There are one or two more performances, later in the week. I can go by myself.' It occurred to her, as she spoke, that Timmie would go with her.

Kit got up. 'No,' he said, 'it would interest me. We shall need dinner fairly early; their shows start at a quarter to eight, I believe.'

'As early as that? It will mean dinner at half-past six. I thought it was later.'

Kit saw her hesitation. There was a feeling of suffocation in his throat. He walked to the window, found himself drumming on the pane, and pushed his hand back into his pocket.

'We'll have dinner at the Crown in Paxton,' he said. 'May as well do the thing in comfort. We'd better start at a quarter to six, I should think. I've got one or two things I'll have to see to now.' He went out of the room.

Down in the consulting-room, unconscious of its icy coldness (the heating had been turned off for the holiday), he sat looking at the top of the desk, knowing that if he went back, even now, it would require only the slightest effort to make Janet change her mind. He found himself dully hating her because she had taken the decision from him and then, at that last instant, tossed it back to him again when his defenses were down. Nothing on earth would have made him plan this for himself. It affronted his whole habit of living, his pride, the instinct for avoiding self-torment which was the difficult growth of years, his common sense. They hammered at him, warning and protesting. All through the dark early morning he had been ruling lines in his life, tearing up records, writing *finis*. It was the second lot of wreckage he had had to clear away; it should, he had proved to himself with monotonous logic again and again, be easier than the first. It was not. Into the edifice that had crashed this time he had been building, little by little and unaware, the dearest stuff of his first love.

Why was he going? He could not take refuge, when he saw her, in cynicism or self-pity or a sense of injury. His mind had already thrown off these drugs, as the healthy stomach rejects a poison. His image of Christie, which they might have dulled or distorted in his defense, burned before him agonizing in its truth. Nothing was to be had from the sight of her but many new kinds of pain and a renewal of the old. Notwithstanding all this, he knew that if Janet came into the room now to tell him she would rather not go after all, neither that nor anything else would stop him.

He put on his coat and went out again, no longer in search of thought but of escape. There were lights in McKinnon's house as he passed; he rang, hoping for an hour's wrangling over Russia, or whatever McKinnon happened to be feeling strongly about today. But McKinnon had his mother and sister from Manchester spending Christmas with him, and was assuming, dutifully, the incongruous character of a jolly young man. They welcomed Kit with enthusiasm, but he felt like sand in machinery and, after the shortest civil interval, drifted out into the streets again. He went home, had tea with Janet, and sat reading, or appearing to read, till it was time to change.

Janet, he saw, had taken pains with her appearance. It was some time since they had been out in the evening together. She had on a new dress of dark red watered silk, with a clear fluent line which emphasized her perfect carriage. Her beauty, like an insult flung at him in the street, pointed past failure and compensation lost. He admired the dress, and listened while she told him where she had found the design and her difficulties in getting it copied. She glanced at him with approval, the same kind of approval she had given to her coat and her other correct accessories.

Dinner at the Crown – a Christmas specialty – seemed the longest and most enormous meal with which he had ever been confronted. He ate it because he knew that if he did not Janet would ask about his health.

There were a great many cars parked round the Abbey, and a bus disgorged its contents as they drove up. It occurred to Kit for the first time that all the seats might be taken, and, now that the moment had come, he sent up a silent prayer that they would. But only the cheaper seats were gone; there were, the box-office girl cheerfully assured him, several seven-and-sixpennies left. Would he like them in Row C at the side, or Row B in the center?

He hesitated, holding up the queue, remembering the smallness of the theater. They would be almost under the stage. It had not occurred to him before that Christie might see him. Expedients for getting away, all of them impossible, raced through his mind. Janet's voice, politely impatient, cut across them. 'The second row, don't you think? The others are much too far along.' He pulled himself together and took the tickets.

Janet admired the theater; the Summer School performance had been in the open air. Kit, staring at the curtain, said, 'Yes, it's supposed to be the third best private theater in England.'

'How do you know?' asked Janet curiously.

'Know? Oh, I don't. I suppose I heard someone say so.'

The orchestra played a verse of 'In Dulce Jubilo', and the curtain rose.

The first scene had a formalized, but weirdly effective, backcloth of peaks and clouds. Kit recognized the touch of Rollo, and accorded it a surprised respect. On the right of the stage, where the clouds were lighter and pierced with gleams, St Michael was standing, white and gold and glittering, leaning on his spear. *So Rollo got someone*, thought Kit, his tenseness broken by a faint amusement; *Rollo would*. St Michael was tall, wore a fair wig which his dark eyes belied, and had a beautiful resonant voice whose rhythms soothed Kit for a moment into calm. He spoke a blank-verse prologue, about the eternal conflict of good and evil and the single combat to come. When he ended, lifting his spear, a distant roll of thunder answered from the left.

Someone behind Kit whispered, 'Satan's coming.'

Kit stiffened where he sat. Among all that he had thought of and dreaded, he had forgotten this.

Lucifer entered, in black armor, lit with green.

Strong make-up, stylized as if for ballet, reduced the face under the visor to a mask. No human traits remained. Kit found himself sane enough to perceive this obvious fact, but not sane enough to remember it. He could feel hatred streaming out of him and battering at the shadowed upslanting eyes, the artificially lengthened mouth. Michael broke into speech again, an exhortation or a challenge; Kit did not listen to the words, but again the calm and lovely voice, with its bell-like solemnity, for a moment smoothed his mind.

Satan stepped forward, and spoke in soliloquy. 'How art thou fallen from heaven, O Lucifer, son of the morning.'

Kit's hatred sprang out to meet the voice, and checked for a moment, puzzled by some quality it had, both of familiarity and the unexpected.

The chatterer behind whispered, 'Isn't he *good?*'

Kit's hatred shook itself free, and rode his mind. The concentration and gathered emotion of the audience gave it a more than earthly life, like the obsessions of nightmare. He saw, with nightmare's clear monstrosity, Christie embraced by a grinning devil, smiling childishly into his slit eyes.

Janet tapped his arm. He realized, as he turned, that she must have tapped it several times. 'Kit,' she whispered, 'are you feeling well?'

He nodded, and whispered, 'Yes, of course.'

Michael and Lucifer were debating, in rhymed dialogue of single lines. While Michael was speaking, vestiges of Kit's moral command would return. He could feel his jealousy like some parasitic growth, external to him. In another moment he would be able to loosen it and be clean. Then Lucifer would begin, and it would become part of him again. He hated it and himself, but he hated Lucifer more. It was all horribly new to him; he had thought that Janet had drilled him in most kinds of endurance, forgetting this in which he had never been tried.

When the curtain fell and the applause began, his mind was sick and bruised, but silent.

Janet said, 'I told you they were good, didn't I?'

'Yes,' he said, 'I didn't know.'

'I'm sorry I interrupted in such a silly way. I thought you looked queer, but it must have been the lighting.'

'Yes, it does that. I've noticed before.'

'Have you the program? We hadn't time to look at it.'

Kit handed it, and glanced over her shoulder without attention. He had a feeling that something was amiss with it, but could not, for a few minutes, summon up concentration enough to see what it was. His eyes fixed themselves on the word *Lucifer*, and wearily rested there. At last they traveled on to the name that followed. It was *Rollo Baines*.

The words above it were: *Persons in order of Appearance. St Michael the Archangel: Lionel Fell.*

Kit stared at the page. Nothing would move in him; only a little, silly voice in his head remarked, *Of course, Rollo couldn't find anyone else tall enough.* He stopped himself, just in time, from saying it aloud. His mind had the dead flatness of a substance whose reaction has been neutralized. No new reaction would come.

The first interval was a short one. Before Janet had had time to notice his lack of conversation, the curtain rose again.

This scene was a winter pastoral. Three shepherd boys were sheltering under a snowy tent, while the eldest played to the others on a wooden pipe. As he played, a hidden orchestra took up the air, and to this music Gabriel advanced and stood before them: Florizelle in all her glory, silvered and lilied. In this, her favorite role, her Rossetti face and figure still brought murmurs of 'Ooh! Isn't that *lovely*!' from the back of the theater. Her voice was too female for the part, and of a cloying sweetness, but it suited the nursery-tale sentiment of the scene.

Afterward, the youngest shepherd boy encountered the caravan of the Kings, and told them of the vision, and they watched the resting of the star. Kit noticed that the indefatigable Rollo was doubling the part of Balthasar. Through all this Christie had not appeared.

Kit longed to get away before his transient calm was broken by the sight of her. He felt that if he did, he might effect some kind of reconciliation with himself, and gather all that had happened into some memory in whose company he could bear to live. So strong was the impulse that he even thought of saying he felt ill, since Janet had already supposed it. But she was greatly enjoying the play; the expedient seemed mean, as well as hysterical and ridiculous. As he was reflecting on it the curtain rose. He wished at once that he had left under any pretext at all, but it was too late now.

This was the last scene, the finale at the Christmas crib. Florizelle's Child-Angels were grouped before a gauzy dark veil, spangled with stars, which was slowly drawn aside. Within it Christie was sitting, her head draped with the blue garment of the Madonna, a baby on her knees.

All the tangled conflicts of the last hour were wiped from Kit's mind. Nothing that happened since he left her was real any longer. There seemed no mockery in this translation, nothing shocking nor unholy. She sat looking at the child, as she had looked at him in the wood, with her tender downward smile. There was nothing false in her face of poise, nothing artificial or even studied. She was herself.

The baby was not, as he had thought for a moment, a property doll, but real. It wriggled in her arm, and gave the beginning of a cry, and she cuddled it into a more comfortable hold so that at once it was quiet, and presently, to the delight of the women in the audience, crowed. Kit looked at her in a timeless moment of revelation, and did not see, till she turned in greeting, the entry of the shepherds and the kings.

She had no lines to say, but her silence seemed to contain her more perfectly than words. A little sigh of pleasure ran through the theater; Kit felt it pass him, like a light wind. In the background of his own emotion he could see like a stranger her rightness in this instant of the story, the only one she could have filled. As Mater Dolorosa she would have been shallow, pathetic, lost; she was a Christmas Madonna, loving and amazed and unsuspecting of grief. As he watched, one of the smallest and fattest angels, too little to have been rehearsed in what it did, pulled away from an elder child who was holding its hand, and, waddling unsteadily toward her, saved itself from falling by clutching her blue robe in its fists.

The shepherds and the kings had made their gifts. The orchestra began the music of the hymn with which the scene closed. Christie stood up, holding the child in one arm, and raised the other in benediction. As he was thinking that this too was like her, that she seemed to caress rather than to bless the crowd below her, she saw him.

For an instant she was arrested in mid-movement; then her smile lit and warmed with gladness, and her arm, moving a little farther, extended deliberately the circle of its gesture beyond the stage. She blessed him, smiling with the anxious love of a mother into his eyes, and the curtain came down.

The sky was dark blue, clear, and powdered with a frosty galaxy, as Kit drove home. Janet was silent beside him; his thoughts were undisturbed. As the schoolmen used to meditate the thorny mystery of the Trinity, he meditated the truth that this, and the Christie whose letter he had in the drawer at home, were both actual, and equal in reality. He did not think about the future, perhaps because the present was enough, perhaps because he knew.

Janet had thoughts of her own. She had seen, for her part, the pattern of motherhood, and her husband's eyes turned to this symbol in worship. Her heart, for a moment, knew its own bitterness. It was during this hour that a thought of escape, formless as yet, touched her mind for the first time.

17

'Hullo, hullo. Happy New Year and all that,' said Rollo. For most of the week he had been acting two parts, been responsible for scenery and lighting to suit costumes, half of which he had designed, in a play he had mainly produced, so he was in particularly good spirits, and when in good spirits he loved to answer the door. 'Haven't seen you lately. Been to the play? Good for you. Oh, nice of you to say so. The notices weren't too bad. Looking for Christie?'

Kit was.

'She's doing hampers upstairs. We're a bit behindhand, with the play and so on. She said, if you came, would you like to go up and talk to her while she finished. She's in the wardrobe room – by herself,' he added, with kindly tact. 'You know the way, don't you?'

Kit thanked him. The sight of Rollo, so unchanged in his dirty gray flannels, but with Lucifer's iridescent green paint clinging unmistakably round his eye-sockets, deepened the dual unreality he had felt all the way there. Side by side with the furious conflict, lasting for days, which had preceded the journey, he had a feeling, equally strong, that nothing had really happened at all. Tossed between these opposites, he groped his way, in semi-darkness, up the twisting staircase that led to the wardrobe room.

Christie was packing for *As You Like It*. When he came in she was pairing off suede thigh-boots, with a list of sizes in her hand. She dropped the list and ran to him, clasping a russet-colored boot to her breast.

Kit had gone over the things they would say to one another till his mind was like a 19th-century letter, with the lines superimposed and counter-crossed. This simple and silent alternative had not entered into his calculations. For a moment, while he kissed her, the illusion of security and continuity was complete, and he rested in it. Then, with compensating violence, imagination woke in him. He thrust her away.

She looked up at him with wide distressed eyes, and dropped the boot on the floor. 'Oh, darling, I didn't mean you to know!' The remorse in her voice was of the kind she might have shown if she had broken something which had sentimental value for him, but had hoped to get it replaced, or invisibly mended, before he found out about it. Words deserted him. He gazed at her, helplessly.

'How did you find out?' she asked.

'From your letter, of course.'

'Not my Christmas letter? But I was so terribly careful not to— Oh, darling, and I was thinking of you so hard and wanting you to be happy. I spoiled your Christmas. I wouldn't have done it for the world. I feel such a beast.'

'That reminds me, thanks very much for the tie.'

'Did you like it? You haven't got it on. Were you too upset with me to wear it? Kit, darling, I feel so bad about you. Look here, I *can't* leave off packing these hampers, they've got to catch a train. Just sit down on that chair there, then I can get on. You don't mind, do you? We can talk just the same.' As he did not move, she pulled him gently by the arm toward it. 'That's right. You can hold the list, do you mind? I don't suppose I shall want it again, but I just might.'

Kit sat down. Christie picked up a ball of string and some scissors and, squatting on the floor, began attaching labels to the pairs of boots.

He said, mechanically, 'Can I help you with anything?'

'Yes, you can call out from the list if I get stuck. But don't worry about it. I'm going to be so nice to you when I've finished this. Oh, just a minute, what size does Jaques take?'

'Nine.'

'Thanks terribly. Darling, you'd understand if you'd been there, truly you would. You see, he hasn't got any people, only the sister I told you about who's got t.b. He lives in deadly sort of digs, and he was going to spend Christmas Day visiting his sister in the sanatorium. He says it's pretty certain that by Christmas next year she'll be dead. So when he said wouldn't I go out with him before, and cheer him up a bit, what *could* I do? On my honor, when I started out I never meant to go home with him afterward. But you know how things happen. Darling, I'm so sorry, but could you look and see if I've put a tick against Amiens?'

'Yes.'

'Size 8 isn't he?'

'Yes.'

'He was in love with a girl once, but he couldn't make up his mind to marry her because of his family history, and while he was thinking it out she got engaged to someone else. He told me all about her. He's never been in love since.'

Kit said, taking a little while to get the words ready, 'Are you in love with him?'

'Oh, sweet, of *course* not. Well, I suppose for a minute, or it wouldn't have happened. But you *do* see?'

Kit turned the list over: Rosalind, 6½; Celia, 4; Phoebe, 5. Without looking up he said, 'Has it – gone on?'

'No. It won't now.' She threaded a label and tied off the string. 'As a matter of fact, I did say perhaps one evening this week. But when I saw you at the play, I knew I couldn't. I lay awake for hours, thinking about you in the night.' She sat back on her heels to look at him, pushing her hair out of her eyes. 'Darling, you look so *worried*. Oh, what shall I do?'

'Could you come here just a minute?'

She came over to him, trailing an odd length of string in her hand. Kit came to meet her, and took her by the shoulders. She said in a small, shaking voice, 'You haven't stopped loving me, have you?'

Kit felt a laugh forcing its way out of him. It took him by surprise. He felt another laugh forming, painfully, in the pit of his stomach. In order not to laugh he kissed her, again and again.

Christie returned his kisses and, dropping the string, patted him gently between the shoulder blades with her free hand.

'There, darling, it's all right,' she murmured. 'Truly it's all right. I love you terribly. I was loving you all the time.'

He said, under his breath, 'You'd better get those things finished.'

'Yes, I won't be a minute. Then we can go out somewhere.' She picked up the scissors, snipped off a couple of lengths of string, and collected Touchstone's pointed shoes. 'Why didn't you tell me you were coming to the show?'

'I didn't know till the day.'

Christie stared at the shoes for a long time, and attached a label to them marked *Duke* in bold characters. With her eyes fixed on the label she said, 'I looked through the side of the curtain at you, after the lights went on.'

'I didn't see you.'

'No. You were helping your wife on with her coat.'

'She wanted to come.'

'Did she like it?'

'Yes, I think so, very much.'

'I'm glad she did.' She snipped off the end of the string and twisted it round her little finger. 'You didn't tell me she was so awfully beautiful.'

He had told her, directly, nothing about Janet at all. He said nothing now. Christie unraveled the string from her finger, and, seizing the remaining boots and shoes in one great armful, flung them into the open basket and slammed the lid on them. She ran back to him and flung herself into his arms.

'Darling, you *do* love me? You *do*? I've been so miserable. Everything's all different when you're away.'

He comforted and kissed her, remembering, like a dream, Christmas morning and the pavements ringing under his feet.

'But swear you do?'

'Well,' said Kit slowly, 'I came here, didn't I? Swearing seems a little superfluous, I think.'

She peered up into his face. Into her own came a glimmering, scared realization. She clutched him more tightly.

'I didn't know. I didn't think of you minding like that. You—' She paused, groping for clarity in her mind. 'You *wanted* not to love me any more?'

Her perplexity suddenly made him smile. 'Haven't you ever wanted that?'

'No, not ever. I always like loving people, right till the moment I stop. Oh, Kit, I will be better to you. I'll never make you unhappy any more. You've stopped minding now, haven't you? Say you have?'

Kit could not refuse her pleading face. He said he had.

'*That's* right. Now we'll have a perfectly lovely evening. The nicest we ever had. Just wait one second while I change.'

'Don't be long.' He looked past her at the hampers. 'Oughtn't those things to have labels on them, or something, if they're going by train?'

'Good heavens, yes, and I haven't tied them up either. My pet, what *should* I do without you?'

The rest of the day was perfect. The magic circle met and closed again. Once more he was welcomed from the cold air into a familiar room. The room had stood empty for him, the fire burning, his chair waiting by the hearth, nothing disturbed. Within an hour the illusion had become more solid than reality. Within three hours, Christie was able to talk confidentially about Lionel Fell without even interrupting it. One merely had the impression that a chance caller had intruded while she was putting his slippers to warm. She described the course of the sister's illness, and was interested in his prognosis of the case. Before he left it was as if they had gone out together from their fireside to take comforts to the needy. She made him, somehow, the proprietor of this act of charity, and surrounded him with a glow of merit. It was not till he was almost home that the spell in some part dissolved, and, even then, he hardly cared.

18

'Yes,' said Timmie uneasily. 'Yes, of course, it must be.'

Janet glanced up sharply at his averted eyes. She was wondering what could have altered him. The change was impalpable, but something had gone, a freshness, a responsiveness. She had been noticing it since Christmastime.

True, when she came into a room his eyes still followed her until the moment when she left it. His attentiveness and eagerness to be on the spot whenever he was wanted for anything were quite satisfactory. But she detected in his eyes sometimes a look that jarred on her, a glimmer of painful questioning, as if a faithful spaniel had been injected with the faculty of criticism, and were still wondering what to do about it. A grudging look, Janet called it to herself.

It was specially apparent when they were walking alone, as they were now. Perhaps a dose of appreciation was what he needed. She gave a melancholy little smile.

'What a natural gift for sympathy you have, Timmie. It will be such a help to you as you go through life. And you're free to make the most of it. It must be wonderful to have one's power for good all untrammeled, not sapped by one's personal problems, and one's own unhappiness. Not perpetually worn down by demands for what one hasn't in one's power to give.' She sighed gently, fully believing every word she said. If anyone had reminded her that it was nearly eighteen months since Kit had so much as implied a request to her, and five or six since he had even looked as if he would have liked to, she would have felt a sense of gross injustice. Her tower of escape was set firmly on its foundations, the walls were thick, and it was very rarely now that anything would lure her outside. 'Your life's all your own to be generous with,' she said with a tired, courageous smile. 'You're luckier than you realize, Timmie.'

Timmie blushed, fingered his tie, and said, 'Oh, I don't know.'

What can have come over him? she thought. It occurred to her that some undesirable person might have been tampering with his mind.

They were walking in the public park. It was the first mild day to bring the promise of spring. Timmie looked at Janet, thinking that every new thing she wore, like this green coat with its collar of soft gray fur, made her look more mysteriously beautiful than the last. He longed simply to look at her, to forget the problems of duty that disturbed his mind. But he had been all over it again this morning, in his quiet time, and had known that his doubts all boiled down to a fear that, if things came out right for her, she wouldn't have time to be bothered with him. Selfishness. Once he had faced up to it like that, he had known he couldn't shirk things any more.

'The first snowdrops,' said Janet. 'Look.'

'They remind me of you,' Timmie ventured, 'if you don't mind my saying that.'

'Dear Timmie.' Unconsciously she drooped her head a little, as the snowdrops were doing. How unspoiled he was.

Unless he made up his mind to it now, Timmie was thinking, he'd never do it at all. 'I've been thinking,' he said.

'Yes?' said Janet indulgently, looking at the snowdrops. She was reflecting that she did feel, herself, a kind of affinity with them – their fragility, their poise, the solitary courage of their beauty in a gray flowerless world.

'I've been wanting to say this for some time, but it's been pretty hard to screw myself up to it. In fact, I doubt if I could now, if it were anyone but you. But you've shown me the meaning of absolute honesty, and facing up to things, in a way no one has before. So I feel I can.'

'But of course, Timmie dear. You know you can say anything you like to me. Anything.' Carefully she collected herself to receive the moving little confession that was on the way. Of course, she would say gently, she had guessed for some time. She respected his honesty in telling her, but why should he think it need make any difference to their friendship? Didn't he think they knew and trusted one another too well for that?

'Yes, I feel I can to you,' said Timmie. He stared at the snow-drops, not seeing them. 'I've been thinking a lot about what you've told me, about your being unhappy with your – at home, and all that. I do see how tough it must have been. But I've been thinking too – of course I don't know myself, but I've talked a bit to Shirley, and she explained to me, more or less, how she and Bill got right with each other. What she said was, before she got Changed she felt absolutely convinced that all the trouble they had was Bill's fault. And of course, as Bill's the first to admit now, it was, to quite an extent. But she said, too, that one day she had a quiet time, and it came to her suddenly that there was a sort of core of resistance right in the middle of her good intentions. And when she got rid of that, it was amazing, she said, how everything worked out. I say, you don't mind my saying all this?'

Janet stared in front of her. If he had taken a packet of French postcards and displayed them suddenly before her, she could not have felt a ruder sense of outrage and shock. Her balance, too, had been adjusted to something so different. Timmie, wrapped up in his own effort, accepted her silence as that of fruitful meditation.

'Well,' he said, 'I just thought I'd put it to you. Matter of fact, it wasn't too easy to square up to it – selfish reasons, and all that.' His blush was lost on Janet for the first time. 'But that made it all the more important I should. That's what I wanted to say, that if you think it out on the lines I've been talking about, and find it – well – brings you and your husband together and all that, and it means you haven't so much time for outside things, such as seeing me, I'll quite understand. If I know you're happy, it'll be all right with me.'

He let out a deep breath of relief. He had done it at last. He experienced, already, the rewarding glow that follows the cold plunge. Somehow he felt that the glow was a good thing in itself, apart from anything the effort achieved. But that must be selfish too. 'How do you feel about it?' he asked her averted head. Because the glow was still upon him, he added in modest deprecation, 'Hope you don't think it's cheek.'

Janet turned. 'Yes,' she said clearly. 'Since you ask, I do.'

Timmie's glow faded, much more suddenly than it had come. She had snubbed him once or twice before, but not just like this, in this cold hard little voice like pieces of china clinked together, the kind of voice which meant that something permanent had happened.

Timmie floundered, chilled, shocked, and bewildered, in outer darkness. 'Well,' he stammered, 'I'm sorry if—'

'Do you really think yourself qualified to pass judgment on my home life? Don't you think you're being just a little ungrateful? Just because I've given you my confidence – a little of my confidence; naturally I couldn't be expected to tell you everything, a boy of your age. Naturally I spared your feelings. And you take it on yourself to criticize me for failing in a relationship of which you know nothing – absolutely nothing.' Timmie heard, terrified, her voice shake with controlled hysteria. 'You haven't so much as met my husband.'

She stopped, breathless. Each surveyed, silent, a separate devastation; each scrambled, in characteristic ways, to salve some cherished object of art from the wreck of fantasy. It was Timmie who came to the surface first, since his had been decorated here and there with fragments of truth.

'I'm sorry,' he said. 'I do feel, really, I deserve this. Not only in the way you mean. I said I was being absolutely honest, but really I wasn't. Not entirely.'

'Well?' A confused hope stirred in her; there was still time for some situation of abasement and forgiveness. The walls of the damaged tower began to rise again before her eyes.

'I ought to have come clean about this before. Of course I see that. But – well, it was a bit of an effort to do the thing at all, let alone talk about it afterward. Actually, I did look on your husband one day. I felt, as one man to another, I wasn't playing straight with him.' He paused, a little fortified by this phrase; it had a round, solid-sounding ring, which made him feel rather mature. Occupied with this, he did not notice Janet's face. 'Not in anything I've actually said to you, I suppose, but in what I've felt. And, as a matte of fact, he was pretty decent to me. That's why I felt perhaps the thing just wanted taking from a different angle.' His spirits began to rise, in optimistic reaction. 'It would be pretty marvelous, you know, if we could get him into the Group.'

Janet drew in a thin, sharp breath. She was as white as the snowdrops, but this interesting comparison no longer occurred to her. Words burst from her, unconsidered, unedited. Gross interference – incredible impertinence – taking sides against her – she should have known better, men were all alike, selfish, insensitive egotists – Timmie's eyes, fixed on her face, momentarily checked her. They seemed to be listening as well as his ears. The unwanted knowledge that he was overhearing not what the words expressed, but what they revealed, whipped her anger to frenzy.

'Please don't stand there,' she said, 'staring at me in that stupid, insulting way. There's nothing for you to wait for. I've made a very foolish mistake and now, fortunately, I realize it. I think that's all I have to say to you. Good-by.'

Timmie muttered, 'Sorry. Meant it for the best. Good-by,' and plunged blindly away. She saw him half trip over the low rail that bordered the grass, recover himself, and wander into the distance.

Janet walked home. She hugged her anger and her sense of wrong around her, desperately, but the chinks of the makeshift structure were drafty with the keen air of reality.

When she came in Kit was taking off his things in the hall. He looked at her, smiled absently, and, as if the sight of her had reminded him, carefully drew the curtain across the alcove where the coat-stand was.

Suddenly and hideously she remembered what Timmie had told her. In a kind of panic revulsion she realized that the elimination of Timmie had not been enough. Kit would be there, daily, to project this horrible thing before her mind. She paused in the passage. 'Kit,' she said viciously, 'when you pull a curtain-hook off the ring, you might have the consideration to put it back again.'

'Oh, sorry,' said Kit. His absent courtesy had undergone no change at all. He reached up easily to the sagging hook, replaced it, and crossed the hall to the bathroom. Janet went to her room and began to take off her hat and coat.

For the first time, she hated him. Immediately, because she had known that the ring was loose before he touched the curtain at all, but (since this fact could not be transformed into anything else) overwhelmingly for his treachery, his loathsome underhandedness, his cold-blooded alienation of her only friend, the one creature who had shown her sympathy and understanding. At the thought

208

of it her vision of Timmie became almost canonized, like the memory of the safely dead. She built up, furiously, an image of the interview, of Kit saying smooth subtly poisoned things. An intuition of the truth, suddenly appearing through this brightly colored transparency, caught her for a moment undefended. She threw herself on the bed and burst into bitter, hopeless tears.

Presently she stopped, remembering that it would be teatime in ten minutes or so, and that she would not be fit to be seen. (Not that he would care how she suffered, she thought, as she dabbed astringent lotion round her eyes; still, there was one's self-respect.) She repowdered, applied her delicate pastel lipstick, and did her hair. There was still five minutes before the gong went. She began to wander aimlessly round the room, straightening small things here and there. In this moment of suspended thought there was a kind of catching and linking in her brain, as of cogwheels that suddenly grip. Small casual impressions, the neglected scrap of months, shook themselves together. The thing they created was there before she had time to shut her eyes. His silences, his absences; his moods of causeless happiness and causeless withdrawal; the mornings when he had gone down, still in his dressing-gown, to take a letter from the hall. In the wardrobe mirror she caught a glimpse of her own fixed face, stared at it for a moment without recognition, and turned quickly away.

No, she thought; *oh, no, no! Nonsense. Of course not.* For the conviction had been followed, instantly, by a vision of decisions, to be taken alone, the choice between private, humiliating acquiescence and public, humiliating revenge. It would end in revenge – her accumulated habits of thought made it a foregone conclusion – but at what a cost! Not only her pretty frame of living would be broken, but what it protected, the picture of herself to which, with the patience of a Chinese craftsman, she had been adding tiny decorative flourishes before she was old enough to use correctly the pronoun 'I'. All this was intolerable, and from this conclusion followed at once, inevitably, its corollary: it couldn't be true.

No, it was impossible that Kit should love anyone but herself. Her mind flew back two years, returning laden with satisfying proof. Of course he was selfish, physical, unimaginative; it was possible that he— Her mind reached down, in shuddering distaste, for the ultimately preferable alternative. Yes, that was conceivable. She had suspected it all along. It was too much to expect a man to be true in body as well as in heart; one must have courage, forgo such illusions. She remembered that she had hinted as much to Peggy one day; so she must really have known it all the time.

Once again the familiar shrine received her, the votive lamp was lit. But at the back of her mind a dread remained that reality would be forced back on her, that some inescapable light would shine through her closed eyes.

She must get away, she thought, escape from this cruelly sordid, unsympathetic background; go somewhere where she would be free again to be her best self. Unhappy wives went to stay with their mothers. She shrank back from adolescent memories of her mother's tinkling laughter, the smell of cocktails on her breath, the jokes of her mother's friends. Suddenly she remembered the Easter house party which Bill and Shirley had asked her to join, the one, she remembered, to which Timmie could not afford to go. True, it was primarily for the purpose of organizing a return visit to the South Africans, but other people were going. In some recess of her mind she saw herself inclining from her shrine to another Timmie (she made him dark, for contrast), understanding, forgiving, adored.

She still had the printed folder with the address. After tea – at which she and Kit were mostly silent – she wrote the letter.

19

'Oh, by the way,' said Kit, 'I've been thinking it would be a good idea if I took a fortnight of my holiday when you're away, if the work lets up. Then we can shut the flat and there won't be all that nuisance of Elsie sleeping with her mother that we had last time.'

'Of course,' said Janet, 'if you like.' Her fingers tightened on the handle of the coffee pot, tilting it. She put it down. Desperately, the sentinel of her tower cried, *No Pasarán.* 'I suppose you haven't decided yet where you'll go?'

'Yes, I thought I'd go up to Cumberland. I haven't been for a couple of years. The Kennards would put me up, I expect.'

All clear! All clear! cried the sentinel; *raiders passed!* As soon as the danger receded, how easy to be sure it had never been. 'Of course,' she said kindly, 'that will be lovely for you. I do hope it won't rain all the time.'

Kit, in the remaining minutes before surgery began, was thinking how little he cared whether it rained or not. In the early spring – and in the middle, incidentally, of a combined epidemic of influenza and measles – Christie had announced, interleaved with passionate assurances, the reappearance of Maurice. Maurice had been in hospital; he was in despair. Kit wouldn't mind – would he? – if she saw him just once or twice? He had written to ask her, but she would refuse if Kit said no. She promised, truly, faithfully, that everything would be all right.

Kit had written to say that of course he didn't mind, and had believed it until the moment when the letter slid from his fingers into the unreturning bourn of the pillar-box. The epidemic reached its peak soon afterward. He did not get an unbroken stretch of free time for three weeks.

In the first week Christie wrote charmingly, protesting fidelity all over again. The protests convinced by their naïve self-congratulation. The second letter contained accounts of two expeditions with Maurice, which were reassuring in their way, but left Kit depressed, also a graphic account of Maurice's knee, containing three surgical inconsistencies and asking Kit's opinion of the case. Maurice was so terribly lonely (the letter concluded) that Christie was trying to think whether she couldn't introduce him to some nice girl. Did Kit know of anyone who would do?

Kit wrote back in the only ten minutes he had to spare next day. He was dog-tired, and his mind ran on measles serum and influenzal complications. He never wrote as flexibly as he talked, and was aware of it; today's effort seemed to touch a rock-bottom of flatness, which he tried to enliven by being funny. The result was dismal, but he had no time to write the letter again.

Christie kept silence for nearly a week. Then he received four pages, written apparently in a hurry and late at night. They were disjointed, full of spelling mistakes, heavy erasures, and a vague, chaotic urgency. The gist was that Christie wanted him to come and see her as soon as possible. Everything was so difficult, she was so worried, so unhappy, it was so hard to know what one felt or what one ought to do. If he came quickly, everything would be all right.

The letter came on a Monday. There was no sign of any slackening in the work, and every indication that things would get worse. He had a dozen cases of bronchitis, most of them potential pneumonias. Quite a number of the youngest measles children were critically ill. He and Fraser were both waiving their free afternoons as a matter of course. He wrote back, struggling in time he could not afford with a medium of expression in which he was inexpert, promising to come as soon as he could, next week perhaps. The core of the letter somehow got left out; he had no time to invent ways of clothing it decently, and was ashamed to present it naked. He got up every morning to look at the post, but no answer came.

A period began during which his only peaceful moments were those in which he was too busy, or too exhausted, to think. He worked unflaggingly; he would have made work if none had existed. The patients thought him wonderful; always on the go, they said, always cheerful and with time for a word or a smile; they wondered, they said, how he kept it up. His smiles, if they had known it, were tokens of gratitude. Better than drink or dissipation, because no reaction followed, they provided refuge from imagining, and he thanked them in the only way he could. In them he could lose himself, decently and realistically. But at night Maurice returned. He knew Maurice intimately and personally, as lovers used to reconstruct their lady from a miniature and a lock of hair.

The next week, by dint of furious work, and still dogged by the thought of work he might have done, he got off for part of his afternoon. On the way to Paxton he took driving risks about which he preferred afterward not to think, and got to Brimpton just before four. Christie met him on the steps of the Abbey, dressed to go out. She said, 'Kit! Have *you* come?' and stared at him in blank consternation.

'I said I was coming.' His mind paused, as the body pauses after an injury before the pain begins.

'But you only said you might. You didn't write.'

'I didn't have time to. Are you fixed up?'

She fiddled with her bag, her face changing, transparently, from dismay to debate, to hope, to longing calculation.

'Well, yes, at least—' She looked quickly up and down the road. 'I really oughtn't – I mean, I ought to leave a message, or a note, or something.'

She looked up at him. Kit read, correctly, the nature of the appeal in her eyes. 'Note hell,' he said brutally. 'Get in the car.' He gripped her by the elbow, bundled her in anyhow, slammed the door, and let in the clutch.

She settled herself, with gasps of breathlessness that settled gradually into sighs of content. 'I oughtn't to do this, really,' she sighed with grateful reproach. 'But you didn't give me a chance. So it's all right. Darling, I *am* so glad you came. It keeps coming all over me. Let's not talk about it, shall we? Let's just enjoy ourselves.'

Kit asked no questions, partly because he did not want to know, partly because he knew that he would hear about it sooner or later in any case. He was used, by now, to the painful tribute of Christie's unexpurgated confidence. She told him, not only what women tell their lovers, but also what – he had been accustomed to suppose – they told their most intimate women friends. She seemed to regard both roles as his natural privilege. He was becoming adaptable. Her trustfulness transformed what, in anyone else, would have been wanton cruelty, into a subtle and somehow pathetic compliment. If he ever showed, by accident, that he minded what she told him, she overflowed at once with tender contrition.

'Oh, darling, don't. You make me feel so mean. I ought not to talk about everything like this. I know it isn't done. But I didn't think it would matter to you, because you *know* I love you best. Besides, it isn't as if anything had actually happened this time. It never even nearly would, if you were always here.'

'I know,' he said. Distrusting her to the depths of his harassed spirit, he never disbelieved her. Truth flourished in her untended, like a weed, like original sin. The lies which her kindness prompted had the ineffectiveness of half-hearted virtue. It made the taste of everything too keen, bitterness and sweetness alike. After it had most hurt him, he missed it most.

As if he had been thinking aloud, she said, 'I'm not like this with anyone but you. It isn't that I don't want to be honest with them, but somehow there doesn't seem any point. If I do tell Maurice what I think, he thinks I'm saying something else. Of course you're nicer than anyone else I know, but I don't think that's all there is to it. I think it would probably be the same if we were both a lot worse than we are. It's something we just happen to make together.'

'You mean, like the right combination of colors producing a white light.'

'Yes, that's exactly it. I don't know why we do. I just know I couldn't talk to anyone else about you the way I talk to you about other people. It wouldn't mean anything, if I did.'

'Well, we need *something*,' said Kit, taking a sandwich (they were having tea in Paxton), 'living the way we do.'

Christie took his cup, and refilled it with tea just as he liked it. 'I suppose,' she said thoughtfully, 'if we hadn't got it, you'd have chucked me some time ago.'

Kit considered. 'Well, I don't know about some time ago. You're too good in bed. I should think, taking one thing with another, I'd just about be chucking you now.'

'That's nice,' said Christie obscurely. 'You *must* have an éclair, they're like heaven. The coffee ones are the best.'

The evening soared like a rocket to a climax of stars. Christie treated him like a returning victor, to whom banners and flowers are appropriate. The fact that they both knew where she would have been if Kit had arrived half an hour later was immaterial, or, rather, added zest to the proceedings. She celebrated his intervention as simply as if he had plucked her just in time from a runaway train. She didn't know, she said, what she would do without him.

'I can tell you,' Kit suggested, 'if you like.'

'No, honestly. Never any more. I can't imagine, now, how I ever thought of it. When are you coming again? You know, if nothing else nice had happened to me all my life, it would have been worth being born just to have you.' She kissed him.

Kit drove back – early, lest more work should have come in – uplifted by a mood whose peculiar quality he did not attempt to explain to himself. It was not concerned much with the past, even the still-warm immediate past, and certainly not with the future. But in the present he had got rid of his last encumbrances of illusion and wishful thinking, with his own consent. It did not, he found, diminish the beauty or excitement of experience, nor did it increase the pain. What he was enjoying was freedom, after many weeks, from the chronic ache of suppressed truth. He had, strangely enough, never loved Christie more.

That was a week or so ago. The epidemic was just trailing off; it and his own exultation seemed to lose momentum together. The soul must pause to breathe, and Kit felt the nagging of his own, and dismissed it with a Greek term.

Next time he saw Christie, while they were walking in the country, he told her he was taking a holiday at Easter time.

She gave a little jump of delight. 'But how marvelous. Are you really able to?'

He looked at her doubtfully, not so much hurt as wary lest something hurtful might be coming. 'I thought it would be a good time, since you're fixed up with the Easter School.'

'But of *course*. It's just right. I never thought you'd make it. Rollo *will* be pleased. We must go in and tell him.'

216

'Tell him just what?' asked Kit, bewildered and still cautious. 'What difference does it make to Rollo?'

'Tell him you're coming to the Easter School, of course, you idiot. You *are* coming, aren't you?'

'What on earth are you talking about?' He said it as kindly as possible, since she seemed excited. 'I'm going to Cumberland.'

'Oh,' said Christie. She slipped her hand out of his, put it in her pocket, and turned to look at something in the hedge. After a pause so long that he had begun thinking about something else, she added deliberately, 'I'm so glad. You'll like that. Shall you climb the mountains? I hope it won't rain.'

'Christie, what's the matter?' He reached after her hand, but she moved out of the way.

'Nothing. It's all right. I knew you wouldn't come really.'

'But, good God, you didn't mean it about me coming, did you? I thought that was just what we said to keep people quiet.'

'Yes. Of course it was. Honestly it's all right. It was only just because you said it like that about having a holiday.'

The whole idea was preposterous, but he wished she had been a little more difficult about it. Her eagerness to conceal her disappointment made him feel guilty in the face of common sense. Arguing with this feeling rather than with her, he said, 'I don't know the first thing about any of it. I'd be like a stuck fish. If anyone I knew saw me, they'd think I was breaking up or something. Damn it all, I can't act.'

'Well, that wouldn't matter, because only about half a dozen out of the bunch ever can. Most of the rest aren't even anything if they keep their mouths shut. You *are* beautiful to look at. And your voice is so attractive.'

'Oh, come off it,' said Kit, deeply embarrassed.

'All right. I was only telling you.'

'I don't even know for certain if I can get away. Easter's a bad time, and Fraser may not care for it. If the flu flares up again, there won't be a hope.'

'I know, darling. I do see. Besides, it would do you good to be out of doors. You've been looking tired.'

'Oh, I'm all right,' said Kit, perversely kicking his best argument overboard. 'But what would be the point? We'd never have a chance to be alone together.'

'That's just what I'd been rather clever about. But never mind. I didn't mean to keep on at you.'

'Don't be so infuriating,' said Kit unreasonably. 'If you've got anything up your sleeve, for God's sake let's have it.'

'Well, I shall be sleeping in one of the dressing-rooms behind the stage. We can't put a visitor in there, because it'll have to be converted during the day. I was going to have put you in the single room just above. No one would notice even if they saw you at the top of the stairs, because there's a washplace halfway down, and there'll be no one at the bottom but me. We'd be as safe at night as if we were in a flat of our own. It's a nice room. In fact, someone who was here last year wrote and asked for it, but I told them it was taken already. I'd better let them have it, now.'

Kit looked round sharply. 'Who?'

'I forget now. One of the schoolmistresses, I think.' Her eyes were as innocent as a baby's.

'It's a mad idea,' said Kit, to himself rather than to her. 'It's idiotic.' But his mind had moved onto a track more easily entered than left. He had prevented himself for some time from asking Christie whether Lionel Fell was coming to the Easter School, and tried not to think about it now.

'Oh, very well,' he said. 'Try everything once, I suppose.'

'Darling, do you *mean* it? No, you want to climb.'

'It'll keep. But look here, you can tell Rollo that if he lands me in for an indecent exhibition with some ghastly woman, or anything like that, I'll damn well wring his neck.'

'Oh, Rollo will cast you beautifully. He's marvelous at casting. And you'll have an audition, of course.' Before he could ask what an audition was, she added anxiously, 'Oh, Kit, I forgot to tell you, the single rooms cost a guinea more. If you have one, it will be six guineas a week. Is that all right? Can you afford it?'

'Oh, yes, I should think so.' He put his arm round her. Her hopeless innocence about money, the innocence of someone to whom an extra shilling has always been the margin of luxury, never failed to move him. *Good God*, he thought with inconsistent anger, *hasn't Maurice or any of those other swine ever given her anything?* It occurred to him that this was the only liberty he himself had so far been afraid to take. Suddenly this thought grew all-important. He recognized something still virgin in her, something unpossessed.

She had started a long story about last year's Easter School. He walked beside her, silent, not hearing what she said. The thought obsessed him, absorbing all kinds of material from past crises in its emotional content. He wanted to give her something with a savage, physical intensity, without knowing why. It was the revenge of nature, which he had pitchforked out with reason and toleration. Returning disguised but insistent, it demanded rape.

'You might listen to what I'm saying.' She jogged his arm.

'I was. Come on back to the car. I want to get into Paxton before the shops close.'

'All right. I want to get some toothpaste, too.'

When they were nearly there he said, 'We're going shopping. What would you like?'

She smiled indulgently. 'Don't be silly, darling. You can't keep on and on giving me things. You've just given me a Christmas present. *And* you gave me those sweets last time.'

'No, I mean really give you something. What do you want?'

'Nothing, honestly. I mean, I haven't thought. I never start thinking unless there's Christmas or a birthday coming.'

'Well, start thinking now.'

Christie withdrew into herself. Her mouth was compressed with the effort of concentration.

'Any ideas?'

'Well, I *have* thought of one thing. I saw a dear little copy of that picture of sunflowers. I forget who it's by, a man called Gough or something. The worrying thing is, I can't remember how much it cost. You're not to buy it if it's expensive.'

'Right,' said Kit, smiling.

The picture cost five shillings. Christie hugged the parcel tenderly. 'You *are* a dear to me, Kit. I've wanted this for ages. I believe you'd give me any mortal thing if I asked you. But I feel mean, letting you chuck your money about. What about your own shopping? They'll be closed in half an hour.'

'Oh, I haven't much,' said Kit idly.

They meandered along the lighted plate glass of the principal street. Christie was constantly interested and excited, but always about something impracticable, like a dinner service or a toy tiger on wheels. The dress shops they passed seemed to be showing nothing but clothes for leisured women, statuesque evening gowns or embroidered housecoats sweeping to the heels. Kit fretted impatiently while Christie criticized them with keen, but entirely abstract, interest.

'Isn't that armchair lovely?' She paused before a huge upholstered throne of rose brocade. 'So voluptuous.'

'Have you got an armchair in your room?' asked Kit with studied unconcern. His heart beat thickly, as if he were planning a crime.

'Oh, yes, a quite decent basket one. But I always sit on the bed. If I had a house I'd have a sort of semicircular divan thing going all round the fire.' She passed on.

The next shop was a furrier's. 'I wonder,' Christie said, 'why they never make tiger-skin coats. Don't you think one would look rather marvelous? On a chic woman, you know.'

'Yes,' said Kit inattentively. On the other side of the window was a loose swinging coat of silky beaver. He recognized the shape as almost exactly that of the tweed coat Christie was wearing; it was shabby, and had never been a very good one, but it suited her perfectly.

'You'd look nice,' he said cleverly, 'in a coat like that.'

Christie turned from the leopard-skin jacket which had caught her eye. 'The one in the corner,' he said, 'I mean.'

'Yes, wouldn't I?' said Christie, pleased. 'If I'd gone to be a White Slave with Mr Cowen, I expect I'd have had a fur coat. If not several. But I suppose in Buenos Aires it's too hot to wear them.' She looked at the coat again. Kit, watching her face hungrily, saw at last what he had been looking for, an inner glow of desire, contemplative, quite remote from aspiration, like the desire of a practical child for the moon.

The price ticket showed. It was forty guineas, more than he had spent on a luxury in his life, or could reasonably afford. He could do it, though, if he made the car last another year; it wasn't too bad. He knew, as he made the calculation, that it was purely formal. He would have had this if it had meant going short of clothing.

'Do you mind if we go in a minute?' he said. 'I've just remembered there's something I've got to see about here.'

'All right. I'll wait and look in the window.'

'No, come in with me. I might want some advice.'

'If you like.' He saw a little hurt look in her eyes which she concealed as soon as its first surprise had gone. He had said the first thing that came into his head, and realized too late that she must suppose he was doing an errand for his wife. Anxiety to make this up to her tangled itself confusedly with his other emotions. They went in.

The shop had concealed lighting and a thick pile carpet. A lithe saleswoman, with platinum hair of incredible intricacy, swam across to them like a black velvet mermaid. Kit was seized with stage fright, and thrust out his jaw to conceal it. Janet had never taken him buying clothes.

'Can I help you, madam?'

Christie indicated Kit with a glance, and began edging away, pretending to look at some stoles on a stand. The plushy texture of everything in the shop made her tweed coat look rough and thin. Kit cleared his throat.

'Could we see the coat at the left of the window? The—' Had he been wrong about its being beaver? There was some other sort of fur which looked rather the same. To say 'The brown one' would, he supposed, be beneath contempt. Christie would know; but she had wandered off. He made a gesture, like a man not accustomed to wasting words.

'The brown beaver swagger coat? Certainly. Madam will like this coat. It's a charming little model. It only arrived yesterday.' She drew back the brocade curtain that divided the window from the shop. As she went, Christie happened to turn round. He raised his eyebrow to beckon her over.

'If Madam will step into the fitting-room?' The saleswoman had the coat over her arm. She was drawing another curtain, showing more concealed lights and a pier glass. Christie looked up at him, waiting for him to clear up whatever misunderstanding had arisen. 'Come along,' he said.

She walked in, patiently puzzled. When the saleswoman took off her coat and lifted the fur one, she submitted in a kind of daze. 'There, sir? Don't you think it suits Madam to perfection? And the coloring, of course, exactly right.'

'Do you like it?' Kit said.

Christie had been looking at herself in the glass, with passive wonder, as if she were admiring some unusual effect. When he spoke, she looked up quickly at his face. Her own was a blur of bewilderment; he could see that she had been asking herself if he had embarked on some elaborate piece of fun, in which she was supposed to be backing him up. At his smile her eyes grew frightened, like a colt's when one dangles a bridle before it. She looked round at the saleswoman, waiting for her to go away so that she could ask him what it was all about. 'Well, do you like it?' he asked again.

'Yes, of course; it's a beautiful coat.' The saleswoman beamed. Christie added, silly with nervousness, 'It makes you want to stroke it all the time.'

'Good,' said Kit to the saleswoman. 'We'll have this one.'

'Certainly, sir. Madam will find this a most satisfactory coat. It's a quite exceptional little model. We shan't be repeating it. Where may I have it sent?'

Kit turned deliberately away, so that he could not see Christie, nor the reflection of her face in the glass. 'We'll take it with us,' he said doggedly. 'Now.'

'Er – yes, sir. If you would just step this way?'

Kit walked out of the fitting-room without looking back. While he was establishing confidence in his check he tried to make his cardiac rhythm settle down. What was there, he said to himself, to get in such a state about? A thing everyone did. He walked, with defiant firmness, back to the middle of the shop.

Christie was going through, in her old tweed coat. It looked thinner than ever after the soft pile of the fur. Her face was white. She walked without looking at him toward the door.

'Miss Bennett, will you pack this coat? Madam is taking it.'

'Don't bother to pack it. We'll take it as it is.' He took it from the assistant and threw it over his arm, overtaking Christie just as she reached the door. The saleswoman bowed them out of it, and, after they had gone, looked after them with raised eyebrows through the plate glass.

Christie had pushed her hands into her tweed pockets. She

walked on for a few yards looking straight ahead, then said 'Thank you' in a small expressionless voice, without turning.

'What's up?' asked Kit defiantly, trying to draw level. She kept half a pace ahead; the coat made him bulky in a crowd. He cannoned into someone, swore silently, apologized, and got up to her elbow. 'Don't you like it?'

'I like it awfully. It was very – kind of you to give it me. I'm sorry I was funny about it, but I was surprised. Can we go back to the car now?'

'We're on our way. Just round the next corner.'

The car park was illuminated by one of those arcs which are supposed, for some reason, to resemble daylight. Under its ghastly glare Christie's face had the pallor of the dead. When he sat down beside her he could feel her shaking. 'You're cold,' he said roughly, and threw the coat over her knees.

'Thank you. It is rather cold.'

He edged the car out, reversing less accurately than usual. While they were driving through Paxton he made the traffic an excuse for not looking round. In the country roads they drove on, still in silence. A few minutes later he stopped the car beside the road.

'Well? If anything's the matter, say so.'

'Why should anything be the matter?' Christie looked out of the far window. 'I'm a very lucky girl. I've just been given a fur coat.'

'Well, what are you being like this for? I wanted to give it to you – I thought you'd be pleased.'

'Did you? I suppose that was why you went about it the way you did.'

'I wanted it to be a surprise,' he said obstinately.

'It was.'

'Christie, look here.' The lights on the dashboard glimmered up into her face. He saw that her lip was pulled in to keep it from trembling. 'No, but Christie, come here.'

'Oh, don't.' She pushed him away.

'Stop being such a fool,' he said, suddenly angry. 'Come here.'

'Let me go!' She twisted, furiously, in his arms. One of her fists, clenched to push him off, glanced up and struck him on the mouth. She stopped struggling.

'I didn't mean to do that,' she said unsteadily.

'It's all right.' His lip was cut somewhere inside; he swallowed the blood till it stopped.

'Did I hurt you?'

'It isn't anything.'

'Kit, are you mad or what? How *could* you do it like that? Not asking me, or anything. And all in front of that beastly woman, so that I couldn't say I minded. Dragging me into a rich shop, all popeyed and not knowing what the hell was happening and wearing a frock with a darn in it, and buying me a fur coat. A *fur coat*. I shouldn't think they've stopped laughing yet.'

'I'm sorry it annoyed you. I hoped it wouldn't. Don't you want it, then?'

'Of course I don't want it. Stop the check and send it back. Give it to your wife. Give it to anyone ... I'm sorry; I didn't mean to be rude. But why did you do it today – just this evening, when everything was so nice? And you'd just—' She felt about in the car round her feet. 'It's gone!'

'What's the matter? Lost your bag?'

'No. My picture of the sunflowers. I've left it in that awful shop. Now I haven't got even that. And I did love it so.' He saw that she was beginning to cry.

'Here, for God's sake,' said Kit. Her tears roused something primitive in him. He pulled her round, using his strength less carefully this time, so that she stopped fighting with a little gasp of pain. 'I'm sick of this. Now shut up.'

'Please, don't, Kit. Don't be unkind to me.'

'Unkind?' he said slowly. 'I could choke you.'

He pinned her arms behind her and kissed her, painfully and unsparingly. She cried out and struggled helplessly at first, then lay still, with wide-open eyes, in his arms.

'God damn you,' he said, his breath coming in jerks, 'you've never done anything but lie to me. I suppose you talk to everyone the same. It must be damned funny for you, telling them all that none of the others count and they're the one. This proves it. Doesn't it?' He shook her unresisting body. 'You can't even take anything from me. You hand me off as if I were someone who'd tried to pick you up in the street. And then you've the bloody nerve to make out I'm more to you than this Maurice swine, or Fell, or God knows who. If it keeps me amused it's good enough, isn't it? You say anything. You don't care.'

He kissed her again, forcing her head back, and let her go. There was silence.

'Kit. Your lip's bleeding.'

She gathered herself up from the corner into which he had thrust her, and, fumbling a little, fished out a scrap of handkerchief, with eau de cologne on it, from the neck of her dress. 'Here,' she said.

She wiped his cheek, and held the handkerchief to his mouth. He bent his head lower, over her hands. Reaching her arms out quickly, she caught it against her breast

'Please, Kit. Dear Kit.' He could feel her breath rise and fall with the rhythm of her words, and a little catch in the pauses between. 'Listen, I didn't mean it. Truly. I've been a filthy pig to you. It's a beautiful coat. It was marvelous of you to give it me. I've been looking at it in the window for weeks and wanting it every day. Say it's all right.'

'What's the use?' said Kit under his breath. 'You're just being kind. As usual. What's the use of pretending. You didn't want to take it, and the reason is you don't give a damn.'

'Don't. It wasn't that. Please; you're making me cry.'

'Of course it was. Cry over Maurice. I can do without.'

'Oh, Kit, stop. Just stop for a minute.' She throttled his face against her, so that he breathed with difficulty. 'Don't you see, I thought you wanted to stop loving me.'

'You're crazy,' he said into the stuff of her dress.

'Why? You said you'd have chucked anyone else by now. I've let you down twice. I thought you'd done it to show me where I got off. Just another bit of fluff.'

Kit twisted his head to look up at her. He gave a blurred grin which hurt his mouth. 'Fluff?' he said. 'What a hope.'

'Say you see. Say it's all right.'

'All right?' He turned his face out of sight 'It's never all right. I lie awake wondering if you know what I look like when I'm not there. Sometimes I think I'd like to mark you so you'll remember.'

'You can if you like. Anything. I wish you would. I wish I were dead.'

'No, you'd better not die.' He smiled, his face still hidden. 'I couldn't come and haul you back from there. While there's life there's hope, I suppose.'

'You're bleeding on my dress. Oh, God, I do love you so. Don't ever leave me.'

'All right. Look out, don't put that bloody handkerchief on your face. Mine's here somewhere.'

'I've stopped now.' She attended to her face, inaccurately, by the green dashboard light. 'My lovely coat. I shall wear it always. Even in Buenos Aires. I'm going to put it on now. Where is it?'

'God knows. There's something round my feet.'

They picked it up, and in the semi-darkness brushed cigarette-ash and dust out of its folds.

'I'm going to make this all up to you. At the Easter School we'll have a heavenly time. No one bothering us all night.'

'The Easter School? Good Lord, I'd forgotten about that.'

He helped her into the coat. 'All right, I suppose I'll come if you can get the room. But mind you tell Rollo I'm not going to be let in for any damned love scenes, or anything like that. Couldn't get the stuff across if my life depended on it. Don't forget to tell him, will you?'

'No,' said Christie, snuggling her face into the coat to hide a smile. 'I'll remember very carefully.'

20

Kit made three separate attempts to tell Janet about the Easter School before he succeeded in bringing it out. It made him feel ridiculous, and he found that to look ridiculous before her was as unpleasant as it had ever been. It would have embarrassed him less to tell her the truth.

'I didn't know,' she said, staring at him, 'that you went in for acting at all.'

'Not lately. I – I used to help with the shows in hospital.' (He had once taken the part of an anesthetized patient in a burlesque operation, quite successfully.)

'Were you still doing that when I met you? I should like to have seen one of them.'

'Oh, well,' he lied desperately, 'they weren't the sort of thing you could take a woman to.'

'No. Of course.' He had guessed that her vague knowledge and general suspicion of hospital would allow this to pass.

Fraser – who had, of course, to be given his address – was even worse. He got this over quite badly, and, when Fraser looked along the top of his glasses, talked rapidly about something else. The weather had turned fine and dry, and the work was falling almost to summer level. He had never taken a holiday so early, but this made the idea sound less unreasonable than it might have done. Fraser probably needed a rest more, and Kit would have persuaded him to take one if there had been any hope of succeeding; but Fraser's custom of starting out in the first week of August was invariable.

Janet left the day before Kit; Bill and Shirley called for her in their car. He was, to his relief, called out to a case at the time. Bill's friendly interest in his plans would have been a little more than he could bear.

After he was left alone, the thought of seeing Christie every day for a fortnight left no room for anything else. It was only when he arrived outside the Abbey – in time for tea, as the leaflet suggested – and saw the other members of the School being welcomed by Florizelle Fuller, that panic seized him. He decided he had better see about a garage for the car before he went in, and took as long over it as was humanly possible. This resulted in his making an impressive appearance in the drawing-room after everyone else had arrived.

Suddenly he saw Christie standing in a group in a far corner of the room. At the same time he perceived that he was not, after all, the junior member present. He had forgotten how late he was; the younger set had already had time to coagulate. There were eight or ten of them, sitting on the back, seat, and arms of a large sofa, the overflow standing about it with cigarettes. A businesslike hum of conversation was going on, broken with laughter. Christie caught his eye as he looked, and Florizelle, relieved to see his face register at last some kind of recognition, piloted him over.

Christie smiled, said, 'Hullo, you've come,' and at once began to introduce him to everyone. He had never been with her in a crowd of her own friends before, and the subcutaneous irritation and jealousy normal on such occasions prevented him from catching anyone's name. The men wore undergraduate tweeds with finished carelessness, the girls had on vivid woolens, against which lips and fingernails correctly held their own. Nearly everyone, he realized in less than a couple of minutes, had been to at least one previous School at the Abbey, and those who had not all seemed to be friends of the others. Their ages would have averaged about 23. He realized quite quickly that he had broken in on a small, self-contained club, which had come not because it expected any unique cultural advantage from being there, but because it had found the place a good setting for collective fun.

Christie, whose work called her almost immediately elsewhere, labored hard for him before she went. When they asked if he had been before, she forestalled his blank negative just in time. No, he hadn't actually been to one of the Schools, but he'd been in and out of the place for months and knew all the ropes. Carried along on the wave of her popularity, he quite believed this himself, till after she had gone. On the strength of one intelligent remark about Rollo, he passed muster for a minute or two; then they began asking him which of the shows he had acted in, and, when that failed, what he thought of this or that play at one of the Sunday theaters.

Tea rescued him, since men were needed to carry plates about. Once Christie passed him. 'Liking it?' she asked.

'Fine, so far.' She smiled and began to move away. In sudden panic he hissed after her, 'What do we do for the rest of the day?'

'Oh, nothing much. Just get settled in.' She hurried off.

After tea, Kit found, as this remark had led him to expect, that everyone seemed to have something to do except himself. When Rollo had showed him his room (dispelling a lingering hope that Christie might do so), and he had unpacked, which took about five minutes, Kit wandered out to a cinema.

At dinner he found he had been put at a table otherwise filled by the younger set. Christie was still doing her best for him. Shamed by this into social efforts, he discovered that the young man opposite was reading medicine at Oxford, and intended training at his own hospital. After this Kit's stock became noticeably more buoyant, and they went off afterward to have a drink together, Kit managing to trade his hospital assets for a little information about the School, only one item of which – that the auditions were held *in camera* – did anything to raise his spirits.

At half-past twelve that night, just as he had decided that she would not come at all, Christie tapped on his door.

'I'm sorry,' she whispered. 'I couldn't come before, I've had such a lot to do. It's always like that the first day; been at it since half-past six. Come down in a quarter of an hour. I'll leave the door ajar so you can see the light.'

Kit looked at his wristwatch a good many times in the next fifteen minutes. The evening behind him suddenly presented itself in mellower tones. It would be all right, he supposed, when he had found his feet a bit. In any case, it was worth it.

At the end of ten minutes he nearly went down. Surely, he thought, she would have done everything she did by now; it seemed hours. But Janet had been a rigid stickler for privacy in the intermediate stages of her toilet; perhaps other women felt the same about it. He had better wait. He started a cigarette, extinguished it on the point of the fifteenth minute, and groped his way down the dark stairs.

Beyond what seemed a rabbit-warren of little passages and doors, there was a crack of light. He found his way to it and pushed open the door.

It was a tiny room, which must have been mostly below ground level, for the window was made of frosted glass, uncurtained, and high up in the wall. The only furniture besides the bed was a wooden chair and a deal table, over which a mirror in a picture frame hung on a nail. On the table a square of shabby brocade, a remnant of some costume, was covered with Christie's oddments: powder, a jar of cream with the lid left off, the green brush and comb painted with flowers. On the bed, a hard-looking collapsible affair, Christie was lying in her dressing-gown and slippers, fast asleep.

When he bent and kissed her she did not stir. Her cheek felt soft, relaxed, and warm against his, and it was as if he touched the hem of her dress, or some other thing belonging to her, when she herself was away. She was drowned in sleep, breathing deeply and evenly, lying on her side with one arm folded across her breast and her hand under her cheek. Her dressing-gown, the Chinese-blue one she had worn at Laurel Dene, had fallen apart so that he could see the soft babyish crease in her bare shoulder. He noticed, under the naked electric light, that the blue silk was beginning to be threadbare at the edges, so that the white cotton padding showed through.

He said her name and kissed her, softly, again, but could not bring himself to any gesture louder or stronger than the rhythm of her sleep. She made a little sound, a deeper breath rather than a sigh, and seemed to slumber more profoundly than before. It occurred to him that the Abbey had been organized to receive between thirty and forty people, and that she and Rollo had probably done three-quarters of the work. He looked round the room. There was nothing with which to cover her except the plaid rug on which she was lying already. He took off his camel dressing-gown and spread it carefully over her, switched off the light, and, fortunately meeting no one, found his way back to bed.

At breakfast it was given out that auditions would be taken during the morning; members would find a list of times on the notice board in the hall. 'You're at ten-thirty,' Christie told him; she had adroitly maneuvered him into a corner on the way out. 'Darling, do be marvelous. I know you will be. Rollo wants you for *Agamemnon*, but don't for God's sake tell anyone I said so. He isn't supposed to have any ideas, of course, till people have been heard.'

'In Greek?' said Kit, alarmed. 'I don't remember any.'

'No, ass, of course not, Gilbert Murray. If you are, you'll wear the Greek armor. You'll look so lovely in it. I've got it all polished up. Darling, I've put your dressing-gown back in your room. Why didn't you wake me?'

'I don't know. You looked as if you could do with a sleep.'

'I thought you'd wake me when you came. You're always so much sweeter even than I think you'll be. Don't be late for the audition, will you? I *know* you'll be good.'

The auditions were taking place behind a door at the top of the first flight of stairs. At 10:25 Kit found himself waiting his turn by the door, next to a stooping, big-boned girl in glasses. She was clutching a piece of exercise-book paper, and her extreme of apprehension made his own look, and even feel, like self-confidence.

'Have you been to any of these things before?' he asked her, to encourage himself rather than her.

She looked up at him with clumsy eagerness, like a carthorse to which a sugar lump is held out. 'No. I haven't at all. Is it dreadful? I expect you've done a lot of it?'

'Never in my life,' said Kit, almost cheerfully. Her admiring awe almost induced him to feel that he had, and was modestly concealing it.

'Haven't you really? What are *you* going to say?'

'Well, actually,' said Kit, speaking with great carelessness to hide his mounting panic, 'I haven't learned anything. I didn't know one had to.'

'Oh, you're one of those *brave* people who just dash at whatever they give you. I do think that's marvelous. I wish I had the nerve to do that.'

The door opened and one of the younger-set girls came out, radiant and evidently bursting with some esoteric joke, to be received loudly by the cabal on the stairs.

234

'Miss West,' said Rollo, looking round the door.

'Oh, dear. It's me now.'

'Cheer up,' said Kit paternally. 'You'll be all right when it comes to the point.'

'Thanks ever so for bucking me up.' She went in.

Kit waited, listening to the indistinct vocal murmurs within. The door handle rattled uncertainly, and turned. Miss West's audition was over. She came out with her bit of manuscript twisted grubbily round her fingers, stumbled over her own feet, and carefully averted her eyes from the faces below.

'Dr Anderson,' said Rollo, appearing again.

'How did it go?' asked Kit over his shoulder.

Miss West gulped. In her soul a longing for comfort warred with loyal resolve not to say anything which could impair this magnificent being's chance. 'Oh, not too bad,' she said, grinned desperately, and strode away down a corridor which avoided the stairs.

Kit went in.

The room was Anna Sable's private sanctum. He was vaguely and generally conscious of Morris fabrics, of a signed photograph of Ellen Terry in doublet and hose and one of Lewis Waller in armor. But these impressions were swamped at once by the vision of Anna Sable, sitting upright on a chair with a tall back like a throne, her blue-veined hands folded, in a perfect attitude, on a book in her lap. Cross-legged on a humpty sat Rollo, taking notes.

Kit acknowledged an inclination from the throne, and shot a side glance at Rollo, in some despairing hope of encouragement or even a supporting wink. But Rollo, bent with the application of a monkish chronicler, scribbled on. Kit's worst fears had not painted anything so awful as this. He had vaguely expected a straightforward ordeal on school lines, with someone – male, he had taken for granted – to be cheerfully caustic afterward. No, he told Miss Sable (feeling his breathing located

235

somewhere in his esophagus), he was afraid he hadn't prepared anything to say.

Anna Sable unclasped her hands from the missal on her knee, delicately fingered its silk markers, and opened it. 'Well, Dr Anderson, suppose you begin by reading me this speech.' She extended the book with her marquise's smile, pointing to the place with a brittle, unvarnished, meticulous nail. Kit took the book, drew himself upright, and, anxious only that he should not have time to forget where the passage started, read rapidly, *'Desdemona's chamber, Desdemona sleeping, enter Othello.'*

'Perhaps,' said Miss Sable gently, 'you might like to read it over to yourself for a moment or two first.'

Kit ran his eye along the passage. Paralyzed by the certainty that Miss Sable's eyes were fixed on him, he took in scarcely a word. Distant recollections of Paul Robeson mingled with the thought that this was one he hadn't done at school. Good God, there were yards of it. Had he got to read it all? He glanced up. Just as he expected, Anna Sable was gazing at him inscrutably. 'Er – yes, all right,' he said.

Miss Sable nodded. Rollo poised his pencil. Kit cleared his throat, and began to read.

> *It is the cause, it is the cause, my soul—*

'Perhaps just a little slower, to get the full value of the rhythm?'

> *—Let me not name it to you, you chaste stars,*
> *It is the cause.*

Suddenly, as sound clothed the disembodied spirit of the words, they began to stir into life in his mind. He saw the small lamplit room, the sleeping girl on the bed, the light catching a gleam in her hair, the shadow leaning forward from among shadows.

236

Horrified by the approach of emotion at so grotesque a moment, he kept it in its place by reading with careful precision and calm.

> Yet I'll not shed her blood,
> Nor scar that whiter skin of hers than snow,
> And smooth as monumental alabaster—
> And quench thee, thou flaming minister,
> I can again thy former light restore,
> Should I repent me; but once put out thy light,
> Thou cunning's pattern of excelling nature—

An aching tenderness pierced his heart. All that had moved him last night without analysis – her sleep, her poverty; the terrifying transience and frailness of mortal delight; the sense of her helplessness, of all her power to hurt him folded innocently like a child's curled hands; the sense of his own strength, which had turned to a painful compassion as he covered her against the cold – all these became crystallized, and, like shapes of incantation, more than themselves. He felt a tightness in his vocal cords. The shocking sensation rallied all his defense mechanisms; with feelings of unspeakable relief and satisfaction he got himself in order, and read on with as little untoward disturbance as if it had been the minutes of the last meeting.

> One more, one more,
> Be thus when thou art dead—

He saw the worn open silk of the blue dressing-gown, the babyish fold between the shoulder and the arm. 'And I will kill thee,' he continued with well bred lack of emphasis, 'and love thee after.'

'Thank you,' said Miss Sable. 'I think that will be sufficient.' Rollo removed his eyes from the ceiling and wrote down a single word, with an emphasis which broke the point of his pencil.

21

The sheep had been sorted from the goats. Produced by Rollo, the sheep were rehearsing for the *Agamemnon*. The goats, including Kit, had been turned over to the pastorship of Florizelle Fuller. They were presenting Justin Huntly M'Carthy's *If I Were King*, a play not only dear to Florizelle's heart, but containing a quantity of very small parts and an elastic crowd.

Kit was Noel de Jolys. His function was to be rejected by the heroine almost at once in favor of the hero, and, principally, to stand about looking effective in tunic and long hose, with scalloped sleeves reaching to his heels. All this he did with very good manners. The younger set had long since, in its private counsels, christened him the Dumb Blond.

He was quite content. The lectures on stage technique, lighting, and so on, roused his mechanical interest; the human fauna fascinated him. In one way and another, the days slipped by. And in the night there was Christie.

They were together till morning. She had chosen his room with perfect strategy, which had passed unnoticed because the fitting in of single and double rooms, with groups who wanted to be together and friends who wanted to share, was a job so intricate that, as with the lady preacher, one wondered not that it was done well, but that it was done at all. In Christie's room, even more remote at night-time than his own, they might have been in a separate building.

There was only a single contretemps, when Rollo drifted into his room for a chat on a night when Christie looked in with the object of telling him she was coming to bed. Kit's heart stopped when he saw her, but he reckoned without his guest; Rollo had not been liaison officer at the Abbey for several years to no purpose. He greeted Christie with a cheerful wave of his cigarette, and at once included her in the conversation. Kit himself was almost persuaded that mixed dressing-gown parties must be an accepted social rite which went on all over the house. The event developed a positive swing. They had a sherry on it.

'Oh, Rollo's all right,' said Christie, when Kit scolded her about it afterward. 'He never gossips. He's as safe as a bank.'

'Never gossips! My God, if you could have heard some of the things he was telling me—'

'Yes, I dare say. But you need to know some of the ones he doesn't tell. You wouldn't get a thing out of Rollo with thumbscrews if he thought it was going to do any real harm. He's like that.'

'It's queer,' said Kit thoughtfully, 'careful as we are, that we've managed to go on so long without getting in some kind of jam.'

'You've forgotten,' said Christie with a shiver. 'Pedlow.'

'Oh, yes, Pedlow. Yes, that was pretty sticky. Thank God it turned out all right.'

'Look out. Touch wood or something.' He laughed, but she pushed down his hand against the framework of the bed.

Kit remembered something. 'By the way, if you're still trying to invest that hundred pounds, I can probably put you on to something slightly more solid than Mr Cowen.' He thought, idly, that it was surprising she hadn't spent it all in one great burst, on clothes, or an ocean cruise.

'Can you? That would be nice. It's all in the bank. I haven't touched any of it.' She changed the subject quickly. He puzzled for some time, afterward, over this oddly uncharacteristic thrift, but presently forgot about it.

As the time drew on for the final performances, tension became heightened all round in the indefinable way that can be observed at such times. The curious, highly charged little intimacies sprang up of people who have known each other only for a matter of days, but who, interpreting emotions as amateurs do with the heart rather than the head, have found out things about one another which might not have transpired in an acquaintanceship of years.

Now, with Christie for the first time in a crowd which included several reasonably attractive young men of her own age, he was aware at last, after months of tormenting doubt, of his power to hold her. She played about with the younger set, in the rare intervals when she had time to play, as if with a gang of school friends. He knew, the more surely because she never troubled to point it out to him, that she never looked seriously at anyone but himself. His debacle at the audition seemed only to have increased her fondness; she behaved to him like a mother whose favorite son has scored a duck in a House match. She had spent, he knew, hours over the costume he was to wear as Noel de Jolys, easing it out where it pulled a little across the shoulders, sponging and pressing it, locking up the best pair of tights in her room, lest they should go astray to someone else. Often at meals or in the evening, when they could scarcely see one another for the press of people between, they would catch one another's eyes for a moment, and without any show of recognition be alone together. He tried not to think about the future. It was something to know that this was his when he was there to claim it. He was sick of the folly of deceitful dreams.

The plays were to be done on successive nights – first the *Agamemnon*, which would attract the critics and the intelligentsia with cars, then *If I Were King*, which would attract the Paxton locals. It was on the eve of the first performance of *Agamemnon* that the Watchman, a pillar of the younger set, went off on his motorcycle to visit a girl of his acquaintance, swerved to avoid a dog in the road, and was removed to hospital with concussion and a fractured femur.

'Well,' said Kit, when Christie, distraught, brought him this news, 'he's got an understudy, I suppose?'

'Don't be silly, darling, how could he have? People who pay to come to a thing like this expect to get parts, if they're good enough. And anyhow, there aren't enough good people to go round. No, poor old Rollo will have to do it. Goodness knows how he'll learn it all in the time. The Watchman's got the first quarter or so of the play practically to himself. He'll be up all night, I should think. Anyhow, he seems in an awful way. I've promised to take him in some black coffee last thing.'

'I've got a spot of brandy somewhere. Better put that in it.'

Kit scarcely realized how much, in a cautious and defensive way, he had got to like Rollo, till he was waiting for the curtain to go up. His own stomach felt quite sick with apprehension for him. Had he really been fool enough to stay up all night, in which case anything might happen? How he would hate to be prompted even once! Kit was finding, in these weeks, an unusual amount of time for the problems of other people; he was experiencing a relief, so deep that he scarcely dared to think about it, from problems of his own.

He could have relieved himself of worry about Rollo as well. His annoyance at being pressed into a major part had been entirely feigned, and, in the course of production, he had learned not only the Watchman's part but most of the play by heart. Moreover, he had the chance to wear a very tall helmet and a very long cloak. It was, in fact, Rollo's night out. His silhouette against the beacon-lit sky was graceful and impressive; his somber voice, hinting at unspeakable dooms, sent through the theater a *frisson* which was almost palpable. While the applause at the end was still going on, a visitor sitting next to Kit turned round and said, 'I wonder, could you tell me who took the Watchman? I didn't have time to get a program on the way in.'

Kit passed his own, looking with a moment's interest at his neighbor, whose face was vaguely familiar. He tried to place the fine-drawn, melancholy profile, which he dissociated somehow from the stoop, the light inefficiency of hair and tie which was forlorn rather than slovenly, and the general air of a lost dog of excessively noble breed. 'You won't find the Watchman there, though,' he said. 'The producer had to do it at the last moment.'

'Good heavens, did he produce as well?' The stranger stared abstractedly before him, rising late for *God Save the King*. When it was over he turned and, without remembering to return Kit's program, went shouldering through the outgoing stream in the direction of the wings.

'Extraordinary chap,' Kit remarked to Miss West, who had contrived to be sitting on his other side.

'Didn't you know who it was?' Delight at having, at last, something really interesting to say to him irradiated her face. 'That was Carlos Traherne.'

'Good Lord,' said Kit, when astonishment allowed him speech. 'Doesn't he look different off the stage!'

Kit dressed in his room in good time to be made up, too much occupied with his thoughts to feel stage-fright yet. Tonight would be the last. Tomorrow the magic island, with its curious inhabitants and its secret cave, would be behind him. Well, there was tonight. He buckled on his gold brocade sword-belt, gave a last tug to the doublet, and went out, feeling a certain pleasure in the deep swing of the sleeves from his shoulders.

On the way down he encountered a tall wall-mirror and was, in spite of himself, a little impressed. For a moment he regretted, in an inarticulate way, the period which could put such a flourish on life with such good taste. It was a costume for huge gestures, for men who polished their passions, set them exquisitely, and wore them like jewels in their caps. It was queer, he thought, that the shifts and concealments which he accepted so naturally would have made squalid nonsense to the wearers of these clothes. The shining extravagance in the glass made thirty years' accumulated convention look curiously like accumulated grime. As he walked on, with his head up and the long folds swinging, he met a handful of the younger set who greeted him with an admiring 'Phew!'

Passing the door of the costume room, he felt a tug at his sleeve. 'Come in, beautiful. I want to look at you.' Christie pulled him inside.

No one else was there. She sat on the top of a hamper, looking him up and down. Mixed emotions chased each other over her unconcealing face: wonder, a tender amusement, a tragic nostalgia. She went up to him, and, when he put his arms round her, his long sleeves covered her from her shoulders to the ground, which made him laugh.

'Don't,' she said, hugging him. 'Don't laugh. I can't bear it; you look so terribly like you.'

'Silly child.' He said it a little shyly, stroking a strand of her hair over the blue cloth.

'Don't laugh at me.' She fingered the chain round his neck.

'It's queer; one does feel different. Everything about us seems all right. I'm only scared I shall forget and suddenly behave as if it were.'

'*Hollo my name to the reverberate hills, and make the voiceless gossip of the air cry out Christina?* Wouldn't it be fun if you did?'

'Not so much fun tomorrow, I expect.'

'I wish there wasn't tomorrow, only tonight.'

'Yes.'

'I wish I hadn't seen you in that. I suddenly feel angry with everything. It seems there ought to be some place, somewhere, where we'd have a right to be.'

'Don't.' He had never kissed her, since the School began, except at night in the safety of her room. The place was likely to become a thoroughfare at any moment, but for a little while neither of them cared. They tried with closed eyes to escape into a golden age of which their little reading afforded them only casement glimpses: banners, a helmet with a token, a song at a window, a glove thrown down.

Voices sounded along the passage; Christie said, 'Look out,' and slid from his arms.

'Dear Kit.' She settled his chain and his long sleeves. Don't be unhappy. Sometime everything will be all right'

'I'd better be getting down.'

'I'll be watching you from the back of the hall.'

'Aren't you going to make me up?' He opened the door.

'Bad luck, darling; Rollo's doing the men. Do be marvelous. I'll be loving you all the time.'

Miss West had broken a tape on her doublet, just after Florizelle had finished her face. In anxious haste to get a repair effected, lest she should lose any possible chance of standing with Kit in the wings, she arrived just in time to hear the last words of the last phrase drift out into the passage, and to see Kit looking over his shoulder in the doorway. Retreating quickly, she managed not to meet him as he went. For her the mediocre stage performance that followed was a cosmic ritual, and Rollo's blues and ambers were a light that never shone on sea or land; pain has its fantasies no less than delight. Kit only noticed that her doublet was fastened with a large safety pin, which showed.

The clothes, the lights, the feeling of unknown emotions

washing up from the shadowy well below their circle of illusion, added themselves to his own mood. After the first sinking when his cue came near, he was amazed to find that he enjoyed it. He even forgot that Christie was watching, absorbed in the thing itself, the curious double life in which one was both the trick and the effect, feeling the dim human mass in front slowly gather itself into a whole whose emotional will, like that of a lover, would suddenly reach out and alter one's own, so that in response to it one would bring out a gesture or a tone which at rehearsals one had not thought of using, and sense, in the anonymous shadows, a satisfied desire. He felt, in interested wonder, the shape of his costume impose itself on his movements. Rollo, who had slipped round to the back to watch for a few minutes, whispered to Christie, 'Damn him, you never can tell with these beginners. If I'd known he was going to ungum himself like this on the night, I'd have had him in *Agamemnon* after all.'

Following the play was a party, which, after it officially ended, branched off into private extensions. Kit detached himself, with difficulty, from the younger set, which had suddenly seen him in a new light and was determined to open its arms to him. He went up to his room, undressed, and opened a book which he believed himself to be reading while he listened for Christie's tap on the door.

It was after midnight when she signaled; she had been kept late clearing up. In Christie's room the women had been made up, and though Christie had dusted it after a fashion, their powder and cosmetics and removing-cream, and the camphor smell of their dresses, still embalmed the air.

'You've taken your costume off,' Christie said sadly.

'Well,' Kit remarked, kissing her, 'I've always been given to understand that when possible it's good form. And this one was rather impracticable.'

'You were so lovely. Rollo was wild he hadn't given you a bigger part. He told me so. Oh, and do you know, when I was at the back I heard one of the women in the sixpennies say at the end, "All the same, if I was 'er I'd leifer 'ave 'ad that fair chap that tried to get off with 'er at first." And the next woman said, "Yes, 'e was a bit of all right, wasn't 'e?" It was as much as I could do not to kiss the pair of them.' She kissed Kit twice by way of compensation.

The mood of the play still clung about them. The parting ahead, like the approaching fall of a curtain, only served to charge the present more highly. When the first cocks crowed, they were still awake. 'You ought to go to sleep. You have God knows what to do tomorrow, getting this place straight.' He pulled her head down on his shoulder.

'You mustn't go to sleep here now. We'd be sure to sleep on in the morning, and someone would come to rouse me out. You'd better go back to your room.' She clasped him more tightly. 'I shall never forget this fortnight,' Christie said, 'I love you so much, I feel I can't have loved you properly before. And yet I did. I could drown myself when I think I've made you unhappy. I never will again.'

'You never have,' Kit said, believing it.

They were both very sleepy. Irrelevant pictures, the beginnings of dream, drifted before their eyes. They lost touch a little with reality, planning impossible stratagems for meeting more often, wandering into futures of vague felicity. Kit, sinking deeper and deeper into drowsiness, listened to the meandering stream of Christie's voice describing a house which began on the top of a hill, but later took to itself a lily-pond and swans. 'And the whole of the top floor,' she murmured with the singsong intonation of someone concluding a fairy story, 'will be the nurseries. And we'll call the eldest Christopher Anthony, and the next Anne Christina, and the next David Julian, and the next—' Her voice trailed away. Kit roused himself, remembering that they must not both be sleeping. The light in the high window was turning gray; the red of Christie's hair looked deep and dusky, her face pale ivory. Her eyes were shadowed, so that he could not see if they were closed. 'Are you asleep?' he whispered.

'Not properly. I always christen my children when I'm going to sleep. Who did I get to?'

'I forget.' He was suddenly roused to wakefulness. With the quick transition that overtiredness brings, his airy castles had turned to an anxiety nearer earth. It was one that often visited him when he was alone, and increased knowledge of her haphazard ways had only served to deepen it.

'Christie,' he whispered, 'you are careful, aren't you?'

She turned over on her arm. 'Careful? What about? Oh, I see. Oh, yes, of course.' She pushed her head into the pillow, so that he could only see a tumble of hair.

'Listen; if anything ever does go wrong, you're not to mess about with these patent poisons, or go to some crook or other. Promise that. You'll come straight to me.' She did not move or answer; he thought she must be afraid. 'Don't worry,' he said comfortingly. 'There are lots of perfectly safe things if you don't leave it too late. And I'll look after you whatever happens, you know that. I just thought I'd tell you— What's the matter, darling? For God's sake don't cry.' A sudden fear contracted his heart. 'Everything's all right now, isn't it?'

'Oh, yes, quite all right.' She went on crying, almost silently, stiffening her body so that he should not feel her shoulders shake.

'What is it? Forget it, darling, I didn't mean to frighten you.' She pushed back her hair, so that he could see her eyes like colorless shadows in a half light.

'If I were going to have a baby, do you think I'd let anyone take it away? If I couldn't have it I'd kill myself as well.'

'Don't say things like that.' He was used to her extravagance, but the fact of her grief lent this a sincerity which frightened him. 'You know you don't mean it.'

'No,' she said more calmly. 'I don't really mean it now. I wouldn't have to now, because I've got the hundred pounds Aunt Amy left me. That's why I haven't spent any of it; it's a sort of vow I've made to myself, till I'm too old to have one. I've worked it out; it would be just enough, if I went somewhere cheap, to see me through and carry me on for a bit till I could get a job. It would mean someone would have to look after him while I was working. I wouldn't like that much. But I know if she was kind, I feel sure I would.'

'But—' he began desperately, protesting not against what she said, but against his own thoughts.

'It's all right. I don't suppose it will ever happen. Don't worry, I wouldn't let it on purpose; for one thing it would mean leaving you. I'd go away, of course, where you couldn't find me, or my people; that would be only fair, if I hadn't done anything to try and stop it. He'd be mine, and I'd see after him; if I decided it was worth it, it wouldn't be anyone else's fault. I'd change my name, or something, and tell him his father died when he was a baby. I'd have to do that, you see, or he'd feel he was different. But I'd let you see him, of course, when he was older ... Darling, why didn't you wake me up? What have I been talking about all this time? You look like death. I say anything, you know I do. Cheer up, precious, I love you more than whole families of the unborn rolled into one. Just be nice to me for a minute, and then you *must* go upstairs and get some sleep.'

Kit went back to his room in the cold light of morning, half an hour before the maids began to move about the house. Over a chair lay his sky-blue costume, with its great sleeves hanging like the wings of a dead bird. He stood and stared at it. Everything seemed to have a slow circular motion, a wheel, an endless band, a snake swallowing its tail. Inescapably it all came round again, the same spoke of the wheel, the serpent's head. He remembered, just in time, to throw back his unused bed before the maid came to call him.

22

The siren sounded again, a spacious, impatient sound. The great ship looked as fixed as the stone to which its gangplanks joined it; one could, it seemed, expect movement as easily from a chain of hotels. But its voice – the voice of a sea beast, pitched to huge distances – convinced. At the sound of it farewells grew tongue-tied, or garrulous, in realization. Some of the travelers sought relief in little panics over books and cases and bags, an escape denied to Janet, who abhorred any form of public inefficiency. She and Kit stood near the gangway, making conversation assiduously, like callers in a drawing-room, while both wondered what the essential thing was that they ought to say.

Kit was concentrated in a last effort to convince himself that this was real. Up till a fortnight ago he had not believed that she meant it; up till a week ago he had been certain she would change her mind. She had made so many gestures, all sterile, all leaving everything as it had been before. When she had got back from the Group house party and told him her plans – to go with the Group party to the Cape, and while she was there spend a few months with her married sister in Durban – it had not occurred to him that they were considering an approaching event. He simply wondered, rather anxiously, what cue he was being given, whether agreement or opposition was likely to offend her more. He had struck a careful balance between the two, and had been relieved when she seemed satisfied. A little later another thought had occurred to him, but when he asked she had said no, Bill and Shirley weren't going, nor anyone else in the neighborhood. He was more sure than ever, then, that when the mood had spent itself, or the gesture taken effect, nothing more would be heard of it, and could not shake himself into realization even when she began buying tropical clothes.

Now here they were; and even now he could not believe that she was doing something real, with effect in space and time. If she meant to draw back now, she would have to make up her mind to it almost at once; already some of the visitors were leaving the ship.

'I suppose I'll have to go in a moment,' he said. It was still at the back of his mind that she couldn't have realized, that it was only fair to warn her.

'Yes. But they tell you when they're going to raise the gang-ways.' She did not look at him. 'I hope Mrs Hackett will make you comfortable. I told you, didn't I, she was with a doctor before?'

'Oh, I'll be all right. Take care of yourself. I hope the Bay behaves properly.' He could produce this sort of thing, he thought, for hours, sooner than throw a real question across the widening silence between their minds. 'You've got the seasick capsules, haven't you? They generally work.'

'Yes, in my bag. But I shan't need them unless it's very rough.' It had been very rough, she remembered, crossing to the Channel Islands the day after they were married; he had wanted to stay with her, and had seemed unable to understand her horror at the idea of his seeing her indignity. 'But, darling, you can't mind me. I've seen thousands of people vomit and thought no worse of them. And anyway I love you.' She had wondered how he could be so coarsely insensitive, and, before she escaped below, had rallied her forces sufficiently to indicate it with a look. Now, as she recalled it, she could only remember how young he had been.

All round them, Groupers were being seen off by other Groupers. Their youth, their crude enthusiasm, their certainty gathered power in this windy place full of sunlight and salt air, ringing with sounds of action and of purpose. Their voices drifted to Janet, charged with reassurance and hope. For months, for as long as she could think ahead, their liking and admiration and belief would be a film of bright flattering color between her and herself. In the safety and freedom of new places she would watch all that she wanted to believe of herself taking on reality in their minds. She looked at the May sunlight; it would be winter before she was back again. 'I'll write from Madeira.'

Kit was looking at the Groupers, feeling envy mingle in him with compassion. He had felt the same sometimes when McKinnon, his dark eyes glowing with defiant faith, was using the words Capitalist and Proletarian as if they were definitions of moral values. He wondered how it felt to be one of these dedicated creatures in their birdlike skimmings over the dull, dull surface of human inertia, so joyfully certain that the heavy mass was rising in their wake. When one worked, as he did, knee-deep in the stuff itself, their effects seemed covetably quick and easy. They could seal a soul to the elect in a couple of afternoons, whereas it might take him months to effect a fine adjustment in the same human being's blood-sugar, and then his work would only be begun. A physician himself by temperament, he had felt a similar unease in the company of brisk and optimistic surgeons. Well, they seemed happy, and there was room for more of it. Perhaps Janet was a surgical case. At any rate, he wished her luck.

'It's queer,' she was saying, 'to think that when I get back it will

252

be nearly Christmas time. Oh, by the way, did you manage to get me a paper?'

'Yes, of course. I've got it somewhere.' He dug into the pocket of his driving-coat. '*Lilliput* – *Digest* – will those do? And a picture-paper. Here you are. Nothing much in it.'

More people were leaving the ship. A party of Groupers farther along the deck seemed to have shed all theirs already; they were all waving over the side. Kit followed the direction of their eyes. He saw, conspicuous by his ginger hair, Timmie Curtis close to the edge of the dock. A qualm assailed him; had the unhappy boy meant to see Janet off, expecting her to be alone? He calculated the chances – and the ultimate kindness – of affording a last-minute opportunity by making himself scarce, but decided against it, because Timmie did not look particularly dejected. Next moment Kit perceived that the brown-skinned girl on Timmie's right was not, as he had supposed, pressed against his side by the denseness of the crowd. She was clinging, with both hands, to his arm.

'Have you seen someone we know?' Janet asked. But already, before he thought about it, he had shifted himself between her and the group on shore. To be her buffer against truth had been his function for so long that, even in this latest minute, he fulfilled it by instinct.

'You wouldn't know him. He used to be a patient of mine.'

23

Kit smoothed out the letter and read it again. This time he smiled a little. He could have written it for her, he thought.

Well, he would be there in good time today. The work had panned out very conveniently. He put the note into his pocket and ran up to his room to change. Burford – Jimmie Burford? Oh, yes, of course. He had been at the Easter School, a rather dim hanger-on of the younger set. A prep-school master, or something similar. It was impossible to work up much emotion about anyone so neutral; Kit, as he wriggled into his shirt, merely hoped that Christie hadn't led the poor little devil too far up the garden path. All from the most generous motives, of course. Probably he worried about his job, or had an ailing mother. Whatever it was, Christie would have had it out of him within half an hour. It had started, of course, in the three weeks or so before Janet's departure, when he had not been able to get away.

What did it matter? This one would be the last for a long while. He would be able to see her, now, every week, and sometimes on a Sunday as well. At last he could begin to make things up to her a little. Whatever she did, now, he would think of it like this. The luxury of forgiveness was denied him. It was he, not she, who was tied to a profession which expelled divorce respondents. It had never occurred to her to question or reproach him, to demand any pity or any compensation. Now at least he could partly fill, with the smaller kinds of happiness, the gap of the greater.

He was wearing a new suit, and paused over it dubiously. It was a lighter gray than he generally had; he dressed conservatively on the whole. It looked all right, he supposed, in its way. Anyhow, Christie would probably like it. He did not actually admit to himself that this thought had visited him when he chose the cloth.

He opened the roof of the car – it was a beautiful day – and started out, feeling happy, not only because he was going to see her, but because he was learning to take this kind of thing in his stride. Apart from other considerations, jealousy had offended the physician in him, like a septic focus. He had attacked the symptoms with a good deal of resolution and some success. The cause remained. It was too deep even for surgery now; he knew that, and accepted it. His mind felt clear and serene. It was not getting her back that was important – he had always done that, and felt less anxiety about it this time than ever before – but getting her back without mess or suffering or indignity.

Christie had asked him to meet her at the outside door of the theater; she had a coaching to work in, she said, before she could get away. He parked the car there and waited for her to come out, wondering what she would have on.

She did not see him for a moment or two. Then she smiled uncertainly, but he expected that. Returning the smile cheerfully, he opened the door of the car.

'I'm so sorry I had to be late,' she said in a small voice.

'It's all right. I've only just come myself.' He took her firmly by the elbow. 'Tea first, I think. Then you can tell me all the news.' He turned the car in the direction of Paxton.

'Kit, not that Paxton place. It's so full of people. Why not that farm where we went before?'

'All right. It's too good a day, really, for town.' He began to reverse down a side-turning. Suddenly she began to search about on the seat.

'Oh, Kit. I've left my bag in the theater. Do you mind?'

He stopped the car. 'I suppose it's no good saying come without it. Probably take another world war to bring in pockets for women. Don't be long.'

'Come in with me. There's no one there. I don't want to be away from you.'

'Well, it might save time.' They went through the echoing theater, chilly now that the heating had been turned off.

'We were in one of the practicing-rooms,' she said, 'behind the stage.' As they went through the side door into the wings Kit sniffed, affectionately, the familiar smell. 'This one,' Christie said.

He murmured, 'It's nice to be in here again.'

'It's all different now.'

'Yes,' he said. 'It looks a bit chilly without the bed.'

There was nothing in the small cell but a piano, a deal table, and a couple of chairs. Christie's bag was on the table. She picked it up, and sat back on the table's edge. He came toward her, but she held him off for a moment, looking at him. 'You've got a new suit on. You look so nice in it. It matches your eyes.'

'It's too light. I chose the cloth in a gloomy shop.'

'Of course it isn't. You always ought to wear that color.' She threw her arms round his neck. 'Oh, darling, I wish you weren't always more than I bargained for – sweeter, or better-looking, or something. You always are. I might have known you would be today.' She gave an unreal laugh, and buried her face in his shoulder.

He stroked her hair. 'Look here,' he said gently, 'if you're going to worry about this till it's off your chest, why not get it over now, before we start? Then we can enjoy ourselves. No point in spoiling your tea.'

She looked up, as if she were frightened. 'Darling, why are you being like this? I thought you'd— Don't you mind?'

'I don't know,' he said, 'yet.' It must have gone further than he had supposed. What had that little swine looked like? If he could – *Look out!* he thought, checking himself quickly. He must, just this once, carry it through as he knew, when he was quiet and alone, it ought to be done. If he didn't spoil this, all the months of happiness ahead would be better for it. 'It's all right,' he said. 'Tell me the worst to start off with, and then how it happened. Like a detective story. Then I'll tell you how to detach the poor wretch without undue suffering. That's what you want, I suppose? Come on. Don't look so scared. After all, I've been there before.'

She drew back. He noticed, then, that her face was white and strained with sleeplessness. He had not seen her like that since Miss Heath died. He sat down on the table beside her, taking her hand in his.

'Kit. Didn't you read my letter?'

'Of course. All but the postscript. You'd spilt a bottle of ink, or something, over the bottom of the page.'

'But all the rest, after. I wrote it out again.'

'I should think you forgot to put it in, then.'

'Oh, Kit, I *couldn't* have. Did I? I remember, I did have to post it in a frightful hurry in the end. So that was why – I couldn't think why you were so—' She stopped. The strain in her face changed, slowly, to relief. 'Oh, well. I'm glad really. It doesn't matter, now.'

Kit, too, felt a moment's sense of reprieve. Need he know about it? It was so much easier without the details that Christie charged with such unconscious vividness; they had a way of taking on a life of their own afterward, when he was driving home, or in bed at night when there was a week to wait before he saw her again. Let it go. In an hour or two it would be nothing to do with either of them ... No, it was too easy. The certainty of truth was the only thing in their relationship that was rare, that kept it above the level of a million furtive philanderings.

'Come on,' he said, putting his arm round her shoulders. 'You know you're bursting to tell me really.'

'I'm not. I don't want to think about it any more. I've got you. Nothing else matters. I don't know now why I thought it did. Things look different when you're alone ... I love you, Kit. I want you more than anything else. I was mad – I want to forget about it.'

'We both will afterward. You know you'll feel better if you spit it out. Fire away. The end first. You slept with this chap, I take it. How many times?'

'Oh, Kit, no!' She had never lied to him. Even if she had, he would have known she was not lying now. His face lightened. He was glad, all over again, that he had kept himself in hand. Just a little good listening, and it would be over. He almost glanced at his watch. She was still talking, however, '—you've no idea how upright and everything he is. He never even said anything till he'd been offered a housemastership. The junior masters aren't supposed to get married, you see. He doesn't believe in long engagements. Poor old Jimmie.'

She smiled reminiscently. It was not till Kit withdrew his arm from her shoulders that she looked up and saw his face.

'Darling, what *is* it? Don't. Honestly I haven't been to bed with him. I promise you. I'd say if I had, you know I would. He didn't even ask me.'

'No. He asked you to marry him.'

'Well, precious, so would you if you could. Don't look so hurt, I can't bear it. It was a crazy idea. I knew I'd realize it as soon as I saw you again. That's why I asked you to come – oh, I forgot, you didn't read that part. Well, you came, anyway. I'll write to him tomorrow.'

'You hadn't refused, then?'

'Well, no, not finally. I hadn't the heart to turn him down flat – it seemed less snubbing, sort of, to say I'd think it over and let him know. Besides – Kit, darling, don't think me a beast, but he'll have twenty little boys in his house between six and thirteen. I couldn't help just thinking about it for a second. Not longer than that.'

He was silent, watching her thoughts run, clear as water, through her eyes. Already the reminder of her doubts had raised them again. She was waiting for him, now, as she always waited, to make up her mind for her in the only way she understood. She was quite near him still. Her hair was soft and fluffy today; she must just have washed it. He said nothing.

'He's fond of children, you see. He wanted somebody who was too. I expect he'll soon find someone else, though.'

'Possibly. Are you fond of him?' He spoke distantly and pre-cisely, as if he had been in the consulting-room. He had learned the manner, however, with Janet. It made him seem older than he was.

'Oh, we get on all right. Kit, what's the matter? You don't sound as if you cared whether I married him or not. Why are you so queer?'

Yes, he thought, *why am I?* A moment's lapse of control, and everything would settle itself. Quite natural, quite involuntary. Or almost involuntary, after the first split second of consent.

'I thought you sent for me because you wanted advice.'

'Of course I did, darling. You've always got me out of all my jams. Look at Mr Cowen.'

'We're not discussing Mr Cowen now.'

'Kit, I can't stand this. Don't be cross. You asked me to tell you. Don't you mind, or what? Kit, look at me, say something.' Her voice shook dangerously. 'You haven't stopped loving me, have you?'

Well, he thought, *that would be one way*. Old-fashioned surgery, dirty and destructive – the Heroic Lie. It mattered, he supposed, very little; still—

'No,' he said, without emotion. 'Not yet.'

'Not *yet*? Darling, what do you mean?'

'I haven't discussed my wife with you, have I?' Surely something would give him away. But he had learned not to make mistakes; it was too late to unlearn it now. 'I'm afraid I may have given you the impression that I was never very fond of her. That isn't true. I loved her as much as I was capable of loving anyone. It lasted three years. That includes the time when we were engaged. Now do you see?'

She looked away. At last she said under her breath, 'But I thought— That was different. She wasn't kind to you.'

She was sitting with her knees screwed up on the table, trying to see his face. He got up, and moved away.

'That's a matter of opinion,' he said crisply. 'She was faithful to me, though.'

He heard a shallow sound behind him, but still stared at the frosted glass of the window, crossed, at intervals, by the jerky shadows of feet outside. 'No one's to blame. Our circumstances are a bit unfortunate, that's all. I think it's only fair to give you the first chance of clearing out. If we left it much longer, it might be me. You can't drag these things on. When they're over, they're over. What about it?'

'I don't know,' she said. She had wrapped her arms round her knees, as if she were cold. 'I don't know anything when you talk like that.' She got off the table, and came, hesitating, toward him. 'Kit – please – won't you be ordinary, just for a minute? I'd feel safer if you would.'

This dependence, this persisting trust, were what he had most feared. Suddenly he feared them no longer. They were what he had needed. She had no one, he thought, to give her things. He could look at her now.

'I am being ordinary. After all, we're separated for fairly long stretches. One doesn't spend all that time in a welter of emotion, particularly if one's got a job to attend to. I've thought for some time this would be the best way out, for both of us.'

'Kit. Is that true?'

'Perfectly true.' He had thought it often, as one thinks how much simpler life would be if one could dispense with the need for food. 'Haven't you?'

'I don't know. Thinking didn't seem to come into it, really, very much.'

'Well,' he said briskly (the tone often worked well with nervous patients), 'I think it's about time it did. You only fancy I matter more than Maurice and Co. because I've been more persistent. You'd have left me several times already, if I hadn't kept making scenes.' (It was amazing what rational material could be produced from bad dreams.) 'Presently we'd both have got sick of it. You'll forget all these episodes, when you've had a kid or two.'

'I always wanted them to be yours . . . You make it all sound so reasonable, you muddle me up. Don't keep talking about me as if you weren't there. Won't you be unhappy – don't you *mind*?'

'Oh, me. It's different for a man, you know.' Phrases returned to him; he could almost have smiled at the faithfulness with which he had learned them. 'These things take a much smaller place. Men have so many other interests. They're naturally more self-centered.'

She looked puzzled, as if she were being set a lesson in advance of what she had learned. 'I don't know about men. I only know a few people. We'd be lonely without each other.'

'For a week or two. It blows over.'

'I shall always want to tell you things.'

'Well, there's nothing to stop your writing to me. This isn't a Lyceum melodrama.' (It would be like her, he thought, to write

261

on her honeymoon. He would read it, too, and be proud that it was possible.) 'I'm always there if you get worried about anything.'

'Yes,' she said. 'Yes, I can always write, can't I?'

He knew that was decisive. He might have thought of it sooner. She only needed to be saved the cold plunge of a decision on the spot. Nothing remained but to get out of the way. The current would carry her.

'We'll meet again sometime. Not for a bit, though; you'll have enough to think about. Well, I'd better be going.'

'Oh, not yet! I haven't – I wanted us to have today.'

'I've got to get back to a case. I meant to tell you before.'

'Kit. Kiss me good-by.'

She had no concealments. It was not a farewell she wanted; it was a decision her mind need not make.

'No,' he said. 'Don't be silly. You know it'll only unsettle you. You'll be all right. Good-by.'

'Kit – I love you—'

He paused with his hand on the door. He had done everything. If, after all—

'—I'll never, never forget you.'

No, he thought; *of course. I wondered for a moment—*

'Thanks for being nice to me.' (That was right, wasn't it? He had seen it in a book, or somewhere.) 'Good-by.'

He went out without looking back.

In the car, driving home, the spurious years dispersed from his face. He might have been 25. But there was no need to look for the horn glasses, since he was alone.

24

Janet wrote from Madeira. She described the weather on the voyage, the deck sports. She enclosed a snapshot, which indicated greater distances than the foreign stamp on the envelope. There was a kind of family resemblance between all the four faces. He wrote back, slowly evolving suitable sentences, as if it had been a home-letter from school.

Christie wrote once, to say how often she thought about him, to tell him Florizelle had a new dress woven by Swedish peasants, and to ask him if he was sure she was doing the right thing. He answered reassuringly.

The shape of her writing on the page was like a physical touch. Before he even read it he could see her writing it, twisted round sideways at the table, in her old smock that smelled of grease-paint, her leg tucked up on the seat of the chair.

It was all over. If he repeated this long enough to himself, presumably it would mean something.

All that remained with him was the satisfaction that springs from having passed a test of strength. It had all seemed quite straightforward at the time, his happiness for hers. But a confused thought was breaking in on him that what was gone could not be divided into hers or his; it was a life beyond them, with rights of its own, a light that had been put out; a soul, different from their separate souls in its weakness and its strength, torn from its body and dispersed into the wind.

He brushed the tangled images aside. He had done the evidently decent thing. There was always his job. The only difference was that once he had looked forward to its intervals when he could be alone with himself.

Early in July the *Telegraph* announced the forthcoming marriage of Christina Heath, daughter of the late Reverend Lucas Emmanuel Heath and of Mrs Heath of 14a Park Drive, Edgbaston, Birmingham, to James Burford, second son of Colonel and Mrs Burford, of the Grange, Winthrup, Hertfordshire. It was to take place at the end of the month.

Kit clipped out the announcement; he need not have troubled, however, as Christie sent him a copy. She was worried, she said; everything seemed different when she hadn't got him there to talk to. She was staying in her mother's flat, preparing her trousseau. The place (she added) was lousy with lingerie, and with hens she had never met in her life coming to stare at it. They seemed to expect her to have *made* the stuff. She felt like a horse being done up for a show. She wanted to talk to Kit. Couldn't they possibly meet just for an hour or two – for half an hour? She wouldn't be a nuisance. She just wanted to talk to him. She supposed she ought not to, now she was engaged, but somehow it didn't seem to make any difference.

He did not answer the letter for two days. As long as he kept it in his pocket, it was as though Christie were on the other side of a door in the same house. He had thought that by now the current would have carried her too far for a backward glance. Even now he could get her back. If she had made it less plain, he could hardly have kept himself from going to her. It would not matter what they had talked about – Jimmie, the bridesmaids' presents, her wedding nightgown. Why not? They would be together and themselves. But evidently that was what must not be allowed to happen yet.

He wrote back saying that it was too bad he couldn't get away; he had a lot of work on hand. Perhaps a bit later. Meanwhile, he would always like to hear the news.

He paused a moment before he added the last sentence, distrusting any concession to himself. It would be a good moment to snip off the last thread. But again he had the feeling that violence was being done to a living thing, and a kind of fear restrained him. He let the letter go as it was.

The Frasers were going to the Isle of Wight for August. They went to the same hotel in Ventnor every year, but Fraser always discussed it judiciously, as if he had made the decision after long doubt and comparison. Kit wished he had decided to go sooner; he looked tired and old nowadays; his digestive trouble had recurred several times. Kit, who suspected that he ate scarcely enough to keep himself going, made several tentative suggestions about taking on a little more of the work. But Fraser's natural obstinacy was becoming complicated with the irritable temper of the gastric subject; it was impossible to insist.

It was a hot July. A few cases of diphtheria broke out; Kit was summoned to everyone in the practice who complained of a sore throat, and did endless inoculations. He had so little time to himself that it always seemed next day would produce the little extra which would make it impossible to think at all. But thought was developing a knack of intruding upon action; every routine mechanical job gave him long enough to see a poky little flat in Birmingham, and Christie staring, her eyes clouded with formless doubts, at heaps of lace and crepe de Chine. He turned the handle of the door, and saw her face clear – certainty and truth spring by themselves, untended, like weeds in sudden sun. *What's the use*, he thought. *It is all so obvious. She'll thank me in a few years' time.*

On the 23rd of the month he woke very early. Either from the end of a dream, or some sudden leap of waking thought, Christie was as present with him as if she had been in the room. Everything was very quiet. The thought of her possessed him – not longing nor imagination, but a contact, as if she had just spoken, or were standing just beyond the range of his eyes. She would be married a week from today.

He lay listening to the noises beginning in the street, as wakeful as if it were noon. His whole mind and body were turned to alertness. Perhaps, he thought, an urgent case was coming in. He had had, sometimes, this odd feeling of expectation. But the only summons that came was the postman's ring. At once, without wondering why he did it, he put on his dressing-gown, and went, for the first time in a couple of months, to take the letters from the hall.

It was there, as he had known it would be without knowing that he knew. It was the longest letter Christie had ever written him, and the most confused. It contained nothing of urgency, nothing but trifles. No separate sentence held the message which reached him from the whole. It was entire, like an animal with a small clear voice uttering a single note of fear.

Suddenly his own mind answered it with a like simplicity.

He did not attempt to think any more. The arguments he had used for weeks seemed to lie about in his brain, functionless, like the crutches of a man who discovers, all in a moment, that he can walk alone. He would never know, he thought, why he was going to her, whether in the certainty of wisdom or self-will. Bill or Shirley, he supposed, would have been quite happy about it. They would have called it guidance, and if it led them where they wanted to go, that would only lend it agreeable confirmation. He had no such trust in his own processes. But he was going.

It would destroy his peace, he knew, for the rest of his life, even if nothing came of it; much more if it ended as it was bound to end. He could justify it endlessly, and without meaning, because his choice, right or wrong, had been entangled in desire. It was a choice that ought only to be made in a moment of freedom from oneself. When he looked back on this he would remember, not that he had done well or badly, but that he had not been free.

It made no difference. He was sure. He would rather have known why, but still he was sure. Whatever it was, was too strong for him, and he would go.

It wanted two days to his free afternoon, the only time when he could possibly make the journey. He sat down, still in his dressing-gown, and wrote to her on a couple of leaves of a notebook he had in his room. He would meet her in the public art gallery, in the room upstairs where the Burne-Joneses were. He did not know Birmingham very well, and it was the only safe place he could think of on the spur of the moment. In a postscript he added that it might happen in the end he couldn't get away; if so he would be thinking about her, and hoped she would understand. He hardly knew why he put this in; he supposed it was a last loophole, in case some conviction came to him that he could trust. He posted the letter on his morning round.

Most of next day he wondered, and sometimes dreaded, whether the clear moment would come. But it was imagination, not thought, that grew clear. By the time it came, he had ceased to open his mind for a revelation. He wanted what he wanted.

Next morning there was no need to think. Expectation penetrated everything, like a colored light. He began the morning surgery, seeing through it the faces of the patients and the instruments he used.

He was letting the second patient out of his consulting-room when he saw someone standing in the doorway. It was Mrs Fraser;

he hardly knew her for a moment – she had always been a red-faced woman, and young for her age.

'Oh, Dr Anderson. I'm so sorry – in the middle of surgery. Could you come? John's been taken ill.'

'Of course. Where is he?' The words formed themselves; he felt dissociated from them. He himself was saying, *No; I've been had like this before. Not this time.*

'He's in his room. We just managed to get him there – the maid and I. It came on in the morning room, just after breakfast. I thought first it was simply another gastric twinge, but then when he went such a terrible color, and couldn't move, I knew it must be something serious. He makes light of everything, as a rule. He seems to have less pain now . . . So thankful you were in.' He did not hear everything she said. She trotted beside him on her thick, stocky legs, wheezing a little as she kept up with his longer strides.

He was thinking, *The old fool's had this coming on him for months. I knew it all along. Why couldn't he get himself seen to? Why should I pay for his pigheaded heroics? Not this time.* His voice, separately animated it seemed, spoke soothingly to Mrs Fraser and asked what her husband had had for breakfast.

'I – really, I don't think I can remember. Just our ordinary breakfast.' She was a sensible woman, as a rule. He did not ask for anything more. They had reached Fraser's room, and he had all the information he needed.

Fraser lay on his bed, staring at the ceiling, breathing quickly from the top of his chest. His hands were clasped behind his head, and his knees drawn upward. His skin looked gray and shrunken, and his eyes were deep cavities ringed with blue. He turned his head as Kit came in, and his face flickered in the way of one who is unwilling to labor the obvious. With a caution that sat grotesquely on her solid frame, Mrs Fraser began to tiptoe from the room. Kit followed her to the door to ask for hot-water bottles.

He went up to the bed, searching for words of reassurance, and feeling the usual diffidence of one medical man in the presence of another. The running, thready pulse, when he found it, was of a piece with everything else.

'This is too bad,' he said quietly. 'No, don't worry, I can manage.' He loosened Fraser's clothes.

In a voice that seemed to form itself on his palate, Fraser said, 'Almost – waste of time. I should say – a classic perforation. I'm afraid – been a little unwise.'

Kit had felt the board-like rigidity of the abdomen, and refrained from uttering euphemisms. Fraser still had an intelligence to be insulted.

'I'll get on to Harbutson right away. You'd like him, I expect? Just time to catch him before he starts for the hospital.'

Mrs Fraser came in with her bottles and blankets. He helped her to pack Fraser in them; she sat down beside him, and took his hand under the clothes, murmuring, as if she were encouraging a little boy, all those heartening platitudes which Kit had avoided. Fraser gave her a smile which made his face look more sunken than ever, and closed his eyes.

The call to the surgeon did not take long; Kit had been Harbutson's houseman at the hospital. He suggested that Fraser be got into a private ward at once; he would look at him there.

An interval followed in which Kit seemed to be in several places at once: explaining to Fraser; telephoning for an ambulance, then for a locum; finding his housekeeper (a small brisk woman who was everything the agency had claimed for her) and sending her off to help Mrs Fraser; weeding through Fraser's patients and his own, asking the urgent ones to wait and the less urgent to come back in the evening. It was not till he had repeated this formula for the third time that he remembered.

For a moment all the interlocking wheels of activity seemed to stop together. The chain of mental and physical habit snapped. Two opposites became self-evident at once. The only difference between them was that what he was doing here could have been done by any one of several hundred men with the same qualifications. His qualifications for what he had meant to do were unique.

Even as he thought it, the chain linked up again, the wheels revolved; his mind returned to Fraser, the ambulance, the locum, the patient in front of him. She was saying that she was so sorry to hear about Dr Fraser, that her little trouble would do tomorrow just as well. The clock on the mantelpiece had not moved.

The wheels of the ambulance sounded in the drive; Kit went up to see Fraser put on the stretcher. His pulse was weaker, but he was still conscious.

'Everything's all right. Locum on the way. It's Garrould – you had him the year before last.'

Fraser's gray-white face made a faint movement of assent and satisfaction. Kit saw, because he was trying to steady his diaphragm with his hand, that he wanted to speak.

'Then – possibly—' (his voice was so shallow that he needed a breath almost for every word) '—you might – manage – give the anesthetic. Always felt – utmost confidence—' His voice faded.

Kit said, 'Of course, if you want me to. I was hoping Harbutson might see his way to letting me. I don't think he'll mind.' The stretcher was ready; he helped the porters and the nurse to lift Fraser onto it.

The negotiation of corners and steps was a longish business, but to Kit it seemed that immediately after he had spoken he was standing alone in the hall. The clockwork had slowed down. Suddenly there seemed to be a great deal of time. He stood staring at a salver with visiting cards on it, thinking of Christie, who an hour ago had been on the other side of an unlocked door. He could hear her voice, saying something familiar. 'You know the way things happen.' At the time he had pitied her incompetence, and wondered how it felt.

He looked at his watch. There would just be time to deal with the urgent cases before they had the theater ready for Fraser. He went into the consulting-room, and found the place in the day-book.

25

'Is he deep enough?' asked Kit.

Harbutson nodded. His scalpel traced its first delicate line across the skin. Kit pulled the gas-and-oxygen cylinder an inch or two nearer. Fraser had become anonymous, reduced to an incision between sterile towels, a faint pulse beating in the carotid under Kit's fingertips.

The warm air of the theater hung motionless; its rubber flooring swallowed the sounds of shifting feet. Each rustle of the theater Sister's crisp gown was audible. From an anteroom the bubbling of a sterilizer came clearly through the quiet, like the humming of a single insect in summer calm.

A faint click told Kit that Harbutson was being handed artery forceps. He did not look up. Just beyond the level of his eyes, four gloved hands came and went, stealthy in their silence and spare movement, but they were nothing to do with him. His field of attention was bounded by the throat where his fingers rested.

'He's a shade rigid; can you get him a little deeper?'

'Sorry, sir.' Harbutson was an excellent surgeon, but not a rapid one. Kit looked at the gas gauge and moved the handle over. His senses were reduced to a fine point, concentrated in his finger ends.

'He'll do now.'

Yes, thought Kit, *he'll have to do; he's got what he can take.* He lifted his eyes for a second; Harbutson had got into the stomach at last. The Sister was extending a needle-holder. Kit thought, *Why doesn't he get a move on? I'd forgotten he was so slow. How many hours does he think he can take over a semi-collapsed patient of nearly seventy? Rigid, hell.*

Harbutson was clucking softly in his throat over the extent of the perforation. *Why,* wondered Kit unreasonably, *does he waste time making damn-fool noises?* He lifted Fraser's eyelids; the limit was very close.

'What's he like now?'

'Not too good, sir.' (*What do you expect, pottering about as if it were a post-mortem? It will be, too, if it goes on much longer.*)

His irritability, the press of an extra sense of urgency, was the only personal trace of Fraser for which his concentration had room. One of the nurses dropped a dirty instrument on the floor. Its slight ring sounded shockingly loud. Fraser's pulse was barely perceptible. He glanced at the emergency hypodermic on the glass trolley beside him. Catching his eye, the nurse who had brought Fraser down came forward and filled it.

At last, at last, Harbutson was suturing the peritoneum. Repressing an audible noise of relief, Kit eased the flow of nitrous oxide. For the minutes that were left, Fraser's chances had risen, perhaps, to fifty-fifty. But the words, *He's not breathing, sir,* still formed themselves, ready, on his tongue. He saw, as if it were happening, the high-pressure machinery they would set in motion.

At last, like a shaken kaleidoscope, the smooth silent group relaxed and broke. Harbutson was stepping back, the assistant putting pads of gauze on the wound, the ward nurse hurrying forward with her wide rolled bandage, the theater nurses whisking instruments away. It was over. Kit unstrapped the mask from Fraser's face; the porters came in with the trolley to take him back to the ward. More instruments were produced, more sterile towels; by the time the trolley had disappeared, the theater was already half prepared for the next case.

Kit stood up, feeling as if something immensely heavy had fallen from his straightened back. Harbutson was having his tapes untied by a probationer while he peeled off his gloves. Kit glanced at the electric clock on the wall; after all, it had only taken a minute or two over the average time.

Harbutson, scrubbing at the sink, looked round at him.

'He should do, with luck. Must have been working up to this for some time, you know.' His voice was faintly reproachful.

'Yes. I suppose he was treating himself; but he wasn't fond of talking about it.'

Harbutson clucked to himself; the sound probably indicated sympathy. 'He ought to have an intravenous right away. I could ask the R.S.O. presently, but I was wondering whether you'd care to do it? We shall be rather pushed with the list today.'

Kit said, 'Certainly, I'll be glad to.'

He threw down his theater coat in a corner of the anteroom (the trolley with the next case was there already) and took down the white one he had been wearing. He hoped the private ward would have the intravenous set ready. With a man in Fraser's condition it would probably be a long job to get into the vein. The sense of time and urgency still pressed on him, the feeling that something must be done in a hurry or it would be too late. He wanted to get rid of the feeling; the operation was over, after all, and an intravenous saline was nothing desperate. But he hurried along the corridors, quickly getting rid of anyone who wanted to stop and greet him, the longing for haste still thrusting him on.

Fraser was just conscious, too weak to do more than follow Kit's movements with his eyes. It was hard to remember who he was; he looked like a hundred old men whom Kit had seen among the same paraphernalia, wearing the same shapeless operation gown. The set was ready; the Sister, who helped him herself, quick and efficient. Everything was done in the minimum of time. He felt a deep, unconscious release in setting his own pace instead of waiting on someone else's. The Sister, who had known him as a houseman, showed signs of wanting to keep him afterward for a chat, but he eluded her.

There were two urgent cases waiting when he got back; he drove straight out to them, and from them to the ordinary round, without stopping for a meal. Speed satisfied him, like a drug to which he was becoming addicted. When he had finished, he drove back to the hospital to see Fraser again.

Mrs Fraser, he found, was already with her husband. They seemed satisfied with his condition. Kit said he would wait till she had gone; there was no hurry. The phrase, as he uttered it, sounded odd and unreal.

Everyone was busy, so he strolled out into the corridor. It was his first moment of inactivity since morning; the muscles of his mind seemed suddenly to sag, and his thoughts, which had consisted for hours of plans for immediate action, were wiped clean like a sponged slate. Voices drifted out to him from the nurses' duty room; for a few moments they were simply noises, like the noises of feet in the main passage outside.

'—that intravenous on top of everything. It saved my bacon, Sister doing it. I will say, she does work.'

'Well, you know why – it was Dr Anderson. She was batty about him when he was R.S.O. here. Walker says the week he got married it was just hell to be on the ward.'

Kit, his ears suddenly opened, began a cautious retreat. Just before he moved out of earshot, the first nurse said, 'No, really? That was before my time. I must say, I thought he was rather a lamb when he came to Collis on Christmas Day.'

Kit passed beyond their voices, into a silence which nothing penetrated. From the memory of that Christmas other memories ringed outward, like the expanding rings made in water by a stone, back to the night when he had first seen Christie, onward to yesterday. For the first time, as if he were looking down from a height over a winding stream along which he had drifted, he saw it all together, without the interference of desire or dread. As a deep sleep clears perplexities away, the absolute removal of his mind during these last hours gave him now, by accident, the knowledge he had wrestled for in vain. He saw that he had failed her. Imprisoned in his own longing, he had been able only to reach for her or to thrust her away; he had not been able to free her or to give her light. She had required wisdom of him, not sacrifice, and he had been wise, not for her but for himself.

He had won a victory in his own will, achieving a discipline of which this moment of true perspective was the reward. He would, perhaps, be stronger and more confident for it all his life. But her he had weakened, because he had made a decision for her which she had it in her to make for herself. Remembering her last letter, he knew that she was groping toward the same realization.

Well, it was finished. Perhaps she would be happy with Burford, perhaps unhappy; it was certain that she would be more alone. Probably Burford, who would not confuse the innermost part of her because he would never find it, would be more use to her in the end.

The door of Fraser's room opened; Mrs Fraser was leaving. He recalled himself to meet her anxiety and her thanks.

She thanked him again next day, when she came back from the hospital with the news that Fraser was holding his ground. He was taking little sips of water already, she said, and had even been able to talk to her for a minute or two. Dr Harbutson, she could see, was delighted, though he hadn't said very much.

Kit knew all this beforehand, having been to the hospital even earlier in the day. He knew, too, why Harbutson hadn't said very much. The critical period was not likely to begin till the second or third day. But Kit, like Harbutson, did not feel that anything was to be gained by telling her this. She was a woman who had lived for forty years a life as regular and predictable as the tick of a grandfather clock, broken by nothing more shocking than the comfortable marriage of two daughters. She was as helpless under what had happened already as a non-swimmer who has been washed overboard. There were several things Kit would have liked to discuss with her, including the question of Fraser's mail, which he could see lying untouched in the hall; but he let it go, reflecting that anything that could wait for the post could probably wait a little longer. He had arranged for Garrould, the locum, to sleep and eat in his own flat, so as to leave her undisturbed. With the arrears of yesterday, both men had more than enough to fill their time.

In the afternoon the news of Fraser was still fairly reassuring, and Mrs Fraser went up to the hospital again. When she got back she looked so much more cheerful that Kit, who still had the mail nagging at the back of his mind (he had just seen a buff Ministry of Health envelope in it), decided after evening surgery that he had better ask her about it.

'Oh, dear,' she said, 'how thoughtless of me. I do hope there's nothing important. Do take them, Dr Anderson. Take anything that comes. Don't bother to ask me. I'm not quite myself, and perhaps I might forget again.'

'If you'd just like to look at these and see there's nothing personal—'

'Oh, yes, thank you. Though really it doesn't matter. Yes, here's a letter from one of the girls; it must have crossed with mine. I don't think the others are from anyone we know; in any case, I'm sure there's nothing John would mind your seeing. If you'll just let me have anything back that isn't about the patients. Thank you so much— Oh, dear, I do hope that isn't another call for you. You've been working so hard.'

'Never mind,' said Kit, who had heard his telephone bell a moment or two before her. 'Better now than in the night.' He ran up to answer it, pushing the wad of letters into his pocket. It turned out to be a call for both of them.

Fraser lapsed into a coma within half an hour of the time when they reached the hospital. There was nothing for Kit to stay for, nothing more of any kind to be done. As he left, the night nurse was settling Mrs Fraser in a basket chair with rugs and pillows, to wait till the worn-out mechanism of breathing and circulation ran at last to a standstill. She sat in the chair looking straight before her, thanking the nurse in vague whispers to which she herself seemed not to be listening.

Kit went home, told Garrould what had happened, and went to bed.

After he had put out his light he stood in the window, as he had stood on the night when he had discovered he did not love Janet any longer, looking out at the street lamp through the garden trees. In a few hours it would be Christie's wedding day. Yesterday he had been making decisions as if other people's lives depended on them. It had made no difference to Fraser. Perhaps if he had gone to Birmingham it would have made no ultimate difference to Christie, either. Probably, he thought, very few decisions made much difference except to the person who decided. If yesterday had begun again, there was nothing different he would have done. Perhaps for Fraser, for Christie, for Janet, for himself, all the decisions had been made years ago, and the moment that brought them to the surface was no more important than any other moment. His thoughts began the circular track of great physical weariness. There was nothing to stay awake for. He went to sleep.

Fraser, he heard next morning, had died at half-past one. Kit found he had exhausted the capacity for feeling anything more about it, and, after counting up the immediate things to be done, could only recall from hospital days that this was the hour at which night nurses preferred a death to take place; later than four in the morning, it upset the whole work of the ward. It was characteristic of Fraser, he thought; he had an old-fashioned courtesy, and disliked giving trouble to anyone. Mrs Fraser, for whom he had got a sedative ready the night before, was still sleeping. He wrote to notify the General Medical Council, and remembered that he would be senior partner now, when Fraser's share was sold; their agreement had provided for it. McKinnon might possibly consider coming in with him. There was something against this, but he could not for a few minutes remember what. Of course; Janet didn't like McKinnon. It was strange that Janet, when he thought about her, should seem so much further removed than Fraser did. There were some letters for her in the hall, waiting to be forwarded. He must remember, sometime today.

At the end of morning surgery, the sight of Garrould about to start on his round reminded Kit of something.

'Oh, by the way,' he said, 'it's just possible something for your side may have come in by post. I've some stuff here that Mrs Fraser turned over to me last night. Would you care to wait a moment while we go through it? It shouldn't take long.'

They went into Fraser's consulting-room and began on the pile. The first two were advertisements, the third a chemist's account. In the fourth, the Ministry of Health announced a minor alteration in one of their forms. Kit glanced at it, passed it on to Garrould, and picked up the fifth, which was in an old-fashioned semi-literate hand; this one would be a patient, he thought. He ran his eye along it idly; he need only read enough to place it.

Dear Sir [he read]: *After considering my duty in the matter for some time, I feel it right I should send you a few words to let you know what has come to my notice with regard to your partner, Dr Anderson.*

During the time I was in service with my late mistress, Miss Amelia
Heath, of Laurel Dene, Victoria Avenue—

Kit lowered the sheet. As he moved, he knew that Garrould
was much too far away to have seen anything, but the impulse
was instinctive. It caused Garrould to look up from the Ministry
of Health circular.

'Anything for me?' he asked.

'No,' said Kit. 'Only a begging letter.' He put it aside.

Garrould returned to the circular, wondering what Anderson
had thought it necessary to lie about. Well, thank God, it was no
affair of his. He had done locum work for some years, and had
long since discovered that odd things had a way of emerging
when people died. Whatever Fraser had been up to, Anderson,
not he, would have the job of sorting it out. The next letter
revealed a visit that ought to have been made the day before; it
was sufficient to crowd the incident from Garrould's mind. Taking
it with him (it was the last of the batch), he departed on his
round.

Kit took the letter into his own consulting-room and opened
it out. There were three sheets of it, very neat and legible. It was
signed at the end *Yours obediently, E. Pedlow.* Yes, he thought; she
would sign it, of course.

Within a somewhat limited style, Pedlow had the gift of con-
ciseness. She had not, in the course of her narrative, wasted many
words. He could not remember, now, the exact number of times
he had been to Christie's room at Laurel Dene, but he had no
doubt that her estimate was correct. The letter contained no sur-
mises, no unsubstantiated accusations, no suggestion, for instance,
that any neglect on his part had contributed to Miss Heath's
death. It was painstakingly, one might almost have said lovingly,
accurate, like a careful historian's research. More than the most
vindictive slander, it sent a chill to the pit of his stomach.

Yet, when the first sick feeling was over, a deep relief succeeded it. He knew that, though not recently, he had expected something of the kind for a long time, without admitting it. He read the letter again, feeling, this time, even a kind of admiration that she could have retained through so much hatred her own kind of integrity. The thing could hardly have been better done. Only the limitations of her reading had kept it from the success it deserved; she had just not known enough to write to the General Medical Council. As it was, addressing the letter to Fraser had been the touch of an eminently practical mind. Ninety-nine women out of a hundred in her class, he reflected, would have sent it to—

A sudden thought struck him. With the letter in his hand, he ran upstairs to the little hall of his flat, where Janet's letters were still on the table, waiting to be readdressed. There were three or four of them. It was at the bottom – the same notepaper, the same handwriting and postmark. He took it into the sitting-room, tore it across unopened, and burned it in the grate.

A very remarkable woman, he thought. He wondered where a few hundred pounds' worth of education would have taken her.

The letter to Janet had curled into hard black ash. He took Fraser's letter from his pocket and lit it; the envelope burned last. The sight of Fraser's name, browning out, stirred the numbness in him to a sharp affection and the knowledge of loss. For the first time he was angry, for Fraser's sake. He remembered his little proprieties, his dislike of discussing, even with Kit, an unsavory case, the humanity that had always been behind them. If this had come before his illness, Kit would have felt forever afterward the guilt of his death. Probably, he thought, if any ultimate justice directed these things, it had operated in Fraser's favor rather than his own.

Picking up the poker, he stirred the ash of the two letters till it powdered. A clock struck the half hour; it was more than time he went to see how Mrs Fraser was, and started his round. As he went downstairs, something jogged at his mind, a puzzled feeling of some incongruity. *I wonder*, he thought, *why she left it so long. I wonder why she picked on me. I should have expected—*

The Frasers' maid was in the hall. Mrs Fraser was up, and would be pleased to see him. He knocked, the question falling into the background before the moment's demand.

26

McKinnon pushed back his rough brown hair from his square forehead and squinted at Kit along his pipe.

'You've forgotten the obvious objection,' he said.

'You can take the big half of the panel,' said Kit, 'if that's what's worrying you. And we haven't got any rich neurasthenics on fake injections to affront your principles. No *Citadel* stuff. Fraser was pretty straight that way.'

McKinnon looked at him, liking him as, even in the heat of their most violent disagreements (which had never been professional), he always did. There was something in him which McKinnon's restlessness and cosmic indignation sometimes envied, sometimes resented, but respected on the whole. He attacked it, when he was in the mood, with various epithets derived from textbooks of the Left, which made as little impression on Kit as they made, secretly, on McKinnon himself. They understood one another.

'We should team up all right. To tell you the truth, it wasn't the work I was thinking of.'

'My ideology bothering you again?'

'You haven't got one, so while there's life there's hope. No, as a matter of fact, it was the domestic side. Look here, Anderson, there's no sense in beating about the bush, particularly as you must know what I'm talking about as well as I do. The plain fact is that Mrs Anderson hates my guts. She always has. I don't see any particular reason why she shouldn't, but there it is; it won't work. It never does.'

Kit put his hand in his pocket for a cigarette. It encountered the thin crackle of the letter he had had the day before. He opened the cigarette case and said, slowly, 'I don't think that question is likely to arise for some time.'

'She's due back from South Africa in a month or two, isn't she?'

'She was – I heard from her the other day.'

McKinnon said nothing. He had learned better, in the course of years, than to hurry Kit if he showed signs of talking about something personal. Only his pipe, which as usual was getting foul, made a gurgle like a note of interrogation.

'She wrote to ask me whether, in view of certain affairs of her own, it might not be wiser to stay put for a time, and asked me what I thought about it. I cabled back and advised her to stay where she was.'

'Oh, you did.' McKinnon slanted a quick glance at Kit's face, which was unrevealing. 'But, after all—'

'I don't think,' said Kit carefully, 'that she's in any desperate hurry, in any case. She says she's very happy out there. The climate suits her. And she seems to have made a great many friends.'

McKinnon sucked noisily at his pipe, partly because his private thoughts were unsuitable for expression (Janet's dislike had been heartily returned), and partly because he hoped that silence might, as had sometimes happened, elicit something more. Nothing came; McKinnon had not really expected it. He had got the information that concerned him; he knew that Kit did not believe his wife would come back at all. He would have liked to know why, and what Kit thought about it, but had not the slenderest expectation of learning either. Kit's private preserves had always been very clearly defined, and McKinnon knew all the fences by heart.

'All right,' he said. 'I'll think it over, and give you a ring tomorrow.'

'Good.' Kit recognized this as an acceptance; McKinnon never needed time to think over a refusal. Since the thing was as good as settled, his mind, as he walked home, drifted quickly away from it, and returned to Janet, who had solved her problems, at last, in her own way.

The letter she had sent him could only have had one answer; that she should have left the responsibility to him he took as a matter of course; he was so used to it that it passed him by like a mannerism, or a characteristic inflection of the voice. He had been interested not in her manner but in her motive. That she knew he had had a mistress he did not believe, and none of her letters had given any sign of it. Between the lines of the last, however, he had read a different reason. Janet had found someone to take his place. The new relationship was likely to be free from the inconveniences of the last, for it was a woman. Janet had begun to write about her friend Rachel some weeks before: her influence in the Group, her sympathy, her understanding, the nursery school she kept for children under five. Later it had appeared that Janet was helping with the smallest children two afternoons a week. In this last letter she said that if she stayed Rachel wanted her to help permanently, and they were thinking of sharing a flat together.

He wondered, now that it had happened, why neither of them had thought of it before. To Janet it offered as much as she was capable of receiving from life, to him such freedom as his profession's veto on divorce allowed. He pondered, as he walked, over the strange and, it seemed, purposeful chain of circumstance which had ensured that it should come too late.

Fraser had been buried some days before. His widow had gone

to stay with one of the married daughters, so that he and Garrould had the house to themselves. They got on comfortably, but Kit was looking forward to the time when he and McKinnon would have settled down. He longed for some resting point in his own life.

Tea was on the table when he got in. Garrould was not back from his round, but they never waited meals for one another. He sat down, glad – since Garrould's conversation, though inoffensive, palled with time – of solitude and peace.

It seemed that he had rejoiced too soon. Before he was halfway through his first cup of tea, Mrs Hackett knocked at the door. 'I'm ever so sorry, Dr Anderson, sir, to disturb your tea. But there's a patient asking for you urgent, she says, downstairs.'

'There would be.' Mrs Hackett reminded him so much of the landlady he had had when he was a student that he found aloofness hard to preserve with her. 'What's the matter, did she say? Because if she isn't actually hemorrhaging or perforating or anything, surgery starts in an hour and a quarter.'

'That's just what I told her, sir – in a manner of speaking, that is, not wanting to be too short with her seeing that you never know. But she was most particular that it wouldn't wait, so I thought, sooner be sure than sorry, I'll let the doctor know, though I do think it's a shame, coming at a mealtime as if they thought you could live like an angel without food or sleep. Just you ring when she goes, and I'll make you a nice fresh pot of tea.'

'Oh, never mind.' Kit seldom found that any annoyance of his own could survive Mrs Hackett's vicarious indignation. 'If it's nothing, I'll soon polish her off. Did she give a name?'

'No, sir. I couldn't get nothing out of her at all.'

Feeling depressed, since this sounded like something long and confidential, Kit got up from the tea table and went downstairs. He opened the door of the consulting-room smartly, and stood, frozen to stillness, on the threshold. Christie was sitting in the patient's chair.

When he came in she got up, smiled shyly, and said, 'Are you surprised to see me?'

'Yes,' said Kit, standing still where he was. His breath felt strangled, as if he had run too far.

'I thought you'd be pleased.'

Still he could not move or speak. He had been, lately, so often solitary that she seemed to confront him like a shape of his solitude, needing an answer only from the mind.

'I'm sorry about pretending to be a patient. You're cross about it, aren't you? I thought it would be more respectable than saying I wanted to see you just like that. Darling, you're thinner. Does that woman give you enough to eat?'

'Yes,' said Kit vaguely. 'She's all right.' His mind had adjusted itself to reality. How strange, he thought, that he should not have foreseen this most obvious of all possibilities; that even afterward she would still come back. She had loved him, but it had not held her; what else was likely to hold her with more effect? Now that it had happened, he was unastonished, not even much shocked that it should be so soon. She must be still on her honeymoon. She was looking up at him, innocently troubled, without a guilty shadow in her face. Why should there be? he thought; some process of her own was sure to be transforming it all to candor and light.

'Why did you come?' he said.

'I thought probably you'd like to see me now.'

'Aren't you happy?' he asked slowly. The words forced themselves out, against his will. He had been settled in himself. He had not believed that he was still vulnerable to anything.

'Oh, yes,' she said with her eager smile. 'Everything's all right now. It's only you I've been worried about. It's been so long. I couldn't get away before.'

'I'm glad it turned out all right.' Everything was clear again. He felt even happiness that he could use, once, the certainty he had not had to give her before. It would be good to look at her for a few minutes, though, before she went away.

'I'd have come anyhow,' she was saying, 'to make sure Pedlow hadn't done anything to you. I didn't dare write, in case— Darling! Is that what's the matter? I wondered why you looked so tired. Oh, she didn't, she couldn't. Tell me, Kit – don't just stand there.'

'No,' he said, staring at her. A sudden surmise stopped his voice. His heart seemed to check, and start again with a jerk that shook him. 'No, she tried, but it didn't come off. Why – do you mean—'

'Yes. That was why.' Something in his face arrested her. 'Kit, you did *know*? You did see it in the paper, didn't you?'

'I've been busy lately,' he said with difficulty. 'I haven't looked at more than the headlines for over a week.'

'But it was nearly at the top of the column. About it not taking place. Oh, God – Kit, darling, you haven't been thinking I was married all this time? Oh, my sweet, come here.'

Even as they embraced he was thinking, *I shouldn't have let this happen; she means something else; it will be harder afterward.* She was bareheaded, and her hair tangled the light, as it always had, just below the level of his eyes.

'It seems funny now,' she said presently, 'that I didn't realize from the start what Pedlow would be waiting for. I had a queer feeling, as it was, when Jimmie would have that announcement thing put in the paper. Though no doubt she'd have found out anyway. She wrote to him just the day before the wedding.'

He touched her hair, silently. His brief rush of joy was borne down by a remorse too great, it seemed, ever to find relief in words – because he had been glad, because he had failed her after all, because even when the truth shouted at him he had not known.

'Oh, darling,' she sighed, 'how glad I am Pedlow had all that money. If I had some more I'd like to give it her all over again.

288

Poor old Pedlow.' Her voice shook. He was suddenly aware that it shook with laughter.

'But—'

'Oh, darling, I can't tell you. Just the very night before, I'd been dreaming I was married to Jimmie, and waking up in the morning was simply like coming back from the grave. And naturally I just tried not to think about it; I mean, the presents had come and the champagne and everything, so it was really as good as over, and I thought after all, probably it would be all right. And then Jimmie arrived looking like an Act of God, and said could he speak to me alone. So silly, because everybody had been leaving us alone as if we had smallpox for weeks and weeks. And he had this letter. He said he'd only come because he knew I'd like to have a chance to deny it myself.'

'Deny it?' There passed through Kit's mind the memory of various confidences: the one in the summerhouse, the one in the wardrobe room – 'Do you mean,' he said slowly, 'that you hadn't told him?'

'Darling, I *know*. And what made it so much more awful was that he'd confessed like anything to me. I did tell him about Maurice, as a matter of fact, because after that it seemed only fair. And he seemed to find that a bit of a pill. But I just couldn't tell him about you. Don't you see, I couldn't talk to someone else about you as I'd talked to you about the rest – as if you didn't matter any more. But when he asked me, of course I said it was true.'

'And that settled it?' He tried, and failed, to create a picture of Jimmie in his mind.

'Well, not at once. You see, then he said well, as I'd confessed freely we must try to forget about it, because of course you were a cad to have taken advantage of me, and ought to be horsewhipped. And when he said that, it came all over me, and I told him I never wanted to forget you, and you were the best person I'd ever known; and if it came to that it was just as much me

289

who'd seduced you, and I was jolly glad I did. And we had a row.'

'Did you?' Kit's mouth twitched. He straightened it quickly, feeling ashamed of himself.

'Yes, terrific. I didn't mind that part; in fact, it did me a lot of good. But it was pretty grim with the family afterward. I don't think I'll tell you about that part – not till it's sort of sunk into the background a bit. Anyway, it's over now. Has it happened – what you thought?'

'Has what happened?'

'That you've stopped loving me. You said you might.'

'I'm afraid that wasn't true.'

'I wondered, afterward, if perhaps it wasn't.'

They said nothing more for a little while. But Kit thought, when her face was far enough away for him to see it, that it had faintly changed. He remembered how he had thought that decisions mattered chiefly to the person who made them. She had made, at last, a movement against the stream, and already it showed a little.

'You know,' she said, 'about this children business; it was really a mistake. I mean, thinking that anyone's would do. I'd have known that if I'd been with you a bit longer that afternoon. But you went away so quickly.'

'I tried to come back. Did you wait long in Birmingham that day?'

'I knew it was because you couldn't.'

'Fraser's dead.'

'Oh, my darling. I am so sorry.'

It seemed quite natural that she should be the only one to realize he had suffered a personal loss. He could not remember having told her anything about Fraser except the most superficial, and often humorous, things.

She rubbed her face softly against his cheek. He closed his

eyes; like a recurring pattern, the memory of the past stamped itself on the future. Nearly all of it would happen again. It was as certain as the approach of death, and as little to be argued with, since death was the price of life.

'Darling Kit. I'm here to look after you now.' Warmly, securely, her voice enclosed him, like the walls of a firelit room. 'Everything's going to be all right now. You're never going to be unhappy any more.'

virago

To buy any of our books and to find out more
about Virago Press and Virago Modern Classics,
our authors and titles, as well as events and
book club forum, visit our websites

www.virago.co.uk
www.littlebrown.co.uk

and follow us on Twitter

@ViragoBooks

To order any Virago titles p & p free in the UK,
please contact our mail order supplier on:

+ 44 (0)1832 737525

Customers not based in the UK should contact
the same number for appropriate postage
and packing costs.